THE METEOR 1

THE METEOR
BOOK 1

JOSHUA T. CALVERT

PROLOGUE

Luc's forehead rested against the small window next to his seat, through which he watched the passing clouds. Actually, it was *he* who was passing *them*, but he liked to maintain the illusion that this majestic world out there revolved around him and not the other way around. He thought about how a little grease spot the size of a quarter would be left right on the acrylic when he pulled his head back.

Luc hated it whenever he arrived at his seat—which was always a window seat, because it was the only place he was spared his latent fear of flying—and discovered such a grease mark. It always brought to mind an unwashed youth with massive headphones and a baggy hoodie who'd sat here in prior to him and pressed his acne-prone skin against the window with a bored look, chewing gum and abusing his jaw like a ruminant.

Clouds. Luc loved them. They looked like cotton balls and yet were full of energy and life. Early on in his geophysics studies, he had become interested in these unique entities. Ranging from sugar-spun water vapor to sulfur colossi on Venus, and planet-spanning blankets on Jupiter, the speeds at which they rotated knew no comparison on Earth. Those that passed before him at the window were admittedly tame sheep, cumulus clouds like something out of a picture book, so romantic that all that was needed was for a flock of birds to pass by—preferably at a safe distance from the turbine.

The plane suddenly jerked as they passed through one of the clouds in descent. The table in front of him rattled and the cabin roared. He closed his eyes for a moment and took a deep breath.

"Sir?" the flight attendant asked, leaning into his semi-detached business class cabin. Her smile was pretty but businesslike, and the red cap on her perfectly coiffed blonde hair was fastened with a white bow under her chin. She pointed to his gin and tonic. "I have to clear your drink now. We'll be landing in ten minutes."

"Ah," he muttered, looking at the glass in his hand, which already felt sweaty. A lone ice cube floated in it, melting with remarkable speed—a tiny climate change between his fingers. Again, it felt like their plane was sagging into an air pocket, and the flight attendant's friendly smile faltered for a split second. Or was he imagining it? Was she worried? Why? Was there a reason for it? Hadn't this been normal turbulence—harmless and every day?

Maybe I should ask her if there's a problem, he thought, but immediately dismissed it. Nothing will happen. No need to be ridiculous. Unless, of course, that clatter up ahead is a bad sign, and what if she doesn't recognize it? It could be that I'm the only one who notices it, and if I'd said something, we wouldn't have crashed.

"Did you know that cumulus clouds are formed by local updrafts? Thermals or orographic updrafts, but that shouldn't be the case here. Their undersides are very flat because of moisture condensation. This combination ensures that when they form towers—you probably know them—they can herald thunderstorms," Luc explained, pointing outside.

"Really?" she asked with seeming interest.

Or perhaps he merely imagined that her rehearsed smile expressed interest. It didn't matter. He was nervous, and he liked her rolling Spanish accent.

"Yes. Everyone likes them because they look so picture-perfect. But they can also get nasty when they hit thermals." He winked at her, hoping it looked casual and relaxed. "Like a Spanish woman, huh?"

The flight attendant's smile faltered, but only briefly. She pointed to his glass. "May I?"

"Oh, sure!" He held it out to her, and she fled after a curt nod.

"Great line, Luc," he muttered, leaning toward the window again. The grease stain his forehead had left was larger than a quarter. Hastily he rubbed it away with the napkin that had served as a base for his drink, now left abandoned with a damp ring in the middle.

Madrid passed under him as the flaps were activated and the plane slowed some more. It went into a steeper approach—it would all be over soon. The many old churches, walls, and gates rose like brown blotches from the modern apartment buildings, reminding him of third-world countries in their ugliness. His schedule was tight, which would leave him no time to explore the sights or take in a few Spanish street bars. Again.

As they landed at the airport and maneuvered down the taxiway to the gate, he followed the row upon row of seat belts clicking open far too soon, as they always did. He pulled his smartphone out of the small storage compartment on the side of his wide seat. He quickly checked Instagram, YouTube, and Facebook before standing up and pulling his carry-on bag out of the overhead compartment.

An awaiting bus took them to the terminal where there was a quick passport check. Even the baggage return at the automated belts was surprisingly quick. He rolled through the exit with two wheeled pieces of luggage—one seemingly as big as a small car and the other big enough that he'd had to pay a surcharge for bulky hand luggage at boarding. A gaggle of taxi drivers and tour guides were already waiting there, holding up laminated name tags for errant tourists. A young man with long hair and aviator glasses, holding out a tablet with @PlanetLuc written in black letters on a white background, stood among them. Luc waved at him and circled the small metal wall that separated the arrivals from the waiting people.

"Hi. My name is Diego," the young man greeted him, extending a hand. Luc reached to take it, but Diego grabbed the extended handle of his suitcase instead before realizing his mistake. He let it go and shook Luc's hand.

"Luc."

"Ah, sorry! How was the flight, Señor?"

"Relaxing," he lied, trying for a genuine smile. "My driver, I'm guessing?"

"Yo! I often do driving for the ground station. My brother works there," Diego explained in a heavy Spanish accent, following Luc and rolling both suitcases beside him. Luc thought the big suitcase looked like the young man could sleep in it.

They exited the airport into a lane with numerous taxis and a few private cars and sedans in the second lane. Most of the engines were running, belching stinking diesel or gasoline fumes from the exhausts. In the heat, the emissions seemed especially acrid and heavy.

During the drive, the young man was surprisingly silent. He steered them so rapidly through the evening rush hour traffic that Luc had to keep looking away to keep his heart from stopping. Only when they had left the last busy roads behind them and were driving west through a dry forest landscape did he relax a little again.

"I'm sure you get this a lot," Diego said after a while, leaning back in the driver's seat with one hand on the steering wheel, "but I've been subscribed to your YouTube channel for two years."

"Ah, a subscriber since the first hour." Luc grinned. "Nice to meet you."

"Your video series on meteors and their influence on Earth's history..." The Spaniard put his thumb and forefinger to his mouth and kissed it, "... really great. 'Our present paradise is the result of cosmic catastrophes.' That's a great line. I'll never forget it, you know?"

"A metaphor that applies to many things, I guess. For example, the asteroid shower eight hundred million years ago upended the entire environmental conditions on our planet."

"The Ice Age, right?"

"Something like that. It coincides with the transition from the warm Earth Age of Tonium to the cold Cryogenian. There was so much dust blown into the atmosphere by the impact that it cooled massively."

"You think it's going to happen again?" asked Diego, overtaking an old pickup truck that sagged under the weight of six goats. "Like you said it would?"

"It's not a question of *if* it's going to happen again. It's a question of *when*," Luc replied, "But statistically, we have plenty of time."

"Really? In your following video series, you warned that the statistics were more of a concern in this case, didn't you? I mean, the series after the impact."

Luc sighed inwardly. "My point was to bring the subject to the awareness of my viewers. I think it's important that everyone thinks about it, and that politicians also take a closer look at near-Earth objects. This is a real disaster scenario."

"I understand." Diego nodded barely noticeably and steered his car onto a one-lane side road that ran between two green hills. The asphalt was dusty and riddled with small cracks, probably due to the heat. After about ten minutes, the Cebreros ground facility came into view—a vast antenna dish that looked like a funnel on a pivoting head joint. Floral white, it contrasted sharply with the green of the trees and against the blue of the sky.

"Impressive," he commented. "Really impressive."

"Si," Diego agreed. "There's the same setup as this in Australia."

"Really?" asked Luc more out of politeness. Of course he knew that. The two deep-space ground stations had been operating for almost 20 years, despite having received little media attention.

"Si, si! This distribution on the globe is probably due to the constellation of stars. Covering the sky or something. My brother always goes crazy when he talks about it."

"What's your brother's name, anyway?"

"Roberto. He's an astronomer. I don't think you'll be working with him."

"I'm only here tonight and tomorrow and probably won't get to meet everyone," Luc replied agreeably, leaning forward to get a good look as they pulled up to a roll-up gate made of chicken wire. A gatekeeper in a blue uniform came up to the driver's window, exchanged a few words in Spanish with Diego, laughed about something, and then waved them through.

The radar facility stood in a football-field-sized clearing in the middle of the forest. The mighty antenna sat directly on a gravel path that led up a hill behind it, where grass grew between the trees. On the left side stood a surprisingly small, one-story building with a flat roof—the actual ground station.

He didn't think it looked the least bit pretentious, but more like a low-maintenance youth hostel. Since his move to California, he was no longer used to the European understatement.

Diego steered the car across the dusty lot between the antenna and the house. He parked next to a good dozen other vehicles, most of which were connected to charging stations via cable.

"Well, here we are," he announced, powering off the car and clapping his hands. They climbed out and set about unpacking. Outside the nondescript front door was a small concrete ramp where Luc could roll his suitcases. Still, he felt like a clumsy tourist as he tried to keep them from rolling back when he had to let go long enough to press the doorbell, since Diego's phone had rung and the young man had stayed behind, conversing loudly in Spanish.

Fortunately, Linnea Daubner opened the door for him. She was the physicist with whom he had spoken several times —including video calls—since the request from ESA. Her black corkscrew curls formed a thick forest around her face, which was quite pretty for a woman her age. He could hardly believe that she was Austrian and not a local, with her southern appearance and brown skin.

"Hello, Luc!" she greeted with a bright smile, holding the door wide open for him. "Welcome to Cebreros! Did you have a pleasant flight?"

"Hi, and thanks. Smooth sailing," he replied, squeezing past her somewhat awkwardly.

Linnea pointed to the floor of the square entryway. "Just put everything down here for now."

"Thank you." The walls were gray and the space didn't strike him as particularly inviting.

"Would you like me to show you around, or would you rather rest first?"

"A little tour would be just the thing," he said. "I've been sitting for a long time."

"Well, come along then." Linnea led him through the door straight ahead, bringing them into a large room. The dropped ceiling reminded him of his school days, but the rest reminded him of a spaceship. Directly in front of them was a work console for several employees, consisting of two rows of displays arranged one above the other in gray and white paneling. Between them were lots of vertically mounted landline phones. Multiple keyboards and mice were arranged across the associated multi-user curved desk area, which stretched over five meters. Half the screens were black, and the rest were running diagrams and complex calculations.

Two men who, thanks to the headsets they were wearing, seem unaware of their entrance were seated at the desk. Linnea gently kicked their office chairs until they turned around. "This here is Roberto. He's an astronomer," she explained, pointing to a man with small cheerful-looking eyes and a full beard. He smiled and waved at Luc.

"Ah yes, Diego's brother?"

"I hope he didn't commit too many traffic violations," Roberto acknowledged with a grin.

"None that I wouldn't have committed." Luc winked at him and then looked to the other man, a gawky blond with a long ponytail and a surprisingly wrinkled face.

"This here is Marcello," Linnea said. "He's a radio specialist and monitors our communication systems."

"Buenos dias. I'm Luc."

"Pleased to meet you," Marcello replied, returning to his work after they'd shaken hands.

"The main part of the staff is in the small mess hall right now, having dinner. They're all leaving soon for the end of the day, though. We share a communal meal every Saturday,"

Linnea explained, leading him past the work area to some individual computer stations.

"And then only the four of us will be here?"

"Yes. Roberto is staying for the realignment. After all, we promised you there'd be something to watch while being quiet enough for you to film a bit and for us to talk. That's what works best today. The realignment, while unspectacular, is great to use as a vivid example of what we're doing here."

"It seems like you've thought of everything," Luc said with a smile. "How about we shoot some footage right away? I was going to break up the post with a few short videos that I'll pop in every now and then that go into a bit of what you guys are doing here. Subscribers don't want to see my boring face all the time."

"Oh, sure. Why not? So we'll continue the tour with the camera then?"

"If you don't mind?"

"Not at all."

Luc pulled out his smartphone and took two wireless microphones from his shoulder bag. He put one of them on the neckline of Linnea's T-shirt and the other one on the collar of his polo shirt.

"You're filming with your phone?" the physicist asked, surprised.

"Most of the time, solo operators do. The quality is good, and I think it suggests a certain immediacy. If the production looks too professional, subscribers get suspicious. After all, they don't want to tune in to a TV station, they want to see something personal."

He switched the camera so he could see himself on the display. His short blond hair was fashionably combed to the side, his big horn-rimmed glasses rode a little lower on his nose, his light three-day beard sat neatly trimmed over his tan skin, but not so clean-trimmed that he looked boring. "Are you ready?"

"I'm ready," Linnea said.

"All right, I'm going to do a quick intro, and then I'll switch over to you, ask some questions and stuff. Okay?"

"Sure."

Luc pressed the record button and grinned at his likeness.

"Hello dear geofreaks, it's your Lucky Luc again, and I'm back today with a very special video, because I flew all the way from San Francisco to Cebreros, Spain, just for you—that's near Madrid, by the way, for all of you who only used your globe to play soccer when you were a kid. As you know, since my video series on the moon and Mars, I'm not just a big fan of NASA, I'm also a big fan of ESA, and they have a really big project going on: Euclid."

Luc pointed upward with an outstretched index finger. "Euclid is the newest space telescope in the world, launched just a month ago from Europe's Spaceport near Kourou in French Guiana on the northeastern coast of South America. It's been a week now since it reached its target point, Lagrange Point 2, on the far side of the moon. If you want to learn more about Lagrange points, just click on the link here at the top of the video."

Again, he raised a hand and pointed to the right above his head.

"Euclid has quite an exciting mission: to find out more about dark energy and dark matter, and it's equipped with state-of-the-art instruments. It's going to get to the bottom of one of the biggest mysteries in astrophysics, and it's going to give us great new insights. To get you up close and personal as usual, and to see firsthand exactly how this works, I flew down to the ground station in Cebreros and teamed up with Linnea Daubner. She's a physicist here at Deep Space Antenna 2 and runs the night shift."

Luc switched the camera and adjusted the image to show her upper body with one of the office workstations. There were some posters of telescopes in the background. Not much, but it would have to do. "Hi, Linnea."

"Hello and welcome to Cebreros," she replied with a smile, waving charmingly into the lens.

"Linnea, you're not just listening for signals from E.T. here, you're also in charge of controlling Euclid and receiving its data, right?"

"That's right. Euclid is the most advanced space telescope of its kind, and we're very proud of that here at ESA. It basically has two instruments, both accessing a telescope that is almost a meter and a half in diameter and has a focal length of twenty-five meters. The first instrument operates in the visible spectrum and the other in the infrared spectral range. Data from both is sent directly to us here in Spain via a moving antenna and then analyzed."

Linnea grinned mischievously. "Luc, your viewers at PlanetLuc like to see real science in progress, don't they?"

Luc switched the camera and made a questioning grimace. "I guess we all know the answer to that, geofreaks, hmm?"

"Well, let's see what Roberto's up to." Linnea nodded to the future audience. "He's sitting at the controls and will be realigning Euclid's eye at the start of the night shift. Our colleagues at NASA have spotted a comet that will pass very close to us. They've asked us to take a closer look at this cosmic visitor. Let me reassure you that it will remain a comet and possibly give us some nice pictures in a clear night sky, but there is no danger. So, would you like to be there live?"

"Oh, yes indeed!" Luc kept the camera on and followed Linnea as she made her way around the back of the huge working console. Linnea was good in front of the lens. Maybe the whole thing here would be the crowning achievement of his series on traveling celestial bodies. Roberto had apparently already been briefed. Luc hadn't thought ESA, the European bureaucratic colossus that always had to reconcile the interests of umpteen member states and their budgets, had that much professionalism and flexibility.

The astronomer grinned most photogenically as they rounded the corner and approached the wide semicircle of stacked displays. In front of him were a mouse and keyboard. Out of the 20 or more monitors, only four were still on.

"Hello, Roberto. What's the deal with the realignment? Can you explain to our viewers what exactly is about to happen here?" Linnea asked, calmly sitting down on the desk that blended seamlessly into the display wall. Luc kept himself between the two of them, zooming in first on Roberto's fingers on the keyboard and then on his face.

"Sure," he replied with his rolling accent. "NASA has discovered a new celestial body, the comet we have internally called Cassandra 22006. It was named after its discoverer, Cassandra Miles, who is based in Houston, and is even on duty today. It won't be called that officially, of course, because there's already a Cassandra, and the sequence number isn't correct, either—it stands for an internal designation of initial sightings with reservations. I have Cassandra's number stored for direct dial on this phone."

Roberto póinted to one of the vertically mounted landline phones under the displays. "She'll want to know where her latest find is headed, of course."

"Cassandra. Catchy name. What do we know about it?"

"NASA stumbled upon it using the reactivated Neowise space telescope as it scanned the sky for unidentified objects. From the looks of it, it's a five- to fifteen-kilometer-diameter chunk of debris and water ice that trails a proud tail behind it."

"That's why comets are sometimes called tailed stars," Luc explained to the camera's future audience. "They don't always have that tail, except when their orbit causes them to pass close to the sun. Usually it's water that evaporates in the process, forming a long jet of exhaust similar to a rocket. It is because the molecules flying around are captured by the radiation of our central star that they shine so beautifully to our eyes or telescopes."

"Right," Roberto agreed, nodding as Luc resumed filming him. "Cassandra is very special. Despite its size, it's from the other side of the sun and has apparently eluded us for a long time, which is really surprising. Its coma is over three million kilometers in diameter on the Neowise image."

"A coma," interjected Luc, "is a kind of nebular envelope that forms around the comet's core when it is near the sun, usually measuring only a few kilometers across. It is exceptionally long, in this case, ten times the distance between the earth and the moon. The tail then forms toward the back, reaching away from it as far as one hundred million kilometers. Unimaginable distances, dear geofreaks."

"Yeah, comets get us all excited every time."

"Joyful excitement," Linnea interjected, and Roberto nodded eagerly.

"Absolutely. A visitor of such magnitude only happens about once every ten years."

"And your job today is to find out more about it?" asked Luc, trying to keep the conversation from getting out of hand.

"We're realigning Euclid and taking a closer look at Cassandra. This is a really recent find."

"Linnea already said there was no danger from it. What makes you so sure of that?"

"Oh, we know that because of statistics. Comets are very fragile celestial bodies, made up of frozen water, rock, and lots of dust debris as was mentioned earlier. They are generally very loose and not as solid as asteroids, which can become meteors or meteorites when they hit the atmosphere. Visitors like Cassandra approach the sun and slowly disintegrate, often breaking apart and fading away. They aren't particularly long-lived once they become visible," Roberto explained, turning away from the camera and back toward the keyboard.

He began typing a whole series of inputs, and the monitor directly in front of him displayed a green line of code on a black background. "I'm going to start the realignment now, which will require me to enter the new coordinates by hand. Euclid's control unit will do the rest."

"What exactly do you hope to gain from this observation?" Luc posed his rhetorical question in such a way that he hoped most of his audience wouldn't see through the obvious info dump.

"The picture from NASA was just that: a picture. One snapshot among many. We now know there's a comet out there, but that doesn't tell us much of anything. Is it long-period, meaning it orbits the sun like a planet, or is it short-period, meaning it has a shorter orbital period between the sun and Jupiter. Usually, Jupiter, due to its tremendous mass, is responsible for them slipping out of orbit. Several things are unusual about Cassandra: normal comets orbit the sun for millions of years and are always visible. This one has only been visible once. Also, the image from Neowise has a mysterious shadow."

Linnea pointed to a display further to the right and made some entries on a second keyboard. An image popped up on it, presumably showing Cassandra 22006 with an impressive tail and large coma stretching backward. But in the middle of the coma was an obvious black spot. Linnea placed her finger directly on it.

"Weird," Luc muttered, moving closer. The camera of his smartphone in his hand followed as if by itself. "How does that even work? A smudge on the lens?"

"We wondered the same thing... Cassandra Miles assured

us that everything was right with the lens even though comparison shots show no such blackening."

"But that would mean there's an object in front of the comet," Luc pointed out. "What could that be?"

"We don't know. If it were an asteroid, for example, it would be many kilometers in diameter, making it a real heavyweight from the Kuiper Belt or the Oort Cloud. Two objects of such mass do not fly that close to each other. Their gravitational effects on each other would be minimal but still impactful. They would probably have been flying parallel to each other in relative proximity for millions of years. That seems most unlikely," Linnea said confidently, pointing to Roberto's display with the lines of code he had entered. He'd just hit the Enter key and a loading bar popped up. "How's it looking, Roberto?"

"The realignment is complete. Now it's a matter of waiting for the results. Euclid will shoot a series of images that the computer then stitches together. Comparison images are taken after an hour and another at twelve hours—then, after three days, a week, and two weeks. So, by then we can say quite reliably how fast Cassandra is moving and in what direction."

"How old is that picture from NASA?" he asked.

"A few days."

"So comparing your first picture to the original might already provide some clues, right?"

"Yeah, we hope so. Are you seeing anything, Roberto?" asked Linnea.

The astronomer had frowned in concentration and was typing away on his keyboard before he looked up, pressed Enter, and slumped back in his chair. A photograph composed itself pixel by pixel on the lowest display, gradually forming the image of the comet. Something was different.

"This is from just now?" asked Luc.

"Yes," Roberto assured him.

"Where's the shadow?"

The two ESA scientists moved their eyes closer.

"It's not there anymore," Roberto said.

"Right," Linnea muttered, pointing her finger at a bright crescent about a centimeter away. "What's that?"

"It looks like a halo of light," Roberto commented.

"Could that be our mystery shadow? An asteroid?" Luc pointed the camera at himself. He spoke in a hushed voice, and the other two didn't even seem to notice. "Guys," he said at normal volume, "I think we're onto something special here. Did we just discover something?"

"We can certainly rule out a lens effect," Linnea countered.

"It has to be a celestial body. The area in front of the halo is definitely darker than the surrounding area." The Spanish astronomer spoke with an increasingly heavy accent—obviously a phenomenon that occurred when he concentrated. "We'll have to wait for the other images, or we won't get anywhere."

As it turned out, Linnea and Roberto took great pleasure in spending the next few hours with their one image, comparing it over and over again with Cassandra's first. The fact was that the shadow was no longer there, and there was now a dark spot with a light effect—possibly backlit—to the left of the comet.

Luc was so tired that he eventually left the room. In one of the offices he discovered a sleeping mat, presumably set up by an overzealous employee. He lay down on it and folded his hands behind his head. When he found the mat less comfortable than he'd hoped, he considered going to Linnea and asking her to take him to the hotel as agreed, but that would only make him feel bad. So he dismissed the idea.

First, he didn't want to disturb the two scientists in their work, which was obviously so exciting to them—a rare occurrence. And second, he would hate it if something new came up and he was in a hotel somewhere, slumbering away to a bad movie after drinking some even worse red wine.

No way—this was exciting. Luc had never heard of two stray celestial bodies from the edge of the solar system getting together and crossing planetary orbits so close to one another. It was a sensation, and if he did well, he would be the first to report it. In his head, he again went over the agreement with the ESA, which basically just stated that he could only record if he were given permission to do so. In return, he didn't have to hand over the footage for a preview and release—otherwise, he wouldn't have consented.

The other point was that he could not use the ESA space agency logo without consent. In this case, they had been very insistent, which puzzled him; after all, NASA's commercial release of their logo had created a worldwide buzz, and ever since, everyone was wearing it on their clothing. But that was the way it was.

So he got up and pulled out his smartphone. He tousled his hair a bit and laid his glasses to one side. In the semi-darkness he found a small battery lamp on the desk, and switched it on so that a diffuse light fell on his face. When he was satisfied, he activated the selfie mode recording.

"Hello, fellow geofreaks, it's your Lucky Luc again," he whispered conspiratorially in a sleepy voice. "I'm currently in the Cebreros ground station building in Spain recording a new video for you to watch in its entirety on Sunday. If you're up for it, give me a thumbs-up, and don't forget to hit the subscribe button if my secret science mission is already driving you crazy!

"Here at the control center, the night shift is currently at work, consisting of just two people—and me. NASA has recently discovered a comet that's extra-large and is just passing by the sun. It's amazing it hadn't already been discovered. But it gets even more exciting. From the looks of it, it's a double, because the image of Cassandra—which is the name of the comet—has a shadow that could apparently be an asteroid.

"We don't know more specifics yet, but I'm telling you, there's a brilliant episode of PlanetLuc coming your way on Sunday! As you know, the series about meteorites and how they have affected our Earth's history has been a real project of the heart. In my geophysics studies, I worked a lot with remnants of former impact events and always found it fascinating how strange visitors from the darkest depths of space have changed and influenced our planet.

"If a chunk like the one we just had on our screens were to approach our beautiful Earth, we'd really be screwed, but I don't need to tell you that after my video series. Just think of the Tunguska event or the extinction of the dinosaurs. If you haven't seen the series yet, just click on the link to it here in the picture above. I'll stay tuned for you guys and keep you posted. Your Lucky Luc!"

He turned off the recording mode, put on his glasses, and began to roughly edit the video and feed it with the appropriate links. Then he added the tags—asteroid, meteor, comet, impact, Tunguska, dinosaur, Armageddon—and started the upload. It took what felt like an eternity with the poor reception here in the boondocks. When the blue bar finally reached its end, he switched off the desk lamp.

Luc peered over the half-height privacy screen of the office cubicle to the back of the control panel, from where the muffled voices of Linnea and Roberto reached his ear. Before he'd started his trip, his fear had been that it would be a bust. He'd already shot with Musk and had been disappointed by everything else since, even when things had gone really smoothly and professionally at NASA.

ESA, however, had always seemed to him like that dinosaur among space agencies. Reliable, technologically significant, and precise in all its projects, but always a little hampered by the morass of too many agencies and ministries through which the Director General had to wade to get his funding. To witness a truly exciting discovery here and now was something he had never expected, even in his wildest dreams across the Atlantic.

He'd been more concerned with opening up more prospects for his followers. Luc had plenty of subscribers from Europe who, while they certainly found SpaceX and NASA sexy, had an underappreciated giant on their doorstep in the form of ESA. In this episode, he expected to show ESA as a bit more open and modern—showing its youthful side. After all, his channel had ten times as many followers as ESA's, and Luc was an individual.

Whether it would pay off for them, he didn't know. With institutions like ESA there was only so much that could be done. You couldn't make a sow's ear into a silk purse. But that wasn't his job, either. He was here to fill his channel with exciting content and add new subscribers, and that plan seemed to be going really well.

When he woke up, he didn't even realize he'd fallen asleep. There was still a gloomy twilight in the control center, but he no longer heard the two ESA employees in discussion. Instead, something rustled very close to him, and he had to blink a few times before he realized what it was. Linnea was rifling through a stack of papers on the desk in the cubbyhole he'd appropriated for an overnight resting place.

"What's the matter?" he asked sleepily, rising to his elbows. Then he felt for his glasses and put them on.

"Oh," the Austrian said with a wince. "I'm sorry, I didn't mean to wake you. And sorry I didn't take you to the hotel. There's just too much going on here right now."

Luc made a dismissive hand gesture. "You weren't going to get me out of here anyway. What's up?"

"I'm looking for a phone number."

"In a stack of papers? Why don't you turn on the light?"

"Thanks." Linnea pressed the battery light, and the flood of photons stabbed his eyes. "Our mathematician's. His name is Filipe, and he's only been here two days. We haven't entered him into the system yet. No stupid jokes, okay?"

Luc raised his hands defensively and ran them through his hair. "Nah, nah. What do you need it for?"

"Roberto thinks we have enough images of Euclid to be able to calculate the asteroid's trajectory with a manageable deviation."

"*Asteroid?* What happened to Cassandra?"

"Cassandra 22006 keeps flying, but Cassandra 22007 is coming our way, if we haven't made a mistake. But to do that, we need to reach Filipe."

"So it really is an asteroid!" said Luc triumphantly. "I knew it!"

"Yes. But I need Filipe's number now."

"You don't want to embarrass yourselves when you ring whoever-it-is out of bed. So you want the math geek to do it all over again?" he thought aloud. Linnea turned around, and her expression looked ghostly, made up of shadows thanks to the lamp's dim light. At first he thought she was angry, but when she spoke she sounded normal.

"Exactly. This sort of thing doesn't happen often, so we'd better be sure that everything's on the up and up. We won't be ringing anyone awake, but first thing in the morning, we should inform the Director General," Linnea said. The physicist turned around and continued to rummage through the pile of papers until she finally shouted, "Ha!" and pulled a piece of paper out of the mess. She waved it in his direction and ran out of the cubicle.

Now that he was awake, Luc used the time to check the reactions to his short video from the evening. It had already received several thousand likes and over six hundred comments—not bad for a few hours. A message popped up. His video was now grayed out, and in the middle of it, in emotionless, small font, it said: 'This video violates guidelines.'

"What's this all about?" he asked, incensed. "Violates guidelines?"

Furious, he began jumping back and forth in the settings looking for the cause, but couldn't figure it out. He hadn't used swear words, said or shown sexist things, and certainly hadn't mouthed the word 'virus.' When the lights in the control center suddenly went out, he didn't even notice at first, still transfixed by his phone's display. "What's wrong with the power?" asked Luc, looking up from his smartphone screen. It was the only light source, as far as he could tell.

"Power outage!" replied Linnea from somewhere.

Luc stood up and peered over the privacy screen of the office cubicle before walking out to the control area. Roberto was still sitting at his keyboard and he raised his arms in frustration. The physicist was using the flashlight function on her own phone, forming a sort of island of light in the darkness.

"Todito muerte!" the astronomer grumbled, pushing buttons frantically, but nothing happened.

"Does that happen a lot?" Luc asked.

Linnea shook her head. "Rarely."

"No generators for cases like this?"

"There are, but they were just replaced and should be hooked up this coming weekend."

"I guess the only thing to do is wait," Luc said with a sigh.

"What fucked up timing!" cursed Linnea somberly, slamming a fist onto the tabletop. Looking up, she grimaced apologetically. "Sorry. I didn't mean to—"

"It's okay, I hear you. It's really shitty timing."

"I was just about to forward all that data," Roberto grumbled. He stopped abusing the keys on his keyboard and threw his arms behind his head. He pulled his own smartphone out of his pocket, and with his brow furrowed in anger, he typed in a number.

"Who are you going to call?" Linnea asked.

"The technicians. Tell them to hook up the new generator now!"

"It's the middle of the night!"

"I don't care." He dialed and held the phone to his ear, only to lower it again and let loose a barrage of Spanish curses.

"What is it?"

"No signal. It's just static and scratching!"

Luc looked down at his phone's display. It still showed three out of four reception bars. As a test, he pressed the speed dial for his brother, but his smartphone only emitted an ugly noise that hurt his ears. "Fuck, what is that?"

"Something's jamming our signal," Roberto replied redundantly. "Maybe it's related to the power outage."

"If it's a large-scale problem, the cell towers could be affected," Linnea speculated. "I guess the only thing to do is wait and see."

Luc squinted at his battery level—50 percent. Not much—he wished it were higher, but still, no reason to pass up an opportunity. He switched to the camera app and pressed selfie mode before hitting the record button.

"Hey, fellow geofreaks. As it stands, my detour to ESA is getting more and more mysterious. First, we discover an asteroid flying in—cosmically speaking—close proximity to a previously undiscovered comet, so it's probably eluded us for ages. It's coming toward Earth, even though it probably won't hit us. It cannot be known with one hundred percent certainty at this point.

"Now the power is out, and all systems are dead until further notice. I'll keep you posted. If you're excited about Sunday's full episode, leave a thumbs up and post in the comments below how close you think Cassandra 22007 will come. For now, I'm going to make sure you see this, and as soon as possible. Your Lucky Luc is not going to be shut down anytime soon. In case my video gets locked again, I hereby give everyone free re-upping to keep it viewable!"

"Really now?" grumbled Roberto, looking at him angrily. "We just make a major discovery, and all our data is gone, and you have nothing better to do than record a message for your followers?"

"No, I haven't," Luc sneered back. "After all, I'm not an electrician or the man with the diesel generator. Or would you feel better if I waved a wrench in my hand?"

"Relax, you two," Linnea intervened. "This is just a power outage—not the end of the world. Luc is here because he's doing something on us for his channel, so he can film all he wants, Roberto. Got it?"

"Yeah, sorry, it's all right," growled the addressee.

"I'll unpack my Starlink receiver," Luc decided. "Do you mind if I put it on one of your cars?"

The physicist looked surprised. "You're a Starlink customer?"

"Uh, sure. Worldwide Internet, no matter where I am? I'm a YouTuber!"

"Cool. Then we can fill in Darmstadt and Paris right away!" Roberto gloated, clearing his throat. "If that's okay, I mean."

"Yo, why not? I'll upload my video. It won't take a minute. And then you can call your people. Deal?"

"Deal." The astronomer visibly relaxed.

"You'd better use my pickup," Linnea suggested. "It's parked next to the dish."

"All right, thanks."

Luc walked to the corridor, illuminating the way with the help of his display, which was just enough to avoid bumping into doors and walls. His eyes had adapted to the more challenging conditions by now, allowing him to make do with what little photons they had available. He could have used the flashlight app, but that would have been at the expense of his battery. Again, he was annoyed that he had used up the power bank during the flight and not recharged it immediately when the opportunity had presented itself. Maybe he should take a seminar against the fear of flying so that he didn't have to distract himself all the time.

In the entryway, his large suitcase still stood as if forgotten in the foyer of a mediocre hotel. Luc tipped it to the side and unzipped it. Directly underneath, on top of his clothes, tripods, and camera bags, lay a flat box, roughly reminiscent of a pizza box in terms of its dimensions. Flipping it open on the sides, he pulled out the receiving antenna for SpaceX's satellite system, which would allow him to access fast Internet anywhere in the world.

Power or no power. The fist-sized battery he taped to the fold-out tripod supplied the built-in router for about four days. Stepping through the door to the outside, he found himself under a clear starry sky, where it was considerably brighter than inside. He put the smartphone away and blinked a few times until he felt he could navigate the semi-darkness well. Two cars were parked next to the door, connected by thick cables to the power columns, which now had nothing to give. The dusty space between him and the huge Deep Space Antenna 2 looked like the gray surface of a lake, and the trees to the right and left resembled dark waves on the horizon with jagged spray.

It took Luc a few breaths before he could make out a downright puny shadow under the mighty complex about 100 meters away. That had to be Linnea's pickup truck. It stood a few meters from the colossus of steel and would give him a slightly elevated position with an unobstructed view of the night sky, so just right. He walked across the square to the short bed, large cab Toyota at a moderate pace. He climbed into the back and, after unfolding the tripod, placed the receiving antenna on the roof. Using the single button on the bottom, he activated the router and waited for the red light to turn green.

Meanwhile, he looked up at the facility, which was much more massive and impressive up close than it had seemed earlier. Like a monster of tangled shadows with all the struts, cables, and little catwalks for engineers, it looked like it had fallen here from another time.

Above the gigantic base, which was as big as an apartment building, the antenna formed a wide-open bowl, as if to catch the stars that twinkled in the darkness above. A few were brighter, such as Venus, and Mars, which stood out for its slight red cast. But a few others weren't stars but satellites, like the first Starlink batches, which were still highly reflective and had drawn the ire of amateur astronomers. Two candidates shone relatively erratically, as if they were trying to send out a Morse code. Sometimes stronger and sometimes weaker, they sparkled in the firmament quite close above the treetops in the west.

Luc looked to the light-emitting diode on his Starlink receiver and hummed in satisfaction when he saw it flicker green. Quickly, he opened the YouTube app to upload his video from a moment ago. The blackout was annoying, but it would also bring him far better viewership than he had hoped for from the appointment with the ESA.

As the loading bar progressed, he looked over the treetops again, only to find that the two stars or satellites were now much more prominent than they had been just moments before. Also, their glow was still erratic but of a deep yellow. The next moment, two helicopters were racing overhead, then abruptly braking. Their rotors whirred no louder than a car with an internal combustion engine, but the headlights they had just turned on were as bright as the sun, fizzling the night into a mere memory where they hit the ground. Luc uttered a curse and jumped from the back of the pickup to take cover behind it.

Helicopters? Where did they come from? And why are they so quiet? flashed through his mind, and his hands were suddenly sweaty. Peeking over the taillights, he watched the helicopters descend on the dusty clearing between the control center and the antenna, kicking up little wind swirls of dust and grit. The swirls hared away from the rotor blades and covered the body of the truck with a soft patter. Luc saw shadowy figures detach themselves from the sides of the cabs, moving in a crouched posture toward the squat building. In their hands, they held...

"Oh, shit!" he cursed in a strained voice and turned away, his back pressed against the mighty rear tire. Breathing heavily, he leaned his head back until it touched the rubber. Those were guns! Soldiers—armed soldiers! The way they walked reminded him of special forces in action movies or thrillers. With shaking limbs, he climbed under the pickup and ducked under the vehicle's chassis, pulling out his smartphone and quickly setting it to silent and the screen to its lowest brightness. Then he pressed the record button on his camera app.

"Guys," he gasped in a whisper, frightened by the fear on his face when he saw his likeness. "It's getting crazier and crazier here! Two helicopters came out of the night sky, some stealthy sort that were hard to hear! They landed and spat out men with guns. I think someone's covering something up."

Luc repositioned the camera so it was facing forward, and filmed the scene from under the truck. A half-dozen shadows with long objects in their hands were headed toward the building, and four others were running toward the antenna, just past him and the pickup. They moved catlike and with frightening speed. He saw someone emerge from the entrance holding a brightly lit smartphone in front of him, presumably with the flashlight activated.

"Luc?" he heard Roberto call out, but Luc remained silent. Something clicked a few times and the astronomer's silhouette slumped! The cell phone in Roberto's hands sailed to the ground, no longer glowing.

"Oh shit!" whispered Luc, and his phone fell out of his hand. He picked it back up with trembling fingers and turned the camera toward him. "Guys, if you're watching this, I'm trying to get away. Someone is trying to kill us to shut us up!"

Hastily, he ended the recording and typed through to the upload process when someone grabbed him by the left ankle and dragged him across the gravel as if he were being yanked along by a horse. Involuntarily, he cried out and lost his smartphone. The pickup's undercarriage sped past his eyes, and then suddenly he saw the starry sky again.

In a moment, he caught sight of a hooded soldier in a black suit and combat helmet, who just let go of his foot and pulled the submachine gun from his back to point at him. He stared into the muzzle in horror.

Luc's last sight was a flower of fire.

1
JENNA

The first thing Jenna had learned about Kuala Lumpur was that it means 'muddy estuary' in Jawi. When she'd flown in on the CIA's Learjet the day before, she'd racked her brains over how the first settlers had chosen such a name. The two rivers, the Gombak and the Klang, were indeed wide, and so brown they looked like sewers. Where they joined the sea they looked like an almost criminal blemish, pouring out into the inviting blue of the southern Andaman Sea as a kind of visual cancer.

However, the city was nearly 40 kilometers away and had nothing to do with this muddy estuary, at least not geographically. Behind the windows of the gleaming skyscrapers and tower-like apartment complexes of the center, however, things looked quite different, or Langley wouldn't have sent her here. While the skyline illustrated Malaysia's rapid rise thanks to its highly productive Chinese minority, the suburbs of corrugated iron shacks and mold-infested terraced houses, which seemed almost to shy away from the banking district, testified to the fact that there were also lots of losers in this development.

It was always like that, and it didn't evoke pity in her.

People were easy to understand. They needed food, sex, and a job, and most of them were content to let it be their job to find substitute satisfactions for the other two things. So they moved to the cities to make money and use it to collect cigarettes, coins for diversion at the slot machine, a Netflix subscription, and an internet connection so they could watch porn when the wife was out of the house while they tried to cover up their dissatisfaction with her unnecessary consumption of cosmetics and clothing.

Had they stayed in their villages and continued to till the field, their only annoyance would have been the hard work behind the plow. But the lure of civilization was too strong, of course. Why toil under the sun for meager meals and do the same thing every day? Why not move to the city where there were supermarkets with plentiful cheap food supplies, where you could eat what you wanted, drive a car, and see a doctor?

Like the Sirens who tried to call Ulysses to his doom, capitalism did the same to them. You could move up. You could afford more if you were more productive. You could be a part of progress. But that progress didn't apply to everyone. When there are large numbers of fish on the reef, the sharks have a feast. They need the fish, but the fish don't need the sharks—except these folks don't know that.

So they go to town, and suddenly they have a hole in them. Nothing is ever enough, none of the multiple distractions make them happy, and the spectacle of human settlements with their concrete deserts and bad air closes them in like a glittering prison.

We're monkeys, Jenna, without hair, her instructor Tony had been wont to say. Some throw shit at you while wearing suits. Others throw shit at you while wearing blue jeans or stained white undershirts. But they all throw shit out of their cages. Then he'd spent several years showing her the various cages, from meetings with bank executives to union negotiations to transshipment points for Mexican drug cartels. The knowledge of the monkeys without hair had come naturally as a result.

"Do you know your way around here?" someone asked. Jenna looked to her left with a friendly smile, leaning further on the rail of the infinity pool on the 52nd floor of the Platinum Suites, from which she enjoyed a perfect view of the Petronas Twin Towers at night. They gleamed like two artfully lit phallic symbols that male hairless monkeys liked to put up wherever they wanted to boast about their economic achievements. Kuala Lumpur had long had the tallest. Not just one, but two. At the time, she was sure the entire enclosure had danced and shrieked.

Next to her stood a Chinese couple with broad grins and SLR cameras around their necks. He was in his mid-50s, badly shaved with thinning hair and sunburn, his watch an Omega, his fingernails too long to pass for neat, and his shoes carelessly laced. His wife was slightly younger with crooked teeth, but they were white. Her red dress begged for attention.

Middle management in early retirement, she thought. He regrets his decision to quit work early, while her regrets go much further back in time, but she can't escape from her prison that may not even be of her own making. So she numbs herself with consumption and small tokens of freedom.

"Not really," she finally replied apologetically, tugging her bikini into place. The pool's water was too warm because the surrounding tropical temperature screamed for cooling rather than a bath. At least she was outside and didn't need air conditioning, which Jenna hated. Just as much, though, she hated being half-naked and having to look up, as was the case right now, to the two tourists who'd bought the view with an overpriced luxury room and were standing on the edge snapping photos rather than getting wet.

"But maybe I can help you anyway?"

"I was just wondering what you were seeing," the retired manager replied in broken English, gesturing downward. "Your gaze was so... focused."

"Oh, that's easy enough. I'm a secret agent and I spy on my targets," she replied seriously, and when he looked at his wife with a furrowed brow, she snorted and slapped a hand over her mouth in amusement. The man's expression cleared, and he made a valiant effort to mask his momentary confusion with feigned amusement.

"Gotcha!"

"You're funny," he said, grinning cheek-to-cheek. "Are you here on business?"

"Yes and no. I'm a business traveler, but I'm off right now. At least for a little while."

"What are you doing?"

Jenna looked at his wife, who was trying her best to look like she was not following their conversation. It was obvious she was listening with her ears pricked up and her fists in her pockets. She wasn't jealous. It was more the disrespect of her husband flirting with an attractive American woman next to her while she stood unappreciated in her red dress.

"I'm a headhunter," Jenna explained.

"Ah, you're poaching talent."

"I eliminate competition," she corrected him, and they both laughed. This time it was his laugh that was genuine.

"Ha, that's good. At the company I worked at, the people in the human res... How do you say in English again?"

"Human resources," Jenna helped him out.

"Yeah, right. They were always as funny as you, too."

"They think I lack a sense of humor in my company."

"Oh, you are too modest. In Chinese we have a saying: the songbird with the crookedest voice has the straightest back."

"You just made that up, didn't you?"

"Yes." The Chinese man chuckled gleefully, and she did

the same, which only made his confidence grow. He clearly thought he was very charming and funny. Jenna judged him as repulsive in character in addition to his unattractive appearance, which openly proclaimed that he had never cared for the state of his body. Others were not always as obsessive as she was, but she expected them to at least care a little.

"You fox, you!" Jenna pointed an imaginary gun at him and winked. Together they laughed as if they were having a good time and an even better connection. Then, as if beginning to lose interest, she let her laughter subside and turned back to the view.

"Do you work for one of the big ones?" the Chinese man asked expectantly. Actually, he seemed to be saying, I don't want this to end. It's got to keep going. It's going so well, after all.

"What do you mean?" Jenna queried.

"Which company sent you here?"

"Ah." She waved it off. "I really don't want to talk about my work. Besides, I bet you've accomplished significantly greater things."

The Chinese man threw his chest out, barely noticeably, but to Jenna, the change in stance was like a flashing neon signal. "Well, I've actually seen quite a bit."

"Let me guess. Defense industry?"

"Do I have a sign on my forehead?"

"No, but you look like a man who can hold his own and knows exactly what he's aiming for." She let her mouth execute a smile she'd practiced many times with lip gloss in front of the mirror.

"I guess you could say that. You're right. I have initiated cooperative ventures with Russia."

"Where have you been? In Russia, I mean."

"Krasnoyarsk, mostly." He hesitated only briefly, then

waved it off. "Ugly, really. Not a place you want to take a vacation."

"I understand. I'm more for sunshine and the beach anyway."

"I'll bet," he replied, glancing furtively at her enticing breasts peeking just over the water's edge and pressing against the pool's railing at just the right angle. He didn't notice, of course, that she had noticed. Most monkeys without hair were the same.

Jenna looked around the pool and saw the rich people with their smartphones and selfie sticks wading through the blue water. In between them, there were also a few backpackers who were doing quite a bit for the right Instastory. Their chatter and giggles were the typical noise in the enclosure, which she barely heard. Instead, she saw what she needed to see before turning back to the would-be charmer, who already seemed disappointed by the moment of her drifting attention.

"Is that your wife?" asked Jenna, and he raised an eyebrow in the direction of his companion in the red dress, expectedly unwilling.

"Ah, yes." He quickly changed the subject. "Are you here alone?"

"Yes. My husband stayed home. But he's not so much a child of freedom anyway."

His eyes gleamed. "What do you mean?"

"Oh, he just doesn't like to travel that much." She raised a hand and brushed a blonde strand out of her face until she had pushed it behind her ear with her index finger. "Nice to meet you, Mr....?"

"Xiami."

"Xiaomi? That's the name of that phone company."

"No, no. Xiami. No o. That's my name."

"Sounds kind of nice," she found herself nodding before turning and wading toward the other side of the pool.

"Hey," he called after her. "You haven't told me your name yet."

"Right," she replied with a laugh and headed for her target, a young man with a well-toned body and tanned skin. He was taking pictures of the Petronas Towers. In the morning, he'd eaten breakfast in the lobby. Alone.

"Well, is it going to be anything?"

"Excuse me?" he asked, about to turn away again before he eyed her more closely and lowered his smartphone.

"Look out!" She pointed at the cell phone he was almost holding in the water.

"Oh. Thank you. Uh, what was the question?"

"I wonder if the photo will turn out. The night is really clear, and the smog is manageable. You're not gonna get a better moment than this."

"Yeah. It's more important to enjoy it anyway. The moment, that is."

"I have a desk calendar that says the exact same thing," Jenna opined, grinning to banish the wrinkles of confusion from his forehead. He was a handsome little monkey, but the furrows in his skin didn't help hide the impression of a rather manageable mental capacity.

"What are you doing here?" the young man wanted to know, now turning to face her fully. A cute mistake, but they were almost all like that.

You see three people... Tony's words came back to her. *One is facing you, looking directly at you, another you only see in profile —he could turn all the way to you, but doesn't yet—and the third you only see from behind. Which one should you be interested in? The one who absolutely wants to offer himself to you, the one who is still undecided, or the one who is turning away?*

Jenna turned her side to him and gazed out at the Petronas Towers. Further down, traffic pushed through the street canyons in endless columns consisting of red taillights and beaded strings of yellow-and-white headlights, a humming organism of sheet metal and gasoline.

"Oh, I'm just passing the time." Out of the corner of her eye, she saw the Chinese man arguing with his wife, who stomped off toward the exit a moment later, leaving him standing there. "What are you doing?"

"Vacation."

"No, I mean professionally?"

"I'm a soldier," he lied. Well, at least it was a half-truth.

"Wow. I like a man who knows what he's fighting for." She grabbed his upper arm and nodded thoughtfully. "And who keeps fit." She let go again and pointed to the rest of the pool. "They're all like greaseballs on soup, if you ask me."

He chuckled. "You're mean."

"My name is Jenna." She held out a hand to him without quite turning to face him, and he shook it a little longer than necessary.

"Brian. Who was that guy?"

"Oh, some rich Chinese prick. Made a really disgusting pass at me." Jenna shook herself as if the mere memory made her uncomfortable.

"You want me to make sure he leaves you alone?"

"I wish guys like that would take a simple 'no' for an answer."

"Been up against a lot of heavy hitters like that." Brian clearly liked himself in the role of the helpful soldier. His shoulders tensed a bit, as if to emphasize the V of his torso. When she didn't answer, he looked to Mr. Xiami. "Hold on a second. I'll be right back."

"Should I get us drinks?" Jenna put a hand on his forearm,

as if to casually restrain him, and yanked at the hairs on his skin.

He grinned.

"Where are your clothes? I'll wait there, then. My skin's all wrinkly."

"The black Adidas bag with the red cap on it!" He then headed out as she made her way toward the bar, which was to the right of the exit: a small bar with blue ambient lighting that matched the pool exactly.

Before she had even exited the water under the gaze of a few surrounding men, she saw Brian and Mr. Xiami arguing with each other out of the corner of her eye. Jenna took the exit and fished her towel off the hook next to the automatic door before wrapping it around herself and walking over to Brian's bag. She grabbed the baseball cap and keycard to his room and headed toward the elevators.

The woman in the red dress was still waiting outside the elevators, which from experience she knew could take a long time to arrive. Her gaze was lowered. When the doors finally opened, they slid into the car with at least ten other happily chattering guests. Xiami's wife pressed 15.

Don't tell me you have a room on 15th, too, her eyes seemed to say as their eyes met. Jenna hunched her shoulders apologetically and avoided her. New hotel guests entered and left along the way, most of them dressed in striving-to-be-casual evening wear to arrange taxis from the lobby for a ride to Bukit Bintang. She took advantage of each new composition to move closer to the doors. When they finally opened on the 15th floor, she stepped out and looked for the metal signs with the room numbers to orient herself.

The walls were dark shades of brown and gray, and the light shone warm and homey from trim without detracting from the dignified look. Before revealing that she didn't know where to go, she found the appropriate sign and turned left. Behind her, she could hear the footsteps of Xiami's wife.

Jenna looked down at the keycard in her hand. Room 17. Of course she already knew it, but it was never wrong to keep double-checking things like that. She stopped just before the large door with 17 engraved on it and turned on her heel. The red dress rustled slightly as the woman in her wake paused, startled.

"Don't worry, your husband isn't my type," she said, grinning lightheartedly. "Besides, I already have another date." She pointed meaningfully at the door beside her.

The Asian woman merely looked at her and then nodded, so Jenna wasn't sure if she even understood English, but she didn't appear confused. That would have to do. She swiped the keycard across the sensor panel and waited for the click before pushing the door inward and disappearing into Brian's room. It was dark because she didn't insert the card into the designated power slot.

She paused until her eyes adjusted to the twilight provided by the streetlights down below bleeding through the darkened windows. Then she went into the bathroom, flicked on the shower light, pulled two clear plastic bags from the dispenser and returned to the main room, setting the bags on the television table. Next she unplugged one of the bedside lamps from the outlet before yanking the cord's other end from the lamp base and placing the length of wire beside the bags. She then went to the door, opened it a crack, and listened.

After ten minutes, during which Brian, as expected, did not return to his room, either being still in the pool or looking for his card, she returned to the nightstand where she placed one of the hairs she had pulled from the ex-soldier's arm and pulled the sanitary bags over her hands prior to reaching for the phone and dialing the number for the bar downstairs.

"Platinum Lounge here. How can I help you?" a young-sounding male voice asked in her ear.

"Oh, hello, room 1517 here. I'd like to speak to my husband, Mr. Xiami. He left his cell phone here," she said lightly.

"Wait, please, ma'am." A tune played, and Jenna eyed the wizened, chlorine-coated skin on her arms until the phone clicked briefly. A gush of Chinese washed through the line.

"Hey, Mr. Manager," she stopped him. "Sorry if that guy down there had to play the gorilla. I don't go for guys like that. I'm more into real men who have accomplished things and know what's important."

"Oh. You?" He sounded drunk.

"I'm staying in room seventeen, fifteenth floor. My favorite wine is Shiraz." Jenna hung up and went into the bathroom, where she turned on the shower and drew the curtain. She tuned the radio to a station that played smooth cheesy soft rock. She draped the white guest bathrobe on the floor in the doorway to the bedroom and wrapped the still-wet pool towel around her right knee before holding the bedside-lamp cord with both hands in the hygiene bags and standing behind the front door. It wasn't five minutes before there was a knock.

It's open, she thought, and after a moment her guest figured it out, too, gently pushing the door inward until the faux wood almost touched the tip of her nose. A black squat silhouette came in and didn't notice her, staring instead toward the bathrobe on the floor, pointing like an arrow into the bathroom from which warm light flowed into the darkness like ambrosia—at least in his mind—of that she was sure.

Hesitantly, perhaps cautiously, he stepped forward and casually kicked his foot back against the door, which slid slowly into the lock. Jenna took two steps forward, threw the cable over Xiami's head, and pressed her right knee between his thoracic and lumbar spine. As he let out a choked cry she pulled hard on the cable, cutting off his air while simultaneously taking away his ability to move back.

"Hello, Xiami Li," she pressed out in liquid Chinese strained between her teeth. "We should talk."

It took almost two minutes for him to stop resisting. Even though she was standing behind him, Jenna's mind could see his reddened face and bulging eyes.

"I'm going to loosen the cable a little now. You scream, I'll tighten it again, you move in a way I don't like, I'll tighten it again. Do you understand me? If so, wiggle your right foot."

His right foot jerked back and forth.

"Very good." She eased the cable, which had dug into her palms, too. "I know about your dealings with Petrolina Krasnoyarsk. Who did you make contact for?"

"What?" gasped Xiami. "I don't know about—"

That was as far as he got before Jenna tightened the cable again. A strangled squeak escaped him before he tried to wriggle out of the trap, but every movement caused her to push her knee further forward and pull her hands back.

"Wrong answer. That was a test question. You made the contact for Chiu Wai, a man about whom not much can be found out. Owner of a medium-sized company in Guangzhou. They make satchels. Why would you want to put someone like Chiu Wai at the same table as Yuri Golgorov, the shadiest oligarch in the Russian Federation? You're out of get-out-of-jail-free cards, Xiami Li. One more misstep and I'll pull the cable up a bit, shattering your larynx, and you'll suffocate. Painful and unnecessary. So... answer."

Jenna gave way again, though a little less than before.

"He... paid me to..." he groaned between raspy gasps.

"I know all that," she replied impatiently. "Why?"

"I don't... know. I don't know! Really! Chiu Wai!"

"Himself? What does Chiu Wai want with Yuri Golgorov?" She pulled a little tighter. "The two of them were supposed to meet in Kuala Lumpur back in 2014, but it never happened. Why?"

"He... He never... arrived."

"Who?" she eased up a little.

"Golgorov. He took Flight MH17." Xiami sucked in a rattling breath between his blue-tinted lips.

"The one shot down by a Russian anti-aircraft missile over eastern Ukraine..."

"Y... Yes."

"You're suggesting that the shooting had something to do with Yuri Golgorov? But then, how could he have met with Chiu Wai two weeks ago?"

"Yuri Golgorov is not a person. He is a... principle." The Chinese man tried to slide his fingers between the cable and his skin, which she quickly put a stop to by means of a quick tug.

"What are you talking about?"

"Yuri Golgorov stands for the fact that certain powers should not be subject to state control alone."

"So someone wanted to make money."

"Don't they always?"

"Where can I find Yuri Golgorov? The current one, I mean."

"I don't... Really!" His voice sounded shrill, almost panicked.

"You made contact with Chiu Wai, so you know a way to contact him."

"A burner phone. I got it from a contact in Shanghai I had already worked with. He promised me ten million yuan if I gave it to Chiu Wai. Chiu Wai gave me another burner a week later for Yuri Golgorov."

"And you went to your contact, who brought you to Yuri Golgorov after you proved helpful," Jenna concluded.

"But you already knew that."

"Golgorov wanted to know if you could operate below the omnipresent surveillance apparatus." She nodded. "Useful and rare. How can I find Golgorov?"

"Not possible."

"Don't tell me now, 'He'll find you.'"

"He's completely paranoid. Even I've never met him directly," Xiami croaked.

"How do I make contact? You have a phone, don't you? You're not here on vacation. Where were you going to meet him? I'm running out of patience, by the way."

"All right, all right! I'm to go to Malacca and meet someone at the marina. I don't know who. They just said they'd find me and pick me up to take the next step. My phone is in the safe in my room."

Crap, Jenna thought. His wife didn't belong in her plan. So what she got from him would have to do. Deviations were not acceptable.

"What car do you drive? What's the license plate number?"

"Black Mercedes, S-Class 500, WHL-888, tinted windows." Xiami's voice trailed off. "What do you want with—?"

Jenna yanked the cable back with a violent jerk and an ugly crunch sounded. She let the Chinese man's body slide off her knee before turning to pick up Brian's baseball cap and drop it next to the dead man. She then pulled the plastic bags from her hands and wrapped them in the towel before quickly leaving the room and taking the elevator upstairs. Just before the doors closed, she saw Brian step out of another elevator. Once in her room two floors up, she buried the plastic bags in the trash, pulled out her cell phone, and called the front desk.

"Hi. I'm from floor fifteen, and I just heard noises coming

from room seventeen. I think you should call the police. I'm really scared!"

She hung up, pulled her wig off her head, and went into the bathroom to wipe off her makeup, speed-shower to rinse off the chlorine, and fix her own hair before getting dressed, stuffing her belongings into her suitcase, and leaving the hotel.

2

BRANSON

"No, that's not a whale penis, that's a piece of the pressure-washer hose," Branson McDee grumbled, and another storm of giggles and outright laughter erupted. He looked down at the gaggle of 4th-graders crouched close together on the floor of the bridge in front of him, hiding their grinning faces behind their tiny hands. Sighing, he shook his head and wrestled a smile onto his face. Another hour and his cheeks would ache. He hadn't worked his cheek muscles this hard in a long time, and he hoped it would stay that way. At least for the next few weeks.

He dropped the piece of tubing onto one of the consoles and disengaged himself from his captain's chair, which was affixed to the varnished wooden floor with four ugly bolts. "So, what do you guys think? Shall we go out back and see if old Joe's found anything for you?"

"Yay!" the little ones shouted excitedly, jumping to their feet. Some even clapped their hands or jumped up and down. The two teachers started shouting again, trying to instill a basic level of order in their charges, which was halfway successful. One of them gave him a reproachful look over the children's heads, and he merely shrugged.

These modern-day 'treasure hunting' outings had been going on for a long time, and by now, Branson knew what the little visitors liked and didn't like. Was he supposed to tell them about how they hosed down and brushed off the finds after dives, only to throw almost all of it back into the sea because it was worthless? How did one glamorize a job that was in reality so uninteresting?

There wasn't a way, he thought, giving a wave to his assistant Xenia, who stood at the door by the starboard railing. At his signal, she quickly opened it. She was still young, not much older than 20, he guessed. Still, she did her job well and had a very high tolerance for frustration, which was more than Branson could say for the many other young people who had hired on with him on and off over the years.

Most just wanted a few weeks of adventure and some fancy photos for Instagram, and they did not want to spend days in the hospital for decompression sickness, or eat fish and chips every day, or go without a shower for long periods of time. This job separated the wheat from the chaff, that much was certain. Besides, she was pretty and didn't ask stupid questions.

The children flowed around her like a storm tide, but Xenia held her ground with loud orders and stern looks, just barely ensuring that the little rascals did not fall through the crossbars of the railing into the harbor basin. Branson followed them, along with the two teachers who kept loudly calling individual children to order and looking visibly stressed.

They would surely scold him, just like the countless others of their colleagues before them. But that didn't bother him. Decisions about primary school children's school trips were ultimately decided at parents' evenings. Xenia, and the children's enthusiastic reports, were there for him to rely on. At least, after Joe's little show.

Marv and Johnny were already waiting on the aft deck of his ship, which was considerably shallower than the foredeck and stretched to the retracted crane at the stern. The two divers were wearing shorts and neoprene shoes but were barechested, which no one here in Hawaii minded. They split the class in two and directed them onto the makeshift, padded, permanently mounted storage benches that lined the aft deck, which was otherwise an open area of scuffed wooden planks. The sunshade, attached with ropes to tall poles, rattled in the light wind, helping to make the humid heat a little more bearable.

When the little visitors and their chaperones were seated, Johnny nodded to him and finger-combed his curly blond mane, which contrasted sharply with his tanned muscles, before—at a signal from Branson—strolling over to the crane.

"So, my fellow treasure hunters," intoned Branson, leaning with his arms folded in front of his chest beside the door from the stairway that led down into the bowels of the *Triton One*. "Do you know what the most exciting part of a treasure hunter's life is?"

"Nooo!" some shouted, while others began to whisper and giggle.

"No? Well then, let me help you out: Why are we going to sea?"

A few hands were raised and shaken wildly with expressions of absolute urgency on the owners' little faces, to ensure he didn't miss them.

Branson grinned and pointed to a girl with red hair and freckles. "What's your name?"

"Lisa," she answered shyly, and he didn't miss Marv's widened eyes, the dark-skinned sea bear staring at the girl as if she were a dangerous predator and not a 10-year-old.

"Okay, Lisa. Why do we treasure hunters go to sea?"

"Uh, to find treasure?" It came out of her mouth as a question.

"Right! Who all would like to see treasure?" he shouted and clapped his hands. Enthusiasm immediately flared up. Wide eyes and widened mouths focused on him, then followed his outstretched hand toward the crane.

"Well. Do you hear that sound?"

At first there was just a little splashing behind the boat, and then the water bubbled and rippled. With Dwight Decker's ship already moored directly behind them, and the damn rich prick stretching his berth to the limit with his ultra-modern fat-cat vessel, there wasn't much room between his own boat's stern and Decker's ship's bow, which loomed as high as a cathedral over a pilgrim. On the right, a few onlookers stood on the harbor wharf watching the goings-on intently as a diver emerged from the water, snorting as he spat out his mouthpiece.

Old Joe pulled the mask off his face, and his white grin shone in contrast to his ebony skin. "Ho, Cap'n!" he cried in his deep, grating voice. "I found something down by the crabs, besides a fat great white shark!"

"Joe!" replied Branson, rushing barefoot across the open quarterdeck. Before he'd started moving, he had reached out a hand to Lisa, who grasped it timidly and came along with him, her eyes wide with excitement. At the end of the rows of seated students, who craned their necks forward, right, and left so as not to miss anything, he continued to hold her hand and braced his free hand on his hip. "Well, I'm glad that shark didn't eat you!"

"I lured him away from the shipwreck," grumbled Joe, his oldest sailor and co-owner of the *Triton One*. "I'm not having my treasure snatched away by a shark!"

"Lisa, do you see any treasure?" asked Branson, pointing to where Joe floated in the harbor water.

She shook her head.

"Should we ask him where it is?"

She nodded and stuck a finger in her mouth before looking away sheepishly. Then she gathered her courage and called out, "Where's the treasure?"

"Oh," replied the sailor, making a rueful face. "I'm a pretty old whippersnapper, you know, and that crate's heavy. I think we're going to need the crane if we're going to lift it. That's a real fat treasure! Maybe you can talk Johnny into helping us?"

They all looked toward Johnny, who was lying next to the crane in surfer shorts with his hands clasped behind his head as if he were asleep.

"Is he asleep?" asked Branson, acting indignant as he looked in the direction of the school class sitting attentively behind him.

"Yessss!" they shouted.

"Shall we wake him so we can bring up the treasure?"

"Yaaaayyy!" The children's high-pitched voices were louder than a hurricane, and swelled even more as he intoned, "Johnny, Johnny, Johnny!" and they immediately joined in. The 30-year-old mechanical engineer pretended to startle from a nap and looked around in confusion.

"What's the matter?" he asked, rubbing his short-shaven skull. His handsome face was only surpassed by his charming grin, which caused the two female teachers to give him dreamy looks. He didn't have to worry about the next class trip for once.

"We need the crane!" shouted Lisa with some urgency, and there was hardly any shyness left.

"Oh, did we find treasure?" Johnny acted confused and looked around as if he needed to get his bearings.

"Yessss!" the fourth graders shouted, and 20 fingers

pointed behind the stern to Joe, who was still floating in the water between them and Dwight Decker's ship.

"Oh. Hi, Joe!"

"Johnny, you sleepyhead, why don't you and our new sailor Lisa here lower the crane so we can lift the treasure!"

"Sure, uh, right away!" The kids laughed as Johnny hurried to get to the control panel for the machine. He eyed the many buttons and rubbed the stubble on his chin. "Lisa, can you give me a hand?"

Lisa ran to him, and he pointed to the two buttons for raising and lowering the load chain.

"I have to control the crane. When I say *down*, you press the arrow pointing down, and when I say *up*, you press the one pointing up, okay? I can't do this without you, so don't leave me hanging, okay?" More quietly, he added, "Or I'll have to keelhaul ya later!"

Lisa didn't understand his joke, and the other kids pretended they didn't hear that part so they wouldn't have to show their ignorance, while the teachers frowned.

I guess I'll have to talk to Johnny again about jokes suitable for children, Branson thought, watching the young machinist wink at Lisa and set the crane, rusted in several places, in motion. Joe directed it with hand signals so the boom chain was sliding down directly toward his head, until he managed to grab it along with the three hooks on it.

"There, now keep it coming down nice and easy," Joe said with satisfaction, putting his goggles back on and reinserting his mouthpiece before disappearing underwater in a white flurry of bubbles. Silence fell until there was a rattling of the chain, and Johnny and Lisa clapped their hands enthusiastically. The schoolgirl pressed her button, and the ship's machinery began grumbling, supplying the crane with enough power to lift the chain with the weight on the other end.

A short time later, there was no stopping the class. Boys

The Meteor 1

and girls, who were done with stretching their necks to try to see, jumped up and ran to the rail as Joe was lifted out of the water, sitting on an ancient-looking crate. His legs dangled casually from the faux wood, and masses of water splashed to all sides of him and the treasure chest. Johnny shouted something to Lisa, who came over to Branson and gave instructions with awkward hand movements so the sailor would steer his shipmate and the precious cargo with precision.

When Joe and the box touched down between them on the last part of the quarterdeck, he shuffled a few meters with his fins and all the gear. The most curious children—to whom he explained things here and there—gazed at him. The majority watched Branson undo the chains, pretending to survey the treasure thoughtfully.

Marv came over and, in keeping with the rehearsed procedure, handed him a crowbar, which he inserted at the tiny mark visible only to him.

"What do you think? Is it safe to open the treasure chest?" he asked the group, and the faces of most of the children were so filled with wonder that they couldn't answer. A few, however, shouted that they wanted to see the treasure.

"All right." He cleared his throat and motioned for them to take a half step back. Then he pretended to use all his strength to push the crowbar down to pry the lid open, quitting as though exhausted. "Whew, pretty heavy. Can some of you kids give me a hand?"

Several boys and girls immediately ran up and grabbed the steel tool he had sprayed with rustproof paint yesterday. Together they pushed it up once more, and this time Branson guided it to the point where he felt a slight click in the metal. The lid popped open, and he beckoned the other kids over as well.

With both hands, he motioned for them to grab the edges and push, or lift, with him. It squeaked and scraped, and a few drops of salty harbor water ran down the planks between their bare feet. The lid landed in Marv's and Johnny's hands, which, seemingly by chance, were suddenly there, making sure no one looked closely enough to notice the rubber edges.

Amazed and clapping enthusiastically, many children's faces bent over the mighty chest, and they were met by the golden glow of finger-sized gummy bears that glittered in their wide eyes.

"Whoooaaa!" they breathed excitedly, and then hesitated. Cautious glances met his eyes. When Branson finally put his hands on his hips and said, "Well, what are you waiting for? You don't get a treasure like this every day!" they started to grab, chattering loud enough for the whole harbor to hear.

"Enjoy," he exclaimed with a laugh, adding, "These gummy bears from Vosko Sweets are really crazy valuable!"

Branson avoided looking toward the teachers, having seen critical looks like theirs often enough. Twice a week, to be exact.

∽

After the kids and teachers left, Johnny and Marv cleaned up the last remnants of the visit and prepared things for the next class on Thursday. Branson stood at the stern with Joe, counting the wad of bills in his hand.

"Don't worry about it," his old friend advised him, crossing his arms—still strong despite his 60 years—over his belly. "At least we can keep the *Triton One*. If you hadn't come up with this idea, we'd be sweeping the parks in Honolulu right now."

"We're *treasure* hunters, Joe," Branson grumbled, sighing as he tucked the bills into the breast pocket of his colorful Hawaiian shirt. A single slip of paper remained in his hand. He waved it in front of his partner's face. "They even want a carbon copy of the bill every time. We get to pay taxes on this pittance, too!"

"It's enough."

"*Enough?* We've gotta make asses of ourselves here for this puppet-dance, just so we can keep on making asses of ourselves!"

"We'll find something again," Joe assured him, pointing into the evening sun, setting behind the pier's walls and bathing the entire marina complex in a romantic warm light. The longing in Branson's chest was intense and still pulsed as much as ever, even in his early 40s. It was as if the sea were calling to him, wanting to reveal all its secrets to him. But he knew her, had sailed her for over 20 years, and knew of her forked tongue, the Sirens' song trying to lead him astray.

"One rusty dagger in twenty years," he growled in frustration, crumpling the invoice copy in his fist. He considered tossing it into the water in a pointless, albeit good-feeling act of rebellion. Eventually he scowled and shoved the paper into his back pocket. This simple act was further evidence of his defeat. The first and most conspicuous was the polished bow that loomed before them as if it was about to ram the stern of their beloved *Triton One*. It was so high that Branson could just make out the wide bridge superstructure with the radar tower behind it. The *Decker I* looked more like a military frigate than a treasure hunter's ship.

"She's ugly," Joe commented, apparently noticing his gaze and now looking up as well.

"No, she looks damn good. Plus, it's already all-electric, goes one and a half times as fast as we do, and doesn't get paint thrown at it regularly by environmentalists."

"I was beginning to think you were going to start again about how they have better sonar and their expensive technology buys them success," his second-in-command laughed, patting him on the back before he started mimicking him.

"Oh, I'm Dwight Decker, the richest fart on Maui. I look for treasure for National Geographic and throw around my million-dollar inheritance because I want to play pirate and score women by the dozen. I can't tell a shark from a ray, let alone know how to pilot a ship, but I just buy the best computers that do everything for me that's harder than clapping my hands."

"He rammed the harbor entrance at Oahu," Branson insisted, reluctantly having to join in his friend's laughter. "I've got a newspaper report in the picture frame on the bridge to prove it."

"Yes, he did."

Together they laughed for a while and then stared at the reflections of the setting sun in the calm docking area. Behind them, Marv and Johnny hummed a song together, and Xenia could be heard on the bridge talking on the phone with her boyfriend. The shouting started at the same time every evening, and when Joe gave him a knowing look, and Branson shrugged wearily in response, they chuckled again.

Branson shook his head. "You know what? Fuck it," he remarked. "We're not just doing this for our dream of being able to go back out. We're doing this to stay together."

"Amen," Joe whispered, and the usually equanimous sea bear sighed audibly. They were treasure hunters, but first and foremost, they were dreamers and adventurers who had been born into a world that didn't have much left to offer such free spirits. They were unconventional and couldn't live in a hamster wheel, and no one appreciated that. What chance did they have but to carry on and hope to set sail again someday?

Joe had ten years left on his parole. Marv and Johnny were wanted in Europe on warrants and protected only by the stubbornness of the State Department, which could change with every turnover in government. Xenia didn't realize it just yet, but she wanted to cut her umbilical cord to the mainland at any cost. They just needed to give her a good enough reason, and that meant cash. She was young and needed to see some perspective to take the leap into the life she wanted.

And Branson himself? He had nothing to keep him ashore besides a failed marriage and a son who wanted nothing to do with him. On the contrary, every time he looked at the ropes that tied them to the quay, he felt like they were chains around his own wrists.

"Hey, you old farts! Stop musing about old times and get over here!" shouted Xenia from somewhere. Only now did Branson notice that her phone call had ended, although the hour was not yet up. He looked at his dive watch and frowned. Joe, too, seemed surprised and looked around.

"Here! Ashore!"

They turned and saw the assistant standing on the crumbling concrete of the dock. Barefoot, she bent under the sunshade of the quarterdeck, which was a little lower than the masonry, and her thick blond braids hung almost through to the floor. Hastily she beckoned them over.

"Come quick! There's a guy here in fine threads who's throwing around some pretty big bucks right now!"

Branson straightened up and looked at Joe. Surprisingly, his older friend with the gray stubble at his temples was almost faster getting ashore than he was.

3

LEE

Lee looked at his reflection in the bulletproof glass, ran his eyes over the reverse-image 'L. Rifkin' patch on the chest of his blue coveralls, and smiled. His creamed-coffee-brown face, with its black short-cropped hair and round eyes with a bit of slant at the outer corners, looked happy around his bright white smile. Really happy. Five years ago, when he'd started his training, that smile had been far from a guarantee. Ten men and women had been chosen, all knowing that only one would do what they were being trained to do, and one more would stand by as back-up. The rest would have to settle for other functions.

Today Lee wondered how he had ever endured those five years with the *Sword of Damocles* risk of failure hanging over his head. Sixteen-hour days, six days a week, was no small feat when you considered that, in the end, it might have all been for nothing.

"But you made it, and now you're up here for your sixth month," he said to himself, changing his focus so that he saw not his reflection but what was outside the window: Earth. Just then, Africa was passing over 400 kilometers below him, with its browns, yellows, and greens unevenly distributed. The view from the cupola, the observation deck of the International Space Station, was mesmerizing and always reminded him how crazy this place was. It was racing around the planet at more than 20,000 kilometers an hour, yet it looked like it was the other way around, like Africa was turning away from him like a shy girl. The bands of clouds over the Atlantic formed a sprawling carousel, spinning around the eye of a massive storm brewing west of Cabo Verde.

"Well, are you feeding your Instagram channel with brag photos again?" a voice asked from behind and below him. It was Sarah MacDougall, who floated in to join him. The astronaut, just like Lee, was part of NASA's current crew of only two. She squeezed herself between him and the many cables, tethered laptops, and handholds until they were perforce very close, and gazed out.

"I don't do that," he replied.

"You can still hope that you'll get your fame on social media, after all." At 34, Sarah was only two years younger than himself, and beautiful. The freckles on her petite nose lent her something youthful, just like her ever-so-slightly mocking mouth, all of which was accentuated by her dark-red braided hair.

"I barely have any free time as it is, and I'd rather spend it here looking at our home planet."

"You never get over that sight, do you?" she asked earnestly, sighing. "It looks so fragile."

"Yes. The atmosphere looks like nothing more than a tiny film of gas, so defenseless against the infinite blackness of the vacuum that surrounds it. It's hard to believe it's merely gravity that keeps everything stuck to that colorful lump of rock." He smiled. "What a wonder."

"That one view changes your perspective. If only more

people from down there could be up here and see it like we do." Sarah sighed, sounding melancholy all at once. "Instead, they fight over which lies from the Internet are their favorite truth, destroying everything our species has achieved over millennia."

"Just six years ago, I was sitting in a cockpit as a fighter pilot, there to shoot down other men who believed in a different flag, if a suit in Washington got his way. Today that sounds terribly absurd to me."

"I'm sure the penguins in the White House wouldn't like hearing that, though."

Lee turned his free hand palm up, the zero-g equivalent of a shrug. "Well, they can come up here and argue with me."

"They love you way too much to do that, you being their Air Force poster boy, now carrying the American Eagle into space. Stoic, conservative, no social media account. A shirt-sleeved Kentucky boy with Native American and Taiwanese ancestry. Darling of social justice warriors and senators, humble, down-to-earth, and emblematic of successful integration and reconciliation with the past."

"The perfect projection screen for anyone," he grumbled. "Nothing more than a screen, so to speak."

"A pretty one, after all," she teased, and her mouth formed an even more mocking expression. "Oh, come on, Lee-boy. Don't be so serious and thoughtful all the time. This is your last month here before you're relieved. You're not going to get nostalgic, are you?"

"I don't really want to leave." Lee looked her in the face, and she returned his gaze before he turned away with a clearing of his throat and a gesture outside. Not wanting to put his body into a rotation that would cause him to bump into her or the work equipment, he hooked his right foot behind one of the blue grab bars. Somewhat sheepishly, he glanced at his wristwatch. "Only three hours until the *Falcon* arrives."

"Finally, back to work," Sarah sighed.

"At least you get to go out this time."

"And you get to dress me, for hours. I know a dozen guys back home on Earth who would have spent a year's salary on that."

"For dressing or undressing?"

"That's all a matter of timing." She grinned and pulled her feet together before pushing herself off the bulletproof glass with her hands and floating through the circular hatch back into the tranquility module.

SpaceX's *Falcon* heavy-lift rocket, scheduled for today, was special: it was the first time the commercial spaceflight provider had undertaken a project for the Russian side. Until now, Musk's corporation had always been able to view itself as the U.S. government's favorite child, but the $500,000,000 order from Russia underscored that SpaceX was not a sister to NASA but a company intended to make a profit, and so the decision was ultimately understandable.

After the initial domestic political squabbles that this move had triggered in Washington, the situation had eased considerably in the last few months before the mission launch, when the Russian corporation RJKK Energiya had struck a deal with NASA: the payload of the currently most powerful rocket on the market was a radio telescope that was to be connected to the ISS.

At first, the plan was apparently for a satellite, but after public outcry from the U.S. and Russia over the deal with SpaceX, it was decided to propose the International Space Station as the deployment site, since the telescope could also be attached to a mating adapter. Russian cosmonauts would maintain it and analyze its data, but in the spirit of science—

according to the press release—they were happy to let Americans and Europeans share in that, too.

So the delivery was taking place today, and so far its preparations had not aligned under a lucky star: Their Russian colleague Anatoli had fallen ill a week ago, right when it came to the first training sessions for the field mission. So, Sarah had been selected to step in to rehearse the attachment of the radio telescope, together with the second Russian on board, Dima.

Anatoli was healthy again but hadn't practiced, so he was no longer an option. RJKK Energiya was not particularly pleased about it, but had apparently decided to exploit this new situation for its own benefit and portray itself as profoundly open. In the service of science, and progress for all humankind, they would let an American woman screw around with their sinfully expensive apparatus.

Fifteen minutes later, together with Dima, they were in the Quest module, the American airlock for field operations, which consisted of an inner and an outer part. Inside, two of the white spacesuits were suspended, and Dima and Sarah were currently squeezing into them by grabbing the circular metal edges and pulling themselves down. Markus, their colleague from ESA, took care of the Russian while Lee assisted Sarah.

The procedure took a total of two hours and was extremely complicated. Again and again they had to connect and disconnect cables and hoses, check data, tighten small eyelet connectors, test Velcro fasteners, straps, and clips, confirm and sign off the correct fit, and connect the individual parts of the spacesuits together and close them properly. It was also extremely cramped with four people and the many cables and computer terminals surrounding them. Every movement in zero gravity had to be made with the utmost care and maximum skill.

Sarah and Dima were condemned to do nothing the entire

time, stuck in the clunky suits without being able to move much, and barely saying anything while they were preparing for the away mission scheduled to last about eight hours.

From his own spacewalks, Lee knew the importance of mental focus. The exertion of such a mission was like nothing else. You breathed processed air, stuck in a restrictive mammoth of a suit, and with your fingers in thick rubber through which you had to perform precise manual tasks. After an hour, every joint from fingertip to metacarpal ached, and after six hours, you felt almost nothing.

Even more challenging, however, was the necessary level of concentration. There were no breaks, and every tool had to be used carefully and with deliberation. Forgetting to hook the carabiners just once could mean that an electric wrench would come loose and drift irretrievably away into the vacuum, where it could collide with a satellite in a few years, or even with their station. And that was potentially fatal.

"Everything looks good," he said as he finished getting Sarah ready, smiling encouragingly at her before taking her big helmet off its mount and pulling it over to them. She almost looked like a young girl under the white-banded hood on her head.

She grinned and gave a thumbs up. "Thanks."

"Good luck out there. I'm always here, okay?" He tapped his headset against his right ear. When she nodded, he put the helmet on the ring latch and locked it. Dima and Sarah did a final radio check with each other as well as with him and Markus. When everything had earned a thumbs up, Lee withdrew with his German colleague, locked the Quest module, and waited until the cosmonaut and astronaut had slid into the outer airlock.

The arrival of the heavy-lift rocket took place shortly afterward. Lee monitored everything from the cupola while Markus operated the Canadarm2 to assist in the final docking procedure. The *Falcon* was acting wholly autonomously, but mission protocol dictated that they had to be able to intervene at any time should something go wrong.

The long cylinder showed as a bright glint, then grew more prominent against the infinite black of space as the earth rotated on its axis below them. Erratic-looking correction bursts from the cold-gas thrusters kept firing intermittent fountains to adjust course. It was approaching the Soyuz docking ring below, which Lee could see clearly. This marked the first time SpaceX had been allowed to prove it could also operate the Russian adapters.

As expected, it worked, and after 20 minutes the oversized white tube, attached to the Russian module like a gas cartridge, slid across the sky with the station. Sarah and Dima had already made their way from the Quest to the other side and were waiting at the adapter for the cylinder to open, which it did in response to a computer input from Lee. The two flaps opened in slow motion, revealing the interior, which contained the radio telescope. In its packed condition, he thought it looked like a dragonfly with its wings laid back.

Sarah floated into the cargo bay with a long umbilical cord and disappeared from his view before Dima followed her on the other side. After about 40 minutes they had released all the restraints, and the 10-meter behemoth of a telescope slid out of its cocoon under their hands. Since it had no weight, thanks to the weightlessness provided by their 'throwing parabola' around the Earth, they could move even an object weighing many tons quite effortlessly.

Still, this mission was extremely dangerous because they had to make it from the Soyuz adapter over to the equipment rack of the Russian part of the station. That meant using display controls on the sleeves of Sarah and Dima's suits to control the maneuvering thrusters SpaceX had attached to the telescope's frame until they could manually connect it to the adapter. That meant 12 meters of flight through space where nothing could be permitted to go wrong, or they would have a massive projectile in close proximity that could seriously damage their station.

"All systems nominal," Markus announced, following the progress of the radio telescope with the Canadarm. The two white, downright tiny, figures of their colleagues clung to the back of their fellow flight 'companion' like drowning men riding a log as they flew agonizingly slowly through the blackness. By now they were over the night side, so the station's lights and their suit lamps created a bizarre panorama. "Nice and slow, guys."

It took a total of an hour to dock the telescope, and in the end it had required help from the Canadarm when a sensor had failed. Ground Control, which monitored every move and gave instructions over the radio, had advised it, and the docking was carried out just fine.

Now the real work began for Sarah and Dima, who were responsible for setting up the radio telescope. The receiving dish—six meters in diameter—had to be unfolded and fixed in place, as did several other systems below it, including the extra solar sails for its internal power supply, since the station couldn't provide enough for operation.

In the end, everything was accomplished smoothly. Markus and Lee followed the operation by eye and via the cameras on the hull and in the helmets of their colleagues. Sarah and Dima followed their instructions, and those of Ground Control personnel who were confirming and commenting on their every move. It was a professionally done job, and nothing less than a first in spaceflight—a stunt of this caliber hadn't been pulled off since the Space Shuttle missions to build the ISS.

Lee knew that Markus and Anatoli envied Sarah and Dima for getting to go out on such an important away mission, but he saw it differently. He was happy for Sarah, and also for Dima. The latter was an extremely smart and hardworking cosmonaut, which was more than could be said for the typical Russian crewmembers, since they usually didn't have much to do up here except to be in space on behalf of their country. At NASA, they were often derisively referred to as janitors who took care of maintenance, and otherwise took photos and played cards while the Americans, Japanese, and Europeans conducted experiments 16 hours a day.

When Sarah and Dima arrived back at the Quest module, Lee was there with Markus, ready to free Sarah from her suit. Her face was pale and completely sweaty, as was usual after the exertion demanded by such a mission.

But she was still smiling. "Whew," she went, "that was certainly a... new experience."

"Yeah, go ahead and rub it in that I wasn't there," Lee joked, undoing the fasteners at her hips and gloves.

"You were close enough, at least with your eyes. I could almost feel your gaze on my ass. Sexy in that behemoth, huh?"

"I'm sure that thought will give me nightmares."

"Hey, Dima, when are you guys going to start this thing up?" she called out to the Russian, who was being taken care of by Markus.

"It's a secret," he replied with his amazingly accent-free English. "You know how it is."

"Are you in charge of that, or is Anatoli?" Lee asked.

"Anatoli, of course. He's a personal friend of RJKK Energiya founder Oleg Snietseva. What did you expect? But if you ask me, I can well do without staring at a monitor for two hours a day and gloating over the fact that I alone got the training for that monitor."

"They won't let you on there either?" asked Sarah in wonder.

"Nope. But I get to analyze the data with you guys when

it's processed. More tables." Dima snorted. "As you Yanks always say, 'Yay!'"

"YAAAY!" Sarah and Lee shouted in chorus, grinning at each other. He loved the exuberant atmosphere after successful field missions when relaxation set in because everyone had come back in one piece. The contrast between suiting up and 'unsuiting' was huge, as if they'd just had a wild party together and were sitting together while things quieted down again. He would miss all of this when he returned to Earth.

"Maybe I'll take a quick peek at the data when Anatoli's asleep, so I can at least see what they're looking at with this little thing that's such a blight on our beloved station," Dima said, chuckling, "or what superior skill my taciturn friend Anatoli brings to the table that I don't have. Apart from his vitamin B levels, of course."

"How illegal," Markus commented dryly, and they shared a laugh.

Afterward, they returned to their respective modules, Dima to the Russian Swesda, Markus to Columbus, and Sarah and Lee to Destiny, where they prepared their mission reports before going to bed. After the relaxation, in this case, came the duty. They wedged themselves cross-legged under their computers until they found good grips and then began typing. Every now and then they discussed their view of things that had happened and complemented each other where one or the other had a short gap in recall, which sometimes happened during such an extended mission.

"When I'm through here," Sarah said at one point, her eyes already nearly closing, "I can get hired as a typist somewhere."

"These reports have got to be the dumbest new deployment policy our guys down there could come up with," he agreed, patting her upper arm. "Go to sleep. I'll finish the rest for you."

"Careful. I'm so tired I won't refuse out of politeness."

"No problem. I wanted to visit Dima anyway and record a vodcast with him," he returned.

"You? A vodcast?"

"Yes, he asked me to do it. It seems he has a successful video stream on YouTube and several times he's asked to interview me for it. You know he dislikes the rift between Russia and the U.S., and we share that opinion. Since I have even less time starting tomorrow, and spent the eight hours during your stint looking out a window, now is my best opportunity."

"How does Dima do it?" sighed Sarah. "I feel like I've been run over by a truck, and he's up to recording an interview with you. At Swesda!"

"He's Russian," Lee replied tersely, and Sarah laughed.

"Touché. I'm going to sleep. Thanks again." She squeezed his shoulder and then floated away toward their sleeping chambers.

Lee finished her report, having long since finished his, and stifled a yawn as he slid to the intercom. He pressed the button for the Swesda module.

"Hey, Dima, buddy, I'm ready. I'm five minutes late, but I'm still awake." He waited for a response but got none. So he tried again, but neither Dima, nor Anatoli, who was supposed to be awake according to the schedule, responded.

Strange. Did they both fall asleep? he asked himself, wondering if he should just go to sleep or go to them. While he wasn't keen on doing the interview, he had promised it to his friend, and the cause was one he really cared about. So he finally made his way, sliding deftly from tether bar to tether bar and flying through the 'Pressurized Mating Adapter' into the Zarya cargo module, which was the first part of the Russian section.

All four walls were covered with cream-colored drawers with latches. Lee was always reminded of the earlier monitors, when computers had just broken into the mass market. It was cramped and felt stuffy. There were plate-sized square lights on the ceiling, like in a school corridor. At the end waited the connection to Swesda, its service module, and the cargo module. The Russians lived and worked across the hall in Swesda, but as Lee was puzzled to discover, the hatch was closed, and the small viewing window draped or taped over.

Locked? he thought, tapping on the window. "Hey, guys. Are you guys okay?"

No one answered him. He pressed his ear against the entrance and listened, hearing clicking noises and a muffled voice, but the passage did not open. The hatch was never locked—part of the etiquette on board—and the fact that now, of all times, it was locked worried him.

He flew back to the nearest intercom and called Columbus. "Hey, Markus, you there?"

"Yo," came the reply after a minute. "What's up, buddy?"

"Swesda is locked and the window is covered."

"What?" The German sounded incredulous.

"And I have a date right now to meet with Dima. Really strange."

"I'll call Ground Control and see if anything's been withheld from us up here. Hold on."

It took two minutes, and then he was back. "Ground Control doesn't know anything. They checked with the Russians, but they don't know anything, either. I'll come by."

"Yeah, you do that," Lee said, staring anxiously at the curtained observation window.

What's going on in there?

4

JENNA

Jenna walked out of the foyer of the Platinum Suites and into the Kuala Lumpur night. She casually heaved one of her suitcases into a passing garbage truck on a side street. The two garbage workers, cigarettes in hand, were arguing amiably and didn't even notice her.

She pulled out her satellite phone and dialed a long string of numbers she'd memorized. When the call went through she said, "In November, the rain weighs heavy," and added the code for an encrypted call: "Eight-four-seven-one-Washington."

It was almost a minute before she heard a deep male voice on the other end. "Jenna. Any news?"

"Yes. I have a point of contact."

"You mean a *contact*, I hope."

"No, I mean a *place*. Xiami didn't know the person, but he was supposed to meet someone at the Malacca marina."

"Do you have a plan?"

"Yes. I'll go to the meeting place and pretend to be Xiami," she said.

"Risky. You're assuming Xiami never came into personal contact."

"Of course he did. I don't intend to show my face."

"Is Xiami dead?"

"Yes."

"Very good. A whole generation in Yemen will thank you for this."

"He was a pig."

"Did you stay clean? Or do I need to call Wolf?" asked the deep voice of the Deputy Director.

"No, I'm clean. A corrupt ex-soldier who was almost certainly involved in a war crime in Aleppo will go to prison for a long time instead of me," she replied without any satisfaction in her voice.

"Good. What do you need?"

"More money."

"Is it ever anything else?"

"Aerial recon on-call would be nice," she joked.

"In Malaysian airspace?"

"Yes."

"How much money?"

"One hundred and fifty thousand in cash. Also, I will need weapons."

"I'll send you a rendezvous point. Give me three hours," the Deputy Director said. She was about to disconnect the call when he added, "Take care of yourself, Jenna."

She left the alley and walked toward Bukit Bintang. She desperately needed something to eat. The night was still young and just getting into the daily exchange process of day-trippers, commuters, night-swarming teenagers, and old guys in suits looking for distraction after a busy day of meetings and appointments. Everywhere she smelled the exotic spice blends used in the many sidewalk cafes and international restaurants of the well-heeled city. The trees on the sidewalks were

The Meteor 1

wrapped in nets of small lights so that they looked like magical creatures, glowing yellowish here and red, blue, or green in the neighboring streets.

Jenna didn't like it and wondered, not for the first time, why so many young people stopped and looked up and down the streets in fascination. The number of impressions merely confused the eye and disturbed orientation. She grabbed an order of pancit at a small diner that seemed somehow out of place with its weathered signs and sticker-framed window, behind which an old Filipina cooked the food and handed it out to the single person who was waiting.

No line, so I don't have to wait, she thought. I hate waiting, but the lack of a line is usually a sign that the food isn't very good. Still, this place has clearly been around a long time, indicating a loyal regular clientele, so at least I shouldn't get sick.

The pancit, which took almost ten minutes to prepare, tasted surprisingly good. She sorted out the onions and left them for the rats, of which there were certainly more in this city than human inhabitants. But she did not try very hard to distinguish the two from each other. She spent the time until she heard from the Deputy Director in the Bukit Bintang Night Mile, which was closed to traffic in the evening and open to pedestrians only. Here, one pub lined up after another, so dense that the many overdriven pieces of music overlapped in an unpleasant mix, as if to insult every nearby ear.

Jenna roamed the crowd, seeing small groups of Western men with beers in their hands fanatically discussing football, Chinese women with flashing umbrellas, and young people in light clothing pushing their way through the throng in search of the one pub that the *Lonely Planet* had recommended to them, and yet which was like all the others. Between two of the pubs was a two-meter-wide façade with closed shutters, and she leaned back against it, just watching the hustle and bustle.

She looked into faces and through them into their potential life stories and behaviors, memorizing patterns of movement and facial expressions, soaking it all up like a sponge. When a beep came from inside her small backpack, she was surprised to find that three hours had passed.

A simple message popped up on the satellite phone's display: 3.146920, 101.707455. Jenna pulled out her smartphone and entered the coordinates into the Google Maps app before stowing the sat phone back in her backpack and setting off toward the pinned site. She had to scour the crowd, mutter an apology here and there, and then squeeze into a small alley near the heart of Jalan Bukit Bintang, where she was alone with some trash cans and a handful of rats. They were fighting over a rotten hamburger in an open McDonald's box and froze in place when she disturbed their munching.

After a second's pause, the vermin scattered, gone faster than she could blink. The coordinates led her to an old dumpster. First she inspected the underside but discovered nothing, then she looked around to the right and left, waited until a bawling group of Englishmen had passed in celebration, and raised the lid. Taking the black burlap bag she found inside, she stowed it unopened in her backpack before leaving the alley from its opposite end and hailing herself a Grab Taxi.

Arriving at her new hotel—an interchangeable five-star skyscraper in Times Square—she examined the submachine gun parts and the three bundles of one-hundred-dollar bills. The weapon she quickly assembled was an MP5 with no registration number and three spare magazines. A good choice, she thought.

She went to the phone and called the lobby.

"Hello, room 102 here," she said after a curt greeting from the receptionist on duty. "I'd like to buy a car, a Mercedes S-

The Meteor 1

Class 500 with tinted windows. I'm afraid I don't have much time, as I have to head south tomorrow. Could you find a salesman for me?"

"Oh, it's already late, and this is a very specialized vehicle. Besides, I'm not a—"

"I understand that," she interrupted the man. "I can take care of it myself, but frankly, I'm exhausted, and I'd rather give the five percent commission to you than to a dealer. They have enough money as it is."

"Five percent? So, I'll make a few calls. If there is one such vehicle, it's in Kuala Lumpur, Ma'am, where there's practically everything."

"Wonderful. I'll be at breakfast at nine."

"All right, I'll take care of it. You can count on that."

"I do." She hung up, used the bathroom, and went to bed.

∼

The next morning Jenna quickly cleaned her room with chlorinated spray, packed her backpack, and headed for the breakfast room, where she didn't touch anything, but trudged straight to the reception desk. A young Malay with short hair and meticulously shaved contours looked at her and returned his attention to his screen until she stood in front of him at the counter and put on a smile.

"Hi. Room 102."

From the bored face, a bright radiance suddenly met her. "Ah! Hello, ma'am. I trust you slept well?"

"Yeah, totally. Thanks. Do you have car keys for me?"

"Of course, ma'am. I'm afraid it won't be entirely convenient, though."

"No problem." Jenna grinned and shrugged. "Is the car here yet?"

"Oh, no, no. But I'll take you," the young man assured

her, beckoning a receptionist over, at whom he threw a torrent of Malay before circling the counter and pointing toward the exit. "Come."

He isn't sure I even have the money, or if this is all just a drunken rich brat's joke, she concluded, smiling.

"All right. I just don't have much time."

"I won't be long!" He hailed one of the taxis outside the door, exchanged a few quick words with the driver, and then got into the back with her. Jenna looked out the window to signal that she didn't feel like talking, but the ride didn't take long. Soon they were standing in front of a Mercedes dealership located on the first two floors of a glass-enclosed skyscraper.

As it turned out, the receptionist hadn't promised too much. With a sycophantic demeanor, an employee presented her with a black S-Class 500 with tinted windows. Not bad. She paid $130,000 in cash and gave the hotel man $10,000. Not only was that amount generous, but it would make sure he kept the whole story to himself so as not to raise any questions, be it from the IRBM or envious people at work. She gave the remaining $10,000 to the Mercedes employee, an elderly Indian, who, in his joyous excitement, added a license plate that belonged to a test-drive car.

She thanked him profusely, then headed south down the highway. Her plan was bold, she realized, but the entire mission was nothing more than an underfunded and under-the-radar CIA attempt to hunt down a phantom that many decision-makers in Washington didn't even believe existed.

They never sent her on the standard missions. She'd gotten used to that early on. So, here she sat in her swanky Mercedes, driving past one palm oil plantation after another, taking less than two hours—once the traffic thinned down the moment she left metropolitan Kuala Lumpur. The former colonial city of Port Klang, which had passed through Portuguese, Dutch, and British hands over the centuries, stood in sharp contrast to the national capital. There were colorful, European-looking buildings amid mosques and pagoda structures, ancient churches, and fortress gates, all set in a winding tangle of individual palm trees and groups of macaques—real monkeys with real hair—that hunted through the city in search of tourists with food.

The docks, long an important transshipment point for the spice trade of the various colonials, were ugly with their rusting cranes and the fat container pots at the jetties. Even the marina further to the southeast couldn't compete with the otherwise beautiful tourist town and consisted of just two quaysides with a few polished sailing and motor yachts moored to them, but mostly wooden barges and poorly maintained small boats on wooden trestles waiting for attention from a technician.

There was a small cottage with a security gate where a scrawny old man in uniform sat, visibly straightening up as she pulled up. He pressed a button and waved her through with an implied bow before she could lower the window.

With tires crunching as they passed over dust and bits of stone on the concrete dock, she rolled onto the right-side wharf, which was wide enough for two cars. If her plan worked, the contact would eventually make himself known in anticipation of Xiami-san. But it didn't happen.

Jenna parked at the very end, where the harbor wall was so high it blocked her view of the sea. The largest ship present was docked there, an 80-foot yacht named *Hamburg* and flying the flag of Mauritius. She loaded her MP5 and stowed it in the footwell, after which she placed her hands where they were clearly visible atop the steering wheel and began speaking nonstop. Her lips moved with great emphasis.

"I don't know, sir," she said, followed by, "I know you're short on time, sir, but the contact will show up," and things like that. There was little activity on the quay—no wonder at 30 degrees and 90 percent humidity. From the Java Sea, heavy swelling clouds pressed over the Malay Peninsula and could be made out in the distance, dark and gravid with rain.

Occasionally, boat owners would come ashore and hop on scooters to head into town. At one point a fuel truck pulled right up behind her, and two port employees in high-visibility vests used a thick hose to refuel the big yacht beside her. That was it, though, so the lone man she saw in the dusky rearview mirrors immediately caught her eye. He looked like a guy who was out for a stroll in loose khakis and a blindingly colorful Hawaiian shirt unbuttoned to the base of his chest.

Jenna draped a strand of blond hair over her face and, dropping a hand between her knees, checked the proper fit of the MP5 one last time before the stranger arrived at her window and knocked on it. He was young, like herself, perhaps in his early 30s and Scandinavian or Central European with fair skin and light hair. However, eyeglass marks at the temples and delicate hands showed he wasn't one for physical labor, but probably more likely to be typing away on calculators and tucking pencils behind his ears.

She pressed the window button and the glass slowly retracted into the door.

"Open up," the stranger said.

"And you are?" she asked calmly.

"A friend."

"Which one? My boss has a lot of friends. He says his friends are usually better dressed."

"I can just go away."

Jenna pressed the window's power switch again and the glass rose. "Have a nice day."

"Wiesbaden," the young man growled.

"There you go." She pretended to listen to a voice in her

ear, bringing a hand up and tugging on her earlobe. "Sit in the back... Other side."

Wiesbaden broke away from the car and circled it. When he got in, she held the muzzle of the submachine gun in his face.

"Hi," she said good-humoredly. "Let's start from the beginning."

The contact's expression froze. His eyes slid to his left, and she heard his grinding teeth when no one was there. He was silent, so he was a professional, or trying to look like one, which was just as well for her.

"I want to meet him."

His left eye twitched.

"I want to meet *her*."

"You can forget that," Wiesbaden replied.

"Not happening." Jenna lowered the MP5 and pressed the muzzle to his left knee. "CIA? MI6? BND?"

He shook his head—individual beads of sweat were forming above his eyebrows. "If I take you there, not only am I dead, but so are you. So go ahead and shoot."

"You sure? It's your knee. Y'know what's interesting?"

"I'm sure you'll tell me."

"Since you ask, there is no surgery in the world that can fix a shot through the kneecap and knee joint. You'll be limping, unable to play sports, and walking with a cane for the rest of your life. Is that what you want? Last chance."

"I told you—"

Jenna pulled the trigger. The bang was deafeningly loud and her eardrums buzzed. Her head reverberated as if someone had struck a gong. The stranger screamed and grabbed at his half-mangled knee. It was a good hit with little blood flow through the patella. Slowly, almost mechanically, she pressed the muzzle to his other knee.

"You still have one. But the bang was very loud. I think

someone's going to call the police. Do you want to be here then? Or will you take me to your boss? A yacht off the coast, I'd guess? The *Wiesbaden*, perhaps?" she asked thoughtfully. He nodded, his face pale and a thick film of sweat on his forehead.

"I h-h-have a m-motorboat nearby," he stammered.

"Fine. We'll take that and say that the authorities ambushed us and shot at you. My boss got killed in the process, and I saved you. How does that sound to you?"

"Plausible."

"All right, let's go!" She leaned back toward him and reached under his shirt, where it was bulging all too obviously. She tucked his pistol into her pants and removed her jacket before getting out and opening the flap for the fuel tank. Then she tucked a twirled jacket sleeve all the way inside, poking it through the backsplash flap so it would soak up the fuel, circled the car, pulled out the young man who limped whimpering at her side as they went back around the car, and then she used a lighter to light the end of the fabric that hung down an arm's length past the tires.

As fast as she could with her new ballast, she hurried down the wharf until the stranger pointed to a stately Zodiac. Just as she maneuvered him inside and untied the rope from the bollard, the Mercedes exploded. With the tank two-thirds empty, there had been enough oxygen to provide a decent whoosh that could be seen and heard for kilometers.

Just what she needed. She tossed the thick rope into the boat next to the whimpering and squirming captive and jumped in behind the small, shaded superstructure before firing up the two 250-horsepower outboards and steering them out of the marina. As they sped out into the endless blue, she heard the first sirens.

"Where do I go?" she yelled over the roar of the engines and the roar of the spray.

"The course is stored in the GPS. The top coordinates!" came the shouted reply.

Jenna used her index finger to scroll through the navigation screen behind the small wheel. It took her several tries because everything was in German, and she'd only taken an introductory course—ten years ago at the university. When she finally found it, she picked up the pistol she'd taken from the contact and emptied its ammo into the water before tossing it to him.

"You fought well!"

He didn't answer.

After ten minutes the yacht came into sight. It was maybe 20 meters long, so not as big as she'd expected, and unobtrusive. The superstructure was sleek and modern, but less ostentatious than the ships of billionaires. She appreciated the coupling of German understatement with a life of crime under the radar.

It was going well so far, Jenna thought as she headed for the bridge at the stern, describing a wide arc. When the radio made scratching noises, she pulled it out of its cradle and tossed it to the contact man. He held it to his mouth and began to speak. She had to trust that his life was dearer to him than his loyalty, but if there was anything to rely on, it was the human instinct for survival.

As she was approaching to dock, she saw two stocky, buzzcut crewmen with camouflage holsters under their windbreakers. This was going to be exciting.

5

BRANSON

Branson climbed onto the wharf and tried to help Joe, but Joe snorted and waved his hand away. The marina in Lahaina in western Maui was relatively small. The main dock for the larger boats had been expanded a few years ago so that tanker trucks could navigate without any problems. Behind a tall wire fence, with tropical vegetation squeezing through it like a pent-up mass of groupies reaching their hands through the mesh to touch the two men, were some ugly utilities and the ring road that circled the island. From there, the gravel road branched off, its roll-up gate leading directly toward Dwight Decker's swank barge.

A GMC SUV was parked in front of it, with a man in a white shirt and khakis trying to fend off a swarm of flies. He might as well have had 'stranger' written across his forehead with his neatly combed hairstyle that belonged to a bygone era, and the polished leather shoes he wore emphasized that impression. No one in Hawaii walked around like that, except for the Mormons who flew here on vacation from time to time. But he clearly wasn't a Mormon.

Ashley, Decker's assistant, who looked like a Playmate

with her curves and brown curls that always seemed to fall like she had a whole team of fans and lights wherever she was, had already hooked the fish and was chatting with the newcomer.

"Who's that?" asked Branson, but Xenia merely shrugged and straightened her stained floral top, which showed more than it concealed. However, it didn't look suggestive on her like it did on Ashley, but rather careless and Hawaiian serene.

"I don't know, but Jim just came by and said that he heard in passing that the schnook there was looking for someone to take him to French Polynesia in exchange for a lot of dough."

"A passage for a man?" asked Joe incredulously, rubbing his graying chin.

"If Ashley's still talking to him, he must be throwing real money around," Branson thought aloud. "Let's get over there before Decker shows up and I have to see his mug."

The sun had already set, but it was still pretty bright, and the sky seemed to be on fire. A distant band of clouds over the sea was bathed in a rich lingering red, making the entire marina glow. The sultry heat, too, though no longer so oppressive, was quite present enough to make him uncomfortably aware of the sticky film of sweat on his skin.

"Ho!" he shouted when they were only a few meters away, pushing his sunglasses over his forehead so they tamed his shoulder-length dreadlocks. The stranger and Ashley turned to him—she with a sour expression, he with an uncertain but not unfriendly smile. "I heard you needed passage southwest?"

"Uh, yes, that's correct," the newcomer confirmed, extending a hand in greeting.

Branson shook it vigorously and clicked his tongue. "Well, you've come to the right place. My *Triton One* is the most reliable ship in all of Hawaii. This is my first mate, Joe, and my assistant, Xenia."

"Uh, *excuse* me? We're already in talks!" Ashley interjected flippantly, making a face as if he'd just slapped her, while Joe and Xenia also shook hands with the stranger.

"Wonderful!" Branson replied good-humoredly, without elaborating.

"You know the rules!" Ashley went on.

"Which one do you mean?" posed Branson, acting ignorant. Of course he knew exactly. When clients came to the marina, whoever made the initial contact always had the right of first refusal. After that, prospective clients were free to solicit other offers. Treasure hunter etiquette was quite clear about this. However, Decker didn't care in the least.

Only last year they'd staked a claim two hundred kilometers west and found a Spanish galleon. Then they had noticed that Decker had followed them and was already searching with his sinfully expensive submarines while they'd still been contemplating how they were even going to manage the 150-meter depth with their diving equipment. Although it had caused some commotion on the scene, no one wanted to mess with the mighty Dwight Decker and his friend the Governor, especially since there had been nothing to find anyway—the Spanish galleon had been empty.

Belligerently, Branson looked at Ashley and put on a curious expression. "Would you like to explain the rules to us for a moment?"

"I'll get Decker," she grumbled, turning on her heel to pull her smartphone out of her pocket and start a conversation in a hushed voice.

"So, mister...?"

"Fred Perkins," the stranger introduced himself. "How do you do? You must be Branson McDee. I've heard a lot about you."

Branson frowned. He loved his ship and his friends and crew, but they had made it to great notoriety at best through their bad luck—at least it looked that way.

"Really?" slipped out.

"Yes, indeed. Joe Kamaka, sixty-one years old, born on the Big Island, served ten years in prison for beating his ex-wife's lover to death. He's been out on bail for the last ten years and has ten more on parole," Perkins explained as if he were merely talking about the weather. "You, on the other hand," he continued, casually pointing at Branson, "are Australian and are on record there as a fugitive prison inmate under your real name, Jefferson Daunton. But since your spectacular escape was twenty-two years ago, and your forged U.S. passport is outstanding work, I don't think that fact, coupled with the fact that your records are gathering dust in some paper archive back home, matters much."

Ashley returned, and Branson took advantage of the moment of absolutely stupefied silence to exchange a sideways glance with Joe, who looked as if he'd seen a ghost.

"He's on his way," she said, giving him a triumphant grin.

Perkins, this stranger who possessed knowledge held, as far as he'd known, by only two people on this planet—one of whom was Joe—put on a carefree face and waited. Branson avoided looking at Xenia, who had just learned things about her bosses and shipmates that would surely give her a headache for a while.

"I assure you, mister, that the *Decker I* can get you to your destination considerably faster."

"Is that so?" asked Perkins, eyeing the spick-and-span ship that had been launched earlier in the current year and into which the *Triton One* would have fit twice. Branson's ship, by contrast, looked like a pirate barge ready to be scrapped, with its wooden superstructure and wide hull. It couldn't hide its age, despite the money they'd sunk into various overhauls and extras over the years.

"Oh, yeah. We've installed B+V's latest electric drive with battery packs that we charge via deployable solar sails while underway. It's not only fast and efficient, but it's also good for the environment!"

"Oh yes, you are *great* environmentalists. That's why you sank the still half-full freighter *Eglund* off the coast so that you could train your new divers. Such a pity that two containers filled with arsenic were stored onboard. Isn't it convenient how you can overlook that with all your environmental awareness?" Xenia derided.

"Wait a minute, wait a minute...," Branson intervened, raising his hands defensively. "It's all right. We're not interested. You guys can have the job."

Now Ashley seemed flabbergasted and eyed him disparagingly. He could all but see the gear-rattling going on behind her brow, wondering if she had missed something when he'd backed down and retreated.so quickly

"What?" finally came from her mouth.

"You can have the job. Mr. Perkins here—that's his name, by the way—is looking for ship passage to Maupiti, and I think a limo ride like this is just the thing for him. At least then we can look for a claim here in peace without you stealing it from us."

The onlooking stranger butted in. "Excuse me, but I'd prefer to use *your* services."

Branson looked to Joe, who gave a barely perceptible shake of his head.

"Sorry," he answered, looking at Perkins. "The trip is quite long and we have too much to do. There are some repairs to be made, and—"

That was as far as he got, because at that moment, the roar of a sports car took over. Seconds later, a bright yellow Lamborghini shot through the driveway and came to a screeching halt in front of Perkin's SUV. Dwight Decker, a sunlamp-brown man in his early 40s with graying temples and pomaded hair, emerged. His three-day beard was so perfectly trimmed it made a statement, and his gold wristwatch and crocodile leather boots rounded out the impression of a playboy who had forgotten that advancing age affected him, too.

"Here I am!" Decker presented a far-too-white smile that dripped with arrogance. Branson knew Perkins wouldn't recognize it and would find him charming instead —that was how phonies came across.

The millionaire extended a hand to the stranger and greeted him. "I'm Dwight Decker." He pointed to his admittedly impressive ship. "This is mine, and I can assure you it's your only choice if you expect professional service."

Branson tried to swallow his rising anger. Decker was always too good to make direct attacks and snide remarks, preferring to taunt indirectly. He was a lying and greedy racketeer who knew how to present himself and spread honey around until someone got stuck.

"So it would seem," Perkins agreed with him—to Branson's indignation—and sighed. "Since your colleagues from the *Triton One* have just declined anyway, without hearing my offer, I suppose I have no choice but to offer you my million and a half U.S. dollars. I'll pay five hundred thousand up front, five hundred thousand upon arrival at my destination, and the remaining five hundred thousand upon return and completion of my mission."

Joe choked, and Branson had to slap him hard on the back to help him get his breath back.

"Besides," Perkins continued, "I don't need a bill, and I'll pay cash."

Xenia cleared her throat.

"A million and a half?" asked Branson hoarsely. In cash. Without a bill.

"Yes."

"Wonderful. You chose the right ship," Decker said,

speaking over Branson, and not even giving him a glance. "When do you want to leave?"

"Wait a minute!" Branson took a step forward. "This gentleman asked for us explicitly."

"But you refused," objected Perkins.

"See?" Decker grinned broadly. "Quality always wins out."

"You don't even know a wrench from a drill!"

"I don't have to, because, unlike yours, my ship doesn't keep falling apart."

"Sure, and if something does, you've got people for that. Not that you're not getting your hands dirty just counting bills," Branson countered.

"Hmm, is somebody jealous?" Decker asked with a pitying look. "Do you know why you're always living at subsistence level, Branson?"

"I'm sure you'll enlighten me in a moment, although I can't imagine a rich pea-brain like you even knowing what subsistence level is."

"You lack an understanding of the market. The best product always wins. Now take a look at your ship, and then take a look at mine. What do you see? Ah, but of course! You see a last-century scrap barge versus a real ship. Money goes where there's value, not where the pity is greatest. By the way, I paid the full year's mooring fee for you yesterday. So don't say I'm not generous. If you've got a lot, you've got a responsibility to give a little to the less privileged."

Decker flinched as Branson rushed at him, face fuming, and Joe intercepted him at the last moment by pressing him to his chest using one of his strong arms like a seatbelt.

"Hey! Easy, brother," Joe exclaimed. "Don't let him provoke you!"

"You're a damned thief and a fraud!" snarled Branson, and Decker's impassive face only made him angrier.

"A hot-head," Decker sighed, giving Perkins a look that

seemed to say, 'See?' "Of course, that's behavior that's a no-go for a captain at sea. A clear head—even in difficult situations—is indispensable for an ocean voyage. The sea is not for hotheads."

"I agree," Perkins said, and Branson cursed inwardly. He'd let that scumbag Decker show him up again. It was time he got a better handle on his emotions. But even if he had, maybe he shouldn't have been so greedy as to reach for Perkins' money, even though his instincts had told him to turn around quickly and go back to hosting school classes, no matter how repugnant that was to him, or how humiliating and frustrating.

This man had to have dug deep to find and even identify him here. And the fact that Perkins knew about his escape from Australia sent shivers down his spine. No one other than Joe knew about that, and now Xenia was a confidant, which complicated everything even more. Then another thought occurred to him: What if the fact that Perkins had put his information directly on the table had been a blatant threat? What if it was his way of letting them know that he knew their secrets and would use them against them should they refuse to take him?

Shit! he thought.

"So you've changed your mind?" asked Perkins in his direction, his expression impassive and businesslike.

"Yes," Branson growled, though everything in him screamed to shout *NO!* He looked to Joe, who nodded.

Xenia kept in the background and remained silent. She was probably busy sorting out what she'd heard so far, and kept bumping into the same hurdle: why was her employer a wanted prison fugitive?

"Okay, we'll do business," said Perkins. "I would suggest we discuss all further details on board."

Decker's grin faltered. "Wait a minute! I thought you'd decided on the *Decker I?*"

"My first choice is the crew of the *Triton One*," Perkins corrected him unemotionally. "The ship is secondary, especially since both are suitable for my cargo."

"Cargo?" asked Joe.

"You realize, don't you, that you'll get into nothing but trouble with this criminal bunch?" objected Decker.

"Trouble I expect, yes. But none from you for not getting my assignment. Or am I mistaken about your self-proclaimed professionalism?"

The rich captain seemed to want to say something more, but instead bit his tongue and grabbed Ashley by the arm to pull her away with him. "Come on, let's go."

"Expecting trouble?" Joe eyed Perkins, but the man merely pointed at the *Triton One* and tossed Xenia the keys to his SUV.

"Could you do me a favor and park my car somewhere? There's a briefcase in the back with the down payment."

Xenia looked at Branson, utterly perplexed, but he merely nodded at her and motioned for their guest to follow them.

"You mentioned *cargo*?" Branson queried, echoing Joe's earlier question.

"Yes. I have a small submarine parked in Big Island harbor. We'll have to take it with us."

"A submarine?" Joe's eyes widened.

"Right. I have to go to a place that's too deep for us to dive without aid. It's no trouble, is it?"

"No," Branson assured him. "If we remove the awning, it shouldn't be a problem. How big is it?"

"It only has one seat, and it's for me. I looked at your ship's measurements beforehand and made sure there's a spot where it should fit."

"You have..." Branson started to reply, but shook his head

and took a deep breath. This man knew things about him that hardly anyone else knew, not even the FBI. So if he admitted he was surprised that Perkins had done his homework regarding the *Triton One* as well, he would only make a fool of himself. "It appears you've done your research thoroughly."

"Of course," Perkins agreed, gratefully taking Joe's hand as he helped him climb under the awning onto the quarterdeck. It didn't escape him how their first customer in ages was embarrassingly careful not to get his pants dirty. Perhaps the *Decker I* would have suited him better after all.

But money didn't stink, and Branson was getting the impression more and more strongly that the million and a half might actually exist, and that would mean he and Joe wouldn't have to bury their dream of going to the Gulf of Mexico just yet.

"A million and a half dollars is not something I take lightly, and—certainly—neither do my clients. Accordingly, I hope that you will carry out this assignment as discreetly and conscientiously as such a large sum would suggest. We know all about you and are sure we have made the right choice. Do you agree?"

Branson decided to swallow his anger at this blatant threat and pretend he hadn't noticed it. "Sure thing. Just one question: you mentioned that you were concerned about me and my crew, not the ship, and that you expected trouble. Did you mean us, or the circumstances of your planned trip?"

"Hopefully only the latter," Perkins replied, looking around the quarterdeck.

Branson was relieved to see that Marv and Johnny had already cleaned up.

Their 'guest' nodded with apparent satisfaction. "It's possible that we'll have to compromise one or two things on the voyage in terms of applicable law, if you understand."

"Uh..." He had already figured on that when he'd heard 'in cash' and that there'd be no physical receipt.

"That won't be a problem, will it?"

"Not if you really have the money," Joe interjected.

"Wonderful. Don't worry about anything in that regard. I also have my own set of satellite phones with me and must ask that you turn off your devices during the trip and hand them over to me."

"What?"

"It's a non-negotiable requirement. Discretion is extremely important to me and my clients, and I promise you that my equipment is reliable." Perkins pointed to the superstructure at the stern. "Would you like to show me my cabin?"

"Of course. Joe, can you take this?"

"Sure, Captain!" The dark-skinned giant gave Perkins a wave, and they were off before Branson grabbed their guest by the arm and held him back.

Perkins looked down at his hand and raised an eyebrow.

"When do we leave?"

"Right away. After your young lady returns, of course."

6

LEE

"It's locked from the inside," Lee explained as Markus floated through the Zarya module and stopped himself with the handholds next to the Russian Swesda hatch. The German with the gray temples and the high forehead furrowed his brow when he saw the blocked passage.

"Did you knock?"

"Sure." Lee tapped against the window. "I've been listening, too, and I heard someone talking, but no one responded. Have Dima or Anatoli talked to you in the last few hours?"

"The last thing I did was talk to Dima. He wanted to take a power nap after the EVA and then prepare for your interview. I told him he was a crazy Russian, and he said that was a pleonasm."

"Funny," Lee replied, floating back through the Zarya to the Unity module, where he freed one of the consoles from its spot in the wall and called up the life support systems. They showed no malfunctions. Markus popped up beside him and tapped a finger through the menu until he'd called up the appropriate hatch. It was marked as electronically locked.

"We could try an emergency override," the ESA astronaut suggested. "That would unlock it immediately."

"The Russians would never allow that."

"Well, we don't have to ask them. What if something happened to Anatoli and Dima? A critical malfunction or something? After all, we just attached a new module to the station, the anchoring of which many have deemed improvised and risky."

"But environmental control doesn't indicate problems," Lee pointed out, shaking his head. "No. If we do that, we're out of a job."

"True—at least the political pressure would be great enough that they'd never let us up here again," Markus agreed with him. "Should we wake Sarah? She's the commander."

"Maybe that's a good idea, but she's really beat. I'll make another call to Ground Control, and if they don't give me any other instructions, I'll wake her up."

Lee shimmied his way, by means of the station's handholds, through the cramped modules crammed with lab equipment, laptops, and cables that looked richly chaotic, all the way to Destiny, where he pulled his laptop out of sleep mode and connected to Houston. Normally they were just in their downtime, letting the astronauts get their sleep, but after informing the ground crew that something strange was going on with the Russians, that shouldn't be the case. And it didn't take two seconds before the screen displayed the face of Michelle Ferguson, who was in charge of the night shift.

"Hey, Lee. What's up?"

"The hatch is locked. I can hear at least one person talking on the other side, but they're not opening for us. Environmental control says there's no problem, though. We're a little worried up here."

"Yes, we have already seen the data. No one is responding

to our inquiries, or those of our colleagues at Roskosmos, either. The director has ordered us to stand down."

"What?" he asked incredulously. "The door is locked, and Dima and Anatoli don't answer!"

"We know," Ferguson replied, shaking her head and not looking happy. "This just came in from the top. We're not supposed to interfere and, according to protocol, we're to stay away from the Russian part of the station," continued the mature-looking, gray-maned physicist, glancing to the side as someone said something in her direction. After a moment, she turned back to Lee. "Hey, we just got a call from Boris Uljana. He wants to come on the line and join the conversation."

"Sure."

Boris Ulyana was the current Roskosmos director—certainly not someone to be ignored—and the fact he called personally was either a very good sign... or a very bad sign.

A second image popped up on Lee's laptop, and now Michelle was sharing the display with a large, shiny face with red cheeks and small eyes.

"Hello, Michelle. Hello, Lee," he greeted them curtly. "Lee, we're giving you permission to use one of our priority codes to unlock the hatch."

"Uh, excuse me?" he asked, befuddled.

"The code is Alpha-Alpha-Bravo-two-two-one-nine-eight-eight-Zulu-Delta," Ulyana continued unapologetically. He looked a little rushed. "You hereby have official permission from Roskosmos to access the Zarya. Furthermore, if there is a problem with the Astron or Anatoli, you have a free hand as far as intervention is concerned."

Astron, the radio telescope. Why did he stress it like that? thought Lee, but nodded at the camera. "Thank you, sir. We'll take care of it. It there anything we should know regarding Anatoli?"

"No. Gain access and make sure everything is okay. We can't reach our cosmonauts."

"Understood."

"Spasibo," the director thanked him and disappeared from the line.

Michelle looked glum. "Lee, you guys need to tread carefully, okay? This is really strange. There has never been anything like this in the thirty-year history of the space station. The Russians won't even let us into their part of the ISS without a cosmonaut present, and now they're giving us a priority code for their systems. You guys are going strictly on Boris's terms, understand? We have his statement on video, but we won't go beyond that."

"Understood," he affirmed, exchanging a concerned look with a wide-eyed Markus.

Michelle looked away from the camera again before returning her attention to them. "We want you to take headsets so we can stay in touch with you."

"It's all right. We'll stay in touch." Lee disconnected and saw that his colleague was already floating to the appropriate cargo compartment, stopping himself in front of it like a monkey dressed in puffy coveralls and positioning himself in front of the drawers so that he was stable and could open one of them with one hand.

Markus pulled out two thin headsets with deep fixed earpieces, put one on himself, and threw the other in Lee's direction in a straight line with a slight left spin. Lee caught it when it came sliding into his fingers and followed Markus's example. "This is really crazy."

"What?"

"That our director strictly forbids us to pursue this matter, and then the one from Roskosmos arrives virtually, and he tells us to do exactly the opposite."

"Yes, that is indeed crazy. It doesn't make sense, and every astronaut knows that. Why wouldn't we try to help, or at least make sure no one needs help? We're the only thing up here keeping us alive. The crew."

"Yeah," Lee muttered.

"Should we wake Sarah?" Markus asked again.

"No. It's probably nothing, or just a misunderstanding or a malfunction, which would be really awkward for me. If something does happen, though, we can always wake her up."

"She's a doctor," the German reminded him.

"If it were a medical emergency, Dima or Anatoli would have informed us by now," Lee countered, typing the priority code into the central control system where it intersected with the Russian system, which displayed in Cyrillic. He then selected the hatch between the Zarya and Swesda modules and unlocked it with the push of a button.

They nodded to each other one last time and shimmied back. Like two fish, they deftly floated past the many sinfully expensive devices, surrounded by the omnipresent hum and buzz of the electrics, hidden behind the panels in the form of cables and switches, a gigantic jumble that kept the space station alive.

In the Zarya, Lee had to pull himself forward and through, due to the narrowness, and then he clamped onto the handhold on the right of the hatch until Markus had arrived on the left and nodded to him. Only then did they pull on it and open the passage to the Russian living module.

The first thing they smelled was ozone and sweat. Anatoli was anchored in front of a laptop hanging out of the wall by means of a screwed bracket with a telescopic arm. He had his legs knotted beneath him on a grab bar and looked up in surprise when he saw them come in. A hint of anger crept into his eyes, but it instantly faded.

"Hey, guys," he greeted them in broken English. "Can I help you?"

"Help us?" asked Lee, irritated. "The hatch was locked, and you didn't answer. We've been knocking and trying to reach you all this time."

"Ah." Anatoli made a dismissive hand gesture. "It's all right, boys."

Lee noticed that while he was talking to them, the Russian kept typing away on his laptop, and his smile looked seriously forced.

"Where's Dima?" Markus asked.

"He's sleeping."

"We need to talk to him about my interview," Lee thought aloud, looking toward the sleeping quarters, which could be reached by a tiny passageway farther back, but which he could barely see from this angle. "It was very important to him."

"He said he was tired, and he'd do it with you tomorrow."

"But I don't have time tomorrow, and he knows that."

Anatoli sighed, paused in his work for a moment, turned the screen a little further away from them, and looked as if he had to explain something annoying to two recalcitrant children. "Listen, guys. I've got to finish the initial analysis on Astron, and it's a terrible slog. The hatch probably malfunctioned, but now it is open again."

"A malfunction? That it locked automatically?" asked Lee incredulously. "And coincidentally, the communication systems also malfunctioned, *and* you didn't hear our knock? What's going on here, Anatoli?"

Something in the Russian's eye expression changed. He was typing away on his keyboard again, and Lee and Markus exchanged glances.

"Can't we analyze this tomorrow? I'm sure we'll figure out what was going on. I'm sorry I didn't hear you guys. I was very engrossed, you know." The Russian pressed a button and then detached himself from the laptop he was about to close.

"No, I want to talk to Dima. He's commander in your section," Lee insisted.

Anatoli paused in his movement. He raised his eyes and narrowed them slightly. "Excuse me?"

"I want to talk to Dima," Lee repeated in a firm voice. "Now!"

"He's asleep, I told you."

"Then you won't mind if I wake him up?" interjected Markus, who was about to push off toward the sleeping chamber when Anatoli stretched out a hand and held him back.

"Wait a minute. You guys aren't supposed to be here. So if you don't want me to call Moscow, you'd better get out of here."

The Russian's downright angry remarks were like a slap in Lee's face. They were all friends here on the station, living in the most inhospitable conditions humans could face, surrounded by vacuum and a cold close to the standstill-point of atoms, 400 kilometers above the heads of all other creatures. Relying on each other was the most important rule, and always welded the crew together in no time.

There was no room for animosity, and only those who were reliably mentally balanced, of a relaxed disposition, and willing to compromise, made it into the astronaut corps. Anatoli was the newest member of the crew and had arrived only two weeks ago on a Russian Soyuz to work as an operator of the Astron radio telescope. But even after this short time, behavior like this was utterly unacceptable and never seen before.

"Boris Ulyana himself authorized us to come here to check on things," Lee growled, slowly losing patience. Something was wrong. He could smell it and feel it. The hairs on the back of his neck were standing up, and the tension in the recycled air figuratively crackled. "And that's exactly what we're going to do. Once we've talked to Dima and are sure you're both okay, we'll help look for those technical problems you mentioned. But not until then."

"The *director?*" Anatoli seemed surprised, his face looking paler than usual in the cool blue light of the half-closed laptop, and the bags under his eyes deeper.

"I'll check on Dima," Markus decided after exchanging glances with Lee. He pushed off with his feet. The Russian shifted his position and held onto a pole between two tethered rubber mats while he watched the German fly through the module that looked like it had been designed in the 80s. Lee waited until the cosmonaut suddenly began to move.

The ESA man was just at Anatoli's height and hovering past him, stretched out, when the Russian jerked forward with the hand he'd been using to hold on. Only now could it be seen that the pole between his fingers had been loosely attached, as if he had prepared it on purpose. He struck at Markus's head with the length of pole, and hit him with full force directly behind the temple.

"Shit!" cursed Lee in horror, reflexively pushing himself off the wall above the hatch. Like an arrow, he shot toward Anatoli. The Russian, thrown into a spin by his own attacking motion, was sent reeling, while balls of blood shot out of the German's laceration into zero gravity. Lee saw the injury only briefly, but it did not look good, and his colleague's eyes were closed. The force of the impulse to Markus's head caused him to spin and hit the wall, from which he was repelled by this new impulse and then came another impact. The longer it went on, the more he would be hurt.

Lee collided with Anatoli's chest and heard the cosmonaut gasp. He pushed him back against the wall and grabbed the laptop's cradle with his right hand to prevent an uncontrolled spin.

His opponent rowed his arms, hitting the back of his hand

on a pin catch. New globules of blood whizzed through the weightlessness, and some of them burst on the wall panels.

"What's gotten into you, you son of a bitch?" snarled Lee, effortlessly catching a punch from the man who was clearly inexperienced in zero-*g*, diving out from under Anatoli's shoulder as he spun too quickly, then grabbing him from behind with one arm around his neck. With the other, he formed a lever under his hand and squeezed while his feet sought an anchor.

Only then did he pull back and increase the force in his choking arm until Anatoli began to gasp and lash out at him ineffectually. It was of no use, for Lee was not only an experienced astronaut, but also a soldier, and he did not even have to think to suppress Anatoli's appropriate reflexes. When the cosmonaut stopped struggling and went limp, Lee waited a few more seconds to make sure he wasn't being tricked, and then let go of him.

He turned to look at Markus, who was still whirling uncontrollably on all three axes. Lee kept his feet anchored and leaned further into the module until he could catch the German. That earned him a painful blow to his temple that briefly made stars dance in his field of vision, but he managed to stabilize his colleague.

Next, he looked around for the closest available first-aid kit, and found it above him behind a net. He pulled it out, wedged it between his knees, and pulled out an adhesive bandage. It was extremely tedious to apply it correctly to the laceration that gaped on the side of Markus's head, as every touch created an impulse and involved unpredictable movements. When Lee finally succeeded, he wrapped a pressure bandage around it and felt for his colleague's pulse. Slow but strong.

Lee carefully set Markus down against a wall that was currently below for him. Then he tied Anatoli up with overhanging cables from above the laptop. Once he was satisfied with his work and had checked Anatoli's pulse, he floated over to the sleeping quarters and stuck his head inside. Dima appeared to be asleep, but Lee didn't trust the sight and pressed two fingers against his neck. His heartbeat was very weak and irregular, and he could not be roused even by gentle strokes on his cheeks.

We need Sarah, he thought, annoyed with himself that he hadn't taken this seriously enough and awakened her right away—especially when Markus had suggested it. Twice.

Only now did it occur to him that he hadn't heard any voices in his ear the whole time, yet Ground Control had wanted to stay in radio contact. Deciding on the fly, he returned to the central area of the Swesda module. He was about to put an arm around the unconscious Markus to maneuver him into the Destiny module when his eyes fell on the still half-open laptop.

A quick look won't hurt anything. What the hell was that guy doing? Lee flipped the screen open. He saw a graph that made no sense at first, until he could read from the fundamentals that it was a sensor test of the Astron telescope. Another tab showed the control program for aligning the dish and a digital memo with exact cosmic coordinates. Lee returned to the chart and tracked the signal strength and relative position of the two axes.

Had they measured something? The data—if it was real—left no doubt: Astron had detected a radio signal. But why would Anatoli get his own countryman and colleague out of the way to do a scientific experiment? And why seal himself off to do it? Lee eyed the coordinates of the signal when suddenly the screen displayed 'Shutdown' in Russian, along with a squiggle that spun in a circle. Then the monitor went black, and the laptop wouldn't turn back on.

"What the hell?" he muttered, backing away. He bumped

into Markus and was reminded that he had something more important to do. He took his European friend to the Destiny module and went to wake Sarah, who looked almost like a dead woman in her mummy sleeping bag that exposed only her pretty face. Thick straps holding her in place were wrapped around her chest, stomach, and legs. The way he floated in, she was upside down for him, relatively speaking, so he spun around his transverse axis first before undoing the fasteners and shaking her shoulder.

"Sarah!"

"Huh?"

"Sarah, wake up!" he shouted.

Her suddenly opened eyes were small and red. Confused, she looked around and then up into his face. "Lee? W-what's wrong? My alarm didn't go off."

"There was an incident."

With that, Sarah was alert immediately and peeled herself out of the sleeping bag. "What happened?"

"Anatoli attacked Markus, and maybe Dima, too. They're all three unconscious, and they need your help."

"What?" she asked incredulously as they slid through the doorway to Destiny, where Markus lay in the air like a dummy with a bandaged forehead. He quickly told her what had occurred—with some relief that she wasn't throwing a tantrum because he hadn't woken her up immediately—while they tended more thoroughly to their injured colleague.

Oddly enough, Ground Control was also back on, assuring him that they hadn't had a connection when he'd been at Swesda. As Sarah moved Markus to his sleeping quarters after treatment and hooked him up to a zero-g drip, Lee returned to Swesda, where Anatoli had by now regained consciousness and was glaring daggers at him.

"You son of a bitch!" Lee snarled at him. "Have you gone *completely* out of your mind?"

The Russian did not answer.

"What have you been doing here? Why is your laptop frozen? You don't want to talk, huh? I'm sure that will change once you get back to Baikonur. And why is there no radio reception here? What have you done?"

Sarah came in then and, without giving Anatoli a glance, nimbly glided straight toward the sleeping quarters of the unconscious Dima. The medical kit on her back bulged like a turtle shell. Lee noticed Anatoli's gaze flick to her and then go up briefly before looking back at him.

"What is it?"

"Nothing," the cosmonaut hissed with a grim expression. But Lee wasn't convinced and floated over to where he suspected the other man's hidden interest lay, where there was a small panel with the Cyrillic inscription for 'Maintenance 2.' How fortunate that astronauts on the ISS still had to learn Russian. He looked for a cordless screwdriver and opened the panel. Behind it ran various cables with identification numbers he couldn't place, since he wasn't trained on that part of the station.

However, what he did recognize was a small device no bigger than a baby's fist. It was an unadorned cube that clung to one of the cables and gave off a pungent, ozone-like smell. For a moment, he considered removing the thing but decided against it. When training for a space station assignment, one was taught, 'Don't do anything you aren't sure *must* be done.' Sometimes, that was considered the most important rule.

"Sarah?"

"Yes?" came the curt reply from the sleeping chamber.

"I'm going to Unity to talk to Michelle. I'll be right back. If anything comes up, just holler!"

"Roger that."

Lee floated back through the Zarya and slid to his work

laptop, where he opened a connection with Houston. Michelle's face was there in an instant.

"Lee."

"I need a private NASA connection."

"This already is. We're not taking any risks at this time."

"Good. I think Anatoli may have sabotaged Swesda's radio equipment. I've..." He faltered and took a deep breath before continuing, "...I looked up what he was doing on the laptop for the Astron when he'd locked himself in."

"Lee, you know that..."

"Yes, I know, but I wanted to know why he knocked Dima out."

Michelle looked uncomfortable in her own skin and glanced around her seat in the last row of the control center. "*And?*"

"The telescope was already online, apparently for a test run, and it picked up a signal. Shortly after I looked at the data, the whole operating system crashed and wouldn't boot up. I saw that an internet connection was active."

"A software-side problem?"

Lee nodded. "I think someone had remote access to it."

"So the Russians put their new toy straight into operation. That seems a little unnecessarily frantic for a research subject, but still doesn't explain—"

"—why Anatoli is acting like a saboteur over this!" Lee interrupted Michelle, earning a raised eyebrow. "I figured you guys could take a look at the coordinates. Maybe the signal's origin will tell us more about this crazy operation."

Finally, she sighed in unhappy acquiescence. "All right. Send them over to me. I'll ask if our people at the VLA in New Mexico can take a look. I'm sure the director won't mind."

"Anatoli is hiding something. He didn't just now go crazy.

On the contrary, he's been very systematic, and when I looked at his calling history, something seemed fishy to me."

"Unfortunately, we have no influence on who they send up. If Roskosmos feels it has to nominate an oligarch's protégé under the influence of the Kremlin, so be it. I guess that includes one of Yuri Golgorov's bodyguards, who will be in space for a few weeks to prove how much power his master has. Lee, it's a farce, but we have to play along with it."

Michelle's gaze slid to the side. "Boris Ulyana is calling. I'll handle it."

He nodded gratefully and ended the connection before returning to Sarah.

7

JENNA

"No time!" shouted Jenna over the roar of the outboards, shutting down the engines. During the last few meters, as the Zodiac glided over the gentle waves and headed toward the knee-high bridge above the waterline at the *Wiesbaden's* stern, she threw her MP5 overboard, rounded the pilot's cockpit, and went to pull the contact man to his feet. Despite his serious injury, he played his part well, still holding the empty-barreled pistol, its slide locked to the rear, and struggling to his feet with her assistance. Jenna ignored the firearms pointed at her by the two crewmen. "Could you guys lend a hand?"

"Don't move!" one of them growled. From his complexion, he was from Europe or North America.

"Even from here you must have seen the explosion!" she screeched back, sitting down on the bridge and pulling the contact man up between her legs onto the yacht. The two gunmen hesitated, each taking a half step back as if she had a contagious disease.

"A trap!" gasped the young contact man as she hoisted him onto the finished wooden planks beside her. "Sniper got Xiami, and then there were police everywhere."

"Who is she?" one of the gorillas asked in German.

"His bodyguard. Got me out when I got hit," he replied in English. "We..." He contorted his face in pain. "We need to get out of here. Now!"

Again there was a pause. Jenna looked up as the two crewmen exchanged uncertain glances, then eyed the horizon where the silhouette of Malacca rose out of the sea. Finally, one of them nodded toward the staircase, at which point the other took off running, pulling out his radio as he did so. Two more men came and carried the injured crewman away a short time later. Jenna nodded at him, but his return gaze was hateful.

You didn't have to play the tough guy, she thought, letting the last guy's rather indecent search wash over her. "Found anything you haven't seen before?" she growled.

"Shut up and move," he snarled at her, pointing the barrel of his pistol toward the right stairwell. He shooed her across a covered outdoor area bordered with weatherproof sofas, through a glass door into a living room.

A stocky man with thinning hair and rolled-up sleeves was sitting on a couch. He held a newspaper in his hands. Gold jewelry adorned his fingers and wrists, and his face was that of a coarse but educated man who had come into lots of money late in life. Everything around him was ostentatious, from the mahogany fixtures to the gold trim to the fastidiously clean floor.

A woman with two small children, whom she was helping with their homework, sat at a dining room table in front of a huge television.

"This's her, boss," the goon at her back said, poking Jenna in the spine with the cold muzzle of his pistol, giving her a shove forward.

The 'boss' looked up and put the paper aside. His look was

hostile and calculating. "Who are you?" he asked in a German accent.

"I'm Xiami's bodyguard."

"He's never had a bodyguard before."

"You just didn't see me before. I'm good at my job," she replied coolly.

"Your client is dead. That's what you told my men."

"It was a trap and it wasn't me. You didn't have anything to do with it, did you? I know lots of people who'd get real pissed if *I* did." Jenna had barely spoken before she took a brutal blow to the kidney area from behind and slumped to her knees. The pain spread like enflamed napalm and nearly caused her to empty her bladder.

"Give me one reason why I shouldn't shoot you right here and now," the boss demanded, acting downright bored but eyeing her closely.

"I have one, but I'd rather share it with the person who's in charge here."

"Excuse me?"

"Spare me the theatrics. You're not in command here, and after what I witnessed at the docks, we should get the hell out of here before helicopters and speedboats arrive," Jenna retorted, annoyed, and stood back up, shifting her weight side to side. The pain was slow to subside.

"What gave me away?" the woman asked, getting up from the table and coming over to them. Addressing the man, she said, "Go down below with the children."

He stood up, nodded, and followed her instructions. The actual owner of the *Wiesbaden* was over 60, with long gray hair woven into a thick plait. She possessed the sinewy, slender build of an ascetic, and her sunken cheeks with the beginnings of a hooked nose gave her the appearance of an ancient witch, had it not been for her full mouth and large, alert eyes. She motioned for Jenna to sit down and then did likewise.

"A criminal who deals in substances that even the CIA can't get their hands on doesn't need to beat up his hostages to demonstrate his power. His Russian oligarch act wasn't bad, but people like that never take off their Rolexes. His slipped, and the skin underneath was brown. No marks, nothing. He put it on specially for this scene," Jenna enumerated. "Besides, he didn't ask the most important question, and a lack of both circumspection and directness doesn't get you a ship like this one or a contact like my boss."

"What is the most important question?" the woman asked.

"What agency I work for, of course."

Her seatmate crossed her legs and smiled. It was a fake smile, calculating and anything but amusing or kind. The flashing white teeth were those of a predator in sheep's clothing.

"So, what agency *do* you work for?"

"CIA," she said bluntly, and a brief flicker of surprise passed across the woman's face. "What—did you think I was going to make up some bad lie? In your line of work, you can spot falsehoods a mile away against the wind, or you'd be dead before you could sail across the sea and make deals with the big kids."

"So what do you think my next question should be, since you're so knowledgeable?"

"Why you shouldn't kill me right now." Jenna almost smiled as she heard the engines start up, and the deck began to vibrate beneath her feet.

"And what is the answer?"

"The answer is that you would gain no advantage from it. Your tough-guy gorilla here," Jenna nodded in the direction of the muscle-bound crewman standing not two meters away with his hands folded in front of his hips and over his pistol like a bouncer, "must have scanned me for bugs when we came up here. Killing me would be a waste of resources, and why would you deal a card from your deck that you haven't turned over yet?"

"A lot of games don't allow a wild card," the older woman pointed out.

"Your game thrives on them."

"All right, then. I'll listen to you... say... for ten minutes before I send you to the sharks. What do you think of that?"

"Quite a bit. I'm sure you want to know how I became Xiami's bodyguard, because he's as paranoid as he is lustful," Jenna said.

Her counterpart looked at her wristwatch and made a questioning face.

All right. Everything rests on one card. As always.

"On April 7, 2016, there was an outbreak of anthrax in Siberia. The first case in seventy-five years," Jenna said. "The small town of Chatanga in the Arctic north was affected. A BND agent happened to be on the scene when it happened. The pathogen had been stuck in the permafrost. Mild temperatures caused it to thaw, and a gas bubble was released.

"Half the town fell into the chasm, and the surviving residents contracted the disease from the resulting exposed animal carcasses, which may have been preserved in the ice for thousands of years. Russia refused WHO assistance in the case, even though the BND agent reported to Berlin that several hundred people may have been infected. We have our own informants on the ground, but the residents have all disappeared, and we've learned that even the Russian government is looking for them.

"Six months ago, dissident Aleksander Khrogashvili was murdered in Paris, and a month later Sergei Morozova and Boris Tatishchev were murdered in Sofia. Do you know what all three have in common? Of course you do: all three are children of Russian oligarchs who have a lot of influence in the Kremlin. But they are also known to have feuded with Yuri Golgorov, who not only owns the pharmaceutical giant Golgorov Sistema, but is also alleged to have sold abroad not inconsiderable portions of mothballed Russian war materiel."

"I always like to be informed, but why are you telling me this?" the gray-haired woman asked calmly.

"All three murders were committed by a person who should no longer exist, because he came from Chatanga and was probably infected with pulmonary anthrax: Pyotr Wolkonsky. While fleeing from the Paris police, he was proven to have been shot and seriously injured, but a month later, he committed the double murder of Morozova and Tatishchev. How is this possible?"

"He probably ate his greens. I am not a doctor, and you are down to three remaining minutes."

"Two months ago, a car-bomb explosion rocked Shanghai. The victim was a high-ranking party member who wanted to start a corruption case against Chiu Wai, an oddly wealthy businessman for someone not making lots of sales. The perpetrator? Pyotr Wolkonsky," Jenna continued boldly. "What is the connection between Chiu Wai and Golgorov, and what does a dead anthrax victim have to do with either one? When we found out that even the FSB had no idea and was turning over half the country, we pricked up our ears."

"Anthrax is supposed to be curable."

"Thanks to a new drug from Golgorov Sistema." Jenna snorted, "which is in the clinical phase, and is supposed to have a cure rate of one hundred percent. That stinks to high heaven."

"Surely you didn't come to talk to me about drug research," the woman commented, glancing at her watch and rubbing her knees, which were covered by her dress. "Thank you for bringing me up to speed on the CIA. That was helpful. Unfortunately, I have more important things to attend to now, and you have an appointment with the sharks."

"Who are you, and why was Xiami sent to make contact between you and Chiu Wai?"

"Oh, come on. You started off so well. Very detached and smart for such a young woman. Don't ruin that impression in your last minutes by being naïve."

"You're not going to kill me," Jenna said confidently.

"No?"

"No. I know nothing about you except what you look like, and that your ship flies the Seychelles flag—like pretty much every other one—and the fact it's an off-the-shelf yacht. If I've never heard of you, neither has the Agency. That means you're doing a good job, and you haven't messed with us yet. You kill me and my agency will turn over every stone. It might take five years to catch you, it might take ten, but you will be caught. And the time in between would be annoying. Give me something to go on, and let me go. I'll follow the lead, and you'll go on your way."

The older woman's face revealed her churning thoughts.

"No good bird dog walks his scent backward."

"I'm old. I can sit this one out."

"You appear to have grandchildren. Do you want to spend your last twenty years on the run? Never visit a city or a park with them? No building sandcastles? What's all that wealth for if you can't use it anymore?"

"I don't know Golgorov, but I had a brief business relationship with Xiami."

"What's your business?"

"You could say I'm in the logistics business in China," the woman replied somewhat vaguely. "That should be enough for you. I'll tell you the place where I met Xiami. What you do with it is up to you." She gestured to her goon, who pulled out a pen and handed it to her. In response to an obvious gesture,

Jenna held out a hand and the woman wrote three Chinese characters on her wrist. "Now get off my ship. Our deal is to my satisfaction, but it will be the only one. If I see you again—"

"All right," Jenna said impatiently. "One more thing. My satellite phone. I want it back."

"Of course you do." The woman laughed and made a waving gesture with her right hand. The man with the gun dragged Jenna roughly to her feet and pushed her toward the door. The yacht's engines throttled back and a small inflatable boat with a tiny outboard motor was retrieved from a canopy and lowered into the water. Jenna was roughly shoved into it. As the *Wiesbaden* accelerated, the resulting wake nearly capsized her and the 'nutshell' outboard.

That could have gone worse, she thought, wiping the spray from her face and grabbing the lever of the soccer-ball-sized engine. It was a long trip to the mainland, and her boat was not very fast. The swell was negligible, though it seemed much stronger to her than it had aboard the much larger Zodiac with its rigid hull. The closer she got to the Malaysian coast, the more frequently she saw individual fishing boats looking for their buoys, to which the fishing lines were attached. They didn't seem interested in a tiny inflatable boat with an underpowered outboard motor.

It took her nearly two hours to reach land, and either she had drifted badly or she'd grossly misjudged, for she was nowhere near Malacca. Instead, she had to sail along an uninhabited stretch of coast until her fuel ran out. She put the boat ashore on the long sandy beach and pulled it up a ways before continuing on foot.

Eventually Jenna found a dirt road that led onto a sprawling palm oil plantation, the kind that were everywhere around here. She came across an elderly man wearing a prayer cap, which many Malaysians wore in their daily lives and while working. He was standing behind a rusty Toyota pickup, loading bast baskets with head-sized palm fruits.

"Hey!" he shouted with a scowl when he saw her. A torrent of Malay followed, of which she didn't understand a word.

"I'm lost. I need to make a phone call!" said Jenna, emphasizing each syllable before pantomiming holding a cell phone to her ear.

"No! No!" the man said, waving his hands defensively in front of her face. She played dumb and smiled before making the sign for a cell phone again. Finally, he uttered a series of unintelligible words—most likely curses—as he walked to the cab and pulled open the rusty door. Turning back to her, he reluctantly held out a very old Nokia phone.

"Thanks!" Jenna beamed blithely and dialed a number. When the connection was made, she said, "The winds of the west bring warmth. Eight-four-seven-one-Washington."

An unusually long silence followed, during which the plantation worker eyed her suspiciously. He did not understand a word, that much was evident from his leathery countenance.

"Jenna? What do you need an extraction for?" the Deputy Director asked after a brief crackle on the line. "And what's this phone number?"

"I got an important clue. However, I'm now stuck in the boonies south of Malacca," she explained with an excited look and wild gestures, hoping the worker would assume she was lost and her boyfriend had to pick her up. 'Always these tourists,' she hoped he would think.

"Are you okay?"

"Yeah, yeah, I'm fine. I had to improvise a little. The cell phone belongs to a plantation worker. Can you get a fix on it?"

"Already on it. Give us some time and I'll see what I can

do. We don't have anyone nearby, but I can ask around among the Five Eyes. The Aussies are bound to have agents on the ground. There's a favor or two I'm good for."

"Thank you."

"What did you find out?"

"Is the line secure?"

"Otherwise I wouldn't ask. Give me a quick update from the beginning," the Deputy Director ordered.

"Yuri Golgorov was the right lead. He died in the downing of Flight MH17, but reappeared afterward, though not directly sighted."

"What about the substance?"

"I haven't found any evidence of that. Neither Xiami nor the person he was supposed to contact here—a woman, possibly German, but maybe that was just a distraction—had anything to do with the substance. If that's why MH17 was shot down, then they either didn't know about it or didn't care. They were both just stooges, just links in a long chain," Jenna said.

The plantation worker was becoming impatient.

"Someone has inherited Yuri Golgorov's persona and is carrying on whatever he cooked up in Siberia. And China—or at least a powerful Chinese person—seems to be in on it."

"So your trail points to China? Very tricky, Jenna. You know how strained relations are with the Middle Kingdom without *this*."

"It's not my job to think about that stuff." She looked at her wrist, once more memorizing the three characters. "This woman I met... she's hard-nosed and smart. Long timer in the business and extremely calculating."

"A shadow?"

"Yes." Shadows were what those in the CIA called big-time criminals who always stayed in the background and magically never made an appearance. Their fingers went almost everywhere, and yet they were hardly ever caught. They were considered the real powers to deal with in this 'game of darkness.' "I made a deal with her, and I rate her as someone who will stick to it."

"She told you something useful?" The Deputy Director sounded incredulous.

"I think so, but nothing that would jeopardize her or her job. Useful to me, expendable to her."

"So either this job is already done, and the initiation by Xiami was for another collaboration, or what you got is worth a wet fart."

"I guess I'll have to find out."

"You want us to smuggle you into China?"

"Yes. I was told a place where I would find answers."

"It sounds like a scavenger hunt."

"You want to know what Compound X is."

"That's right. I'll send someone to you. Go to the next intersection. The phone is located."

Jenna hung up and tried to delete the number she dialed, but the phone was set to Malaysian, so she gave up trying and handed it to the unfriendly guy.

"Thank you so much."

She continued down the path until she came to a small, paved road, sat under a palm tree in the shade, and waited for four hours until an old pickup truck, not unlike the plantation worker's, pulled up and stopped beside her. An Asian woman, well-toned and with an alert expression, sat at the wheel. They nodded silently to each other, Jenna got in, and the woman drove off. Reaching into the backseat, Jenna grabbed the backpack laying there, along with a shoulder bag containing a passport, smartphone, five thousand dollars in cash, and a makeup kit. She set up the phone and Googled the three characters.

Hmm, she thought, this is going to be interesting.

8
BRANSON

Branson stood on the gangway behind the bridge with his arms folded, staring down at the quarterdeck. Marv and Johnny had converted the awning into a tarpaulin with which they had covered the five-meter submarine, which was now moored between the benches like a shrouded cylinder. The heavy tiedown straps were anchored in the thick cargo eyes in the deck to ensure that it did not move a centimeter, even in the current, considerable swell.

"Looks like a Christmas present, doesn't it?" commented Joe, who joined Branson. Joe lit a cigarette and held the pack out to him. Branson took one as well, lighting it on Joe's held-out storm lighter.

After a few deep puffs, Branson answered with a nod. "True. Even though I'm not completely comfortable with the job."

"Why not? At least we don't have Russian torpedoes on board or anything."

"No, but the thing itself is certainly worth many times our wages."

"I know where you're going with this. Don't go that way, old friend," Joe sighed.

"I'm just sayin'. He rubs our noses in the fact that we're criminals and then trusts us with his sinfully expensive toys?" Branson shook his head and propped his forearms on the parapet, which was sticky from the salt water. "We also know he has at least another half million in his cabin. Who would voluntarily seek out criminals with whom to set out for the middle of nowhere in the Pacific with a cargo like that?"

"Well, he seems to have done his due diligence. He knows for a fact that you did time for a bank robbery in which someone died, but only because you jumped through the wrong window while rescuing your accomplice. I caught my ex-wife cheating on me and assaulted her lover in the heat of the moment, and he fell awkwardly, hit the back of his head, and died. I found Jesus in jail, and you and I are supposed to be the bad villains he's got to be afraid of?"

The old sea dog waved it all off before continuing. "Forget it, Branson. We're the Diet Coke of evil. We may be tattooed to the hilt, but the tattoos are fading and they're no longer a sign of what we left behind back then. The little bit of black money we make? The few barrels of oil we've been secretly dumping? Even a square from the San Francisco suburbs laughs at that these days."

"Still, there has to be a reason he wanted us so badly," Branson insisted.

"Well, sure. He knows we're eating out of his hand. With me, all it takes is one oil drum and I'm back in jail for ten years. And with you, all it takes is one tip to the Australian authorities and you'll never see the light of day again. He couldn't have found a better pair of service providers. But you know what?" Joe put a paw on his shoulder. "None of that should matter to us, because the way I figure this Perkins guy, there's a valid reason why he doesn't ask for a bill, and why he wants to be on the least noticed and most unsuccessful treasure-hunting ship in the Pacific."

"Hey, you take back the *least noticed* part!" grumbled Branson, grinning. "After all, we are famous for our lack of success!"

Together they chortled and watched the sun sink diagonally into the horizon behind the stern. The silhouette of the Hawaiian island chain was just visible past the waves, peeking sharply out of the sea in front of the red disk. The scent of the ocean breeze wafted around Branson's nose, reminding him once again that this was right where he belonged. Joe was like a brother to him.

Marv and Johnny were like sons, even though not so many years separated him from them in age. They were good boys, could lend a hand, and were content with the simple life they led here. They appreciated the evening beers and endless card games with bad jokes as much as he did and never asked uncomfortable questions. He knew they were both drug addicts and drank too much, but as long as they smoked their weed outside of their working hours, or were at least functional, he didn't care. Nor did he care that they'd smuggled coke in Europe to fund their trip. They weren't dangerous or aggressive or unpredictable, and that was enough for him.

Xenia, on the other hand, was a special case. He felt responsible for her and wanted to make sure she did something decent and didn't become a loser like himself. She could sugarcoat her adventuring life all she wanted, but in the end, it wouldn't be enough to support a family or find a real home port in life.

"What's the matter, old fellow?" asked Joe.

"Oh, I don't know." Branson took one last drag on the cigarette and stubbed it out on the parapet before packing the stub into the small metal box in his trouser pocket and sighing. "I sometimes think about how freedom is just a nice word for captivity."

The fact that Joe didn't reply, but stared thoughtfully into the waves, told him once again that he had the best possible friend by his side. *Home* was anywhere you were as long as you had the right person beside you.

"Come on, let's go down." He pointed to his dive watch. "We've got a briefing in five minutes. I'm guessing he's already waiting for us."

Together they walked back to the mess hall, leaving Marv and Johnny in charge of the bridge. The two had donned linen shirts and were discussing the merits of Hawaiian women over South American ones and seemed to conclude that a joint was the better companion. Through the stairwell that led down through five decks to the engine room, they went to Deck 2 and toward the door straight ahead of them, where Xenia was already waiting.

"Xenia! What are you doing here? Weren't you going to clean the bilge pumps?" he asked, surprised.

"I want to go to the interview," she protested, crossing her arms in front of her chest.

"You can't."

"Why not?"

"Because..." Branson looked helpfully at Joe, but his partner didn't acknowledge his gaze and instead watched the young woman. "Because you just can't. It wouldn't be fair to Marv and Johnny. Perkins said just me and Joe."

"Oh, come on! There's five of us on this ship! Besides, this guy knows more about you guys than I do! Is it true what he said?"

"Shhhh!" hissed Branson, pursing his lips. "Not now, okay?"

"I want in!" she insisted. "Look, I don't care what you've done. I know you're good guys. But I'm building my life on this shit ship, and I want to be integrated, all right? I'm going in there with you!"

Their gazes met and remained intertwined for a while. Her eyes sparkled like opals, and Branson already knew he'd lost. Besides, she was right. After all, they had her to thank for the idea of the school classes, and without that they would have been broke a year ago.

"All right," he relented, reluctantly. She didn't smile or display a triumphant expression on her face, which he appreciated. Instead, she walked through the door into the mess hall she had cleaned up in the morning when they had docked in Hawaii to load the submarine. There was a hand-sized projector on the large table set into the wall opposite, like a small bench-lined cave, and the two pieces of training equipment were on the kitchen counters to the right and left, creating a considerable open space. Branson couldn't remember the place looking this neat before.

Fred Perkins waited beside the door until they were seated, then slid a portable screen in front of it before using his smartphone to turn on the projector and turn off the lights. "Nice of you to be so punctual," he said, watching them make themselves comfortable on the horseshoe-shaped bench seating.

Branson was almost ashamed that the place reeked so much of cigarettes, looking at their passenger's expensive clothes and genteel demeanor.

"As you know," Perkins continued, "we are bound for Maupiti, a rather small island in French Polynesia. Our exact destination is seventy-eight kilometers to the northwest in a relatively shallow sea area. That's where we need to stop and I'll make my dive. If all goes well, it will take me about three hours."

"Is there some wreck we don't know about?" asked Joe.

"No, but I will—assuming my mission is a success—

salvage something from the bottom that we need to get to Vladivostok."

"Vladivostok?" asked Branson. "Where's that?"

"Russia," Joe replied. "Nasty shithole."

"There was no mention of that!"

"Is this going to be a problem?" Perkins inquired with a neutral expression.

"No, not necessarily."

"Wonderful. This mission is of utmost importance to me and my clients. Therefore I am authorized to disclose to you all details of our undertaking. But I warn you, once you have this knowledge, there is no turning back."

"What are you saying? That you'll blow the whistle on us if we go to the media?" Branson smirked.

Perkins' expression remained serious. "No," he said. "I'm afraid the consequences would be considerably more... final."

While Branson was still pondering what this man had just said—his words didn't seem to fit his contained appearance—Perkins was already continuing.

"But I'm sure you'll keep our appointments, and your combined history of secrecy is proof enough of your abilities in that regard. After all, you and your crew are the best examples of how to keep secrets. On the bright side, if this works out well, we'll hire you for at least two more years, and for considerably more money."

Branson exchanged a glance with Joe.

"Have you ever heard of underwater grain circles?" Perkins asked the group.

"Nah," Joe replied, and Branson and Xenia shook their heads as well.

The screen displayed the image of a strange and complex pattern in the sand, clearly at the bottom of the sea due to suspended particles. It was reminiscent of a mandala waiting to be colored in, with spoke-like struts and small circles in between.

"This pattern is about two and a half meters in diameter and was discovered in the Pacific Ocean off the coast of Japan in 1995," Perkins continued. In quick succession, he showed more of these patterns in apparently different places. "Mexico, Argentina, Kamchatka, Alaska, Sulawesi, Palawan. Until recently, it was thought that these were formations made by puffer fish, that they put together for mating purposes. NASA, however, has debunked that theory—and did so only two weeks ago."

"Uh, *NASA?*" asked Joe, scratching his head.

"Yes. The new satellite constellation MASTA—Magnetic Anomaly Sensor and Tracking Array was intended to detect peculiarities in the Earth's magnetic field lines, originally to better study the migration routes of some herd animals and migratory birds. In the process, however, unexpected results emerged."

Perkins pressed his smartphone, and an animated globe popped up. It spun leisurely on its axis, showing flashing red dots in multiple locations. One was off the coast of Japan, one somewhere in Russia, and others off Argentina, Kamchatka, Alaska, Sulawesi, and Palawan. "Oddly enough, these strangely extremely powerful magnetic fields are in the exact locations where underwater crop circles have been found."

Branson raised a hand.

"Yes?"

"But that marker in Russia. It's not underwater, is it?"

"No, that's where it gets weirder. This anomaly is in the center of the place commonly known for the so-called Tunguska event," Perkins explained, looking at three perplexed faces. "Tunguska is a river. Podkamennaya Tunguska, to be exact. There was a massive meteorite impact there in 1908 that destroyed tens of thousands of square kilometers of forest land, and nothing grows in its impact crater to this day. The anomaly is in the center of the crater. We don't understand what it's all about, but we also don't know anything about these anomalies as such, except that the Russians have already investigated off the coast of Japan."

Again the images changed and now they saw a grainy shot of a ship using a crane similar to that of the *Triton One* to retrieve a roughly spherical object from the water. Due to the poor quality, hardly anything could be made out.

"What's that?" asked Branson.

"We don't know, but an informant has told us that it was recovered from under the Japanese underwater grain circle. The U.S. government is setting up its own recovery missions right now," Perkins said. "We need to move faster."

"Wait a minute." Joe made a dismissive gesture. "I think I'm in the wrong movie! NASA shot up some new satellites there, and they have found out that there are magnetic anomalies on Earth that just happen to match up with those weird alien circles there? And we're sitting here on our ship going to a place like that?"

Branson had to confess that it did sound funny, and if he hadn't counted the five hundred thousand dollars himself, he would have thought it was all a bad joke, especially as it could hardly sound more absurd than when Joe, that sea-bear of a man with his small eyes and martial looks, recited it.

"That is correct," Perkins replied unapologetically.

"Where did you get this data from anyway?" Xenia made her presence known for the first time.

"My principals have a source at NASA. She was well paid."

"And who are these principals?"

Perkins merely smiled and shook his head. "Our job is to find, near Maupiti, what the Russians found near Japan. Whatever is responsible for that magnetic field there: I want it.

When we're ready, we'll take it to Vladivostok and you'll get the third and final portion of your payment."

"At least now I understand why you hired us," Branson commented. "You're not supposed to know anything about this data."

"Originally, the satellite data was even available on NASA's website, albeit somewhat awkward to access. However, only for two days. When U.S. government agencies got wind of the Russians' recovery operation, everything went straight to secrecy. I'm sure the NSA is working meticulously to erase all traces from the Internet and figure out if the Russians were just carefully reading NASA's site, or if they got to the data through other means. Also, they were on the scene amazingly quick."

"What exactly are we dealing with here?" asked Joe. "Any Chinese stuff?"

"I don't think so."

"What else?"

Perkins didn't answer and merely shrugged. "We won't know until we find something. But as of this moment, none of this need concern you. You've installed, if I'm not mistaken, an unauthorized secondary engine and installed unregistered extras that will make the ship a total of eight knots faster."

Branson did not answer, and when his employer looked at him questioningly, he acted surprised. "Oh, I didn't hear a question."

Perkins smiled. "Good. I suggest we go full speed because I learned an hour ago that a research vessel escorted by the U.S. Coast Guard has departed Honolulu. It looks like it's heading for the same position we are. I'd appreciate it if we were gone before they show up. Do you think that's possible?"

"That shouldn't be a problem." Branson wiggled anxiously in his seat. "I'd rather we didn't get in trouble with the Coast Guard, that's for sure."

"Then we are in agreement. Very well." Perkins seemed about to finish his presentation, but Joe held him back.

"Your principals—I realize you won't reveal anything about them—but they are undoubtedly powerful. Are they members of the U.S. government?"

"No." Their passenger smiled humorlessly. "No, Mr. Kamaka, they are not." Perkins packed up the projector and screen and disappeared from the mess hall without another word.

"That was the shortest and least informative talk I've ever heard," Branson grumbled.

"Have you even heard one before?" asked Joe.

"I was married." They laughed briefly, but it wasn't a joyous laugh, more one that indicated the need for an outlet for their tension.

"You're right," Xenia replied. Her expression betrayed a mixture of concern and excitement. "He didn't tell us about our mission so much as he did about how powerful he is and how insignificant we are. That was pure intimidation, wasn't it? All that about him wanting to involve us and share details with us. All we know now is that it's about some magnetic stuff at the bottom of the ocean, and he's hoping to find some artifact there because a horribly pixelated shot from somewhere shows a ship's crane holding an orb."

"Mm-hmm, that's right," Joe agreed with her solemnly. "I can't shake the feeling that we've stumbled into something bigger here than this schnook lets on." He glanced around uneasily. "Who knows if he's bugged the place yet? After all, he's been in here alone all this time."

"Now calm down," Branson said, though he had to admit that he couldn't ignore the uneasy feeling in his stomach. Something about this Fred Perkins fellow frightened him. At first he'd seemed like a clueless tourist when they'd been standing in the harbor. Since then he'd turned out more and more to be an extremely confident and calculating operative, like a puppeteer who watches with satisfaction as everything dances to his tune.

"He's paying well, and we're to take him to the southwest. That's a week's travel with a bit of effort, maybe some bad weather the day after tomorrow. We could do worse than that. Whoever he's working for, we could care less. Magnetic fields? Russians? NASA? I don't care about any of that."

Branson tried hard not to look into the corners of the room despite the urge to check for bugs.

"I may still be young, and you're welcome to call me a naïve landlubber," Xenia objected, "but I've always been able to trust my intuition, and this whole thing smells like trouble. The job may sound easy, but I'm sure it will be anything but."

"I'd like to disagree with the little lady," Joe said in Branson's direction, "but that coincides with my gut feeling. We should be careful, one way or another."

"We always are," Branson said lightly, giving them an encouraging wink and standing up. "Time for supper! I'll go relieve the boys on the bridge, and remember, you still owe me two big blinds!"

Joe and Xenia played along with his game, teasing that he was going to lose tonight, and they had only let him win. And yet even Branson could not rid himself of the stone that had been in his stomach since they had left Hawaii. He remembered all too well what took place back in the harbor, the silent men who had loaded the submarine and then disappeared in a black van.

What have I gotten myself into?

9

LEE

"An *asteroid*?" asked Lee, staring into his laptop's camera. The Destiny module suddenly seemed much more cramped to him than it had up to now—the walls and panels packed with research compartments, fittings, and machinery felt even more chaotic and dense.

"Yeah." Michelle nodded wearily. "And it's already pretty close and pretty big."

"How close?"

"Just under thirteen million kilometers, according to our calculations so far, though they're pretty vague. Our telescopes almost missed it, although we were aimed directly at it."

"Thirteen million?" Lee shook his head in disbelief. "That's... *very* close."

"I know. The director is in quite a tizzy. True, Cassandra 22007 will skate past Earth—at about twice the Earth-moon distance—but we'll still have to explain how the NEOWISE missed such a chunk. After all, it measures at least twenty kilometers in diameter."

"NEOWISE is an infrared system. It could misread or miss something, given the vast sky. It happens regularly," he objected. "ATLAS should have sounded the alarm by now, though. It's responsible for very close objects."

"Yes. But the fact is, *none* of our early warning systems have kicked in, and we don't know *why*." Michelle's voice sounded like a whisper. The dark circles below her eyes were deeply gouged. "Cassandra 22007 is very dark and should reflect sunlight. But it doesn't. Walter's department marched through and wedged all the coffeemakers under their arms and locked themselves up over in the hangar. They've been poring over it for hours, and they've got some theories as to what's causing it."

"But nothing concrete yet."

"No. That's not the problem though, Lee. A huge rock is hurtling past the Earth in a few moments, far enough away you couldn't adequately draw the scale on a chalkboard. The media will run reports again for a bit of clickbait, and then that'll be it."

"Same as always," he grumbled.

"Same as always." Her brow furrowed, and her right eyelid twitched slightly. Lee knew that reflexive trait all too well. When an EVA was due and she was on duty, Michelle had always been tense, yet outwardly calm. The physicist was good at not letting her emotional state show. It was probably because, in a male domain like NASA, and despite all the female accomplishments in the agency's history, you still had to act like a man to get ahead.

"What is it, Michelle?"

"Huh?"

"There's something else on your mind, isn't there," Lee probed, and silence fell for a while—except for the murmur of electronics around him.

"We'll keep it a secret. For now," she finally said with some reluctance.

"What? Since when do we keep discoveries like this

secret?" Lee felt a fist clench in his stomach. He hated secrecy, which had been one of the reasons he'd applied out of the Air Force and into a civilian agency that had embraced transparency and progress. NASA continuously published its discoveries on its website without much political influence. Sure, there were regular attempts from Washington to somehow harness the space agency for itself. Still, transparency had never been taken away—apart from a few special cases during the Cold War.

"I know how you feel about it," she replied in a placating tone. "But the matter is extremely delicate. One of our astronomers, Cassandra Miles, recently discovered a comet that she wanted to have imaged using the ESA's new Euclid space telescope. Its coma showed a *spot*. This spot was, apparently, a previously undiscovered planet-killer-class asteroid."

"Cassandra 22007," he thought aloud, snorting. "I'm guessing someone's not happy about a discovery being named after her, especially since the name isn't even allowed. There's already a Cassandra."

"Nobody cares about that anymore since the video. To the whole world, it's just Cassandra. What's worse is that it's being called 'meteor' everywhere. And—worse *yet*—we only know about the ESA discovery because of this video by Luxembourgish YouTuber Luc Breusch."

"Lucky Luc? The geophysicist?"

"Yeah." Michelle nodded, looking like she was slipping into a microsleep. She reached for something out of the camera's view, and a moment later a white coffee cup with dried brown stains came on screen. After a slurp, she screwed up her face in disgust and sighed. "He was going to Spain to record a new video for his channel from Euclid's ground station. Thanks to him, and the Internet, a growing public now knows about Cassandra 22007.

"It was only a preview video he uploaded, but he had it in

spades. Retrospective. All the while, he was merely talking about how he was in Cebreros and how it was an exciting clip that would be released next Sunday. If he hadn't mentioned the discovery of Cassandra and coupled it with the question of whether it could strike us..."

"That sounds like typical influencer clickbait." Lee waved it off and held onto the grab bar next to the laptop with his other hand to keep the wave's impulse from causing him to drift away. He was getting too tired and really should sleep. If only he could.

Sarah had brought Dima to join them at Destiny and tucked him into the spare sleeping space next to Markus, where she could monitor him more easily. She obviously felt more comfortable treating her friend and patient 'at home.' After Roskosmos instructed her to do so, they had restrained Anatoli in his own sleeping chamber, giving him something to eat and drink twice a day.

He was to return to Earth with Dima as soon as the latter was fit and able to pilot the docked Soyuz. The cosmonaut kept waking up, but judging by the bump on the back of his head, his comrade hadn't held back when he punched his lights out. Dima was complaining of nausea and dizziness and exhibiting some neurological deficits that had shown improvement over the last 24 hours, but did not yet allow for a conversation from which more details could be drawn from the incident at Swesda. Sarah was optimistic, however, that the symptoms of the severe concussion would improve. Time was the relevant factor here.

"Lee? Lee!"

"Huh? Yeah? Sorry." He blinked a few times and snorted. "Really tired. What did you say?"

"After the announcement video, nothing more came, and YouTube had even blocked the clip initially due to an alleged policy violation. But some users had already downloaded it and uploaded it to competitor platforms like Vimeo and so on. Since then, it can be found on YouTube again.

"A few days ago, the control center in Cebreros was completely burned out. From the rubble they recovered the bodies of Linnea Daubner, Roberto Camacho—and—yeah, hold on—Luc Breusch. No data was recovered, and the circumstances are extremely mysterious. Apparently there was a phosphorus source there, and the flames were hot enough to melt bones and metal parts. Also, fifteen minutes earlier, some kids were rioting at a nearby substation, causing a power outage that supposedly triggered the fire."

"They all died?" Lee confirmed sadly. "Damn."

"Yes, and combined with the oh-so-mysterious video message from the late Breusch, it all makes for a super picture for all sorts of conspiracy theorists on the Internet."

"And now you don't want to give them new fodder by saying, 'Ta-da! It's real, the asteroid, but it will miss us.' And then the web will boil over with even worse conspiracy theories, and we'll be accused of hiding the impending apocalypse so as not to cause panic. Then even the mainstream will believe that, and there will be real panic."

"Something like that." Michelle nodded. "You can't blame people, either. It's such a curious chain of unfortunate and mysterious circumstances that led to the deaths of our European colleagues, especially since it's still not clear why they didn't make a run for it when the fire broke out. Investigators in Spain are still sifting through the scanty debris, but we shouldn't count on many answers. The authorities there have already revealed that much."

"If this incident hadn't happened, the public would have been informed long ago. At least that Cassandra 22007 existed."

"Yes. And now we find out that RJKK Energiya's new toy

is aimed directly at the asteroid in question. No one in Houston or Moscow believes in coincidence anymore."

"What are the Russians doing?" Lee asked. "Has Ulyana let anything slip?"

"They were quick. The Kremlin has had FSB working on it, and special police units are searching the group's Moscow premises. But that's all still ongoing, and we think they mainly want to know what the connection is between Golgorov and RJKK Energiya, and who's to blame for someone like Anatoli —apparently under the guidance of a third party—being able to travel to the ISS and pull some secret crap."

"Astron doesn't interest them?"

"At least that's what it looks like. From all appearances, they think it's either unimportant or a coincidence, that the new radio telescope is pointed directly at a previously undiscovered asteroid or that it's also picking up a radio signal from there."

"Do the Russians know anything about it? Is it radiation from the rock?"

Michelle shook her head decisively, and her thick mane of curls swung back and forth. "No. They didn't get any data. Whoever Anatoli was in contact with before his laptop gave up the ghost—that person wasn't sitting at Roskosmos."

"That's why the searches." Lee sighed. "I don't need to tell you, do I, that I don't sleep very well knowing that Anatoli gave an unknown faction access to the ISS EDP?"

"No, and that's also what we're currently most concerned about here. But we're on it, and our IT fuzzies don't think there's any danger due to the lack of integration of the IT infrastructure from the Russian and Western sides of the station. At least not a big one."

"But we can't rule out the possibility that Anatoli has done something to get around this."

"No, we can't. But if he was serious about sabotaging the

station, surely something would have happened by now. So, let's assume—for now—that it was more about Astron's first data sets." Michelle smiled mirthlessly at the camera. "Then hopefully you can sleep better, too... which you should start doing, by the way. You still have strict daily routines, and all of us here agree that you should stick to them."

"It's not so easy after the first violent crime in space occurred in humanity's closest and most dangerous shared apartment." Lee yawned, no longer thinking to put a hand over his mouth. "Sorry."

"Go to sleep, Lee. We'll wake you as soon as there's news, all right?"

"Roger that." He ended the video call with the press of a button and detached himself from the laptop. For a few moments he closed his eyes in exhaustion and let himself drift in the module, tightly bending his knees and hugging them to himself with his hands so that he floated along in the fetal position. Rotating slightly on his long axis, he focused on the smell of grilled steak that was always up here. Even now, he could not fathom where this odor came from and why all astronauts and cosmonauts shared this association since the ISS came into existence.

Anatoli's apparent attack on Dima, whom he had come to esteem as a good friend, had staggered Lee. Anatoli had robbed him of his illusion that they were up here as an example of how friendly and constructive togetherness could work. Beyond all languages and cultures, beyond all the conflicts that seemed so important and dramatic to their fellow humans down on Earth. Space put so many things in perspective, but that seemingly didn't apply to Anatoli and those who had managed to lobby for his training and flight up here.

Lee didn't even want to know how deep into a very well-stuffed pocket someone had dug to make that happen, and how many officials in Moscow were guilty. That their corrupt arm had made it up here to join them in the ISS made it all feel like a fraud, tainting the entire project in such a way that he felt like a damaged human being.

"Hey." Sarah's voice snapped him out of the dozy state in which he had hoped to withdraw from everything that was happening around him and take a moment of silence. He'd tuned out even the hum of computers and other machines.

"Hey," he croaked, clearing his throat and opening his eyes. His colleague was hovering— upside down from his point of view—in the passageway to the Columbus module, eyeing him anxiously.

"You look exhausted."

"It's not just looks." As if to punctuate his words, Lee yawned so that his jaw cracked. He pointed to the bags in her hand. "Those are for Dima, I guess?"

She nodded and looked down at the IVs. "He's doing well. Responsive, but still a little confused. But that's to be expected. How's the asshole?"

Since the incident, Sarah had only called Anatoli 'the asshole,' which she'd made clear to the Russian in two short outbursts. His affectless silence had only made her barely suppressed anger worse.

"He ate, and said nothing. Like before." Lee raised both palms upward. "The restraints were still tight and well secured. He's not exactly comfortable, and he'll be pretty well atrophied from lack of movement when he leaves, but he deserves it."

"He's lucky we don't throw him out the airlock," she grumbled, pushing off to float past him to the sleeping chambers. Lee intercepted her with his arms, causing her to come to a halt in front of him and look at him in surprise.

"We're not going to let him make us do anything stupid, okay? You, Markus, and I are still a team, and we're going to handle this, too," he said earnestly, looking her in the eyes intently. "Not even a violent Russian can make us forget our training and lose our heads."

"I have nothing against Russians," she replied gravely, until a tired smile stole onto her expression. "But they're all Klingons."

Lee snorted in amusement and shook his head. "And Dima is our Commander Worf, I know."

"And I have to take care of our Worf now. Don't worry. I'd love to rip Anatoli's head off. Not just for attacking and hurting our friend, but especially for—"

"—that he has defiled this place, and we will never be able to rid it of that taint," he finished her sentence.

She nodded after taking a deep breath. "Yes. I'm sure it's best if we take such good care of him that he lands in Kazakhstan unharmed and is welcomed by the FSB." Sarah's face took on a gloating expression. "I don't think I can make him anywhere near as uncomfortable up here as Russian domestic intelligence can down on Earth, where after a week of being motionless up here he'll feel like an old man with glass bones."

"I guess you're right."

"But to do that, I need to make sure Dima is fit to pilot the Soyuz again." She glanced past him and pointed at his laptop. "Didn't you just get done?"

Lee turned and saw a budding video call. It wasn't from Michelle, but from Ulysses Keinzman himself.

"Ulysses?" he asked aloud, grabbing the cradle of the laptop and pulling himself closer with one hand as Sarah disappeared into the sleeping section. He accepted the call and saw the face of the NASA director, who had only been in office for a year, almost filling the entire screen. To the right and left, the glass cases lining the walls of his office could just be made out, making it look like the interior of a turn-of-the-century Southern mansion.

"Lee?" Ulysses began. It was a rather young-looking, rosy-cheeked face that stared at Lee, which had already led many a political opponent to make the mistake of underestimating him, his ambitions, and especially his contacts in Washington.

"Hello, Director."

"Not so formal. It's important, and this is a direct channel."

Not so formal. In other words, *off the record.* Much of Lee's fatigue disappeared as if by magic, and he tensed barely noticeably.

"I see." He looked around to his right and left, feeling like he was giving his superior the impression that he was ensuring discretion, even though he knew Sarah could probably hear them. But he didn't think much of secrets anyway.

"I want you to do a little maintenance."

"An EVA?" asked Lee in surprise, but the Director shook his head.

"No, no, inside the station. Our IT has a proposed improvement for controlling the security hatches," Keinzman explained. "I want you to try using their proposal and tell me if it's feasible and makes sense."

"Now? I was supposed to be asleep two hours ago to keep my rhythm."

"I know, I know, but I think it will be quick. I'll send you a file. It's all in there. Just work through the items, you understand?"

"Uh, sure," Lee replied, irritated. A file?

"And Lee?"

"Yes?"

"I want you, and no one else, to work on it. And I want you to put the file into the Eraser when you're done reading it."

You want me to delete it completely? "Understood," he said, though he didn't understand a thing. What was all this secrecy about? Of course, it had to do with the tense situation, and no one knew what it all meant for cooperation between them and Russia.

But after all, they were taking care of Dima right now, and the only ones who were even responsive at the moment were him and Sarah, as well as Markus from the ESA, which was something like their twin agency from Europe. So Keinzman's call and the manner of the conversation could only mean either that he was acting on his own, or he had been commissioned directly from Washington... or they feared a mole.

Or something else I'm not thinking about right now just because I'm dead tired, he thought, but nodded at the camera.

"Good."

"I'll be in touch when the work is completed."

"It will be quick," the Director was confident, leaning back a little until the U.S. flag at his back was also visible. "You don't have to report. Good luck."

The screen went black, and Lee saw the distorted reflection of his own face, as if he had been left alone in the void. And that was precisely how he felt.

"Sarah?" he called, waiting until her head appeared in the doorway to the sleeping chambers.

"Yes?"

"If you've taken care of Dima, I want to show you and Markus something," he muttered, looking again at the text document that had just been emailed to him. It was from the Director, and it included a rather large file that the program was still downloading.

Five minutes later, Markus and Sarah were hovering next to him, staring at the lines. They were currently on scheduled time-out—per the duty roster—so that allowed them privacy during sleep and rest periods—and there wasn't much privacy in space. Ground Control was neither on the radio nor the cameras.

"Is he serious?" asked Sarah incredulously. "They want us to plug a USB stick with a computer virus into Swesda?"

Lee nodded with a somber expression. "Yes." The instructions in the document were clear enough. Director Keinzman, and whoever had programmed or unearthed the backdoor, apparently wanted just that. In sober lines of text, it described how to download the file from Keinzman to a portable data storage device and plug it into a USB port on the Russian main bus. Everything else would then happen by itself. Written at the top and bottom in capital letters, it informed them this document had to be destroyed with an eraser program.

"You've got to be kidding! There's an incident, and the first thing Ulysses thinks of is spying on the Russians?" Sarah snorted like a buffalo. "You're not really thinking about going through with this shit, are you?"

"Yes, I am, but I'm coming to the conclusion that I don't like it."

"Wait a minute," said Markus, who had remained very still the whole time. The bandage that stretched around his head like a bulging white snake made his face look kind of funny. "We should at least discuss this."

Lee and Sarah turned to him and gave him surprised looks.

"Not only are we spying on the Russians, but this gives us the most promising opportunity to follow up on Anatoli's leads. After all, he did give someone on Earth access to our systems. Having the techies in Houston search all the files isn't a bad idea if we want to find out what's going on." Markus's expression turned somber. "It's still possible he's been planning sabotage, and if this remote contact is still in place, we're all in danger. The Russians no longer have access—if they're telling the truth, and right now, nothing is being recorded. There's no better time."

"Mmm," Lee murmured. "I wish you weren't right."

Sarah sighed and turned away.

"And I wish I didn't have to be right and we were in a different situation. But the fact is, we've got an externally controlled cosmonaut on board who took a swing at me, and Dima too—only he got it worse than I did. On the other side of this corridor," Markus pointed in the direction of the Zarya, "lies the problem, and we must shed light on it... for our safety and for the station's."

"I'll do it," Lee announced reluctantly, pulling the large file onto the thumb drive now that his email program had finished downloading it.

"We'll come with."

"No, Sarah, you won't. He wanted me to do it, and all it takes is one of us to cross red lines and get his hands dirty."

"Do you always have to be so damn... good?" she grumbled.

He smiled. "How many astronauts does it take to put a USB flash drive into a slot?"

"Okay, then. Go ahead."

10

JENNA

The flight to China took over six hours, a surprisingly long time. As always, money had solved the problem of urgency, and Jenna had electronically obtained a 14-day tourist visa in short order. During the flight, she read everything she could download onto her smartphone about Xinjiang Province and its capital, Ürümqi.

As it turned out, the three characters from the woman on the Wiesbaden referred to a remote village far to the west on the Kazakh border. However, there was no more information to be found on the Internet, which was probably due on the one hand to the restrictive censorship policy of the communist party and on the other hand to the special status of the autonomous province.

Xinjiang Province was home to the Islamic minority of the Uyghurs, many of whom lived in 'reeducation camps,' where they were compelled to learn the culture, language, and political views of the dominant Han Chinese. Men were also forced into compulsory service, and women were allegedly sterilized, while at the same time, Han Chinese from other regions were relocated there to slowly displace the Muslims. Beijing didn't like the aspirations for autonomy and the dangerous religious zeal, so they tried to reshape the facts.

Jenna didn't care. She didn't care about politics or religion any more than she cared about human rights. Whenever she thought about it, she wondered how people could claim that there was such a thing as universal and inalienable rights for them. Who said that? As far as she was concerned, this was just another made-up concept to be believed in, the sole truth for which one went to war. Earth would be a better place if more adults admitted they didn't have the faintest clue about the world and its complexities. People would take situational moral action and walk around without 'flipping others off,' and instead, observing with unbiased eyes.

She looked at her seatmate, a New Zealander, as she could hear from his accent. Up to now he had been silent. "Have you ever been there?"

Jenna pretended to be happy about the conversation and smiled. "No, first time. And you?"

"For me, too." He was a few years older than her, maybe 40, but there was something youthful about him with his short haircut, nerd glasses, and strong, tattooed forearms. "What do you do?"

"Excuse me?"

"Not many Westerners fly into Xinjiang. It's not exactly the tourist paradise in the Middle Kingdom," he said with a smile, gesturing past her out the window. They were already on approach to Ürümqi.

"Oh." Jenna slapped her forehead and chortled artificially. "I'm a nature filmmaker hoping to take lots of good photos and short films."

"For a TV station in the U.S.?"

"No, I'm not there yet. I'm a stock photographer for nature subjects. But I prefer to call myself a nature filmmaker.

That sounds more exciting than an underpaid photo machine."

"Either way, it sounds exciting to me because my photography skills are limited to whipping out my smartphone and pointing it everywhere. After that, I don't see the pictures again until I have to purge the phone's memory because of their overwhelming quantity." He grinned and held out a hand to her. "My name's Thomas. From Auckland, I'm sure you've heard of it."

"Julie." She shook his hand and pretended to tap an imaginary hat. "From Texas."

"Did you check your guns in or smuggle them in your carry-on?"

"Both."

They chuckled together until the landing gears deployed and the plane's engines sharply cut thrust.

"Are you staying in Ürümqi?" Thomas asked.

"No, I'm traveling farther west by train."

"Oh, funny. Me, too! And after that? North or south?"

"North."

"Ah." He shrugged his shoulders in disappointment. "For me, I'm heading southwest. It would've been nice if I wasn't the only Westerner the locals keep wanting to take pictures with, like an alien descended from outer space."

"You'll be fine."

"Have a good onward journey. Nice meeting you."

When the AirAsia plane had landed, Jenna quickly ran to passport control and left the airport via the metro toward the long-distance train station. She had to get used to the crowds, because every corner was full of people, like in most Chinese metropolises. Even though it was a large city, and despite her blatant exoticism, hardly anyone paid any attention to her. She was just another frantic person among millions.

The long-distance train station looked like a large-scale

commercial area whose simple low-rise buildings had been placed too close together. It squeezed in between the many ugly concrete residential towers the government was trying to add to their country's ever-growing cities.

Since Jenna could read hanzi pictograms, she could use the signs to squeeze through to the train she'd picked out while in Malaysia. The paint was peeling from the carriages, and the window frames were rusted, which told her a lot about the region she was heading to. The New Silk Road project, which China had been aggressively pushing for many years, had given most of the remote areas of the country much better infrastructure and transport links than one might have expected.

This was also the case in Xinjiang, which had only had a proper highway for the past five years, and which would eventually stretch through Kazakhstan and Uzbekistan to Duisburg, Germany. But even from this lifeline of asphalt and rails, her destination was not only many kilometers away, but also several decades.

She was stared at, and understandably so, on the train. Her compartment smelled unpleasantly of human odors and disinfectant. Besides the typical Han Chinese, she also saw many women with hijabs and men with more Kazakh and Mongolian features. The atmosphere was not tense, but it was as if there was a wet blanket over this place. No one was talking loudly, their gazes were locked, and the soft background music blaring scratchily from the speakers seemed disturbingly loud.

"Nǐ hǎo," she murmured politely as she settled into her reserved seat next to an older Han Chinese man. He smiled kindly and made a small bow.

The train journey took eight hours to reach the northern border region with the city of Altay. Most of the time she slept or leafed through her Mandarin dictionary, which she had bought at the airport in Kuala Lumpur. Her Chinese was not bad but had grown a bit rusty, and she wanted to use the little preparation time as effectively as possible.

Altay was a small city by Chinese standards, with a population of just under 200,000 and a peculiarity among peculiarities. Namely, it was the capital of a Kazakh autonomous district within the Uighur autonomous province of Xinjiang. Here she saw countless Kazakh-born people on the streets among the many Han Chinese who had moved in and were supported and encouraged by the government in their resettlement. The buildings here were more reminiscent of Kazakhstan or Russian Siberia with some candy-striped style buildings and colorful facades.

Since it was already autumn, the many trees in and around the city all but exploded with color. Shades of brown, green, and even orange alternated on individual branches, and the cool east wind blew fallen leaves through the streets. It was crowded here, too. There were loads of cars, most of which were still internal combustion engines, and just as many bicycles and even some donkey carts, underscoring the rural character of the town.

Although Jenna was dead tired, she immediately started looking for a taxi, which turned out not to be so easy. She stopped passers-by several times and soon realized that no one understood her Mandarin. It wasn't until a kiosk owner who was trying to sell her some chicken finally did, though she wasn't sure if she'd accidentally asked him for a crowbar instead of a taxi. He kept nodding and grinning from ear to ear before pulling an old Nokia out of his pocket and talking loudly to someone.

"Wait here! Taxi coming!" he beamed, offering her a Chinese Coke. She nodded gratefully, wanting to give him a few yuan, but he refused, raising both hands almost indignantly. "No, no! A gift! We don't often have tourists here."

"Not often?" she asked, more to make sure she understood him correctly, as his dialect was extremely difficult for her to understand.

"Never, actually." He laughed as if he'd made a good joke, and kept nodding with half-closed eyes. Finally, a white sedan that had seen better days pulled up in front of the kiosk. Jenna wondered for just a moment if it was such a good idea to accept a ride in a strange car, not licensed as a taxi, to the most remote areas in the region. If the driver wanted to try to kidnap her, she wished him good luck.

"Xièxiè!" she called out to the kiosk owner, holding up the Coke can to him in a salute as the driver got out to open the door for her. He was Han Chinese, nearly a head shorter than herself and quite slight, leather shoes on his feet and a white shirt under his jacket. Judging by his advanced age he was of the type who, although he didn't have much money, always left the house reasonably stylish.

"Xièxiè," she said to him as well. Jenna sat down in the rear, its unsurprisingly sagging bench seat covered with a white blanket that smelled a little like sheep or goat.

"My name's Li," he introduced himself as he got back behind the wheel and eyed her in the rearview mirror. "Where would you like to go?"

"My name is Julie, and I would like to go to Hemukanasixiang."

"What was the name?"

"Hemukanasixiang," she repeated more slowly and with more emphasis.

"Oh no, lady. You must have it mixed up. There's a town that's pronounced quite similarly, but..."

"No, I want to go to Hemukanasixiang. That's north of here near a river."

"But lady, that's over four hours from here. Only Kazakhs live there. They don't even have electricity, I don't think. No, no, that's very dangerous!" The driver seemed seriously worried.

"I'll pay you in dollars." She reached into her backpack and pulled out a wad of fifties, waving them toward the rearview mirror. "Can we go?"

It didn't take long to convince him—just a call to his family that he wouldn't be home until very late tonight. The drive took them west on a reasonably good country road before turning north. They followed that road for about two hours before heading northeast on a dirt road lined with dense woods to the right and left.

Villages or even towns had been scarce before, but were now nonexistent. They were alone in the untouched vastness of nature. Densely overgrown hills and mountains in warm autumn colors looked downright homey to Jenna and reminded her a little of her home in Montana. Snow already covered some of the higher peaks. At the time of the Cultural Revolution, the entire region—especially to the north—had been explored for mining and many tunnels were dug. As she had found out, the communist leadership eventually abandoned the project. The uncovered veins of ore were not worth the effort of connecting this remote area to the infrastructure of the then-still-extremely-poor country.

"This place is really no good, lady," Li said after a long period of silence. The gravel stones crunched under the tires, creating a constant roar in the car.

"What's wrong with it?"

"People live here very lonely and secluded. They're Kazakhs who don't want anything to do with China, you know." He shook his head. "The CP has an office here, but it's rarely staffed, and they say the official in charge is from the village himself. There isn't even a supermarket here."

"Oh, they won't kill me, will they?" she asked rather jokingly, but he made no effort to laugh.

"These are criminal people. They know no law."

"Have you ever been here?"

"No!" Li shouted indignantly.

"Then how do you know that the people of Hemukanasixiang are so bad?"

"Everyone knows that. Kazakh separatists live as secluded as these."

Of course, she thought, and sighed to herself. When they finally reached Hemukanasixiang, she was at first stunned by its natural beauty. To the left was a vast, naturally dammed river that looked like an elongated lake in the middle of a tub-shaped valley lined with tall, densely vegetated mountains.

The village consisted of long one-story wooden houses, their gray slatted roofs reaching almost to the ground. They all faced west to east and were surprisingly numerous. There had to be at least 50 of them, with dusty paths running between them like little streams. There were knee-high fences, roughly timbered and half-dilapidated, and everywhere goats, cattle, and even a few horses were grazing. She could hear dogs, and as she rolled down the window, an eagle called from aloft. Everything looked very peaceful and almost idyllic—but very run down.

"Where is everyone?" she thought aloud, looking at the clock. It was only four o'clock.

"They're Kazakhs. Maybe they're already asleep." Li sounded tense and stopped at the edge of the village next to a well. Jenna gave him the agreed amount, got out, and was about to slam the door behind her when he called after her, "I'll stay another ten minutes, in case you change your mind."

"Thank you, Li," she said, walking over to the well. An old watering can had caught her attention. It stood on the edge of the parapet of rough-hewn stone and was perfectly dry. With a furrowed brow, she looked to the winch and turned it out of curiosity. It squeaked loudly, but worked. A glance at the village revealed absolute motionlessness, if she disregarded the animals trudging unhindered through what with squinted eyes could be called front yards.

It was weird. Jenna walked up to the first house. Its tiny bull's-eye windows were just below the edge of the roof that reached her waist. An open dog kennel stood outside the front door, and the fence around the yard seemed to have been collapsed for some time. Weeds sprouted everywhere, and a homemade wooden rocker moved squeakily in the cool breeze that sang in the grasses. She knocked on the front door.

"Hello? Is anyone there?" she asked in Mandarin.

No one answered.

When she pushed lightly against the door, it turned out to be unlocked. The house's interior consisted of a large room bathed in unnatural twilight. The tiny, curtained windows barely let in any light, and she was blocking the best source of illumination. She looked for a light switch but found none, so she took the flashlight from her backpack.

In front of her was a large table, and behind it was a living area with a fireplace and an old sofa adjoining a platform on which lay thick mattresses and blankets. Probably a whole family slept there. Jenna approached the table and was surprised to find plates and pots, and putrid ham on a serving board. Some of the cutlery was on the floor, some dirty on the wooden top, and the smell grew more unpleasant the closer she got. The leftovers had to be at least a week old, if not more.

Just where were the inhabitants?

She walked over to an open, well-stocked tool rack. Finding a machete, she took it, checked its sharpness, and gripped the handle so tightly her knuckles cracked. The hairs on the nape of her neck stood up, and the goosebumps on her arms didn't diminish as she walked to the next house. It also looked as if its occupants had left it in a hurry—the only difference being the table here had been overturned and the food was lying on the floor.

Just as she was checking the dusty ground for tracks, she heard something at the door and wheeled around in a flash.

"Whoa, don't beat me to death!" The voice was familiar, and so was the face with eyes narrowed in the glare of her flashlight.

"Thomas?" she asked, flabbergasted for a moment. Then she raised the machete.

"Hey, no need for violence." There was no doubt about it, this was the New Zealander who had sat next to her on the plane, now holding his hands up in a defensive posture!

"I'll give you three seconds to tell me the truth. Why did you follow me?" she growled. "Three."

"I changed my plans. You were really friendly, and I thought—"

"Two."

"—I'm looking for inspiration for my—"

"One." Jenna leapt at him, swinging the machete at head height. Thomas deftly dodged it, diving under her blow and trying to grab it from the side. She'd been expecting that, though, and hadn't shifted all her weight onto the blade side, so she danced around him and stomped her heel on his right foot.

He grunted in surprise and staggered back, but he anticipated her thrust with the grip into his stomach and parried with a cross block of his forearms. Again he tried a grab and got a grip on her around the shoulder. Jenna rammed her elbow into his solar plexus, whirled around, and took him off his feet with a foot sweep. Breathing heavily, she pressed her left knee to his chest and aimed the tip of her weapon at his larynx.

"Last chance," she hissed, ready to stab.

"MI6," he gasped in a sudden British accent, putting on a

pained smile as she felt a gentle pressure in her side. A glance down showed her it was the barrel of a pistol. She acted unimpressed.

"Why is an agent of British Foreign Intelligence following me?"

"Yuri Golgorov. Compound X. We want to get our hands on it, too. Now, could you please get off my chest?"

"No."

"Hey, I could have tried—"

"I don't care. Why are you following me?"

"I had no leads, but an informant tipped me off that Mr. Xiami, at the top of my list, was murdered in Kuala Lumpur. So I looked into the case, since I was on the scene, and..." He paused and tried again with a charming smile. A raindrop trying to smash through a windshield would have been equally successful. "...I'm not as dumb as the local cops, let's put it that way. I know intelligence work when I see it."

"You've been nipping at my heels to get to Yuri Golgorov?"

"Yeah. But you found the Black Widow, so that wasn't bad, either."

Jenna narrowed her eyes to slits in irritation. "The Black Widow?"

"The woman on the yacht."

Jenna froze. "*She* is the Black Widow?"

The Black Widow had long been nothing more than a phantom, a specter to the intelligence services. She was allegedly responsible, directly or indirectly, for 40 percent of forced prostitution globally, having created an underground network through which young women around the world were lured, abducted, and trafficked to work as prostitutes in wealthy countries.

As recently as 2016, Scandinavian authorities managed to free 600 sex slaves from Russian trucks that had been headed to the port of Oslo disguised as food shipments. As in previous cases, investigations into the masterminds had revealed little except noting that the arrested crooks had opted for prison rather than testify and hope for mitigated sentences, for fear of being 'Black Widowed.'

Thomas tried to laugh. With her weight on his chest, it sounded like a gasp. "Apparently, it might be worth it if we swap information. Preferably without that." He tapped his free hand against her knee and lowered his gun.

11

BRANSON

Branson walked past Perkins' cabin and couldn't help grinning when he heard loud gagging noises through the closed door. The *Triton One* was rolling violently in the storm, and the ups and downs were so powerful that he had to keep holding on. He'd come from the galley with a bottle of bourbon jammed in his belt. The stairs led back to the bridge, where his two crewmen awaited him.

Marv sported blond, surfer curls. Johnny was a dead ringer for his best friend, except for his broad face and the thick full beard that made him look considerably older than he was. Both wore white linen shirts and harem pants as if they were going to an Indian ashram. Branson had long ago stopped making jokes about their appearance. One downside to their weed use was that they were so relaxed that he had a hard time exciting them over anything.

"Yo, boss," Marv shouted, standing at the helm and repeatedly turning the wheel left and right to point their bow head-on into the waves rolling toward them, while still trying to keep them sailing in the right direction. In the glow of the bow headlights, Branson saw surge after surge of spray spraying up in front of them like a ghostly gray wall.

The waves were striking so rapidly that the spray splashed right up against the bridge windows and the wipers had to be running at maximum speed for him to make out anything. Lightning flashed again and again, and the thunder that followed was loud enough to temporarily drown out even the smashing of the waves and the thumping of the diesel engines.

"Best weather for a bourbon," Branson said with a grin, and took the bottle from his belt. He swayed back and forth on his way to his place, the tightly riveted captain's seat at the helm, deftly smoothing out the roll of his beloved ship and gratefully shooing Marv away as he took the wheel himself. "Y'all want a drink, too?"

"No way, man!" said Johnny, standing between the radar screen and the electronic map, making minor calculations one after the other. "That stuff is pure poison!"

"True!" Marv agreed with his best friend and walked a serpentine line to reach Joe's seat, which was unoccupied because the first officer was still asleep.

"Johnny, how's it look on radar?" Branson inquired. "And what's the weather report?"

"The real rough weather will be with us for another fifty kilometers or so. With the little headway we're making, it's going to take a while. It should get better after that, though."

Branson grumbled discontentedly. His souped-up engine was doing them very little good in these swells, and he winced inwardly every time one of those monster waves broke against the bow. His old lady was working too hard for his taste, but he had thought the same thing plenty often before, and so far, she had never broken down.

"All right." He took a swig from the bottle, then slipped it into the leather holder he'd specially fitted a few years ago to hold his favorite bourbon bottle. The bottle fit inside perfectly and didn't come loose even in the worst weather. "Marv, why don't you fire up the TV? With the new dish, we should be able to get something in, even in this shitty weather. At least we'll find out what Oskar's promises were worth."

Marv nodded, jumping out of the seat right next to his and swaying for a moment with outstretched arms while trying to find his balance, and then pulling the small flat-screen TV out of the dashboard console that ran across the entire width below the bridge windows. He detached the remote control, temporarily attached to the display with duct tape, and climbed back into his seat.

"Any program preferences, boss?"

"Nah, just fire up the box."

Marv did, and sure enough, they got a picture, though it was grainy and repeatedly interrupted by white noise. So Oskar had only half lied. Branson had hoped for something quite different even during the worst weather. However, he could at least recognize and hear things, which was already a hundred percent improvement over their previous antenna.

"... disappeared under mysterious circumstances. Spanish authorities believe..." said a female voice, while hard-to-recognize photos were shown in the picture.

"Go on," Branson grumbled, and Marv switched to the next station.

"... residents of the village have also confirmed that on the night of..."

"Go on! Is it all news?"

"They all seem to be talking about the same thing," his crewman replied apologetically.

The next station had slightly better reception. Branson saw a blurry night shot showing indistinct figures with guns, running in a crouched posture from two helicopters toward a shadowy building.

A female voice off-camera, sounding almost the same as

the first woman, narrated, "The well-known YouTuber Luc Breusch is from Luxembourg and has been living in San Francisco, California, for the past two years, and had traveled to Cebreros to shoot video. In an initial statement, ESA Director General Dietrichs expressed concern about the scenes that have gone viral on the Internet since that night."

The image switched to a slew of tweets from celebrities that said things like 'Save Luc Breusch' and 'Truth must not be hijacked.' "Questions," continued the newscaster, who was now fading in from behind a studio table and was extremely attractive, "are raised primarily by the circumstances of Breusch's disappearance.

"The geophysicist, with more than two million subscribers, who was also a regular guest on West Coast TV shows, reported—in a clip available on YouTube for only a few hours—the possibility of a previously undiscovered meteor hitting Earth.

"YouTube blocked the video a short time later due to alleged violations of the platform's guidelines by the content. Several users who had previously downloaded it keep uploading it, so it is still available. In response to a request from the editorial team for a statement, we have received a single reply via email stating that this case is currently being reviewed internally."

"It's called an asteroid," Johnny murmured, not looking up from his screens embedded in the armature.

"What?" asked Branson.

"It's called an asteroid, not a meteor. Chunks aren't called meteors until they've entered the atmosphere, and this thing they're talking about is obviously still in space. So it's an asteroid!"

"Don't you know that nobody likes a *smartass?*"

"No, enlighten me, *wise guy*," Johnny shot back.

Branson laughed at the comeback as he continued to

turn the wheel now and again, still steering them head-on into the waves. He motioned for Marv to turn the volume up.

"Spanish federal police are searching for the body of Breusch, as well as that of Linnea Daubner, an Austrian physicist who ran the Deep Space Antenna 2 control station, who is also missing. One body has been recovered from the extinguished flames of the building, identified as Roberto Camacho. The astronomer had recently been appointed by ESA to Project Euclid, and leaves behind a wife and two children. Aguirre Fuentes, president of Spain's federal police force Cuerpo Nacional de Policía, spoke to reporters in the afternoon about the case, which is currently dominating worldwide news."

An overweight man in a suit and tie, his hair clearly thinning, emerged at a podium in front of a portico and began to speak. "At this time, I cannot reveal any details about the ongoing investigation. What we know so far is that the victim, Roberto Camacho, was a Spanish citizen and had been killed by two shots to the head and three to the torso before the control center burned down. All the evidence points to a paramilitary unit or covert foreign forces being responsible for the murder and double kidnapping and trying to make the fire look like an accident."

Loud voices shouted wildly, and the police chief pointed into the camera. Silence fell, and a single woman began speaking in Spanish, simultaneously translated by the news station. "Señor Aguirre, what do you know about the blackout in the Cebreros area? Is there a connection?"

"Yes," the politician replied, nodding. "We can confirm that three cellular reception and transmission towers have been sabotaged, as well as the West Madrid substation. Currently, we are looking for clues to the saboteurs and have offered a reward of one hundred thousand euros for information leading to the apprehension of the culprits. Accordingly, I ask all residents for their support."

The newscaster came back on the screen. "Responding to a request for comment on the possibility of Cassandra 22007's collision with Earth earlier in the morning, a NASA spokesman said the following."

The pretty newscaster disappeared, and a young man with slicked-back hair and a NASA badge emerged, standing in front of numerous hanging microphones. His voice was soft as velvet as he began to speak. "Together with our European friends at ESA, we have our eyes on Cassandra 22007 and, based on calculations so far, can give the all-clear. The asteroid, we've determined, will miss Earth by more than one hundred and eighty million kilometers. That's close in cosmic terms, but still far enough away that you couldn't even see it with an expensive hobby telescope. So, you have nothing to worry about."

The picture broke into white noise, which became stronger and stronger and finally filled the entire TV screen. It seemed the antenna wasn't doing as well as Branson had hoped.

"You go south once and a second-rate James Bond movie spins out on the news," Branson laughed, turning the wheel to the left as a particularly large breaker appeared in the ghostly light of the front headlights. The spray whipped deafeningly against the bridge's windows, and the windshield wipers struggled under the weight of the masses of water.

"I know Lucky Luc," Marv said, turning off the TV at a nod from Branson. "It's a cool channel. You really learn a lot!"

"Never heard of him," Branson replied.

"He explains a lot about the Earth. How the continents evolved, how volcanoes work and changed everything over the course of Earth's history. Also, significantly, he did a series on meteorites. Did you know that at least one was responsible for an entire ice age?"

"Nah. But I didn't study much, either."

"Don't pretend. You're smarter than your Crocodile Dundee exterior suggests. You don't need to use your underestimate-me strategy with us."

"Okay, so this guy's a big deal on YouTube and a smart physics-head," Branson summarized. "He saw something at ESA and thinks there's a previously undiscovered chunk coming our way. An asteroid."

Branson squinted at Johnny, who seemed busy with radar and satellite images. "He says it's going to hit us, then sinister characters from Big Brother come and bag him, but not before he uploads an evidence video. Now, half the world is looking for him and spinning a bunch of conspiracy theories. We had that just a few years ago when Democrats allegedly used pizza parlors as secret entrances for their vampire rituals and kiddie porn binges."

"Gross that you can see the kidnapping on YouTube. Or at least the beginning of it." Marv seemed thoughtful, which was pretty rare. "I hope the authorities catch these guys."

"Unbelievable that something like this could happen in the middle of a country like Spain. It's enough to give you the heebie-jeebies," Johnny mused, moving the zoom control for the satellite images with his left hand.

"I'm more worried about all those airheads in our own country who spend their afternoons shooting shotguns at dirty cuddly toys in the backyard and sipping Mountain Dew through the gaps in their teeth," Branson retorted, squinting his eyes as his vision was so obstructed by the spray on the windows that he could barely see for a few seconds at a time. "They'll be all over this thing, talking about some big government conspiracy to keep the truth about this meteor from us at all costs."

"Asteroid," Johnny corrected him.

"Yeah, yeah, all right. I can already see the riots in the South in my mind's eye. You'll see. It won't be long now."

"I'm afraid you might be right about that. On the other hand, it wouldn't be the first time they've kept something from us," Marv agreed.

"Boss, I got something on my radar here," Johnny spoke up again.

"What?"

"Two ships astern, thirty kilometers."

"How did we miss them?"

"The storm." Johnny shrugged and waved him over. "You take a look at this. A minute ago, they had automatic radar detection after transponder matching, but now they're suddenly blank."

"Marv, take the wheel," Branson ordered, sliding out of his seat onto the polished wooden floor, which looked colorless from the many decades of countless boots and shoes. Swaying, he walked over to his crewmate and bent beside him over the radar screen that lay at an angle in the dashboard. Sure enough, two relatively closely spaced dots appeared there at two-second intervals. "Hmm, they're not small."

"No. Oddly busy for sailing in the middle of nowhere in a storm."

"You can say that again." He eyed the two dots that kept appearing and fading until the radar circle caught them again and solidified them as if to burn them in. "Did we miss any restricted sea area we should know about?"

"Nah." Johnny shook his head and rubbed his wiry blond beard. "There's really nothing out there. The nearest radio station is three hundred and twenty nautical miles away. Eighty to starboard are two container ships, another to the southwest. These two, though," he pointed his finger at the two dots, "are on the same course as we are, if I'm reading it right."

"And there's the matter of the transponders. You can't turn them off."

"No, but we've done it before."

"That's precisely why it makes me wonder. Can you remember the identifiers?"

"There were four numbers on the back and two letters on the front. I think they started with U, but I'm not sure."

"We'll keep watching them. First we have to get out of this storm, and then we'll see if they're still on the same course," Branson decided before walking back to his captain's seat. He had to hold on twice along the way as the *Triton One* rolled right and then left. "It wouldn't surprise me if they took a little detour to avoid getting caught by that swell. That doesn't sit well with any ship. Except for those container monsters, of course."

The storm continued for another 12 hours and then moved on toward Japan, which lay many thousands of nautical miles away to the west. The seething dark cloud mountains with the sun behind them looked almost romantically beautiful on the horizon. There was nothing to indicate that they had previously caused the sea to rage and foam and be alive with energy.

Branson enjoyed the hours after rough weather very much, which was probably due to his days as a crabber, when several times a year he had thought he was going to capsize and his luck would run out. But he had always returned with a catch. The *Triton One* had never let him down, and time after time he had soaked up vistas like this and known that once more he had been spared.

Treasure hunting wasn't like crabbing. It was considerably less dangerous because you weren't under as much pressure—you didn't have to go out at any cost in any weather and risk your neck. Unless, of course, some snooty, rich guy came along and waved a million and a half dollars.

The rest of the trip was relatively uneventful. Perkins had confirmed the two ships on the same course were indeed their pursuers. Through the binoculars, the Coast Guard's white and red one with its gun turret had been easy to spot once the storm had cleared. The research vessel, more reminiscent of an oversized whaler, was following in its shadow. But without the fierce winds and large waves, the *Triton One* was able to play its only ace once again: Speed.

Thus they shook off the government ships without effort, losing them from sight after a day, and even from close-range radar after four. It took them ten days in all to reach the waters of French Polynesia, during which time it became increasingly hot and humid. Perkins stayed in his cabin most of the time, and when he wasn't there, he sat in his mini-submarine playing with the instruments.

Since Branson rated him a hundred percenter, he figured Perkins went over his dive day and night, as often as he could. About once a day he came up to the bridge to make sure they were making maximum speed, having noticed earlier that they were reserving about five percent. The ensuing discussion had been brief and heated. Perkins insisted on full speed to get there first at all costs, while Branson pointed out that the fuel consumption would then be too high and they might not make it to Vladivostok in one go, despite all the extra barrels they had strapped to the deck on the right and left of the submarine.

Finally Perkins had prevailed because he had threatened the money, so they resumed full speed. Branson was almost physically hurting from the enormous fuel consumption, but there was no way he was going to risk the huge payday. In the end he took some risks. When he was sure that he knew exactly the times when Perkins was in the submarine he searched the guy's cabin. Inside were clothes, three smartphones, which irritated Branson, a notebook with a fingerprint sensor, and a satellite uplink. He had already seen the suitcase with its combination lock when Perkins boarded, and he hoped that the rest of the payment was inside.

All in all he found nothing suspicious, but he also didn't know what he'd expected to find. In the end, it was his innate curiosity and the compulsion to know just what he was getting into. Not for his own sake—he was a bitter old sea dog—but for the sake of his crew.

On the tenth day, they finally reached the GPS coordinates Perkins had provided them. It was an inconspicuous spot that looked like any other in the Pacific: deep blue sea, unhurried rise and fall of the waves, flocks of cotton-ball clouds in the equally blue sky, and nothing far and wide, except for the barely recognizable silhouette of Maupiti, which stuck to the horizon like a mirage.

Marv and Johnny had the bridge when Branson went to get their guest from his cabin, but no one answered his knock. "Joe?" he asked over his walkie-talkie.

"Yo, what's up?" came the tinny reply through the small device in his fist.

"Have you seen our passenger?"

"Yeah, Xenia and I are watching him get the sub ready right now," Joe answered.

"My, he doesn't waste any time, does he?"

Branson was about to join them when the radio beeped and Marv's raspy voice rang out. "Yo, boss. We've got company!"

"Visitors?"

"Other ships bearing down on our position."

"From which direction?"

"Feels like all of them. I think you need to see this."

"I'm on my way," he replied, face screwed up. The middle

of nowhere, my ass. Instead, they had arrived at the Pacific's new hotspot. For the first time, he wished they'd fixed the antenna that must have taken a hit during the storm. But he hadn't considered it particularly important. Now, however, he felt sure he'd missed something.

What the hell was Perkins looking for in this place?

12

LEE

Lee felt bad after—according to the director's instructions—he plugged the USB stick into the Swesda module. While it hadn't taken anything more than plugging it in, waiting two minutes, and pulling it back out, it had felt wrong, like a betrayal of his home above the clouds. He'd also been startled by how efficiently and surreptitiously he'd gone about it.

According to Roskosmos, the systems in the Russian part of the station were no longer controllable from the ground station, although he had no way to verify that. So he had paused for just a moment in the passage between Zarya and Swesda so he could slip the stick into the USB slot he had already seen in the document's drawing. He had then flown on casually, as he was on his way to deliver food to Anatoli. The fact that there was a handhold next to the connection had helped him act as though nothing else was happening.

On the way back, the whole thing had worked as easily in reverse, and he had gone straight to sleep. The next morning—which differed only by his own internal thoughts from any other time—everything had been strangely normal. Sarah and Markus didn't let on, playing out their usual routines, altered only by the care and control, respectively, of Dima and Anatoli. Lee, too, threw himself into his work so as not to constantly rack his brains over what he had done and what was going on with Anatoli, RJKK Energiya, and this asteroid Cassandra 22007.

So, three days dragged by, taking care of the scheduled experiments he was doing for some universities. These were new drugs that were concerned with the behavior of blood cells on nutrient media in weightlessness, and changes in the permeability of the blood-brain barrier without gravity. Everything required his full attention and concentration, and it was only during his daily two hours of training that he could choose to let his mind wander.

Dima felt much better by the morning of the fourth day, although he couldn't remember what had happened. The cosmonaut was furious when they told him that Anatoli had knocked him out, but he stuck to Sarah's instructions to resume only light training against the atrophy, for the time being, and to get as much sleep as possible otherwise.

Lee received a call from Michelle just as he was scrolling through the plan for the day again.

"Hello, Michelle," he said as her face came up on the screen. She still looked as tired as when they'd last spoken, and the worry lines on her forehead had deepened.

"Hello, Lee. Would you get Sarah and Markus to join us, please? We have something important to discuss."

"Uh, sure."

Markus approached from Columbus, and Sarah from the other side of the Destiny module. They took positions where they could anchor themselves a short distance from the laptop.

"I want to get straight to the point," Michelle said after nodding to acknowledge them. "There are new findings that we want to share with you first."

"Oh, we won't be the last to find out, for once," Sarah

joked, but Michelle didn't respond to the line, adding to Lee's uneasy feeling.

"Cassandra 22007 is on a collision course with Earth."

There was silence for a few moments. Something in Lee's brain didn't want to understand what that simple statement meant, and another part could not process its implications.

"But wasn't it going to fly past us at some distance?" Markus muttered in shock.

"That's what we thought. Evidently, our calculations were wrong. Now that the asteroid is closer, we can see it much better, despite its strangely reflectionless surface."

"Is it possible that there's been a mistake?" Lee bit down on his lower lip, knowing his question sounded woefully naïve. He barely noticed the pain.

"No. We've already gone over everything three times. In about five days, Cassandra will hit near the Okavango Delta in northeastern Botswana."

"But that means that..." uttered Sarah, her voice failing.

Michelle nodded. "I know."

"How are the people on Earth taking it?" Markus asked.

"They don't know. We haven't informed anyone yet. Ulysses hasn't even called Washington. He's trying to buy time by ordering another round of calculations."

"But he must be—"

"No," Lee interrupted his friend and colleague. "He knows that Democrats and Republicans will tear each other apart, and there is no solution. No nukes can solve this problem, nor can drills or solar sails. Five days is nothing. The Senate can't even get an emergency bill together in five days."

Lee looked to Michelle. "What are the projections?"

"Not good," she replied, shaking her head. "If we go by our estimated size of twenty-five to thirty kilometers in diameter, then Cassandra 22007 is the end. The dinosaurs were nearly wiped out by a ten-kilometer chunk, along with seventy percent of all life forms. The impact crater was a hundred and eighty kilometers wide and smothered the entire Earth under a layer of ash. So a chunk three times that size? We can only imagine."

"We need to know," Sarah said in a quavering voice.

Lee felt transfixed. He thought of his brother and his nephew Charlie, his old friends he had been so looking forward to spending time with when he returned. He would never see any of them again. That thought was so surreal—*nothing* seemed real to him anymore. Even the hum of electronics seemed distant and bizarre. It had to be worse for Sarah and Markus. Sarah had her parents and several siblings, while the German was married with two children. This could *not* be true.

"Ulysses has said that if the final run doesn't give the all-clear, we'll inform the president in six hours—but an all-clear is highly unlikely. The team here in Houston and our friends in Munich and Cologne have been muzzled, as have you, by the way. No one here is going home until we have instructions from Washington and Paris, respectively, so there won't be any leaks to the media," Michelle explained, the clarity and directness of her voice making Lee even more nervous. "By then, hopefully, we'll know more."

"We're not allowed to talk to our families?" asked Sarah.

"Sorry, no. Maybe tomorrow, but not today. Please forgive us that this action was necessary."

"Do the Russians know?" Lee tensed up, and strained for a neutral expression. Normalcy. He had to keep normalcy going if he wasn't to lose his emotional bearings completely in this storm of consequences and scenarios spreading through his mind, leaving little room for anything else if he didn't maintain concentration.

"No. We don't know how they will react. But we've read the Swesda system and analyzed the data." Michelle put on a blank smile. "Ulysses has informed us. It doesn't matter now, anyway. I can still send you the results. Whatever they did there is extremely strange, but what's behind it will go down with all of us."

"Send it to me, please."

They exchanged a long look, and finally the head of readiness at the Houston Control Center nodded. "I think it's best for all of us to continue our work for now. We're the ones keeping an eye on Cassandra, and we may have to make sure the politicians don't do anything stupid tomorrow—which will be hard enough."

"We're not dead yet," Lee agreed, and was surprised to realize he was holding Sarah's hand. His colleague looked as if she had seen a ghost, pale and with a lower lip in constant motion. Markus, on the other hand, had gone as still as stone and said nothing, even when Michelle said goodbye and disconnected.

"I'll look at the data," Lee announced as an oppressive silence filled the module. He pushed off with his feet against the drawer of the small CT unit to fly toward Unity, where he climbed into the cupola and opened the armor segments with the push of a button, the plates detaching from the windows like chunky lotus leaves. Ironically—given the circumstances—the armor had been designed to protect them from micrometeorites.

Determined and methodical, Lee proceeded to boot up the laptop there and accessed his secure personal account. Once his gaze drifted upward, he saw the day side of the Earth, that blue paradise amid endless darkness, covered in bands of blinding white clouds. It looked as peaceful as ever, and at the same time, much more fragile and precious. It was easy to see the big picture from up here and at the same time lose sight of the fact that tiny creatures—people—lived, loved, suffered, and died down there, engage in very mundane pursuits.

While out of the darkness, death rushes toward them without them knowing it, he thought, swallowing several times as the thick lump in his throat made itself known again. I must not even think of pulling the covers over my head right now! Where's the data?

Lee clicked on the inbox and, at that exact moment, received an email from Michelle, which he opened and quickly skimmed. It consisted of a copy of an internal report from NASA's IT and Cybersecurity Division marked Top Secret and addressed to Director Ulysses Keinzman. The familiar salutation could only mean that this document was never meant to be seen by official bodies.

Ulysses,

After analyzing and breaking down the Russian system from the inside, we noticed some interesting things: From the looks of it, when cosmonaut Anatoli Timoshchuk set up his account after his arrival, he uploaded files that nestled deep into the code infrastructure.

In addition, there is evidence to suggest that a radio signal jammer had been installed. There were more than two dozen contacts from Timoshchuk's account to a disguised IP address in the Philippines. Each time the initiation was in Cyrillic and extremely terse, the actual conversations were short and spoken, so unfortunately we don't have any information about that.

Things will get interesting once the Astron has been installed. Apparently the unknown faction that had their fingers in the pie was very aware that there would be a signal and where it would come from, however, not in the way we previously suspected. The Astron radio telescope did not pick up radio waves emitted from Cassandra 22007, but rather ones from the Earth's surface, aimed directly at the asteroid.

The Meteor 1

Lee rubbed his eyes and skimmed the last few lines again before continuing to read:

We found coordinates in hidden files in Timoshchuk's account that exactly match the center of the crater in Siberia widely known as the Tunguska Crater and epicenter of the Tunguska Event early last century. The direction of the signal was also known, and instead of merely picking one up, there was apparently a narrow window of time in which Astron had to be activated, since it is directly over the coordinates with the station only once every 14 weeks.

The telescope flew into an existing signal sent from Siberia, and received a response in a mere two seconds. This sounds normal at first, since an asteroid is a passive transmitter, but the captured signal is very reminiscent in its basic structure of the one emitted from Russia. The processing of the signal data did not produce any image, which it should have.

Now Lee was utterly puzzled. The typical purpose of radio telescopes was to throw out a radio signal and evaluate the signals reflected from objects—like asteroids—to produce an image with a clear outline and shape, like an echo. But this echo had obviously not taken place as expected, or at least was so alienated that it did not produce this image, but perhaps something else. Why didn't this cosmic lump of rock behave as it should, and why was something from the Tunguska crater transmitting exactly in its direction? He was not aware of a radio telescope there.

And how was it possible that someone knew of Cassandra's existence without NASA or its partner agencies having the slightest clue? Even if there was some truth to the conspiracy theories about a cover-up of the discovery that had been spreading since the fire at the ESA facility in Spain, that still didn't explain why someone had known weeks, months, maybe even years ago that they needed to build Astron and get it to the ISS.

Lee returned to Sarah, who was in Destiny and going about her daily tasks as quietly and precisely as a robot, just like Markus, as if nothing was happening. Her hand movements were snappy but controlled, her face rigid with concentration.

"Sarah, there's something really weird here," Lee said, having to tap her to get her attention.

"You think?"

"Seriously. I looked up what the computer geeks back home found out. The Russians—or at least someone in Russia—already knew about the asteroid."

"What? What are you talking about?"

"The Astron," he explained impatiently. "It was built two years ago and prepared for transport months ago. A cosmonaut was fast-track-trained and approved, and he was tasked with getting the radio telescope into operation at a fixed time to pick up a signal from Cassandra during a window of two seconds after the asteroid was previously bombarded with another signal from Tunguska. Someone *knows*, and I wonder how that's even possible."

Sarah frowned and accepted the tablet he held out to her. After what felt like an eternity, she broke free from something like a thought-trance and took a deep breath. "We need to take a closer look at this. And we need to have another serious word with Anatoli."

They did, although the Russian was still not particularly talkative, and his physical condition was declining due to the lack of movement while in weightlessness. Even though he barely said anything, his silence revealed a lot. For example, it hardly seemed to irritate or surprise him when they informed him that Cassandra 22007 would crash into Earth in a few days, thus destroying it. Either he didn't care, or he knew something they did not that led to a different reaction. Either was troubling.

So they had no choice but to go over and over the letter to the director and discuss it—only during scheduled time-outs, of course, when every breath in the station wasn't being monitored.

Another call came in the next day, again from Michelle, only this time the director was sitting at her side. They two were obviously in the control center, because Lee, Sarah, and Markus could see the white walls with glass windows behind the two of them. In a departure from normal, it wasn't quiet around them. Instead, they heard loud conversations, scattered arguing, and the rustling of paper.

"We have news," Michelle said, tension audible in her voice, like a guitar string stretched too tight, creating too intense a vibration with each touch.

"Cassandra 22007," Ulysses Keinzman interrupted her. "It's slowing down."

Lee thought he had misheard and looked first at Markus, then to the right at Sarah, who both seemed just as confused as himself.

"Excuse me, sir?" Sarah asked.

"The asteroid is slowing down," the director repeated, shooing someone outside the frame away with a stern gesture.

Michelle took advantage of her superior's brief pause for thought. "Everyone's freaking out. We're trying to run parallel calculations while simultaneously running scenarios where a celestial body like that—"

"—*brakes?*" Lee jumped into her sentence. "That's utterly impossible!"

"We don't know why or how," Keinzman rejoined, pointing an outstretched index finger at the camera. "But that doesn't mean we have to resort to absolutes yet. Cassandra's slowing down, that's pretty much a given. Ever since we spotted it, we've been pointing every telescope at our disposal toward this deadly giant. I've already briefed the President, and all I can tell you is that I'm extremely relieved he hasn't gone public yet. It looks like the end of the world will be a long time coming for now."

"What do we know about its deceleration rate?" asked Markus.

"Not much. But we know it's gaining weight."

"This thing is supposed to be speeding up because it's being pulled by Earth's gravity funnel," Michelle needlessly explained. "It's doing just the opposite, though, and that's making us pretty nervous around here."

Lee understood what she meant. Instinctively, he wanted to be relieved, hoping that Cassandra 22007 wouldn't collide with Earth after all, or would fly past it due to its altered velocity, or would be deflected by the moon. At the same time, the behavior of this cosmic visitor contradicted everything they knew so far about celestial bodies and orbital mechanics, and *that* was never a good sign.

The director took over again. "Some here have suggested that extreme solar winds that have escaped us could be causing outgassing on the side facing us, slowing Cassandra down, but there's nothing to suggest that, and we do not see evidence of any such activity. However, the fact remains that we are now dealing with an asteroid that is slowing down, and we must respond to that."

"What can we do?"

"We have involved the Russians and Europeans after consulting with the President. Since the Kremlin fast-tracked the Astron from RJKK Energiya, they have given us permission to assist Dima in reactivating it and photographing this strange visitor. Anything that helps, helps."

Lee, Sarah, and Markus nodded.

"Good. Best to get started now, and let us know the minute you've got something."

"All right." They ended the connection and exchanged a few looks in silence before Sarah broke it. "This is really creepy, " she said.

"You can say that again," Lee agreed. "I feel like I'm stuck in a dream, and I can't wake up."

"Just one crazy event after another." Markus nodded. "But we are up here, and what is happening is somehow actually happening. I have no idea how it's all connected, but I don't believe in clustered coincidences. It's got to be something we're not seeing, and I want to know what."

"Then why don't we start by looking at this mysterious object itself, which is somehow decelerating in our direction," Lee suggested.

"You don't think that's an alien spaceship, do you?" Sarah looked at them wide-eyed and made a tortured face when they didn't reply. "Oh, come on."

"No," Lee assured her, "I don't believe in an alien spaceship. The rough structure of an asteroid has already been confirmed, and I don't believe that living beings who have developed technology to enable them to get here wouldn't report in. At the very latest, once we've locked on to them."

"Besides," Sarah added, "aliens would hardly be in contact with the Russians."

"The Russians?" asked Markus, confused, and Sarah pursed her mouth.

"We got the results back from the USB stick thing." Lee glanced around conspiratorially. "There was a signal sent from Tunguska to Cassandra 22007, and somehow there was a response. But that may have simply been an unnatural echo."

"*Unnatural* sums up everything about this. But Tunguska? Oh, man." The German exhaled a long, drawn-out sigh. "I hope all those conspiracy theorists down there don't hear that."

"If this keeps up, I'll be one of them soon," Sarah grumbled. "Come on. We need to talk to Dima. I want to see this hunk with my own eyes."

13

JENNA

Jenna stood with Thomas—no, Colin, he'd told her, if that wasn't another alias—under the overhang of the abandoned house.

"The owner of the *Wiesbaden* is the Black Widow? How can that be?" she asked, feeling anger bubbling up. Had she missed something, maybe even let the woman double-cross her? She hated it when someone played more shrewdly than herself.

"You know that foreigners can't do business in China without Chinese involvement?"

"Yes. Except for Musk."

"Exactly. Normally it works like this: General Motors, for example, wants to set up its business in China and has to accept a fifty percent shareholding from a domestic partner company. In this way, the Communist Party protects land as well as jobs while siphoning off technologies and know-how," the MI6 agent explained.

"In return, it opens up China's vast market, more significant than that of the entire West. This applies on a grand scale, ironically, to Western criminals, who are, after all, nothing more than businessmen who don't play by the rules. This one directive, however, they can't get around, because as Westerners they immediately stand out. Chiu Wai is an insignificant nobody, and at the same time one of the best known human trafficking racketeers there is."

"Chiu Wai is a no-brainer middle-class entrepreneur who makes pretty much the most innocuous thing imaginable—satchels," she said thoughtfully. "Not big business, but no big waves either. The perfect strawman for someone who needs a legal and actionable person for their illegal business. But who is the woman behind him?"

"We don't know her name, but we believe this is the Black Widow."

"So Chiu Wai is kind of like her mailbox in China," she concluded.

"Right. At least that's what we're assuming."

"Where did this information come from?"

"We were able to tap Chiu Wai's phone connections and noticed that he always dialed the same untraceable number before and after meetings with contacts considered to be criminals. We then tried to make a connection so we could evaluate his account activity. This wasn't easy for our analysts because Chiu Wai is extremely good at disguising his finances."

"Otherwise, I'm sure the Black Widow wouldn't have picked him."

"Yes. There have been two major waves of abductions in China, mostly of boys. Both times it involved several thousand who were abducted from three industrial metropolises simultaneously and never reappeared. Mostly they are sold to new families after the one-child policy in the Middle Kingdom has made children a rarity. They grow up with others, with new names, and change quickly enough that they are virtually untraceable to the authorities. Both waves have made Chiu Wai rich—his business took extreme upward swings at those same times," Colin explained. "That's when we took notice."

"You have an informant," Jenna said, nodding her head. "Otherwise, you wouldn't have been so quick to pick up on a phantom of the kidnapping trade."

"Yeah," he finally admitted. "We do have someone."

"And now you want to catch him."

"Of course. But that's what a lot of my colleagues are concerned with. I'm sort of on the bench after a somewhat unfortunate stint last year, and I'm supposed to be chasing a pipe dream. A formula."

"You don't think it exists?"

"A Russian oligarch developing a substance that's a miracle cure? The one responsible for the very low numbers of infected and dead in China?" The agent snorted. "Come on. Compound X is a fantasy. We don't have anything more than a part of a chemical formula that doesn't make sense, and the alleged inventor was shot down on Flight MH17 over Ukraine."

"My investigation into this fantasy has put me on the trail of your Black Widow. If someone like Yuri Golgorov—who is supposedly dead but still effective—is buying the services of someone like that, don't you think something is up?" asked Jenna rhetorically as she heard engine noises and reflexively ducked into cover. It wasn't until she glanced over the waist-high weeds of the front yard that she saw it was Li, her cab driver, turning around in the dusty lot and making his way home.

Jenna wondered if she'd just made a mistake, since she'd come without much gear, carrying only a little water and a few candy bars. "How did you get here?"

"On a motorcycle. It's standing by the river."

"We should keep looking around. Did you see anyone in the village on the way here?"

Colin shook his head. "No, it's like it is extinct."

"Surely there must be something like a village center. The place is secluded and backward, but not particularly small. There will have been a small local economy—farmers selling their produce, butchers, carpenters, a meeting place. Let's take a look around," she suggested, and he nodded. She had to admit that while it annoyed her that another agent had used her as a stepping stone, at the same time, it comforted her to not be alone and to have his pistol within reach.

This place was as eerie as the silence that surrounded it. Knowing that they were wholly secluded and even the almighty CP was barely active here didn't necessarily improve that impression. Walking toward the center, deeper into the village, only made their goosebumps more uncomfortable. Little dust devils flew across the barely trampled paths, and every now and then they came across tracks of tightly packed shoeprints, all of which led east. Most were made by adults, but many were small enough to have been left by children.

The sky drew ever closer, plunging the previously idyllic landscape—which contrasted sharply with the eerie scenery—into a dreary gray, as if someone had draped a shroud over the valley. A few cows gawked at them from the front yard of a collapsed house, pausing their constant chewing until the two of them had passed. A couple of horses shied between two dark sheds and dashed away as if they'd seen a ghost. Jenna felt like a foreign body, a spike protein, like someone who wasn't supposed to be here. Although that feeling pretty much always came to her during missions because of the nature of her work, here it was different. The houses seemed to have eyes, and the mountains seemed to have ears.

"Where is everyone?" whispered Colin, as if worried about waking anyone—or anything—that was better left sleeping.

"I don't know. But an entire village doesn't just disappear," she grumbled.

The Meteor 1

When they reached a spacious square, about the size of two tennis courts, they stood before a horseshoe-shaped, stately building. Its walls consisted of wooden slats blackened by the damp, assembled rather more roughly than artistically, and a roof that had been patched several times. The wind had already caused some dust drifts under her feet, but they could still make out lots of shoeprints, some of them aiming in different directions. Where paths led between the other houses, they also found tire tracks that had dug themselves surprisingly deep into the earth.

The large building was also deserted, and there were no food scraps or overturned furniture. On the contrary, the simple tables and chairs were neatly lined up. Something else caught their interest as they walked across the creaking floorboards: a scrawl on the back wall between the antlers of two deer.

"Can you read Cyrillic?" she asked.

"Yes I can, but not hanzi characters," the Brit replied, smiling. "You see, we complement each other perfectly."

Jenna scowled and pointed at the frantically or carelessly written sentences on the moldy wooden wall.

"Down with the Beijing dictatorship. Return home to the bosom of the nation," Colin read aloud, shrugging his shoulders. "Then, below that, it's hash marks. Maybe a vote was held or something."

"You said, 'Return home to the bosom of the nation?' They must mean Kazakhstan, right?"

"That's where I'm going with this. The residents here would all have to be of Kazakh descent. But that doesn't make sense. They've lived in China for centuries, probably because they were a persecuted minority in Kazakhstan, or the borders were unfavorably drawn. Either way, surely they could have gone back at any time if they'd been welcome over there."

"Maybe Chiu Wai wanted to make it look like they left

voluntarily," Jenna speculated. "He's behind this, isn't he? Chiu Wai, who's working for the Black Widow, if you will?"

"If anyone can make an entire village in China disappear, it's them. Just like you, we have whole shelves full of evil people who are eligible for this or that, but very few are ever eligible for the really big things in the various industries of evil. This number here definitely has her signature on it."

"That is strange. After all, she was the one who put me on the scent of this place," she said somberly, feeling all at once like the loneliest person on Earth, as if someone had zoomed out very far. "I didn't even know who she was, after all."

"Mm-hmm," Colin said thoughtfully, looking gloomily out the window. "That can only mean—"

"—that she wanted me right here." Jenna followed his gaze and fumbled for the machete she'd tucked into her belt. "There's no better place than this to take out unwanted agents who stick their noses too deep into matters whose continued existence depends on remaining unseen. I made a mistake coming here. If they kill me, I'll just disappear, and where all hell would otherwise break loose if a U.S. agent were assassinated, I'll remain missing somewhere in China."

"Who is foolish? The fool, or the fool who follows her?" asked the British agent, clicking his tongue. "Which do you think? Snipers? A hit squad?"

"I'm not sure. If she still had forces on the ground, or at least in China, she should enjoy a decent time advantage. If not, anything is possible," Jenna added. "Snipers in the mountains, claymores between houses, a strike team... I should never have made this faux pas."

"You're being pretty hard on yourself. After all, I'm the one who nipped at your heels and now I'm in this mess with you."

Jenna was tired of his constant comebacks, so she distracted herself by thinking. "Snipers are a possibility, but they always mean a mess. Blood and DNA traces everywhere, bodies to make disappear. In this environment, it's hell to get rid of human remains without a trace. If my government reports that a U.S. citizen is missing here, I'm sure Beijing will send investigators. Booby traps are hardly an option, either, since they can't talk their way out of it by claiming you accidentally wandered into a hunting ground. This place seems perfect for an ambush, but the circumstances are more difficult than they seem at first glance."

"Shh. Do you hear that?" asked Colin.

Jenna had heard vehicle noises at the same moment. They ran to the door, stood right and left of the frame, and peered out. Sure enough, two police cars with strobing blue lights rolled by.

"So this is her trap," she grunted in frustration. "That woman is even more cunning than I thought."

"She obviously has good contacts in the CP."

"That's what these people do for a living. She outmaneuvered me. She probably sent them a picture of me and exposed me as an agent. The local police chief will be pleased to have gotten his hands on a U.S. spy—maybe including a promotion—and *she* will be sitting pretty without getting her hands dirty. Elegant, I must confess. Once we end up in a black site here, we'll never see the light of day again, and chances are our governments will drop Compound X investigations. The topic is already being treated like a stepmother as things stand. This will finish off the whole thing."

Jenna watched as the cars angled toward the entrance and braked rapidly. The meeting house they were in had no other exits, and as all four doors of each vehicle opened, she also knew they couldn't fight their way out. The trap was indeed perfect.

"Chūqù!" shouted one of the officers, who had all taken cover behind their doors with their weapons drawn and aimed at the entrance to the house. They were wearing the dark green uniforms and sweeping hats of the Chinese military police.

"I'm guessing that doesn't mean I look great today?" asked Colin, sighing as he looked at the pistol in his hand.

Jenna shook her head. "Military police. That tells us a lot about the Black Widow. Eight people, one with the rank of captain, which is unusual. They never go out with their teams except on big missions. So my guess is he's her contact and took a few people he trusts with him. If his tip from his criminal friend turns out to be correct, he doesn't want any senior officers with him to snatch away his success. That's why they came here in regular street-cop patrol cars, a sedan and a minibus. So he wants the action to be under the radar for now, has bribed, threatened, or known the local cops, and doesn't want anything to be pinned on him just in case. He's cautious, maybe even nervous."

"And is that a good thing in your eyes?"

"Chūqù!" the captain roared, louder and more aggressive this time.

Yeah, yeah. We'll come out.

"Possibly."

"You want me to shoot him? At least we'll have eliminated the Black Widow's contact."

"Then when the others start shooting, we're mashed potatoes." Jenna shook her head. "No, we surrender."

"Just like that?"

"Just like that."

"What if I'm against it?" asked Colin. She shrugged in response. "Great."

"Wǒmen yào chūláile! We are coming out," she shouted, raising her hands.

"I'm guessing you didn't just tell them I was looking particularly good today?"

"I would never say that." Jenna cautiously walked into the

The Meteor 1

open doorway and looked to the police officers, who immediately tensed and extended their pistols and submachine guns.

"Bùyào kāi qiāng! Don't shoot! There are two of us!" She stepped forward slowly, walked down the two flights of stairs, and allowed herself to be handcuffed by strikingly young police officers. Two more approached and surrounded her. A moment later, she heard a click behind her.

"In the name of the people, you're under arrest!" barked the captain, an older man with a bulging belly and gray temples under his hat. He put his pistol back in its holster and came at them from the passenger door of the sedan with the blue lights.

"What's the charge? I'm a tourist. I have a visa," Jenna returned. It was a game, a farce, but even if you lost, you kept rolling the dice. That was just the way it was.

"Espionage. Get her out of here, and that one, too." He held out a hand and pointed at Colin, who was being roughly dragged beside them.

"I guess you won't be making a call to the ambassador?" the Brit asked with a sigh.

"No."

"Because you don't have reception, probably. I see. When we get back in range, then."

The policemen pushed them to the minibus and opened the rear doors. In the large back end were two bench seats against the walls. To the front, the driver and passenger seats were in plain view. A small crew minibus, then, not a prisoner transport. That indicated that the captain hadn't been able to prepare perfectly and was improvising. It could have been worse.

They were seated on the benches, each accompanied by an officer on the right and left, so that there were three of them sitting on each side, she and Colin with their hands cuffed in their laps. The driver got in and put the vehicle in reverse, then stopped until the passenger got in, and drove off.

"You've got the New Zealand accent down pretty well," she said in Colin's direction. "How about your Irish?"

"Oyrish?" he asked in a broad dialect.

"Yes," she answered. "When I give you the sign—"

"Ānjìng!" one of the military policemen yelled at her, giving her a painful jab in the side.

"—then hold on tight," she completed her sentence and caught a fierce blow to the mouth that made her lips split open. She sensed the metallic taste of blood in her mouth and fell silent. Colin bared his teeth angrily, but said nothing.

Two on his side, two on mine. One driver and one upfront passenger. That makes six bad guys here in this vehicle, she thought. That leaves two in the sedan. We're not strapped in, so we're not restrained. But we are sandwiched between these aggressive young guys. They're fit but probably inexperienced and not very bright.

The minibus rumbled over the gravel and sand roads, clearly having suspension problems as it was not designed for this terrain. Jenna was barely able to move as her handlers held her forearms from each side, in addition to the handcuffs. But she had to do something. Once they reached the graded dirt road south, it would be smooth sailing, and they wouldn't stop again until they arrived at some hole where the captain could question them.

There would be a call to the Black Widow to confirm her identity, and one to a CP official to tell of his great success. After that, the real heavy hitters from Beijing would surely take over. An American secret agent wasn't snatched up every day, and she was more valuable than her weight in gold. That automatically meant she would never see the light of day again, and would have some very unpleasant experiences.

She wanted to do without that, especially since this was the first time she had been paraded like this. Unacceptable.

Jenna sought eye contact with Colin, who nodded barely noticeably. A glance to the right between the driver's and passenger's seats through the windshield showed her that they were heading toward the last houses before the square with the well. If she remembered correctly, there was a large puddle in the collection of deep ruts there.

She began to exaggerate a little with every hole and bump the old minibus hit, rocking hard, bobbing forward a little—just far enough that it didn't seem intentional. The military policemen's grips reflexively tightened at first, but eased after a few times. So the typical habituation effect set in fairly quickly for them as well.

Jenna briefly considered trying to reach for one of their guns—since as soldiers they didn't wear safety tabs over the grips of their pistols—but quickly dismissed the thought. For one thing, they held their submachine guns in front of their chests with their index fingers across the triggers so that no shots would go off, but no one could reach in, either. For another, they might overreact to a direct attack. But she had to act. So, she did.

When they reached a puddle, it made itself known by a sharp jerk as their minivan was slowed by the water and the mud within. As it did so, Jenna rocked forward and lifted slightly off the bench with her rear end. As expected, when she reached her apex, the two soldiers pulled her back like a seatbelt.

Then came the first rut, and she did it again, but this time it was like the minibus was riding a wave. It bucked, and she moved forward, catapulting herself up as she got enough leverage with her legs. When they pulled on her sides again she first gave way, then used the brief downward motion of the front axle to throw herself forward with all her might and wrench her hands from the grips.

Jenna sailed between the two front seats, bumping her shoulder hard against the driver's seat as one of the soldiers tried to pull her back, but she managed to pull her hands to the left. They found their target as she crashed painfully onto the steering wheel. Her fingers gripped the old leatherette and she used her downward motion to yank it to the right.

The minibus swerved and broke through a fence. There was a crash and a clatter, throwing Jenna around. There was screaming and yelling from behind her, and the grip of the one military policeman who had still held her slackened somewhat. She opened her mouth and bit the passenger's upper arm with all her might, not letting go.

With her hands still bound, she grasped the lever of the handbrake and pulled it up in a jerk. Since it happened in the middle of a skid to the right, the sudden emergency braking locked the wheels and the vehicle rolled over, everything happening as if in slow motion. Jenna saw the hands of the men beside her fly up as if they were in zero gravity. Small objects and pebbles from the footwell flew up and seemingly changed direction.

The passenger screamed and tried to hit her, but the vehicle landed on its roof and crashed, sliding toward a wall of a house that seemed to come hurtling toward her like a dark shadow. She'd pulled her knees up to brace herself against the front seats before the impact, but it couldn't replace a seat belt. She flew upward into something hard, gasping as all air was forced from her lungs and a sharp pain drove through her ribs. Her right cheek impacted the light in the ceiling of the minibus and was ripped open.

As soon as she hit the floor, she spun around and found herself in a tangle of arms and legs. Someone was on top of her, trying to pull her up. Unlike her captors, she had mentally prepared herself for the accident and acted immediately. She pulled her head to the side and saw that she had a torso lying across her. Its upward movement brought some light between them, and she quickly recognized the pistol she'd been seeking.

The handcuffs now turned out to be to her advantage, as —unlike the soldier's on top of her—her hands hadn't been twisted or trapped but were pressed together just in front of her stomach. She pulled the gun from the holster, flicked the safety lever away with her thumb, and raised the muzzle. Her index finger pulled the trigger twice in quick succession while she was simultaneously twisting to the side. The BANG was brutal and her ears rang.

The screaming around her became more shrill. The bleeding man, now lying powerless on top of her, formed enough cover and her twisting motion had brought her hands and the pistol out from under him. She saw a face topped by a police hat and aimed a shot between the eyes. Then she fired in quick succession at the driver and passenger, who were still trying to free themselves from their seat belts, and saw the windshield turn red from the splattering blood.

Another shot rang out, then two more in quick succession. A hot pain drove through her left shoulder, as the weight on her chest suddenly eased. Jenna jerked the gun up and almost pulled the trigger before she recognized Colin. His face was bloody and so was one leg, but he stood between the bodies and helped her up. There was no hint of his permanent smile.

He climbed to her and squatted down. "Great plan," he groused, and she realized he was missing his top front teeth.

"Shh!" Jenna heard an engine howl nearby and dropped back down to lay behind and partially draped over the man who'd been on top of her. Keeping her eyes half-closed, she rested the pistol seemingly at random, but aimed toward the rear door. "Get in front!" she hissed with a matching head flick.

It took what felt like an eternity for the doors to open. No one stood there, and for a minute or more nothing happened. Then a soldier peeked around the corner with his machine gun at the ready. Jenna allowed him some time, acting dead while waiting. Only when he'd cautiously ventured inside did she shoot him in the head. His impassive face looked as if he had seen a ghost just before he died. Silence fell again. Behind her, on the edge of audibility, she heard a door click and something rustle.

When a hand holding a grenade appeared at one side of the open rear doors, she cursed inwardly.

"Come out, or I'll blow the whole thing up!" the captain barked in Chinese. Jenna pursed her mouth and tossed her weapon out before standing up and daring a glance over her shoulder. As soon as she stepped out the door into the gathering dusk, the muzzle of a pistol was in her face. The captain's hand trembled slightly, and his mouth quivered with anger. Then he heard a safety being clicked off, and his eyes grew wide.

"Drop it," Colin muttered firmly, pressing his outstretched pistol against the Chinese officer's temple.

Jenna sighed in relief when the captain complied with the demand. *I hope they brought first aid kits*, she thought, eyeing her counterpart grimly. *And tools.*

14

BRANSON

"*Four* ships?" asked Branson incredulously, staring at the radar screen. Two were approaching from the east, one from Maupiti to the southeast, and another from the west.

"It looks like it," Marv affirmed with a shrug as he stood beside him. "If I judge the distances and current visibility correctly, we should be able to see the first ones with binoculars in about an hour."

"It could work. They're all moving pretty briskly." Branson grabbed his walkie-talkie and pointed a finger at Marv. "Hold us in position. I'll try to put a little pressure on our guest." He then hit the send button and held the little radio right in front of his mouth, "Joe? We're going to have company soon. Perkins better get a move on."

"Why? Are you expecting trouble?" his friend asked as he stepped out the side door into the open air and walked along the side rail toward the quarterdeck.

"Yes. Our guest expects some, and how often do you think it happens that there are five ships headed for the same point here in the middle of nowhere? Not to mention those two from Hawaii."

"Touché."

"Be right there." Branson clipped the walkie-talkie back on his belt and climbed down the spiral steps behind the bridge superstructure to the open aft deck. Without the awning it was unfamiliar looking, reminding him of a long tray on which a poorly shaped sausage was served. Perkins was already scurrying about on it. Xenia stood by the crane, listening to Joe's instructions as he walked back and forth behind the sub, directing her with gestures and wild shouts.

The towing harness, with its robust chains and hooks, jingled like a menacing trap above the fragile-looking underwater vehicle. Typically, they used the harness to retrieve larger finds like crates or ornate wall sections from old galleons and sunken merchant cogs from the bottom of the sea when they could not use gas balloons. Well, at least they hoped to use it as often as possible for just that. The crane's last few missions had involved oil barrels they'd sunk for well-paying customers, in addition to pseudo-treasure chests of candy for the kids.

Branson wasn't proud of it, and still resented the fact that he'd contributed to the destruction of the Pacific, no matter how small it might have been. He would even have preferred to sail around in an electric ship like Dwight Decker's, but a new purchase was currently nothing more than an unrealistic dream. Last year, the money from that shady contract with the two barrels they hadn't been allowed to open had saved the *Triton One*, because otherwise they wouldn't have been able to pay for the necessary maintenance in dry dock.

Whatever bad karma he might have brought upon himself —they had even debated whether it might have been two bodies hidden in the barrels—the alternative would have been the loss of his home. Everything in his life revolved around the old lady, and once she was gone, he didn't know what he would do. He'd probably stick the muzzle of a shotgun in his mouth and not call his own bluff.

"Perkins!" he called to their guest, who was just poking his head out of the submarine's hatch, about to climb out.

His eyes sought Branson and then he looked at him questioningly as he took the last rungs two at a time and landed on the deck.

Branson moved two steps closer to the glassed-in cockpit of the submarine and then pointed back with his thumb where the ship's superstructure towered several stories high. "We're going to have visitors, and they'll be here in the next few hours. I suggest you hurry."

Perkins didn't seem surprised and merely nodded.

He knows a lot more than he's saying, Branson thought—not for the first time. This man looked so boring and normal, yet Perkins was so confident and composed that the guy scared him time and again. An asshole like Decker was one thing, but a guy he couldn't size up, whose appearance and behavior didn't match, and who came from a world completely distant from his own, he was quite another.

"I'll go down at once. Everything is ready. You make sure the ship stays put. Under no circumstances are you to be driven from here, understand?" Perkins gave him a stern look and waited until Branson nodded before pointing to the crane. "Tell them to hurry up. My dive will take at least four hours, and the other parties won't be sleeping during that time."

"The other parties?"

"Yes. You want the artifact, but I'm not interested in that. What I need is *under* the ocean floor."

"Artifact?" Now Branson was bewildered. "Different from the one you're looking for?"

"Listen," Perkins snorted impatiently. "I pay you to do your job, not to ask questions, okay? I'm not your friend, I'm your business partner. You do your part of the deal and I'll do mine. Your job now is to maintain this position at all costs.

Have divers standing by so that when I return, the submarine will latch quickly. If anything should happen to me, dial the number I left on the table in my cabin. It belongs to a satellite phone."

"I don't suppose you mean a diving accident with your submarine?"

"No, I don't mean a diving accident with my submarine," Perkins confirmed. "But even then, dial this number. And remember, the object has top priority."

With that, the strange passenger climbed back inside and closed the hatch over himself and took the pilot's seat. The glass dome was highly reflective, so Branson could only dimly make him out as he pressed a few buttons and moved the control stick back and forth, examining it. Joe had already climbed to the top and was attaching the final hook to its designated point. Xenia was operating the crane's controls with steely concentration and seemed relieved when Branson joined her and took over.

"Well done," he said, and she nodded in satisfaction.

"Did I understand correctly that there are other ships coming toward us?"

"Yes." Fortunately, she left it at that, and seemed to interpret his grim expression correctly. Branson raised the submarine, and the entire crane structure groaned under the unaccustomed weight it had to lift. Joe instructed him with brief waves of his plate-sized hands to make sure he didn't bump the sub against anything, and then he was lowering Perkins down into the gentle waves. The passenger raised his hand in a thumbs-up with a stoic expression and then slowly sank into the deep blue of the Pacific.

Branson disengaged himself from the rusty controls and put a hand on Xenia's shoulder. "You stay here in case we need you. Does your radio have enough battery?"

She nodded.

"Fine. Joe?" he barked at his friend, then gestured toward the bridge. Together they walked up. "I don't like this one."

"Tell me about it," Joe grumbled, pointing to the horizon to the east. "But it's not all bad. It looks like tonight is going to be our first clear night since we cast off."

"Wonderful." Back on the bridge, they stood at the radar and looked at the dots moving like metal beads toward a magnet. Toward *them*. "Guess who's coming to dinner."

"That's a lot of traffic," Joe agreed with him thoughtfully. "Have you tried hailing them yet?"

"No, and I don't know if we should, either. Marv?"

The man he'd addressed was currently sitting in a cross-legged contortion in his captain's seat, and he looked tired. "Yo, boss?"

"Go up on the roof and fix our antenna, will you?"

"Whew, I don't know if I can handle that. I'm an electrician, not an electrical engineer." Marv unknotted his legs and slid off the seat. "I'll see what I can do."

"Do you think *now* is the time for listening?" asked Joe.

Branson asked a counter-question. "Did you ever hear of underwater grain circles before this putz showed up here?" When his partner shook his head, he pointed to the radar dots. "I'm sure the same goes for whoever is sending all these ships here. I can't shake the feeling we're missing something. Hey, Johnny?"

"Yeah?" asked the machinist from where he lay on the floor in front of the pinboard of hero photos from the last 20 years, smoking a joint.

"Do the comm check with Perkins. I want to be sure the cable is working today. He'll be on the bottom in an hour, and I don't want to wait until then to find out if we can talk to him or not."

"You got it," Johnny sighed, getting to his feet.

"Joe, we'll get the diving equipment ready."

"Ours?"

"For all of us. If the waves get heavier, or we get pressed for time, we'll both go down. Otherwise, Xenia and Marv," Branson decided. "We're taking care of that now. Things are getting weird around here, and I want to be ready for anything."

"No objections."

They went back to the stern and opened the lids of the diving-equipment storage compartments they had converted into seats for the children's visits. One by one, they checked the BCDs and the automatic dive machines for functionality and proper fit before putting everything into their designated spaces by the exit. He answered some questions about the operation of the crane for Xenia and went through the steps with her until he was sure she would have no problems. When an hour had passed, Johnny radioed in.

"Yo, boss. The first two ships are in sight now. Starboard. And our Freddy has reported in. He's reached his destination and is digging around or something. He was pretty curt. The connection was really crap, too. He said something about magnetic field and interference, but I have no reason to think anything's wrong."

"Thanks for the info." Branson retrieved a pair of binoculars and knelt on the seat by the starboard railing. With the artificial magnification before his eyes, he slowly scanned the horizon, where light blue faded into a jagged dark blue. Then he spotted the first ship. It had a tall, steel gray superstructure, as far as he could tell from this distance. Several smaller add-on structures rose from the hull, and on deck was a low turret with...

"Holy shit!"

"What is it?" asked Joe, coming to join him.

"It's a fucking warship!"

"Marines?" Joe took the binoculars from him and looked

The Meteor 1

through them after Branson pointed him in the exact direction. Without setting them down again, he muttered, "Must be Chinese."

"Chinese?"

"Sure—who else would be coming at us from the west that is not allied with our country, which has already sent the Coast Guard after us? Unless they've got more in tow." Joe paused. "But where's the second one? There were supposed to be two ships coming from that direction."

"I don't know. I only saw the one. Marv?" he asked over the radio.

"Yo, boss?"

"How close are the two western contacts?"

"I don't know. I've only got one signal left on the screen."

"What? Where's the other one?"

"I haven't a clue. Gone."

"A submarine, I'm sure," Branson joked, and his smile dried up like a drop of water in the desert when he saw Joe's worried face and realized it was no joke.

"Uh, guys?" called Xenia from the crane's control panel. "Are you guys seeing this, too?"

"Seeing what?" Branson asked. When she didn't answer, he elbowed Joe. They walked across the swaying deck to his assistant, who stood there in shorts and a billowing T-shirt, looking upward with sunglasses and one hand shading her eyes. "What are we supposed to see," he repeated as they arrived next to Xenia and looked up at the sky, too. If she showed him another wandering bird, as if it were the miracle of Canaan, he would have a serious word with her.

"Look at the moon," she replied, pointing with an outstretched arm toward the milky-white structure that stood as a pale, nearly full disk approaching the zenith, while the sun was already approaching the horizon in the west and would be gone in a few hours.

At first Branson did not understand what she meant, but when he looked at her, she was still pointing to the moon. Earth's satellite looked the same as always, he thought. Then he saw it—something was wrong, something he hadn't noticed all day because its outline was as natural in the sky as ever: near the center was a black spot, where the deep craters in the surface were dark shadows. It was small, but large enough and dark enough that it could not be missed. Branson would have dismissed it as a personal visual-field defect if the others hadn't seen the mark, too.

"What is that?" muttered Joe in his deep bass.

"I haven't a clue, old friend. It looks like the moon is... broken."

"If I didn't know that was impossible, I'd say something had moved in front of it," Xenia agreed. "Do you see that little dot of light there, too?" Her slender index finger moved downward.

This time Branson saw it at once. A red spot with a long tail, lower in the sky than the moon, slowly growing larger and glowing with variable brightness.

"Am I stupid, or is something coming at us?"

"I'd say both," Joe said, his voice sounding distorted because he'd also craned his neck to keep an eye on the object, "but that one's getting bigger."

"Is this a plane crash?" asked Xenia tensely.

"If so, we're about to get a close-up look at the horror."

Branson had to agree with his friend. It was becoming more apparent that the red glow was flames. Something was plunging out of the sky, growing into a fireball with a long tail that seemed to tremble barely noticeably, as if it were being shaken by an invisible hand. But perhaps that was just an optical illusion caused by the erratic atmospheric heat effects.

"Not a plane," he said aloud. "It's a shooting star."

"But shouldn't it be burning up?"

The Meteor 1

"Actually, it is."

"Guys," Joe interjected. "I don't want to spoil your fun, but that thing is getting dangerously close. I'd say we should fire up the engines."

"You're right." Branson reached for his walkie-talkie, pulled it off his belt, and put it to his mouth. Before he pressed the send button, he froze. "But the cable! We can't leave."

The three of them eyed the finger-thick cable that ran from the bow superstructure over the stern into the water, their only communication link to Perkins. He glanced back at the fireball, which was now as big as a ping pong ball in the sky. Then suddenly the flames were gone, and a white ring formed around a teardrop-shaped object that streaked away from him and rapidly dissipated. Branson stared up with his mouth open until there was a loud bang, as if someone had set off a firecracker next to them. He winced and hit the send button.

"Johnny! Marv! Full speed ahead! Now!"

"Yo, boss, what's up? What's up with the ka—?"

"NOW!" he roared, nearly tumbling off the deck as the *Triton One* lurched forward, her engines roaring to life and thundering deep in the heart of the ship. Dense spray splashed off the stern, mixing with the churning bubbles of air from the propellers. Joe helped Branson up, and Xenia pulled herself to her feet by one of the columns of the crane's console. The cable struggled under the strain and snapped at the same moment with a loud crack of the whip. Only centimeters away, the frayed end whistled past Branson's ear and disappeared into the churning waters.

Then the object came. After another sonic boom, it grew larger and larger, became a shadow the size of a minibus, and crashed with a deafening roar into the Pacific Ocean at the exact spot where they had just been. Not 30 meters astern, a fountain of saltwater shot up at least 100 meters as if a torpedo had detonated. A tidal wave spread out in a ring from the epicenter and spilled over the stern as well, but it wasn't strong enough to sweep him, Joe, and Xenia off their feet.

Soaking wet and shivering, he wiped the water from his face and stared in disbelief at the field white with spray from which they were fleeing.

"Shit! Did we just get bombarded by a fucking meteorite?" cursed Branson breathlessly, coming to a halt from his crouched position before yelling into his radio, "Johnny, full power astern. Take us back to the Perkins drop point!"

"Shouldn't we first..." put in Joe, but Branson shook his head and pointed to starboard, where the outline of a large gray ship was peeling out of the horizon. It was now plainly visible to the naked eye. "Oh, damn! That's the Chinese, isn't it?"

"Yes." Branson stared again at the point of impact of the lump of rock that had nearly sunk them. The spray was slowly clearing, but the circle, some 25 meters across, was still visible, and a dense mist of tiny water crystals were leisurely settling over it like a veil. "Is that what Perkins meant by the artifact he's not interested in?"

"I don't know. That guy gives me the creeps."

"Guys! A meteorite just fell out of the sky!" squealed Xenia. She was shivering all over. Since she was also dripping with water, you might have thought she was freezing, but the air was exceedingly hot and stuffy. "We almost got killed."

"Yeah, and there's about to be a really weird crowd here."

"Boss?" rattled Johnny's voice from the radio as the *Triton One* moved agonizingly slowly backward, as if using the spray circle as a target point. "We've got a problem."

"Another one?" grumbled Branson. "What's the matter?"

"Listen!"

The radio clicked and clacked, and then a muffled voice

with a heavy Chinese accent rang out, "This is Captain Li San of the frigate Jiaxing. Make yourself known immediately."

"Give them our identification and tell them we're a damn civilian ship in international waters," Branson shouted.

"Okay, boss. But now the guy wants us out of here," Johnny replied.

"On what grounds? These aren't Chinese waters!"

It took time for the machinist to answer, and Branson could hear voices in the background. Finally, it clicked and scratched again. "Yo, boss. He didn't respond to our info, but instead he threatened that they'd take firm action against our alleged illegal presence at a Chinese military maneuver if we didn't leave immediately."

"Shit!" His money and his mission. Branson stared at the impact site slowly calming before his eyes and thought of the miniature submarine rising there, somewhere in the depths.

"What do we do now?" asked Xenia anxiously.

Joe eyed Branson, who didn't answer, and nodded in understanding. "I know that look on your face. We're doing our thing."

15

LEE

Lee stared out of the cupola, pressing one cheek against the center window and looking through the one on the side toward the moon, which just barely appeared at the bottom edge as a glowing disk. Directly in front of it: Cassandra 22007, a round object slightly less bright to the naked eye. Of course, he knew from the Astron images of the last few days that the asteroid wasn't *round*, in fact it looked more like an ugly lump of mud that extremely clumsy hands had sculpted. But from here Cassandra 22007 was merely a tiny twin of the moon that had been there for 12 hours.

From photos taken in Houston and playing on social media and news streams around the world, he knew that to the people of Earth, it was more of a smudge that marred the moon, a black mark on their planet's satellite that had for centuries been the source of numerous myths and legends. The public seethed with speculation as to what it was, as informed governments and space agencies kept remarkably efficient seals—until now. Theories discussed on all the front pages ranged from a new and particularly massive crater on the moon, to a gas mixture stuck in the atmosphere, to extraterrestrial visitors, and—to some—a divine sign.

Lee had seen photos of crowds in the squares of the world's great metropolises gathering to look up at the sky at night and share this wondrous yet somewhat eerie sight. He did not know whether it was due to the long time during which they had barely been allowed to attend any large events due to the past COVID-19 pandemic or the need to feel the warmth of fellow humans in times of uncertainty. But this much was certain: something was moving in on Earth. And it was something very different from what he had expected a few days ago. Instead of the apocalypse, there was a cosmic mystery to solve.

He could still feel the excitement in his chest that he had felt when evaluating the first Astron images they had viewed with Dima. Even though he wouldn't admit it to Sarah, it hadn't escaped him that part of him had believed they might be dealing with aliens, until they had seen the first images from the computer. Cassandra 22007 was an asteroid, there was no doubt about it. Its surface was extremely dark and dull, however, unlike any traveling celestial body that humanity had been able to study so far. Admittedly, there hadn't been very many, but those that probes had landed on or at least flown past had shown no such deviations, but had always roughly agreed with what had been predicted.

Geologists and geophysicists would undoubtedly be busy for a long time, looking into what this one's texture was all about, but Lee had one overriding question: what was this signal that the faction operating in the shadows had picked up, and that had puzzled NASA's cryptographers? Nothing in the pattern made sense, intuitively suggesting a natural but unknown origin.

The Department of Defense was already working on launching a satellite to be positioned over Tunguska to intercept the signal, should it be prove to be ongoing. The hope was that it might have changed somehow, or that the snippet picked up by Astron was just a slice of a much larger one that only made sense as a whole.

In short, they were still in the dark.

Cassandra's surface was rough and rocky, as expected, an ugly lump of rock whose origin the astronomers suspected was the Kuiper belt. From the recorded trajectory, which had been as anticipated from first contact to Earth—apart from the inexplicable braking process—they had been able to deduce precisely where it had come from, and how long it had been traveling. At least 110 years in all, give or take a dozen or two months.

He'd already talked to Sarah about the fact that the point in time from which Cassandra had been knocked out of the belt—perhaps by a collision—pretty much coincided with the Tunguska event of 1908. But that had merely given him goosebumps and doubts about his sanity. Indulging in conspiracy theories and fantasy was not a direction he wanted to go. He was still an astronaut and a scientist, not a nut job.

But the fact was that there had been far too many coincidences and unexplainables over the last two weeks, none of which they could make sense of so far. Lee had to accept that, just as he had to accept the sight of that dark spot between them and the moon, positioned exactly 197,000 kilometers above the Earth on a direct line to the satellite, where it had remained fixed for half a day.

Well, not quite motionless. The first three *fragments*—as Markus had called them—had come loose two hours ago. Tiny pieces had broken from the surface of Cassandra and hurtled toward Earth. On NASA's radar screens, which got their data from the Goldstone Deep Space Communications Complex in California, they looked alarmingly like torpedoes fired from a warship. They weren't moving particularly fast, but they were moving fast enough not to be deflected by the atmosphere like flat stones skipping off a lake's surface.

The first fragment, which had been five meters long and two meters wide at its thickest point, had pierced the outer layers of the atmosphere as a glowing fireball over Tierra del Fuego and had come down somewhere in the Pacific, near French Polynesia.

The second had hit southeast of Japan.

The third had been shot down over Siberia by Russian air defenses using an S-400 guided missile. Judging by the television footage on Russian state television, which played up the launch as a remarkable feat of the armed forces, it had been destroyed, shattering into hundreds of stone-sized chunks. The images of the missile tail, the explosion, and the glowing meteorite shower spread rapidly on the Internet and looked surreal, like a clip from a war.

The world was now in an uproar, feeling under fire, although NASA, ESA, and Roskosmos, along with the Chinese government, were trying to nip abstruse theories in the bud. The experts did not tire of emphasizing that it is not unusual for smaller fragments to detach from an asteroid and fall from the sky as shooting stars. At the same time, with careful observation, it was clear to viewers that these experts did not feel particularly comfortable in their skins.

The fact was that even they had no clue what was happening, or why. But the public needed to be reassured, and basically, there was no serious problem, either. Yes, a celestial body not doing what it was supposed to do and thus baffling them all was scary, perhaps, but no one had been harmed, and an impending doomsday scenario was off the table. For now.

Strictly speaking, it hadn't been on the metaphorical table long enough to be fully grasped. The fragments were potentially dangerous because of their size, and because the sonic booms could be heard on the ground many dozens of kilometers away. This time they had come down over the sea and uninhabited territory in Siberia, but over a city would be a different story, which was why air forces worldwide had been put on high alert. It was crazy times on Earth, that much he could glean from the media, to which he had been virtually riveted since Cassandra had become a part of the night sky.

"Lee!" he heard Sarah call out. "It's happening again!"

He freed himself from the tether bar and pushed his way back into the Unity module, from where he returned to Destiny, where Dima, Markus, and Sarah were already crowded in front of a deployed monitor they had repurposed from the liquid crystal research unit. It showed real-time data from the NASA radar they used to monitor Cassandra around the clock. More fragments had detached and were beginning their journey to Earth, just as their three predecessors had done two hours ago.

"Five this time," he muttered.

"What is that thing shooting at us?" asked Dima.

"Stones," Markus answered dryly. "Have you noticed that a veritable gold rush has broken out in the Pacific? Navy ships, treasure hunters, converted fishing trawlers—everything motorized is looking for the crashed fragments. They're on it like flies on shit."

"It's obvious. There's a damn black dot in front of the moon, and it's dropping artifacts. I'd want to go off and get my hands on one of those, too," Sarah commented as they all gazed transfixed at the radar contacts regularly popping up in new positions, like a squadron of Cassandra 22007s heading toward Earth. Unspectacular in the form of pixels but incredible in the form of real objects heading for their home planet from some unexplained location.

"Maybe they're smart rocks."

Now all eyes turned to Dima, who raised his hands defensively. "What?" He pointed at the monitor. "If that looks like a natural process right there, I'll eat a garbage can."

"A broom," Markus corrected him.

"In Europe, maybe." The Russian sighed. "That one scares me, okay? A huge fucking scare."

"The first calculations are coming in," Sarah announced. "Suspected impact locations two in the Atlantic, plus one each in the Indian Ocean, the Pacific, and the Antarctic Ocean. Flight times about two hours."

"If the trajectories stay like this, the outermost fragment will be just 20 kilometers away when they go past us," Lee commented, and Sarah nodded.

"That's really close."

They spent the next hour and a half at the monitor tracking every radar contact. The countries involved in the ISS had agreed at short notice to publish the data in real-time to give the people in possible impact locations some advance warning, so the images were broadcast live on television in most countries. Their televisions carrying nothing but special broadcasts about Cassandra 22007, people talked about nothing else.

When 20 minutes remained, Lee retreated to the cupola carrying his SLR camera with its most powerful lens. He wanted to see the fragments with his own eyes. When he arrived at the viewing canopy, it occurred to him that he must have forgotten to raise the protective flaps. This would be an unforgivable mistake under normal circumstances, which served to make him realize what an exceptional situation they were in, and how tense he was.

He kept rechecking the exact direction he needed to look, but then spotted them by accident as he scanned the space surrounding them through the lens. The ISS was flying straight over the night side of the Earth, which almost blended into the blackness of space, had it not been for the reflection of the moon and the many lights of the cities that stretched across the continents like a luminous rash.

The lack of sunlight made it easy to see the five fragments when they were still beyond the terminator line in a direct line with the sun. They hurtled past the stars like glowing coals until they dipped into the planet's shadow. He snapped a series of photos and growled in surprise when one of the fragments flashed for a split second as if it had pierced a nest of fireflies. The effect was extremely brief.

The changing perspective made it look to Lee as if the objects were splitting up, and then they penetrated the upper layers of the atmosphere. At first, the effect began as a barely perceptible haze that trailed behind them like a thin mist, but it intensified until becoming trails of fire as the friction-induced heat grew increasingly more intense. It was a sight both beautiful and terrifying, as he knew these things were intruders forcibly invading the biosphere of his home planet.

When their glows disappeared again, he returned to Unity, pulled out one of the laptops, and followed what was happening on CNN. The fragments were coming down over the world's oceans right where predicted. There was even subsequent footage of two impacts that showed vast water fountains. In the Indian Ocean, a confrontation between Indian and Australian naval ships took place during the race for the meteorite that came down there. However, very little data was available about the conflict. Shots had reportedly been fired, but the station was keeping a low profile.

Later, as Lee was on his way to his sleeping cabin, he looked through the hatch in the Zarya, which was now always deliberately left open, and saw Dima hovering in the Swesda module. It looked like he was unconscious, but when Lee floated over to check, he relaxed again. The cosmonaut stretched and beckoned him in.

"Hey, Lee. Are you okay?"

"That's what I was going to ask you."

"Ah, well. The call came in." Dima sighed. "Tomorrow we go back to Earth. I'm bringing back our shithead Anatoli. I guess the FSB can't wait to get their hands on him, and I'm considered a risk in case the blow caused a brain hemorrhage or something."

"I'll miss you, my friend," Lee said with honest disappointment. "This will be the first time in a long time that there will be no Russians on the station, huh? At least for a few days."

"It's going to stay that way."

"Why?"

"The president doesn't want to send a replacement, not even to the moon. It's obvious everyone just wants to see Cassandra now. Why spend so much money on this shared flat?" Dima's mouth twisted as if he'd bitten into something bitter. "Crazy times. I'm going to hit the hay, but I'll check on Anatoli first. He's supposed to be fit, after all, when the Secret Service guys tie him naked to a chair and unwrap the ropes."

Lee's giggle sounded more like a snort. "I'll see you tomorrow."

Back at Destiny, Lee was about to turn into the sleeping chambers when Sarah, who was opening a packet of steak with mustard sauce so she could suck it out through the mouthpiece, beckoned him over.

"You're supposed to report to the director."

"What is it now?" he sighed. "I was supposed to be asleep."

"I don't know. He wouldn't tell me. But I wonder if it's about an unscheduled EVA they want to assign you to."

"All right." He gently pushed himself off the wall with his feet and caught himself by grabbing the support bar next to the NASA computer before turning it on and requesting a connection with Michelle. All hell seemed to be breaking loose again in the control center, as noisy as it was. Several people in white shirts were walking together, crossing behind her seat.

"Ah, Lee. I'm patching you right through to Ulysses. He wants you to use headphones. It's important." Before he could even say anything, NASA's logo appeared as a 'wait' screen. It took about a minute, then Ulysses Keinzman appeared on camera in his office, even before Lee had stuffed the earbuds into his ear canals.

The director wasn't looking at the lens, brusquely shooing someone away before rolling his chair to one side. A gray-haired man dressed in Air Force blues took a seat next to him. He wore the three stars of a lieutenant general and the humorless expression of a staff officer. Lee stiffened—a trained reflex.

"Lee, I want to get straight to the point," the NASA director tossed out. His eyes looked anxious, and his tone of voice betrayed that he was unhappy about something. "We did shoot up a military satellite with the last Atlas, didn't we?"

"Yes, AF-117—it was launched the day after Astron arrived." Lee's eyes shifted back and forth between his superior and the general.

"Exactly. When one of the fragments came down, it hit a Japanese weather satellite and created a shrapnel cloud that hit two other satellites. It doesn't look like there will be a large-scale chain reaction, but AF-117 was damaged."

The general added his voice for the first time. "Preliminary analysis indicates that it hit one of the automatic control thrusters essential for maintaining orbit. We would like you to fix it."

"Fix it?! A satellite?!" Lee was taken aback and shook his head as if he had misheard.

"In exactly sixteen hours and forty minutes..." the director began, looking anything but happy, "... the ISS will be in a favorable position relative to AF-117. It won't be easy, but it can be done. We'll reroute the ISS so it stays close, and you can get back every ninety minutes. SpaceX has already agreed to let you use their docked *Crew Dragon*. This is a matter of national security."

"Sarah is much more qualified for this kind of—"

"No, colonel," the general said firmly. "This is military hardware, and because of your background in the Air Force, only you qualify."

"Sir, I'm willing to do my job at any time, but sixteen hours is far too little to safely prepare for an EVA. I need information on the planned repair, an accurate plan of the satellite, and time to calculate the flight and approach maneuver. If you'll pardon the expression, you don't just do these things on the fly—"

"We know, Lee," Keinzman cut in again, "but it's urgent. Our guys have been sitting on the math for a long time. I've got eighty people on it, getting everything ready. It'll be a cinch."

Lee didn't think the director looked like he believed his own words. But apparently the pressure on Keinzman was significant enough for him to agree to such a reckless and unreasonable undertaking—he must have been given no choice.

"Dima and Anatoli have been ordered back," Lee stated. "They'll fly back to Baikonur tomorrow. That leaves only Sarah and Markus with me. That's a pretty small crew to be working on an away mission, especially since it's not even at the station. If Sarah pilots the *Crew Dragon* and I go out, Markus will be here alone. That's way too dangerous. There must be someone in the cupola, and someone on the Canadarm for docking."

"That's right," the director affirmed, "and for that reason Sarah and Markus will stay aboard."

"You want me to fly the *Crew Dragon* by myself *and* do the repairs?" Lee shook his head. "Come on."

"We want no one but *you* near that satellite," the general said.

"Lee, you can do this," added Keinzman. "You are qualified to do the repairs, and you're also trained on the *Dragon*. Get some rest, and then we'll start preparing you. An internal team consisting of our people and some experts from the Air Force are already sitting down together and getting everything ready for you. When you're awake, say in four hours, they'll brief you on everything, and you'll go over everything in detail. You'll fly over, fix the nozzle, and fly back."

"Understood," he sighed resignedly.

"Good man. Well, get a good rest. Oh, and before I forget: The repair details are secret. The others don't need to know what it's about. Just tell them it's an important GPS satellite."

Lee swallowed his anger, nodded, and ended the connection.

16

JENNA

After the captain had been willing to credibly assure them that his police minibus, which was now lying on its roof, did not have a GPS transmitter, and after they'd agreed that the age of the vehicle made this likely to be true, they had put him in the car and driven to the end of the village, which was dead silent. In the trunk were all the guns, magazines, belts, and cans of mace they'd recovered from the minibus before consigning it to flames to cover their tracks. Jenna didn't think anyone would be looking for the captain and his subordinates here anytime soon, no matter what the captain tried to make her believe.

The house in front of which they had parked was the only one situated a little higher up, on the slope of a shallowly rising hill that offered an unobstructed view of the entrance to the valley. A gravel road beyond the many rooftops divided the endless forest in two like a firebreak. Colin had tied their prisoner to a chair, and Jenna had found needle and thread in a small box in the closet.

The damp house smelled of mold and unwashed clothes, not exactly antiseptic, but it was the best they could do for now. As it turned out, Jenna had taken a graze to the shoulder, a laceration to the forehead, and a three-centimeter gash to the cheek. The multiple bruises on her legs and hip were painful but would have to heal on their own. So would the cracked rib. What bothered her was the disgusting taste of blood from the passenger's arm, which she had misused as a 'mouth guard' before the accident.

Colin cleared the table, sweeping aside all the objects with his arm and spreading a blanket from the sleeping area on top of it. Jenna lay on her back and held out the disinfectant spray from the military policemen's first aid kit.

"Almost like a doctor's office," joked the Brit, who looked like a plucked chicken himself. He disinfected his hands, then the needle, and set to stitching her shoulder wound after disinfecting it as well. "Are you positive you don't want a bite stick?"

"Sure," she replied, staring at the ceiling beams, which looked so rotten she wondered if, after everything she'd been through, she would die now—ironically—from a collapsing roof.

"All right. I'll try to be like a good doctor," he assured her, placing the needle. "This may hurt a little."

The feel of the tip poking through her skin was more pinch-like than painful, as was the tugging when the thread tightened. She wanted to watch his fingers, but the angle wasn't right, so she had to trust that he'd gone through field training similar to hers, and thus he shouldn't have any problems with wound treatment.

"It's been a long time," Colin mumbled.

"You need to—"

"Shh. I'm just kidding. Six stitches. That's it. Now your cheek."

It pinched more badly this time, but the accident had been more painful, and Jenna kept her mind riveted on the bruises on her legs and on her teeth, which still felt like they were a bit loose. When Colin was done, she nodded her thanks and waited for him to put bandages over the freshly stitched wounds.

Then Jenna got up and tended to Colin. He'd gotten off surprisingly well, though his head appeared to be bleeding, and blood was still dribbling from his mouth. After she used a drinking glass to rinse his hair with water from a small well next to the house, she found that the blood wasn't his—but the three big bumps were. She thoroughly cleaned the glass with disinfectant and then made him gargle and rinse with it.

"Three missing front teeth. I'll have to stitch you up," she said.

"Great," he grumbled. "I'd like a bite stick."

"I should think so." Jenna tilted his head back and began closing the wounds with precise sutures. The man was either brave or macho enough to react as little as possible. When she was done, she took a rolled-up gauze pad and laid it across the sutures in his mouth. "Bite down on it carefully and maintain pressure."

"Mm-hmm."

She nodded her satisfaction at his compliance, then turned to face the Chinese captain, who met her gaze her with eyes wide and his pupils dilated with fear. She recognized this expression and was glad to see it, not out of sadism but sheer necessity. People who were afraid usually turned out to be surprisingly talkative—just what she could use right now.

Jenna went to the toolbox she'd also brought into the house from the trunk of the police car and set it down in front of the officer. Slowly and deliberately, she raised the lid, letting him take in every detail. She brought one hand to her chin and looked at the hammer, screwdriver, and pliers as if she couldn't decide, and finally took the hammer.

"Do you know the game about the little pigs going to

market?" she asked in Mandarin, slowly removing the captain's shoes before pulling his socks off and setting his bare feet on the dirty floor.

"What?"

"Some piggies are going to market." Jenna pressed the head of the hammer down on the little toe of his right foot, and he jerked back, startled.

"I... I'll tell you anything you want to know!" he stammered, tears streaming from his eyes. "Please!"

"Ah, wonderful." She put on a smile and set the hammer aside, close enough that she could easily reach for it. She stood up so he had to look up at her. "How did Chiu Wai contact you?"

"He called and said that an American spy was on her way to Altay to travel to Hemukanasixiang and..."

"Yes?"

"...and look around there."

"You wanted to grab me and get a promotion, right?"

"Yes," he admitted reluctantly. "Please, just let me go. I won't do anything—"

"Of course you won't," she interrupted him. "Who else knows I'm here?"

"No one! I only brought people I trusted and gave them money."

"That you got from Chiu Wai?"

"Yes."

"What happened here?"

"I don't know."

"Where did the residents go? Chiu Wai kidnapped them, didn't he?"

"I really don't know!" he assured her in a quavering voice.

Jenna sighed, knelt down in front of him, picked up the hammer and raised it to take a swing.

"WAIT!" he screeched in shock, causing her to pause at the apex. "He's taken them away."

"Aha. So now he's *taken them away*, hmm? That's a different story." She let the hammer fall downward, guiding it toward the little toe of his right foot, but her arm was blocked halfway. Colin had snatched her wrist. He merely shook his head.

"What?" she asked in a broad Irish accent. "A lie merits a punishment. I'm sure you learned that in your training, too."

As he was about to reply, she put an index finger to her lips, signaling him to be careful not to loosen the pressure on the gauze roll, and turned back to the captain.

"You were very fortunate. However, I like to assert myself, so don't try that again. You covered up the kidnappings because you're the district commander in charge of the military police for this region, am I right? As far as I know, you have more authority than the local police, so you were the best guy to be bribed."

"Yes," he admitted reluctantly, looking down at his feet with flared nostrils as if afraid they'd already been beaten to a pulp without him realizing it. "They merely told me to make sure no one came here on a certain date for at least a day. I ordered the road leading here closed for an exercise, that's all."

"And what did you get in return? Money?"

"Money and a promotion." The officer didn't even try to sound contrite. That was a good sign—he had stopped playing the game. She surmised that he wasn't ashamed, probably because he harbored racial resentment against the Kazakh minority.

"So there are higher-ups behind this. Someone in Beijing?"

He nodded.

"Where were these people taken?"

"I don't know." As she was about to reach for the hammer again, his voice cracked and he stuttered so badly she could barely understand him. Then he managed, "I really don't know. Honestly. I merely provided the roadblock and came here to arrest you. After all, you're operating illegally... All right?"

"Did you see any vehicles coming here? Before the barricade, I mean? You had to get all this ready."

"Y-y-yes. Vans, lots of them, maybe twenty of them."

"What make?" she inquired.

"Lada."

"Russian, then."

"Yes." He nodded, and the beads of sweat on his forehead rolled onto his nose and dripped from the tip. "There are a lot of those around here, you know."

"Did they come back?"

He shook his head.

"They could have gone to Russia or Mongolia," she said in Irish and turning to Colin, who was half-sitting on the tabletop with his arms folded, watching them. "Toward Kazakhstan, the mountains are pretty impassable. Besides, my money's on the Black Widow being involved with Golgorov. That's why the contact via Xiami-san."

Jenna pointed at the captain and looked at her 'partner' questioningly. "We'd best bury him somewhere around here."

WHAT? the Brit's eyes seemed to say.

"I was joking," she retorted dryly. "We'll leave him here. If no one finds him, he's earned his fate. If someone does find him, what story do you think he'll dare to tell them without the risk of ending up in jail himself?"

Jenna poured water over her prisoner until he shook his head, then packed up the tools and the remains of the first aid kit, while Colin took two blankets, a lighter, and a tarp. They stuffed everything into the trunk of the police car and then returned to their prisoner. After Jenna snapped two photos of him, she nodded in satisfaction.

"We're going to clear this thing up, just so you know."

"You can't just leave me here!" protested the Chinese man with a horrified expression.

"No? Why not?" she asked. "Don't tell me this is unfair or cruel. After all, you tried to kidnap us, and you have the blood of an entire village on your hands."

Jenna picked up one of the crude knives that had fallen from the table and, in one smooth motion, threw it at the opposite wall, where it stuck, briefly vibrating. She then walked over and rubbed her sleeves over the blade where she'd gripped it. "You've got a chance here. It won't be easy, but at least you won't get bored."

She walked back to the car where Colin was waiting at the driver's door, carefully feeling his mouth from the outside.

"I'll drive," she said firmly, and to her surprise, he showed no resistance before walking around to the passenger side.

Their route led north through the village to where the valley narrowed between the converging mountains. As expected, the river ran through the deepest part, with a gravel path beside it. She could hardly imagine that the former inhabitants of this place had ever owned vehicles, the way the paths here looked. True, there were tire tracks in the packed earth where some rainwater had collected, but they were probably all from the Lada vehicles in which the people had been taken.

"This is all crazy," she thought aloud as she steered the car over the bumpy dirt road. Dusk was slowly setting in, creating thick shadows between the ubiquitous trees.

"What exactly?" mumbled Colin, "You translated for me, remember?"

"A Russian oligarch develops an unknown chemical and is sponsored by the Kremlin. Then the government shoots down Flight MH17 over Ukraine, and along with the plane, down goes Golgorov with an aluminum suitcase containing the first samples. Sure, every high-end intelligence agency wanted to get their hands on it, but why would the Russians shoot down an entire plane and not just poison him with Novichok like they usually do? And why did Golgorov want to fly to Malaysia? To meet Xiami and make contact with the Chinese? Hmm?"

"Malaysia is dependent on China. That could be. Neutral ground," came the British man's barely intelligible reply.

"Good. Golgorov is making a deal with China, or at least people in China. There's a new wave of kidnappings, but it's merely a bit worse than usual in 2018. That's not news. In 2020 COVID-19 breaks out, and China, despite its huge, often densely packed population, gets off so lightly that everyone thinks of manipulated numbers. Russia, on the other hand, comes off badly, though mostly in the West."

"Sure, that's where most..." Colin made a slurping noise, "... people live."

"We're assuming Compound X is an unapproved drug," she said. "And you?"

"Nerve agent."

"Mm-hmm," Jenna nodded. "We thought so too at first, but there's something to be said for a drug with military applications. Otherwise, the results of the study phases would have been published."

"Something like stimulants for soldiers? But why would Russia share those with China?"

"*Russia* wouldn't, but Golgorov would. In the end, it's all about money, and if you want to do illegal drug trials that no one wants to participate in, you forcibly use people that no one will miss and no one will go looking for."

The trail went into the mountains for a few kilometers and then split into two narrower dirt roads. One turned further north and one turned east. Jenna got out and knelt in the headlight illumination to examine the ground closely. Since they were a little higher up now, it wasn't wet and the ground was fairly hard, so there were no deep ruts. On top of that, darkness was already laying its hand over the idyllic land, and the bright headlights were almost blinding even when she had her back to them. After a while she was convinced it was the eastern track that gave the clearest indication that lots of vehicles had passed through in recent days, maybe as long as a week ago.

Jenna returned to the car and turned it to face the east route.

"Did you find anything?" asked Colin, his lips smacking a little from trying to keep the gauze in place.

"They seem to have gone this way."

"Won't we be into Mongolia soon?"

"Yeah. Where there's plenty of room for pretty much everything and hardly any people," she replied. "It's a perfect place to make a village disappear. Open your mouth."

The Brit followed her request hesitantly and cautiously. She pulled his chin in her direction and eased his upper lip upward to check the wounded area before nodding. "It doesn't look good, but considering the circumstances, not bad, either."

"A dentist wouldn't be bad."

"Do you want to turn back?"

"Not in this lifetime."

She put the car in gear and drove on, both remaining silent, for more than four hours. The gravel road led them along a mountain that snaked eastward. The night was dark and cloudy, meaning their headlights were the only light source. The trees on both sides cast bizarre shadows that seemed to lean over them like ravenous demons, and the path appeared cold and gray, as if they were passing through a tunnel. At some point, soon after the car's low-fuel-alert light had indicated their diesel was getting low, the road simply stopped. It ended in a clearing where the ground was pitch black and hemmed in by the dense forest.

"Weird," Colin grumbled, opening his door and spitting out a gush of slimy blood and saliva.

"Extremely weird," Jenna agreed, grabbing one of the pistols they'd taken from the military cops, tucking it back into its belt holster and donning both before grabbing her flashlight, turning it on, and stepping outside. The cold, damp air hit her like she'd smacked into a wall.

Shivering, Jenna zipped her jacket up to her chin and walked into the clearing. The headlights formed two glaring funnels of light on what had once been grass. The beams of light were lost 20 meters away in the forest, whose shadows seemed impenetrable.

As she knelt and rubbed the stalks between her fingers, she frowned. "Burned," she muttered.

"What?" asked Colin, who had appeared beside her as if from nowhere. She was getting tired, which was not good.

"The grass was burned." She shone her light toward the trees. The branches and leaves facing the clearing were also charred, but the rest beyond them looked normal. "Strange fire, don't you think? Grass doesn't burn very well, and flames don't just stop when they hit trees."

"Then this was done with flamethrowers. To cover their tracks?"

"Possibly, but where would the Lada buses have gone? They didn't go through the trees, anyway." Jenna shone her flashlight around the edge of the forest as if to prove a point. The trees were too close together. "Wait a minute."

"For what?" mumbled Colin.

Instead of answering, Jenna walked toward the steep rock face to their right. It looked like a giant had hacked off part of the mountain with an ax. "Does this look natural to you?"

"No, but this used to be a prospecting area for mining." The MI6 agent shrugged. "So in a way... yes."

The wall was rugged and formed many small, jagged shadows wherever she shone her flashlight. Although dark brown and gray rock stood out here and there, most places were covered in moss, lichen, and tufts of grass. The dampness of this place and its dense vegetation had apparently quickly ensured that nature had successfully resisted the human encroachment of the 60s. She searched everything, going right and then left all the way to the edges, but could find nothing conspicuous. The call of a tawny owl snapped her out of her thoughts after a while, and she switched off the flashlight.

Vans don't just disappear like magic, she thought, walking back to the car.

"What are you doing?" asked Colin. "Are you going to turn back?"

"I don't do that. Stay right there." She got back behind the wheel, started the engine, and moved the car to the far left of the clearing, at the furthest point relative to the bluff face. From that distance, the front headlights illuminated nearly the entire width of the rock wall. Jenna left the ignition on and stepped out. With squinted eyes she scrutinized the rock, and then she saw it: from a distance, a small section about halfway down looked just barely different from the rest. She had to look and squint several times, but now that she knew what she was looking for, she finally recognized the outline of the square area.

"Move a little to the left," she called out. "Okay, now step forward."

Colin did as he was told and soon stood directly in front of what she perceived as a black line. He reached out and felt along the tiny crevice. She wanted to run to him and help but feared she might lose sight of her find, so she practiced patience. After what felt like an eternity, she heard a high-pitched whirring sound, and a square area opened in the bluff, just big enough for vehicles the size of minivans. Like the yawning mouth of an animal, the dark cutout lay before them, and Colin stood directly in front of it as if he were about to be eaten. The camouflaged door had swung open to the outside and now lay there in perfect silence.

"Let's hope it's not too far. We don't have much fuel left," Colin called out, coming toward her at a trot. They got back into the car and drove into the maw of the creepy beast they'd found in the middle of nowhere. "Do you think this is a good idea? Whoever can pull this off sure isn't going to like getting visitors."

"I don't think there's any other choice," she replied, steering the car into the narrow tunnel.

The darkness swallowed them.

17

BRANSON

"What does the sonar say, Johnny?" shouted Branson, not taking his eyes off the Chinese frigate that was still heading toward them, growing larger on the horizon as if to threaten them—which it was doing quite blatantly.

"Our Freddy is surfacing. He's still a hundred meters down," replied the machinist from the bridge. "It'll be another fifteen minutes. But boss, there's another problem."

"Another one?"

"Yes. Do you remember two radar contacts coming at us from the direction of the Chinese?"

"Which were then only one. Are they two again?"

"No. But a sonar contact has been added."

"So it was a fucking submarine," Branson concluded in frustration.

"It sure looks like it."

"Bloody hell! What about that other one?" He looked to the hazy silhouette to the southwest. "Make radio contact."

"I already did. It's a French guided-missile destroyer," Johnny explained.

"And did they threaten us, too?"

"Yo. They've advised us that we are in the exclusive economic zone of the French Overseas Territory of Polynesia and to leave immediately."

"This is ridiculous! The EEZ is over two hundred kilometers away. What are they all doing here?" grumbled Branson, forcing himself to calm down.

"There's one more thing, boss."

"I don't want to hear it."

"That meteorite... I got it on sonar, and its dot and Freddy's dot were in the exact same spot. I don't want to sound like the devil, but I wouldn't be surprised if he got hit."

"What about his rate of ascent?" he asked.

"Slowing down."

"We're going down."

"Down below?" Joe pointed to the sea, which had calmed again after the impact. The *Triton One*'s engines were no longer howling, just rumbling subliminally to keep them in place.

"Yes. We're going into the water. If his sub is damaged or he's hurt, we may have to help put the latches on the crane harness." Branson spoke into his radio again, "Johnny, Marv, you have the bridge. We're not moving from this spot, all right? Joe and I are going in the water. Xenia's got the crane!"

"Yo, boss. We got it! Be careful, all right?"

"Will do." A lump formed in his throat as the machinist's words struck him. Johnny was relaxation personified and never worried—which from time to time bordered on otherworldliness. His telling them to be careful was nothing short of a pivotal point. But if not now, when?

They were traveling in the Pacific while an obscure contractor rose from the depths in a high-tech mini-submarine, they'd nearly been sunk by a meteorite, and the Chinese and French navies were moving in and openly threatening them. Add to that the U.S. Coast Guard behind them, the absolute horror of semi-legal treasure hunters like Branson and his crew.

He hurriedly squeezed into his six-millimeter, deep-dive wetsuit and slid his already wetted feet into the long fins. The Pacific was warm here but got quite cold further down. He could stand it down to 120 meters but didn't dare go any deeper.

"Do you want me to operate the crane all by myself?" asked Xenia nervously. She paced back and forth in front of them like a tiger, constantly glancing over at the approaching warship. Branson stood up and grabbed her by the shoulders so he could look into her eyes. Every fiber of his body wanted to hurry, but he forced himself to speak in a measured manner.

"Kid, you can do it. We're old farts, and we're better at telling tales of the olden days than we are at accomplishing anything. You're smart and the only woman aboard. We all know you're tougher and smarter than we are. You get on that crane and do the same thing you usually do. Just stay steady on every steering pulse. Joe will stay on the surface and pass you signs so you know how far to lower the harness. Okay?"

"Yeah, fine," she replied, nodding. "I'm good."

"Here we go."

Xenia returned to the crane, and Branson slipped into his BCD with the two oxygen tanks on his back and the small O_2 pack on his chest. Once he had the mask, snorkel, and mouthpiece attached, he quickly checked Joe's gear and vice versa. Like penguins, they awkwardly waddled their long fins across the open deck and jumped from the low end into the deep blue waters. It turned white, then blue and still, then roiled and white again, before Branson and Joe floated to the surface with their vests puffed up, washed out their masks, and put them securely back on their faces.

"We'll go down and see what's going on. I'll dive down as quickly as I can and tack on the sub," Branson instructed as they swam up and down in front of each other in the light swell. "You stay halfway up and wait for my signal, then go back up and let Xenia know. As soon as I'm in sight, I'll give you instructions for the crane harness."

"It's too dangerous." Joe shook his head. "The ship needs its captain."

Branson smiled. "Sorry, old man. You've got nearly twenty more years on you than I have. This is going to be an emergency ascent, and if anything goes wrong in the process, my lungs are more likely to take it than yours. No discussion."

He put the regulator in his mouth and pointed his thumb down to make his point. With the deflator held over his head, he let the air escape from his BCD and exhaled at the same time. Thus he descended rapidly, and the warm blue closed over the top of his head. Unlike on reefs, where they usually dove for sunken treasures of old, it was pretty quiet here. There, coral, snails, shrimp, and crabs usually lived and made a great concert of clicking sounds, but here it was downright serene.

There was a sound layer of soft crackling, but it was somewhat restrained by the sea. Added to this, however, was the low hum of distant propellers, which gave Branson goosebumps on his arms and legs. Water conducts sound more than four times as fast as air, so the threat of the approaching war machine sounded even more immediate. Feeling uneasy, he gazed into the dark blue around him and saw Joe sinking considerably slower a few meters away. Like the last two people in eternity, they sank lower under constant pressure. When he could barely make out his friend as he left him further and further behind, he turned on the high-powered lights on his BCD and pulled the flashlight from his belt clip.

The blue was turning into black, and his dive computer was already reading 50 meters when he saw a faint glow beneath his feet.

Perkins' submarine, he thought, and continued to sip his oxygen supply sparingly, quickly gaining depth. Only when the lights became more prominent and took on the contours of lamps did he use his inflator to force air into the BCD to create some buoyancy. Concurrently, he began to breath a little deeper so that his accelerated rate of descent would not cause him to collide with the ascending sub.

By the time he could clearly make out the submarine, it was only about five meters away—like a ghost appearing from beyond the grave. Its glass cockpit was lit from within, and the grappling arms extended directly in front of it held a perfect sphere of such blackness that it seemed to swallow even the little light that struck it. The sphere was no bigger than a medicine ball, and yet it looked so heavy that it ought to act like an anchor.

Branson unfastened the first of the two oxygen cylinders, separated it from the harness with a backward grip, and watched it disappear into nothingness, a gray projectile passing near the rising submarine. Then the sub met him, and he tried to angle his body so that he would land like an insect with feet and hands on the uneven surface. Even though he had slowed down, it felt like he'd been hit by a truck, the impact was that violent.

Growling, he grabbed the metal rails running lengthwise on his right and left and lay flat, facing the pilot's cockpit. A sideways glance at the dive computer on his left wrist told him that the ascent rate was very slow. He pulled himself closer to the cockpit and waited until the bubbles from his exhale were gone before looking in through the glass. Perkins saw him and gestured wildly forward to the object in the grasping arms' clutches.

"The object," his lips formed over and over.

Branson reached a hand out and raised a thumb, but Perkins shook his head and pointed at his small sonar screen. It was hard to see anything because the lens effect of the water was distorting his vision. So he turned his head upward and saw Joe's lights above him—at least he hoped it was Joe. He made a repetitive twisting motion with the index finger of his right hand and did not stop signaling until his friend was rapidly moving away upward.

"The object!" again Perkins mouthed to him. It was eerie to glide upward through the darkness in the silence disturbed by the hum of the engines, with no sense of movement. The odd stranger was only a few handbreadths away from him, and yet he was in an entirely different world, an artificial capsule filled with oxygen and electronics that seemed downright alien.

"Branson! Take the object!"

Branson was sure that Perkins had said that. His lips had moved slowly and emphatically. The object. Was that all he was supposed to take? Then he suddenly realized what the man had been pointing at all along. There was a dark dot on the sonar, approaching rapidly.

Shit! he thought in panic, and hurried forward, pulling himself along with his hands on the metal edge above the cockpit and sliding like a fish toward the grasping arms. Reaching overhead, he bumped against the left arm and held on like someone falling from a tree might grab onto a branch. The pitch-black orb was within his grasp now, hovering like an eerie planet beside him. Branson felt his heartbeat slow down and become strangely heavy, as if an oppressive aura was emanating from the thing.

A glance upward showed him, as if in the far distance, the unsteady surface of the ocean, from which a confusing construction of shadows and moving parts glided toward him.

The crane harness! He climbed up onto the grapple arm and hooked his feet between two of the metal struts on the forward section before inflating the BCD to get more buoyancy. He then switched on his six-liter oxygen pack at his chest and flooded his regulator with pure oxygen to counteract the dangerous decompression of his upcoming much-too-rapid ascent, to be made without stops.

The harness was rapidly approaching, but it would land too far behind. Hastily he spun through the water, which seemed to resist his movements like resin, and gestured in Perkins' direction for him to turn the sub. The latter, however, shook his head and pointed aft. Only when he looked up did Branson see that the entire left flank of the craft had been destroyed. As if a huge predatory fish had bitten into it, a large part was missing, and dense gas bubbles poured out through small holes into the water like blood from a wound.

Frustrated, he looked up at the harness. He didn't have much time. Without further ado, he pumped up the BCD, pulled his feet back from the arm, and shot up before squeezing the deflator and exhaling, sinking back down, this time with quick flippers to the stern. He deftly spun and grabbed one of the harness's four chains at the last moment. Then he swam back, scraping across the wounded side of the sub, slicing his belly on a protruding, badly bent piece of metal and gulping against the sharp pain.

Back at the grappling arms, he had to anchor himself again, tugging at the metal chain before he began wrapping it around the sinister sphere and then hooking it to the other three. He used clamps—which were intended for steel struts the diameter of a forearm—to fasten the chains into a tight network.

Before he could finish he noticed movement in the cockpit and looked up. The rushing breath that sounded hollow through the regulator in his mouth, as if he were trying to drink from an empty glass with a straw, intensified the growing sense of urgency.

Perkins looked upset for the first time. With wild gestures

he pointed to the left, and as Branson turned his head with a furrowed brow, Perkins uttered an unheard cry. A mighty shadow raced up from the dark blue of the sea, a freight train of pure darkness. Like a nightmare come true, it thundered past the mini-submarine by a hair's breadth, and then everything happened in a flash. Branson was hit by strong turbulence in the water and swept away. Something cracked in his foot, sending a sharp pain through his entire leg.

One moment he saw Perkins' submarine flipping over in all directions at once, like a piece of paper in a storm, then the surface of the water, which seemed far too far away to him. The huge shadow turned into a gigantic propeller, its wake of vortices worsened his situation. The mouthpiece swept out from between his teeth, and only with difficulty could he keep himself from inhaling water out of reflex. Up and down lost meaning, and an ominous nausea spread through his stomach.

Quick-witted, he reached an arm down and then pulled it back like a windmill, catching the tubing of his octopus and forcing the mouthpiece back forward, in front of his chest. While still spinning on several axes simultaneously, he groped for the mouthpiece and put it back in his mouth. Two deep breaths, then he stretched his hands and feet far from him, saw a thin thread of blood spiraling before him, and slowly steadied himself.

Orient, he thought, and his chest pumped violently. Reluctantly, he forced himself to take in sips of the oxygen so as not to endanger himself. He briefly closed his eyes, then opened them again. What could he see?

Perkins' submarine was visible only as a circling point of light, moving away from him and descending, its lamps flickering ominously and dimming. The big shadow—the Chinese submarine?—had disappeared, but there was still the black sphere hanging from the crane harness, swinging back from far away at that moment like a wrecking ball in slow motion.

Branson felt like an astronaut in a vacuum, watching while the world was ending in relative silence all around him. He took half a breath to assess his situation, then shot forward with violent flippers. Ahead of him was nothing but the dark blue of the Pacific. To his left and below him, Perkins descended into a watery grave, while above him the surface of the water waited like a distant promise that seemed beyond reach.

Again and again he turned his head, adjusted his course slightly, and then the black sphere, hanging from the crane's chain, passed him. Although the object had been gashed in two places, not much was missing. He feared the thing would loosen and sink into the depths, but it seemed to be securely fixed.

Branson stretched his arms out in front and got hold of a chain link, clutching it with all his might. As if being pulled by a motorboat, he slid to the right, the artificial current tugging at his mask. His dive computer still read 20 meters. There was no time for a decompression stop, so he had to rely on the O_2 pack on his chest.

Above him, Joe floated on the surface of the water. From the looks of it, one hand was pointing out. He could picture— could almost hear—the crane straining and groaning under the load the sudden turbulence had caused. But the connection was still there, and that was all that mattered. The more the pendulum movements slowed, the faster the object went up.

There were barely ten meters to go when he heard a deep roar. *Triton One's* two screws began to turn, and bright spray whipped backward. The chain tightened, and at its lower end Branson was driven back, clutching the sphere that seemed to constrict his chest again.

He was beginning to fear that he would break off and be as forever-lost as Perkins, but when everything around him was white and gurgling wildly, he suddenly poked his head through the water's surface. Someone—or something—grabbed him around the shoulders with some force. Snorting and inhaling sharply, he struggled to hold his breath, wanting to pump his BCD but not daring to let go of the object.

"Gotcha!" someone shouted over the roar of the machines.

"J... Joe?"

"I'm here, old friend. Hold on tight!"

"Why... Why are we taking off?"

"There's trouble," was all Joe replied. Confused, and plagued by an oppressive headache, they reached the stern sideways, got out of the flow of the screws, and then slid out of the water. Someone reached out and helped him stagger aboard. Joe ran to the crane controls and maneuvered the sphere to safety while Xenia briefly examined Branson, lifting his eyelids, then removing his BCD and weight belt.

"Are you okay? Are you dizzy? Nauseous?"

"No, I'm fine," he lied with a groan. He struggled to get up, not realizing that he had ever been lying down. A glance around told him that things hadn't gotten any better since he'd started the dive. The Chinese warship was heading straight for them and was barely more than 100 meters away—reason enough for Marv to fire up the engines. Further to the right, the other naval vessel—presumably French—was approaching. From somewhere, the wail of a shrill siren sounded as if to herald the end of the world.

"Where's Perkins?" asked Xenia, who was as white as a sheet.

Branson merely shook his head. She understood and swallowed hard.

"Get that object below decks. I need to get to the bridge!"

"You came up far too fast!" his assistant protested, but when he gave her a sterner look than he'd intended, she nodded and ran across the deck to free the sphere from its chains. He swayed violently as he got to his feet, blaming it on acceleration and wave action, before he rushed staggeringly to the stairs and made his way across the three decks to the bridge railing. He saw the Chinese ship to his right, looming high and veering in their direction as if to ram them.

"Turn off your engines and prepare to be boarded and inspected!" a voice with a heavy Chinese accent boomed over the scant 50 meters that still separated them.

"My ass!" growled Branson, wrenching open the door to the bridge and seeing Marv clinging to the helm like a drowning man. Johnny shouted something unintelligible at him, and infinite relief spread across his expression when he saw Branson.

"Marv!" he barked. "Go help Joe and Xenia with the object."

"What a—"

"Go!"

Marv ran, Branson took the wheel, kept on course, and kept looking over his shoulder through the dark wood framed side windows. The Chinese destroyer stuck to their left stern and was clearly faster than they were.

"Damn gooks almost rammed us with their sub!" he cursed angrily.

"They probably just picked up Perkins on sonar and didn't want to use torpedoes with the Frenchies nearby," Johnny thought aloud, sounding tense.

"I don't care. I won't let any of them even touch our railing."

"We're too slow, boss!"

"Yeah, but we've got other advantages," Branson growled, snatching the radio and its coiled cable from the ceiling. "Everybody hold on for hard starboard!"

He jammed the radio back on its hook and silently counted to three, took one last look at the Chinese ship, which was still diagonally behind them but rapidly catching up, and then turned the wheel to the right as fast as he could. *Triton One* banked into such a tight turn that he had to shift his entire body weight to the side to keep from falling over. A few loose objects tumbled to the deck with a clatter. They described a short arc to the right, bringing the destroyer's bow dangerously close.

"Boss, they're running us over!" shouted Johnny shrilly.

"No. They want what we've got, and they don't want to see it go back to the bottom of the ocean, not with the urgency they seem to be operating under," Branson said, hoping he was right. A fresh look out the side window confirmed his assumption. The Chinese ship slowed down and pulled to port to avoid a collision, giving him and his *Triton One* a clear horizon for the time being.

Again he picked up the radio and dialed the frequencies Marv had pinned to the ceiling with sticky notes.

"This is Captain McDee of the *Triton One* for the French destroyer," he said in a pressed voice. "We have been attacked by a Chinese submarine and are being pursued by your destroyer. We are a civilian ship requesting assistance. They are threatening to board us. We are breaking out toward Maupiti. We are damaged and have a medical emergency on board. In accordance with international maritime law, we request assistance. *Triton One*, over."

He adjusted their course and steered toward the French warship, glanced at the radar, and saw more ships approaching.

Let them settle it among themselves. Whoever shoots first will surely have the others against them. He thought and prayed that he was right about that, too.

"Johnny?"

"Yo, boss?"

"Go get me the phone number from Perkins' cabin. I think I need to call someone."

"Is he—?"

"Yes. And with what's going on, we will soon join him, if we don't get help. Let's hope his employers are as powerful as we feared."

18

LEE

The preparations for his flight to AF-117 were surprisingly swift and professionally managed. The ground teams must have been no less blindsided by it, yet no one seemed overwhelmed to him. The many people he talked to on the radio had seemed tired but on top of their jobs.

Lee went over the planned flight several times with a team from SpaceX, the repair of the damaged nozzle with engineers from the Air Force, and the orbital mechanics of his approach and return with NASA mathematicians. He had to sign a confidentiality agreement with the Department of Defense, and then the 12 hours were over and his head was buzzing with information.

As expected, Sarah and Markus had protested, annoyed by the unscheduled assignment. His friend and colleague had even gone so far as to call the director to try to change his mind, or at least ask to be allowed along, but he seemed unwilling to give an inch. So she and Markus supported Lee where they could, and made conspicuous little attempt to point out the risks of such a last-minute and poorly planned away trip. They knew it, and so did he. Stating those facts added nothing positive to his situation.

They got one of the American EMUs into the *Dragon* and attached it according to the improvised mounting solution the SpaceX team had proposed. The spacecraft was geared for flights in simple pressure suits, not spacewalks. Since no high acceleration forces were expected, Hawthorne engineers had been optimistic that attaching the clunky EMU behind the seats wouldn't be a problem. For the flight itself, he would be wearing one of the futuristic SpaceX suits, which offered much more freedom of movement than the EMU with its huge satchel containing oxygen, and cold gas supplies for the maneuvering thrusters.

The stiff joints made it difficult to move efficiently indoors, and getting out would take a long time and he would be uncomfortable once he reached the satellite. Lee would have to take his time to avoid making mistakes. The dressing process typically took an hour or two in advance of a field mission with the assistance of his colleagues. He would have to do it all by himself, without checklists and without the second pair of eyes rechecking every step.

The schedule was so tight that he barely had time to think about the asteroid, the fragments, the political upheavals on Earth, or Dima and Anatoli's departure. It wasn't until Lee, along with Sarah and Markus, said goodbye to their Russian friend and colleague two hours before his own mission was to start that everything sort of became concrete. Anatoli was wrapped up like a package, visibly thinner and weaker but still silent, with sunken cheeks and deep circles under his eyes. He looked like he wouldn't survive reentry, but Dima joked that only the good die young. He hugged them one by one before, with help from Markus, he strapped his prisoner to one of the three Soyuz seats and then settled himself while Markus

The Meteor 1

floated back. When the hatch closed, it suddenly became a little lonelier on the station.

"You'd better come back," Sarah muttered to Lee as they waited to monitor the Russian space capsule's descent on the computers and from the cupola windows.

"I'll be repairing a satellite. How hard can that be?" Lee asked, watching the Soyuz detach from the station. Weightlessly, it drifted away centimeter by centimeter, as if everything was happening in slow motion, then the first correction thrusters fired. It took 30 minutes before it was correctly aligned and accelerating on a new vector. Most of the work would be done by the Earth's gravitational funnel to bring it to entry velocity on the pre-calculated route, and then to land —by parachute—on the Kazakh steppe about an hour later.

"They've all lost it, haven't they," his colleague sighed. "We've got an asteroid that's been traveling for over a hundred years situated between us and the moon, dropping little meteors on us, and they've got nothing better for us to do than fix a GPS satellite."

Lee pursed his mouth. He hated not being allowed to tell her the truth, though he could read in her sidelong glance that she knew something bigger was going on. She didn't press him, though, and he was grateful.

"It must be crucial," he replied neutrally. "The repair seems straightforward if I go by the engineers' instructions. I don't think it will take an hour. It looks like a metal socket around the exit valve of a maneuvering nozzle was bent or punctured by the impact of shrapnel from the Japanese satellite because the satellite doesn't respond to changes in direction like it used to. So there is some drift. Worst case, I'll weld a new socket on it."

"Is there any other kind of 'case' currently?"

"Hey, Cassandra could have hit Earth. Now it's stuck in

front of the moon. That's kind of creepy, but it's still better than a mass extinction and the end of humanity."

"That's right. Now everything is as it was, and we can continue to ensure our own extinction and that of other animals," she grumbled. "We do like to have the scepter in our own hands."

"Don't be so misanthropic." He made his voice sound conciliatory.

"Do you think about it much?" she sighed.

"About what?"

"About this thing."

"Cassandra?" Lee shook his head. "I'm trying not to. It's misbehaving, turning our understanding of celestial mechanics upside down. And these fragments... They're just chunks of rock, but they shouldn't come off it like that, and certainly not in coherent groups. Besides, there's been no indication that Cassandra would be porous and shatter like a comet. It's not like we're even close enough to the sun for that. It scares me, but this thing with the Russians' radio telescope does that even more. Somebody down there knows about what's going on out here. How could that be possible?"

"I definitely don't know."

Half an hour later, Lee was sitting in the *Crew Dragon*, feeling lost in the pilot's chair with the spacecraft's touch displays at head height. The seat next to him was occupied by the strapped-in EMU unit, as if he had a co-pilot. Knowing that there was only emptiness behind the large visor didn't necessarily help.

You're an astronaut, he reminded himself as his rubber-gloved fingers flew over the controls on his screen.

"All systems nominal," he announced over the radio.

"There's a green light from here, too," Markus replied. "Houston is taking over now."

"Understood. See you soon."

The Meteor 1

"Good luck!" the German said before there was a crackle in Lee's ears.

"Hello, Lee. This is Megan," the young engineer he remembered well from his mission prep to the ISS greeted him. "I'm sitting with General Oliver Marsden of the Air Force in Briefing Room Four. We've set up a makeshift little control center here with a staff of four,"

"Hello, Megan. General?"

"Hello, Colonel," he heard a male voice.

"All right, then. Let's get going, Lee." Megan paused for a moment. "Sights down."

Lee flipped the visor closed. "Sights down."

"Release docking clamps."

He selected the capsule view, then tapped on the brackets and released them after the system asked if he was sure. "Docking clamps released."

"Check autopilot."

"All systems nominal. Autopilot engaged," he commented in time with his actions, lowering his hands as the *Crew Dragon* moved away from the station on its own with well-measured bursts of cold gas. On the screen one spot further to his left he saw the animation of his upcoming flight, which would take him nearly 600 kilometers toward the North Pole into a much higher orbit. This fact had puzzled him, for normally satellites in such a high orbit relied less heavily on maneuvering thrusters than those in lower ones, where the gravitational pull was stronger.

The flight vector would take him around the Earth twice before bringing him to his destination, two and a half hours later. Until then, he had to equalize the orbital velocity and approach the artificial satellite in parallel at the same time.

The *autopilot* has to, he corrected himself, and put his hands in his lap. From now on, it was just a matter of monitoring the systems and intervening if there was a problem, which wasn't likely.

Megan queried every move and he acknowledged each time, doing his duty as scheduled and following protocol closely. This helped him fight his fatigue, as he had barely slept and then worked nonstop. Things got strange when there was nothing left to do and he was in the flight-only phase. General Marsden stepped in and went over the repairs with him again.

"You're approaching the satellite from the rear," the staff officer began. "You will stay on the rear side *only* the entire time, do you understand?"

"Understood."

"Then you'll use the recesses in the heat dissipation panels to move to the lower left side of the main cylinder to conserve your EMU's cold gas supplies. You can tell the directions by the satellite's identification number on the back, which—from your perspective—will be above."

"Mm-hmm."

"There's also half of this unit's solar sail on the left side, the attachment of which you can use to hook into," Marsden continued. "Don't forget to set the line very short so you don't get too far alongside, or even in front of the unit."

"What do you have there? A microwave emitter?" asked Lee, but the general didn't respond and continued undeterred.

"The nozzle is easily identifiable as a bulge that looks like a small pot. We manually shut it off from the ground, so you don't have to worry about it accidentally detonating. When you've done your job, you'll return, via the back of AF-117, to your spacecraft, which will be held in position throughout by the autopilot."

"Roger that," Lee replied, suppressing an annoyed sigh. In addition to the fact that he couldn't remember the last time an astronaut had repaired a satellite, it was definitely the first time a spaceman had disembarked while his spacecraft was

The Meteor 1

autonomously holding itself in position. So, he had to trust that the control software was working perfectly.

At the moment, several NASA and SpaceX teams were researching how to use robots to repair satellites, but he never thought he'd be their first guinea pig. When radio silence ensued, he unbuckled his seatbelt, set aside his helmet, and floated over to one of the large portholes rimmed with blue ambient light.

With his nose against the inner pane, he looked down at Earth. Below him he saw the Iberian Peninsula in summer brown with small green speckles. The first bands of cloud followed farther out on the Atlantic, where scattered storms were brewing as usual. The blue of the ocean was as deep and luminous as a globe lit from within, and it fascinated him as always.

As a young boy, he had often gone sailing with his father off the coast of Maine and had always seen the sea as a gray, cold place. They had enjoyed fishing together, the wriggling of a fish on a hook and the raw power he felt in his fingers. Even then, he'd been more interested in the exciting, new things, hardly understanding why his dad had always raved about the quiet out there.

When his dad died of cancer a few years later, Lee's attitude toward the ocean had changed. Every spare minute he would sail the *Ariadne* out of their village's small marina, looking for what his father had apparently found. He had wanted to see and understand it, in the secret hope that after his dad's death he might be able to make a contact with him that he had not succeeded in making in life. They had been strangers most of the time, one an administrator with a clear focus on security and ritualized living, the other a hot-headed teenager drawn to the world and adventure.

Today, Lee sometimes imagined himself returning to Maine in retirement and sailing out to sea every day to get closer to his father. But it hadn't worked then, and it probably wouldn't work two decades from now. Some things would forever remain unspoken and misunderstood, and the older he got, the more he became comfortable with that idea.

As the American East Coast came into view, a brief stab to the heart hit him, because he couldn't help thinking of his mother. She lived in a nursing home in Connecticut today, the state's dirty-looking shoreline reminding him of what he'd given up to be here. Others had to compromise with family because they didn't see their children enough, or live in constant fear that their wives would seek attention elsewhere, but not Lee. He'd had to choose between his mother, who had Alzheimer's, and his dream of exploring and pushing the boundaries of humanity as an astronaut.

Putting his mother into a nursing home had been the most horrible thing he'd ever done, and he was ashamed of it to this day, not thinking it was a mistake, but still second-guessing himself. The day it had happened, unlike usual, she had recognized him first thing in the morning and had been glad he was with her. That recognition had given way to a mental blankness as soon as the nurses had taken over. His mom had talked about the weather and how her dear Walter—his long-dead father—would be home from work soon and needing his lunch.

Everything had pointed to the illness not letting her understand what was going on, but part of him couldn't shake the impression that she was just playing it so he could leave without feeling guilty. He knew that was probably a spin his grief was putting on him, but the mere possibility that it might have been true made his insides feel leaden.

His wristwatch snapped him out of his musings after a while and reminded him that he still had 30 minutes until the scheduled exit. So he returned to his seat, lowered the seats, and got the EMU ready. Lee split it in half above the waist ring and then attached the top one to the headboard with a rope before checking all the functions again. Finally he sat down, put his helmet on, and sealed it, then made the connection to Megan.

"Ready for the final approach."

"Understood, *Dragon*. We're with you, and we'll back you up any way we can. Good luck!"

"Thank you, Ground Control."

When the time came, the spacecraft braked slightly to synchronize speed with the satellite to within two decimal places before making cautious approach thrusts from its cold gas thrusters until the two objects were separated by only two meters. That was so close in space that the trained astronaut in Lee inwardly cried out in protest.

A green light on the display signaled that they were now in synchronous orbit with AF-117, so he began to squeeze into the EMU spacesuit. It took him over 40 minutes to do so, despite being in a hurry. After that, he requested clearance for the mission, and with a few safety inputs, allowed the atmosphere to escape from the capsule, which took another 15 minutes. He then shimmied up the handles on the wall with the windows to reach the hatch, before counting through the tools on his chest harness and finally informing Ground Control that he was starting his deployment.

He felt chills as soon as the hatch was open. It happened every time he was on an exterior mission. The sight of the blackness in front of the tiny passageway, the infinity that lay before him, and most of all, the indescribable silence, were something that could not be explained to anyone who had never encountered this scenario. The vacuum was as mesmerizing as it was hostile to life, and so absolutely empty that it was impossible to comprehend. One could only sense it, and this made every sentient being feel small and insignificant.

Feeling the slightly rushing breath in his helmet, he

grabbed the outer edge of the opening at the top of the pimple-shaped spacecraft and carefully pulled himself outside. There he held on to the hatch with one hand, folded himself to the side like a hat, and checked the attachment of his umbilical cord, a finger-thick connecting line at his hip that linked him to the *Dragon*.

"Out now," he radioed between deep breaths, turning cautiously. The first thing he noticed was the sheer size of the satellite. It consisted of a gray metal cylinder, the dimensions of a bloated advertising pillar. The unfurled solar sails to the right and left were at least 20 meters long and gleamed dully in the earth's shadow.

At first he thought the structure was a spy device with a massive lens at the front, which would explain why the general had repeatedly impressed upon him not to go there. However, he saw a ring of smaller cylinders at the rear that resembled fire holes. The engineer in him recognized capacitors, but wondered what the ring of holes at the back was all about, and why an observation system needed so many of them.

It's not my job to understand the Air Force's new toy, he reminded himself as he detached himself from the *Dragon*. After gently pushing away from the spacecraft, he carefully navigated around the satellite with the mobility unit on his back until he reached the rear side. Silently, he felt for the edge with his left hand and carefully pulled himself along the shiny metal. They were currently flying over the night side of the Earth, one thousand kilometers above brightly lit Japan.

Breathing raggedly, he peered around the corner, forcing himself to make the most minimal of movements so as not to cross a certain threshold of momentum and get himself into trouble. Once he was hovering calmly, he looked for the maneuvering nozzle and spotted it not far above him. It looked like the nozzle of a hairdryer with a dented opening. How the shrapnel shower had damaged it without also catching the rest of the satellite was beyond him—they'd probably just gotten lucky.

Lee allowed himself a glance into the blackness beside him, staring at the terminator line of Earth curving far out into space. The stars glittered like mother-of-pearl, full and far as the eye could see. He imagined the cloud of debris from the destroyed satellites racing around the planet at over 20,000 kilometers per hour, sparkling just so, but deadly rather than being beautiful.

An urgent sense of danger and haste wanted to rise within him, but he allowed it no room and instead methodically set to work. He hooked a carabiner onto his umbilical cord and latched the other side into a magnetic socket, which he attached to the condenser just in front of the maneuvering nozzle. After that, he gave the cord a few test tugs and nodded in satisfaction. Only then did he give his full attention to the damaged part.

"Well, let's see what we can do," he muttered into his helmet, flexing his fingers that had little sensory perception in the bulky gloves. The maneuvering nozzle consisted of a simple steel ring that sat on a ball joint that could turn 45 degrees in either direction.

"I'll have to cut the ring off and replace it, as you guessed," he said with his visor directly in front of the damage. "The shrapnel must have caught it on the very outside. Not something you'd want to have a hole punched in."

"Right," the general said. Lee would have preferred Megan in his ear, but presumably the Air Force was taking over now. After all, he was fiddling with their favorite new toy, which must have cost a few hundred million dollars.

"Can you see the fine weld where the nozzle was attached on the joint?"

Lee blinked and moved closer until the visor almost touched the metal. "Yeah, I can see it."

"All right. Best put it there, but make sure the plasma doesn't point into the opening in the center of the joint."

"I get it." He pulled out the welder and set to work. On Earth it wouldn't have taken him 10 minutes under normal conditions—20 if he wanted to make it extra good—but up here it took him almost 90. Again and again, he had to pause and clench his hands into fists and then unclench into a stretch, as his fingers quickly became fatigued. Gripping the welder sapped strength because he had to fight the stiff gloves, which were under pressure like the entire suit.

Finally, he held the damaged ring in his hand and then almost lost it due to his exhausted fingers, but he caught it and jammed it into his belt. He then fished in the small cargo compartment in his belt to get the replacement he'd made on the ISS from the remains of a broken freezer, and set about attaching it.

Again, the tiny plasma lance in front of his downed sun visor glowed like a distant star. He commented briefly on each step as it was initiated and completed. He knew that Ground Control was connected via cameras in his EMU, but the protocol wanted it that way because it was proven to be safer.

When he had finished his work, he checked everything and was startled when the Earth-facing quarter of the satellite began to move. The ring of capacitors that was just behind the suspension of the solar sails was turning. Not far, just a small correction to the right, like a gear. Then all was still again.

"What was that?"

"The satellite's system rebooted itself and factored in the new weight ratios."

"The system?" asked Lee.

"Yes," was all he got in reply from the general.

What the hell is this thing?

"Return to your spacecraft now, please."

"Sure, I'm on my way." Following an impulse, he tapped

The Meteor 1

the camera button on the armpiece of his satchel and switched off the picture link.

Megan immediately spoke up. "Uh, Lee? We have a problem with the camera here."

"What's wrong?" he asked innocently, pulling himself close to one of the capacitors by the umbilical cord before catapulting himself forward with a careful jerk past the solar sail connection.

Someone else was talking excitedly in the background.

"We don't have a picture," Megan told him.

"I don't know why, and I don't see a problem here. I'm on my way back to the pod right now, and I'm about to unhook from the satellite."

"Understood." She didn't sound happy.

Lee searched his fingers for a grip on the front of AF-117 but found none, so he placed his hands on the joysticks of his armrests, using the cold gas thrusts of his mobility unit to move freely. He spun around the satellite until he hovered directly in front of it and came to a stop.

To his surprise, the cylinder was hollow, at least for the first meter. Behind it was a sort of drum two paces in diameter or more, with at least 100 cones stuck close together like bottles in a box. They shone brightly in the light of his helmet lamps.

"Holy shit," he snapped as he stared in horror at the massive tungsten bolts, each the size of a child's forearm and weighing several kilos. A single unpowered projectile dropped from this height would be enough to incinerate an entire swath of land with its kinetic energy gain as it fell to earth.

"What is it?" the general immediately asked. He sounded alarmed.

"My EMU has a malfunction on the right side. Ironically, one of the jets. It seems to be stuck."

"Can you fix it?" inquired Megan.

"Yeah. I think so. I'm still on the backside giving myself a push toward *Dragon*," he lied as he quickly maneuvered with the joysticks to return to the first carabiner.

They've put weapons into orbit, he thought, suddenly feeling very, very cold.

19

JENNA

The tunnel was just wide enough that she didn't scrape the jagged rock with the police car's side mirrors. Wet streaks shone on the walls in the illumination from the headlamps, whose cones of light gained intensity in the narrowness. She sensed they were going downhill, but because she had to concentrate to keep from scraping against either wall, she couldn't be sure. If she were claustrophobic, this would have been the worst place she could have imagined. Cables ran along the ceiling, connecting individual construction lights hung from crude hooks.

"It looks like someone went to some trouble here," Colin opined casually.

"At least those lights weren't put up during the Cultural Revolution, that's for sure," Jenna replied, not taking her eyes off the tunnel. Several times she licked her lips in tension. If they had to get out here, the doors wouldn't even open enough to accommodate them. She didn't necessarily trust herself to back out either, especially since they would be running low on fuel if this former prospecting shaft turned out to be very long.

"Do you see that?"

Jenna followed her passenger's outstretched index finger and looked up. Slowing down a little, she realized what he meant. The old tunnel, which up to now had been very roughly blasted from the rock, changed abruptly. The walls were no longer craggy and damp but smoothed and a bit wider. Instead of a roughly square shape, it changed to a roundish one, and reflector strips conveniently showed the tunnel's boundaries in the headlights.

"No fans," Colin said.

"Excuse me?"

"There are no fans," he repeated in an effort to make his voice clearer. The gauze bandage between his front teeth made it hard to hear him well. He pointed to the ceiling again. "Normally there should be fans hanging there to bring in fresh air, right? You certainly wouldn't have any fun here on foot."

"Or if there's a fire," she agreed with him. "No emergency exits."

"Are you thinking what I'm thinking?"

"Anyone so intent on remaining unseen and who can afford a camouflaged front door to a secret tunnel, can also afford cameras?"

The agent nodded. "We've been inside this thing for ten minutes now. Granted, we're going very slowly, but if there was a warning system at the entrance, they've known about us for at least ten minutes. I don't know if I should really be hoping we'll find the way out soon."

"There are two more grenades in the trunk," she said almost flippantly, and he grinned, looking somewhat bizarre with the bloody gauze and his missing teeth.

"I'll get us a way in there." Colin climbed past her into the rear and set about folding down one of the back seats to gain access to the trunk.

"I think I see the exit!" she exclaimed. There was a circular black spot at the end of the headlights, and multiple glints of light beyond it, which looked extremely strange. Jenna slowed the car down until it was moving forward at walking speed.

"Got it!" Colin squeezed into the trunk like a worm.

Jenna shifted into neutral and climbed into the back as well after flipping the switch to open the trunk lid. Crawling over the leather of the back seats, she got hold of a submachine gun and magazines and tossed them out. Then she slung the first aid kit and tools after them, climbed into the back, and waited for Colin to do the same. She looked forward over the car's roof and saw they were nearing the exit. There was no door here, and no crevice. On the contrary, the illumination of the headlights showed a dirt road, trees, and a diffuse glow in a valley.

"Ready?" she called over the loud engine noise that reverberated in the tunnel. He nodded, and she took the two grenades, pulled the pins, and tossed them into the trunk before jumping. Since the car was rolling downhill but not particularly fast, she could break her fall to some extent. Still, she growled in pain as the bruises on her left side made their presence known.

Colin was already crouching and loading his submachine gun as she grabbed the rest of the gear and ran to the left wall. He took to the right, and after exchanging a curt nod, they jogged after the car that was just now rolling out of the exit. A roar sounded, followed by a metallic screech. The grenades exploded, and the windowpanes shattered. Like a rolling fireball, the car moved away faster and faster as Jenna and Colin ducked out and immediately ran off to the side into the woods, where they jumped over a root sticking out of the ground and hid behind it.

"Did you hear that?"

"The shot?" she asked breathlessly, hugging the submachine gun tightly against her chest.

"Yesss," he hissed back. "They were expecting us. Do you think they saw us?"

"I hope not, because then the grenade plan worked and they think they got a lucky hit and the car blew up. Let's hope that by the time they've cleared everything and figured out there are no bodies to be found, we'll have gotten a decent head start."

"What was that light in the valley?"

"I don't know." Jenna shook her head. "Before I could see anything, the grenades exploded and temporarily blinded me. We should get away from here and hide for now. When it's light out, we'll be able to see more. No flashlights."

"I'm not an amateur, remember?"

"Right." She was silent and listened for a few more moments. The blaze of flames grew quieter as the car rolled down the gravel road into the valley before clattering and then crashing loudly. Jenna nudged Colin with her elbow and moved along the mountainside deeper into the woods. It was so cold that her breath condensed in front of her face, and far too dark for them to make rapid progress.

They crept on carefully and with deliberate steps, proceeding parallel to the rising terrain and always keeping one hand forward so as not to accidentally collide with a tree. The ground was surprisingly wild with knotty brush, roots that became natural tripping hazards protruding erratically from the soil, and plenty of bushes and young shoots that kept whipping into her face.

Jenna still remembered how, in her field training, she had been abandoned for several weeks in the Thai jungle with nothing but a knife and the clothes on her body. It had taken her many days before she got used to the darkness and lack of tools, but the knowledge that she gained had never left her.

So she kept quiet, kept walking, forcing herself to be calm and level-headed, paying no attention to the shouts in the distance. Either they were already being searched for, or the kidnappers were gathering around the burning wreckage of the car. Neither of those options mattered to them now, since they couldn't go any faster without falling.

After several hours of walking like the blind among the gnarled trunks, they finally paused. Jenna felt as if her entire body was on fire. The escape incident had affected her more than she wanted to admit. She knew she'd been fortunate to have gotten off so lightly with her reckless plan. But that didn't mean she was unhurt, and two stitched wounds and at least one cracked rib usually put an athlete out of competition for three weeks. If she pushed herself too hard and too fast now, she was only jeopardizing her mission, which was unacceptable.

They chose a spot with a little less undergrowth as a resting place and sat down after Colin had spread out the blanket he'd wisely brought from the car. The ground was damp enough they would otherwise have gotten wet—potential bad news at this time of year.

"It should be light soon," the Brit whispered as he checked his gun. "We should wait until then."

"Agreed," she said, "As soon as we can see something, I suggest we find a spot higher up, above the vegetation so we can overlook the valley. I don't fancy stumbling blindly around for days while they're also out here searching for us."

"How are you feeling?"

"Excuse me?"

"How do you feel," he repeated softly.

"I'm fine. I'm ready to go."

"My goodness, you sound like a robot sometimes."

"What is this? Are we an old married couple now just because we survived a kidnapping attempt by a corrupt Chinese officer?"

"Whoa," Colin reacted, raising his hands defensively. At

least she thought he'd done so, given she could see next to nothing. "I'm not the enemy here, okay? I just wanted to know if you were okay. I stitched you up, don't forget, and you looked pretty banged up."

"Sorry," she said more mechanically than insightfully. She'd never understood this kind of talk. She was here and on assignment. What relevance was there in how she felt? "I'm fine, considering the circumstances. No swelling, no fever, no pain in the wounds beyond the normal, so probably no inflammation. The cool climate is helpful."

"A robot," Colin sighed, "I've been nipping at the heels of a robot."

"HK-47. Nice to meet you. My mission is to wipe out all the sacks of shit."

"Excuse me?" he parroted her, audibly irritated.

"I'm kidding." She shrugged and took a drink from a canteen they'd brought with them. Then she passed it carefully to the Brit, leaned against the tree trunk at her back, and closed her eyes.

∽

The call of an eagle owl woke her. Jenna opened her eyes and saw the small clearing where Colin sat beside her, breathing steadily. The trees around her were thick, the open space no more than a few square meters, and bushes surrounded them like a protective cocoon. It was still dark, but dawn was breaking. Her watch read five in the morning, so she had slept for almost two hours. Her limbs felt heavy, like they were molten lead, and everything hurt.

With a gentle elbow nudge, she woke the MI6 agent, who opened his eyes and nodded at her.

Jenna pointed to an oak with low-hanging branches. "I'm

going to climb that tree. Maybe I can see something from up there."

"You be careful. I'll hold down the fort here," he mumbled, wiping dried blood from his chin as she pointed it out with her index finger.

Leaving her submachine gun and the rest of her equipment with Colin, Jenna set about climbing up the trunk of the oak tree. The bark was rough and old, but also offered long grooves that her fingertips could fit into, so she didn't have much trouble getting to the top. Her palms were burning, and she got minor scrapes and scratches where damp wood had broken away. Still, she reached the top of the tree without falling or making any noise, and carefully poked her head out of the orange oak leaves.

The valley that spread out before her was round, almost like a caldera with rapidly rising mountainsides all around. Only a few kilometers wide, it was small and squat, with dense vegetation and no visible entrances or exits. In the middle was a clearing about the size of two football fields, which she quickly spotted as it was exactly square, with large piles of tree trunks piled on top of each other to the west.

Inside the open area were four huge gray 'tents' that looked like inflated hemispheres with lights burning inside them. The glow was not obvious, but it was still easy to make out in the early morning twilight. At the corners of the cleared area she saw poles that pointed outward at an angle, rising at least 100 meters. These anchored a gigantic camouflage net that stretched over the valley. The edges of the net aligned with the tops of the trees on the ascending mountain slopes, so that one would have to look with great care to spot anything from the air.

It was the perfect place to hide: a valley with only one secret entrance, in a region away from pretty much everything and with nothing in the surrounding area, and camouflage as simple as it was effective for random overflights at high altitude. Jenna was amazed at the resources and effort that must have gone into this place.

The initial construction activities would have required heavy equipment flown in by cargo helicopters. So, either Chinese airspace surveillance was patchy out here and they had flown extremely low, or the right people in the right places had been generously bribed. Since this was the border area with Mongolia, there was the possibility that such flights had come from there.

She needed binoculars to see better, but even with her naked eyes she saw small figures walking back and forth between the giant tents, illustrating just how big these futuristic bubbles of light actually were. Beyond them, on the east side, she spotted another structure, much smaller and more of a block shape. With thick cables running from it, she assumed it was there for electricity production.

Colin had already packed up weapons and equipment by the time she climbed back down, and he looked ready to leave. "Well?" he asked.

"The valley is isolated with no visible entrances or exits. Maybe they have a tunnel, like the one we came through, but there are no roads. In the middle, further down, there are four large tents and a small power supply building. The whole area hides under a huge camouflage net. I've only ever seen such big things in football stadiums," she explained.

"Have you seen the Lada buses anywhere?"

Jenna shook her head.

"Strange, isn't it?" Colin pointed a thumb behind him. "I wonder if they even went through the tunnel."

"They could have just dumped the Hemukanasixiang residents and sent them through on foot."

"What do you think we're dealing with here? A secret bio lab for testing Compound X on humans?"

"Quite possibly." She nodded. "This place is merely an unknown spot on the map, and they've gone to great lengths to remain undiscovered. Compound X's full formula is still unknown many years after it first appeared, and you only achieve that by keeping your tests and studies secret—impossible these days, actually."

"Not if you own a hidden valley," Colin objected.

"Exactly. We don't have much time, though."

"The Black Widow."

Jenna nodded again. "They'll be waiting for a call with good news from the captain. The fact that Hemukanasixiang is most definitely in a huge radio hole gives us a bit of a buffer, but if she hasn't already, I'm sure she'll pick up the phone and start tapping her contacts soon."

"Yes. We can only hope that people like her never have the nerve to admit mistakes or even admit that they passed information to the authorities. Her business partner Golgorov—whoever that may be now—won't care if she had good reasons and a plan. He'll see it as treason, and that would be damaging to business at the very least."

"I wouldn't count on it, though," Jenna replied. "Two possibilities: Either she calls after all, and warns Golgorov—and thus probably this facility, which I'm sure belongs to him—or the security personnel have wiped the car and didn't find any bodies while rummaging through the remains. Either option leaves us with no time to waste."

"What do you suggest?" Colin asked.

"We need to see what's going on and get the information out of here somehow."

"There's no reception here. And I'm sure there's a decent interference field that's turning everything that anyone wants to transmit out of the valley into white noise."

"True, but I can't imagine there being no contact with the outside," she objected. "Such an elaborately raised and operated facility is far too valuable for that. Maybe there's a landline they've laid."

"Or we can find the jammer and disable it."

"Also possible. The little house where I suspect the power supply is might be a good place to start."

"At least one thing in our favor is that they probably didn't install any cameras except at the tunnel."

"I think so, too." Jenna looked at his mouth. Every time he opened it, it looked like he was grinning crookedly because the blood-soaked gauze was changing his facial expressions. "Tilt your head back. I want to check the wound."

"All right." He followed her instruction, kneeling first because otherwise he would have been too tall. She sanitized her hands, then carefully removed the soaked bandage to look at the stitching. It was still holding, and there was little blood flow.

"It looks okay to me. You should drink something."

While he took his canteen, she pulled a fresh piece of gauze from the first aid kit, rolled it, and, when he was done drinking, she placed it over the wound and indicated he should go back to keeping pressure on it. "I suggest we walk a half-circle until we're on the other side of the valley behind the powerhouse. It will give us a new view, and we can start from there. With any luck, we can cut the power and create enough confusion that we can sneak in."

Colin shook his head. "No. Then they'll know where we are right away."

"Have you got a better idea?"

"Yes, indeed. I'll stay here, wait for a sign from you and distract them, shoot around a bit, have a cat and mouse game with them, and hope they send as many forces my way as possible. Then you should have less trouble getting into the facility."

"Mmm," she murmured. She hadn't even thought about

that possibility, because if she were him, she would never accept doing the dirty work and risking another intelligence agency's agent getting away with the information without receiving it herself. "You would do that?"

"Yes, if you promise to share anything you find out with me," he said seriously, looking her straight in the eye.

"I promise."

"And if I die in this shithole, then in the spirit of the Five Eyes, share your knowledge with MI6."

"I'll do what I can, I promise. Best not to get yourself killed."

"I'll try." He grinned, and it looked grotesque with his missing teeth and the still half-white gauze roll in his mouth. "So, let's wrest this place of its mystery, Agent Julie."

"Jenna," she corrected him, surprising herself by her spontaneous impulse toward honesty.

The Brit raised an eyebrow and smirked. "Nice to meet you, Jenna. My name's Feyn."

20

BRANSON

"Boss, I got the number!" shouted Johnny breathlessly, handing him a piece of paper containing a very long phone number.

"What kind of area code is that?" grumbled Branson, motioning Joe to keep looking at the radar.

"I don't know." The machinist rubbed the back of his head and shrugged.

"Joe, how does it look? What are our pursuers doing?"

"Coming about and giving chase. Sorry, old friend, but we can't outrun a navy ship, even with our souped-up engines."

"What are the French doing?"

"Going to intercept the Chinese."

"Let me know if anyone shoots," Branson growled, indicating to Johnny he wanted the satellite phone brought from the charging station. The sea ahead of them had grown choppier and the *Triton One* began to roll slightly, as if refusing to play along. When he finally had the forearm-sized phone in his hand, and while holding the steering wheel straight on the side, he dialed the number on the slip of paper and waited.

It beeped several times, then a voice with a Russian accent answered. "Perkins?"

"Uh, no, this is Branson. Fred Perkins gave me this number in case something happened to him."

"You're the captain?" the voice asked impassively.

"Yes. We got the order from Perkins—"

"I know that. Why are you calling?"

"I'm afraid your friend is swimming with the fishes. We have recovered the object. With some difficulty and quite a bit of—"

He was cut off again. "Do you have it on board?"

"Yes. However, we are being pursued by the Chinese navy right now."

"I don't care about that. Bring the object to the rendezvous point we agreed upon. I will transmit the exact coordinates to you following this conversation."

"I don't think you understand. We've got naval ships stuck to our ass trying to sink us," growled Branson.

There was silence in his ear for a while, and he looked at the small display to make sure the connection was still open.

"We're willing to pay you ten million dollars above the agreed upon amount. I think that should encourage you to find a solution."

"Uh. Yeah, that sounds good. We can always think of something. It'll take us at least a week, though. We're that far from the nearest landmass."

"Just bring the object here undamaged. If you're in danger of being boarded, don't let it fall into alien hands. Are we clear?" the voice asked, getting a touch harder.

Who the hell are we dealing with? Branson wondered. "We follow through on every job we take, once we take it."

"Wonderful." The connection was severed.

He tossed the satellite phone to Johnny. "We just negoti-

The Meteor 1

ated ourselves an extra ten million dollars," Branson said loudly.

"Ten million?" Joe sounded incredulous.

"Ten million."

"We'll have to make it out of here first to get it, though."

"That's the plan. Johnny, take the wheel!" Branson turned it over to the engineer, snatched the binoculars from the bracket on the forward dashboard, and ran to the left bridge window. With the rubber sockets to his eyes, he scanned the sea, letting his gaze glide over the churning horizon, and then linger on a gray silhouette. "Damn it, that must be the Coast Guard."

Back at the radio, he dialed the frequency of the U.S. Coast Guard of Hawaii, which he knew inside out but usually just listened to.

"This is the *Triton One*," he called into the microphone. "I'm calling the U.S. Coast Guard ship. Come in, please."

"This is Captain Diller of the *Gettysburg*. Transmit your transponder identification. Over."

"Shit!" raged Branson, closing his fist around the small device that crackled, begging for mercy. Pressing the send button again, his mouth quirked. "Ah, sorry, *Gettysburg*, we're having trouble with our computers. We were rammed by a Chinese naval submarine and have sustained damage. Also, we're being tracked by one of their destroyers right now. They're looking for something on the ocean floor, and they think we have it."

For a while there was just static. Branson looked to Joe, who merely shrugged.

"Have you got it, then?" asked Captain Diller at last.

"What?"

"Did you recover anything from the bottom of the ocean?"

"No," he lied, adding quickly, "But a meteorite came

down here and almost hit us. They're all going nuts here. We're a civilian ship requesting assistance."

"We are already in contact with our allies on the ground."

"You mean the French, I hope?"

"Yes. Maintain your course toward Maupiti and request permission to dock. We'll come aboard later. Do not run off before then, do you understand?"

"Sure," Branson grumbled. "*Triton One* over and out." Angrily, he latched the radio back into its cradle and shook his head. "They've all lost their minds, haven't they? Before I volunteer to wait for the Coast Guard, I'll eat the barnacles off my keel."

"It will take us another six hours to reach Maupiti at our present course and speed," Joe announced. He sounded very tense and looked Branson in the eye for a long time before turning to Johnny. "Kid, go join the others and help them get the object below deck. Hide it well, all right?"

"Aye!" The machinist ran down the stairwell and was gone a moment later. It was extremely rare for him to be so snappy—just another indication that this whole situation was crazy.

"Branson," Joe said. His tone was that of an even much older man, which meant that now would follow a discussion he was not looking forward to.

"Out with it."

"Do I even have to say it?"

"I won't force you," Branson replied with a pained smile, glancing to his left into the large rearview mirrors mounted outside the bridge. The silhouette of the Chinese destroyer pursuing them was growing larger, already filling a third of the mirror.

"Perkins is dead. I was suspicious of the fellow when he was here on board, but by the cross of Jesus, he's dead, man! Killed by the Chinese Navy!"

"Maybe it was an accident."

The Meteor 1

"Oh, come on. You can tell the Coast Guard that," his second-in-command grumbled.

"What are you trying to say? Should we face the Chinese and throw them this damn sphere?"

"No." Joe tapped the radar screen with an outstretched index finger. "All I'm saying is that we've got a Chinese destroyer on our tail right now, and a French one right in their lane. Now we've got the Coast Guard coming in to give us instructions, too. If we refuel in Maupiti now—even if we don't get arrested—we won't be allowed to sail."

"But we still have to do it," Branson objected.

"Yes, but is it worth the money? Whether it's five or ten million, if we get sunk or arrested, we can't exactly spend it, can we?"

"You don't want us to turn ourselves in, but you don't want us to keep going, either. What do you suggest?"

"Let's just throw that thing overboard." When Branson rose to protest, Joe made a placating gesture. "Listen to me. We don't know anything about it except that we're supposed to deliver it to Perkins' contacts in Russia's easternmost port. There's a lot of money on board for us to make off with. Xenia's only in her early twenties, and the two guys have their whole lives ahead of them, too, not like us old farts. Don't make this decision for them."

"We've been through worse," Branson insisted.

"Worse than two destroyers and the Coast Guard rushing after us like dogs because they think we're a chicken bone?" snorted Joe.

"Sort of, but they don't know for sure, and they distrust each other, too. Listen up—I have an idea!"

"An idea... Does that include how we're going to get out of this mess?"

"What we're missing is a good lead, right?"

Joe didn't answer and instead raised a brow.

275

"We'll get that lead." Branson went on to explain the plan to his friend.

"You're completely insane, as usual," Joe commented, shaking his head.

"But it *could* work."

"Yes. If we pull this off, either we die or we become legends with our mugs over the whiskey pours at the waterfront bar."

"It's all or nothing," Branson agreed.

Ten minutes later, he handed the wheel to Joe and left the bridge to the right. Over the rail and up the stairs he ran to the quarterdeck, where Johnny and Marv were frantically attaching the small dinghy to the crane. In the middle was a tarp that looked like it was covering a ball—Xenia's exercise ball. She was in the process of attaching the two-hundred-meter rope, wrapped in thin steel cable, to the red distress buoy.

"How's it look?" he called over the roar of machinery working at full power. Johnny distractedly raised a thumb and ran to the crane controls. Xenia beckoned Branson over to help her. Together they grabbed the heavy rope at the end with the buoy and again checked the other end, which was attached to the stern rail by a substantial retaining clip. After a nod, they lifted the float and tossed it into the churning spray of their wake. Then they jumped back as the arm-thick reinforced rope unwound and left the stern like a startled snake.

Branson pulled out his radio. "Joe, now!"

Johnny lowered the dinghy with the decoy into the water but didn't cut the connection yet. When the rope had uncoiled itself and was trailing behind the *Triton One* like a long thin braid, Branson raised the walkie-talkie to his mouth again.

"One click to port!" he ordered, and Joe adjusted their course with great sensitivity. When he was sure that the rope was just to the left of the bow from the Chinese destroyer, which was gaining on them some 300 meters behind, he gave Xenia a wave, and she released the holding clip. The reinforced rope slipped under the naval vessel and grew shorter and shorter until it finally disappeared. Then nothing happened for a while, except that the gray hulk came even closer and looked even more menacing. Just as Branson was about to curse it suddenly slowed down, only a little at first, but then it came to a stop and the gap increased.

"YEAH!" he roared triumphantly, and Johnny released the dinghy to drift alone and lonely behind them as the *Triton One* sped from the scene. "I hope you all saw that! All eyes on the object, eh?"

"I hope they don't shoot us out of the water for jamming their screw," Xenia said anxiously.

"They won't shoot when there are two NATO ships around. Trust me, kid!"

"Now I finally know the point of that multi-ton rope that you guys used to load on the quarterdeck."

"Charles Bronson always carries a rope," Branson said with a wide grin, wincing as something resembling thunder resounded, followed by a mighty hiss that sped past them so fast it seemed like an auditory hallucination.

"Shit, did they just *shoot* us?" shrieked Xenia.

"No, or something would have blown up already. *Joe?*"

"You're damned right, girl, they're shooting at us!" his first officer bellowed, his face gone pale.

"I'm coming! Get below, now!" Branson shouted to the others and sprinted back to the bridge. As it turned out, they had taken a shot across the bow, only 20 meters away, which was nothing at all from a nautical point of view. He seriously considered cutting the engines and surrendering. He'd always been willing to take personal risks, but he did not carelessly risk the lives of his crew.

Then came a new twist. The French destroyer fired across

the bow of the temporarily hobbled Chinese naval vessel, and over the radio they could hear a subsequent storm of indignant communication full of threats and accusations from the three pursuing ships.

Branson's plan had worked. The pursuers no longer cared about the *Triton One*, and when they were almost out of range of the spyglass, he could just make out the crewmen launching tenders to pounce on their diversionary mock object. All that mattered now was that the port at Maupiti didn't give them any trouble, and that they were able to turn their lead into something useful.

He tried not to think too often about the promised extra reward if they made it to Vladivostok, lest he feel like a money-grubbing Dwight Decker, but he found it challenging. After 20 mostly luckless years, curiously enough, it was this crazy trip that first gave him hope that in one fell swoop they could rid themselves of the misery-causing financial curse that weighed them down.

I can still dream, can't I?

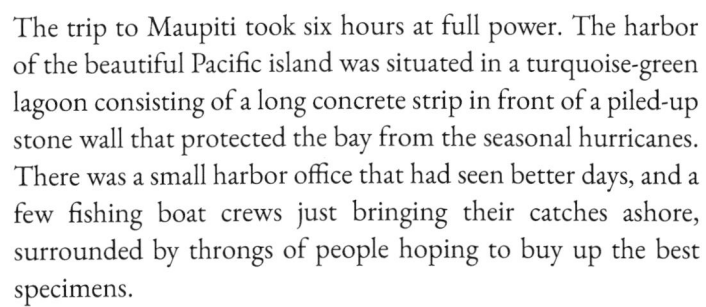

∼

The trip to Maupiti took six hours at full power. The harbor of the beautiful Pacific island was situated in a turquoise-green lagoon consisting of a long concrete strip in front of a piled-up stone wall that protected the bay from the seasonal hurricanes. There was a small harbor office that had seen better days, and a few fishing boat crews just bringing their catches ashore, surrounded by throngs of people hoping to buy up the best specimens.

The sea in the lagoon was very calm, being surrounded by the reefs and sandbars in the distance that enclosed the island proper like a protected paradise. The sun was already setting, bathing the scene in a homey yet eerie atmosphere that made

Branson feel like he was in the middle of nowhere. Somewhere out there, beyond their radar range, were the navy ships. Which one had found the exercise ball first, and cursed them in absentia? Why hadn't they seen anyone on the horizon or on the screens?

In his mind, Branson imagined how the fight had played out, and how the world was heading for the long-feared, hot conflict between the West and China. Perhaps it was much simpler than that, and no one wanted to be the first to shoot, while making sure no one else got their hands on the object—and with it, the *Triton One*.

The harbormaster came to them as soon as the helpers ashore had caught their ropes and lashed them down. He was a friendly local with a fleshy appearance and a smarmy look that didn't quite match his open smile. Concerns about being held turned out to be unwarranted. Though the harbormaster had received calls from both the U.S. Coast Guard and the French not to let them go, he eloquently explained that he belonged to the Independence Party, and in the end, was content to settle for a bribe of $50,000.

So just two hours later, fully fueled and with 20 extra tons of ship's diesel on the quarterdeck, they set off again in a northerly direction, scribing a wide arc around the meteorite's impact site, and then heading northwestward.

The mood on board was mixed. The fact that they had been fired upon by a warship—even though it had only been a warning shot across their bow—had not failed to leave its mark on Xenia, Marv, and—in particular—Johnny. All three appeared tense and were monosyllabic in their communications during the following days, and only loosened up again when they could see after several days that they had no pursuers on their heels.

The money in Perkins' suitcase—which they had no code to unlock, but which Joe was able to jimmy open—put them in a positive mood again. When they were still five days away from Vladivostok, they sat gathered around the table in the mess hall with the autopilot on. Thanks to Johnny's infamous coffee, on which even a horseshoe could float, they were still reasonably lively at midnight.

"It's nice to have us all together for once," Branson said, rubbing his hands together. He had to admit to himself that he was a little nervous. "What we went through was gnarly, and I think you guys feel the same way I do. We got really lucky."

Murmurs of agreement.

"But," he continued, "the most significant part of that was us—as a crew. I could count on you guys, and hopefully you could count on me. I put a lot on you guys, and I also know that not all of you agreed with us taking such a considerable risk. Was it luck? Maybe. Did it work? Yes.

"But I don't want to toot my own horn because it could have turned out differently. I'm your captain, and that makes me responsible for you. I appreciate the fact that you trusted me, despite everything. You're not just my crew, you're my family, and that's why," he slammed a plastic bag on the table, "I want to give you something back. The captain gets a twenty percent cut. Thirty percent is reserved for the ship—maintenance, fuel, bribes. You know, all that pesky stuff."

They all giggled, but the tension was still palpable.

"None of that applies today. Here is a million dollars." Branson dumped the contents of the plastic bag on the table. Thick stacks of dollar bills, held together with rubber bands, tumbled onto the scarred wooden top. "Two hundred and fifty thousand for each of you."

"What about you?" asked Joe, looking in amazement at all the money, as did Xenia, Marv, and Johnny.

"I'll do without this time. We'll get another ten million and five hundred thousand when we've delivered. But I know you guys are worried that we got involved with the wrong people. That's why I'll take the financial risk myself. I make the decisions, so I take the responsibility, too."

"Thanks, boss," Johnny said, looking him in the eye with genuine appreciation. "Fine move. For real."

"Thanks," Xenia agreed, and Marv nodded.

Joe put a hand on his shoulder. "We'll see this through, old friend. You got us out of there, all right, and don't you worry about it... Of course, I'll still take the money," he said with a smirk.

"Figures, you greedy son of a bitch!" growled Branson, and they all shared a laugh.

"Yo, guys! I fixed the Starlink system, by the way. We should be getting reception again now!" said Johnny, pointing in the direction of the old TV bolted to the wall above the fridge.

"Well, let's see it." Branson joined in the round and toasted each in turn.

They traded friendly insults for a while and then began a rollicking hero's rant about their adventures so far. That Perkins was dead lay like a gloomy veil over everything but it hadn't affected anyone all that much, probably because he had been suspicious to the crew. As treasure hunters, they had often been confronted with even close colleagues not returning or having accidents. The best way to deal with having gone through something so surreal and dangerous was still to brag, joke, and exaggerate.

A few hours later, as Johnny and Marv took over the bridge and Xenia headed for her bunk, Branson sat alone with Joe and turned on the TV, which they hadn't gotten around to earlier.

The news on CNN showed a smoking valley or a volcanic crater. Branson was not sure. Only gradually were other images and videos played in, showing from a distance a colossal explosion and subsequent hurricane of dust and dirt rising from a wooded area. All the footage had been taken from very far away and was blurry and pixelated due to the extreme zoom.

"Shit, did a nuclear bomb go off?" asked Joe in horror.

"Shh!" went Branson, turning up the volume.

"Initial reports suggest the massive explosion in China's far northwest in the sparsely populated Altay region may have been a small meteorite that broke loose from the asteroid Cassandra 22007. When asked by Reuters and AP, the Chinese government confirmed that the impact site is uninhabited and there are no casualties. Nevertheless, Beijing has announced investigations.

"This latest incident of smaller fragments breaking away from Cassandra and entering Earth's atmosphere has caused further protests around the world. Many people continue to point fingers toward the moon and expect answers from their governments. While some experts point out that it is unlikely, but not impossible, for an asteroid to decelerate between the gravitational funnels of Earth and the moon and remain in a high orbit, conspiracy theories are spreading faster and faster on social media. Where did Cassandra 22007 come from?"

21

LEE

Lee pulled himself by the umbilical cord toward the open nose of the *Crew Dragon*. Due to the high mass of the spaceship, his position barely changed as he moved closer hand over hand.

"How's it going, Lee?" asked Megan tensely.

"I'm approaching *Dragon*," he replied curtly. Earlier, the general had asked him something, but it had taken him nearly two minutes to realize that someone was talking to him. The shock of seeing the ballistic projectiles was too profound. He couldn't believe his government had dared to take that step. The Outer Space Treaty only prohibited the deployment of weapons of mass destruction in orbit, not kinetic projectiles like these, but the implications were still far-reaching.

With a satellite like this, the Pentagon could incinerate any place on the planet in no time without anyone being able to do anything about it. Of course, there were anti-satellite missiles, but they had to find their target first. Since the tungsten rods were certainly unpowered and just got a quick push at the right time, there was hardly anything to locate. No government should have such power, and no government should set this precedent. If China, Russia, and maybe even the EU got wind of this, they would undoubtedly have to follow suit, much like they did with the nuke, to establish a balance of power.

"Colonel Rifkin," the officer spoke to him again. He sounded different somehow. "Describe your actions so far."

"I... lost one of the jets on my EMU, so that made me a little uneasy, but I was able to compensate and unhooked from the satellite. That took a little longer than I planned."

"The nozzle on the left side of your pack, right?"

"Right," Lee replied absently, and at that same moment got a grip on the top edge of the *Dragon's* open hatch. Because of his speed, his legs flew on, and he pulled them up as close as he could—which wasn't particularly impressive—to swing inside with his feet.

"But you said it was one on the right."

"Yes, right is correct." *Damn it!* he scolded himself in his mind. *Focus, Lee!* Knowing he had just repaired a military weapons satellite, that wasn't so easy.

"Are you not feeling well, Colonel Rifkin?" the general echoed in his ear, and if his voice had not sounded particularly friendly before, it was even less so now.

"No, I'm fine. I'm just overly tired from the mission and the preparation. I haven't slept very much, as you can probably imagine. Can I talk to Megan again now, please? The work on your toy is finished, and I'm back on *Crew Dragon*. We should think about giving it a better name than AF-117, though."

"Lee, it's Megan. Did you close the hatch behind you?"

"I'm just about to." He squeezed through the opening and twisted, bumping his hips and shoulders against the metal ring without particularly feeling it, and in perfect silence. When his thick boots had hooked somewhere—trying to look down would have been about as successful as jogging in zero gravity—he grabbed the manual shutter

The Meteor 1

wheel and pulled it toward his helmet. A few centimeters in front of the visor, the hatch clicked into place, and he turned it to the left several times until the lock was engaged before releasing his feet and floating down as if in slow motion.

"Hatch locked. I'll get to work on restoring the atmosphere now."

"Very good. We're with you, Lee."

"Thank you, Megan." He floated over to the touch consoles and pressed the big red flashing button for the life support systems. Nothing happened. With a furrowed brow, he released his finger and pressed again, but still the button flashed red. Following protocol, he turned slightly to the left and flipped the manual life support switch, which served to function even in the event of a display failure. However, it didn't. The red flashing was still there. He glanced at the oxygen reading on his chest display: two hours to go.

"Um, Megan? I have a problem here."

He got no answer.

"Megan? Hello?"

"Lee, it looks like someone put the control software into maintenance mode. Did you do that?" She sounded distraught. In the background, he heard choppy, loud arguing.

"No, of course not." He peered at the display, and sure enough, in the upper right corner he saw the symbol of a wrench in a yellow circle. "I see it, too. That wasn't me, though. This had to come from you guys. What do the SpaceX guys say?"

"Here in the room, due to the high secrecy of this mission, it's just me and Henry and four Air Force personnel," she explained. "I just had to inform the general that the mission is over, and we're taking over again now. I already have the Hawthorne people on the line, and we're patching them in now."

"Everything worked on the way here. Is it possible that one of you made a mistake down there?"

"I don't know. Give us a few minutes to sort things out. How's your oxygen supply?"

"Two hours."

"Good."

Lee's hands and feet were tingling. What was going on here? "Are the general and his men still there?"

"Yes, they're still refusing to hand over their workstations, but I've already spoken to Director K—" The connection broke.

"Megan? Megan!" Lee looked at the display and realized that the radio had been rebooted. "Son of a bitch!"

He waited anxiously for five minutes, but radio silence persisted and the reboot icon seemed frozen in place on the screen—just like the one for maintenance mode.

"Don't tell me you crashed. A triple-redundant software system," he growled, knowing full well that a crash in this form was all but impossible.

A nasty suspicion flooded his mind as he looked around in the silence of the pod, rotating on his long axis.

"All right, then. Situation analysis." Lee mentally reviewed an age-old ingrained plan that he'd learned in his fighter pilot training and repeatedly used in astronaut training. "I'm in a very high orbit, and my spacecraft is off life support. The computers are down. That means no autopilot, no flight aids. I can't get back to the station without computers, and I'm going to suffocate in two hours. Contact with Ground Control is down, and I have no indication that it can be restored. So the only way is back to Earth. With manual controls."

Lee spun around the two pilot seats and pulled the controls out of the armrests. He then performed a hard reset of the computers, at which point they only rebooted into safe mode. While they no longer loaded any control software, at least they turned on the most critical displays as required for the emergency procedures.

"All right, what have we got here? Heat control, power supply to thruster, combined propulsion system, motion control, course rendezvous system, reentry actuators, landing system. All green. Navigational computer..." He sighed. "By hand, then. You learned all that, Lee. Just remember it."

He pulled out the emergency protocols log, attached to a long cable in the compartment under his seat and began to look into calculating the thrusts necessary for an emergency reentry. Reentry was a tricky business and possibly the most dangerous thing humans could currently do. This was due to the many factors required for a successful maneuver—which was why they usually planned them well and always had at least two brains working on them.

First, he had to leave orbit, which basically meant slowing down. Since there was still over 90 percent of Earth's gravity up here, and the weightlessness existed only because of the 'throwing parabola' that included his ship and all the other equipment and even the ISS trying to maintain an orbit, it took orbital velocity in excess of 20,000 kilometers per hour. To achieve his goal, he had to turn the ship around for a precisely calculated time and virtually fly backward with the orbital maneuvering thrusters serving as brakes, taking him out of orbit and back toward Earth.

Then came the trickiest part: reentry into the atmosphere. For this, the *Dragon* would use its flat underside to exploit the friction from the air particles it encountered to create a further braking effect. The angle of inclination had to be around 40 degrees for everything to work. Then flames of up to 1,600 degrees Celsius were created by the brutally charged particles. If any part in the hull wasn't seated properly or there was a hairline crack, he wouldn't even have a chance to note the fact before the *Dragon*—and he—died in a fiery explosion.

Lee made the appropriate calculations, double-checking them even though it cost him valuable time, and only sipped the air in his helmet to bring his breathing down as much as possible. That limited his brain oxygen, producing a good effect and a bad effect: thinking was more challenging, which could negatively affect the mental work he had to do. At the same time, though, that was positive news, because his thoughts were less likely to spin over and fill with panic. He must remain calm.

When he was sure he had done his calculations to the best of his ability, he strapped himself into the pilot's seat and placed his hands on their respective control sticks. The feeling in his fingers was barely existent, and that was going to be a problem. With little time left before he suffocated, he had calculated everything very tightly, choosing the quickest and riskiest reentry, but he had no regrets because there was no alternative. In the absence of good options, the least bad one remaining was the best.

As expected, deorbiting was unspectacular. After the initial thrust, Lee waited for the specified time, which he had stored on the armature of his EMU's jetpack, and then initiated the rotation. With the help of the three-axis position controls he was able to get all the readouts close enough to right using the small joysticks. The *Dragon* slid diagonally like a projectile toward the outer layers of the atmosphere. His visor almost touched the displays, which in safe mode showed only white numbers and lines on a black background.

Unable to remove the jetpack satchel from his back without help, the pack and its accompanying harness that extended under his arms and over his shoulders forced him to sit much too far forward. It caused his arms, bent unnaturally

The Meteor 1

backward, to lose feeling as this posture squeezed off blood in his armpits. But he could not change that now.

"Commencing reentry," he shouted, just in case anyone could hear him. The small spaceship began to jerk and buck as the air particles of the outer layers of the atmosphere resisted its violent intrusion, and soon the first flames were leaping outside the windows. "A meteor. I'm a meteor."

Lee laughed out his tension as an ironic thought occurred to him. "Good thing I'm coming down over Europe and not Russia. They'd probably shoot me down," he muttered to himself.

The wriggling of the capsule and the hard *g*-forces created by the heavy braking pushed him into the straps. He prayed that none of them cut into his suit, designed for working in a vacuum, not for use inside a starship. When the pressure finally let up, he could hardly believe he was seeing blue outside the windows—a very dark blue, but blue.

"I'm still alive. Houston, if you can hear me, I'm still alive. I can only guess who tried to sabotage my return, but I can say this much: it didn't work. Someone needs to get word to Sarah and Markus. I'm sure they're worried. But I'm still around. Ha!"

Lee drummed his fists on his knees, feeling how exhausting these normally minute movements were under the relentless gravity of the earth. It was as if he were in an invisible jelly that he had to fight against. Even breathing was harder with all the weight on his chest.

"This is definitely more uncomfortable than I'd imagined," he muttered. "A wheelchair wouldn't be so bad."

As he raced through the top layers of clouds in the sky above the Suez Canal, he closed his eyes for a few minutes until a slight jolt went through the capsule. He exhaled in relief. The parachute's automatic deployer had worked. It was keyed to specific pressure ratios, which, if exceeded, ensured that the release mechanism would kick in and eject the chutes, regardless of any input from pilots or software.

To keep the braking effect from becoming too intense, the special rip-stop fabric deployed very slowly so that the occupants didn't end up as bloodstains on the ground. Even so, the forces acting on him were enormous, and the long time in zero gravity had overtaxed his cardiovascular system. His muscles were whimpering for mercy as he growled and groped for the ring clasp on his neck. His oxygen supply had been depleted. He searched and searched, finding something, fumbling impatiently with it, growing more and more panicky as he gasped ineffectually like a fish on land.

Something finally gave, something hissed, and he was able to take a rattling breath. As a violent jolt went through the *Dragon*, the helmet flew off his head and ricocheted into his temple. For a few moments he saw bright stars dance before his eyes and felt blood running down his cheek.

"What a bummer," he muttered absently. He still registered that his fall had slowed considerably, and the capsule had entered its final descent at only 20 kilometers per hour. An unpleasant spinning sensation overcame him, and as it jerked vigorously and choppily one more time, there was a sudden silence. The smell of smoke and ozone assailed his nostrils, acrid and heavy.

You're not supposed to fly without a helmet, Lee reminded himself as if through a thick haze of sluggish thought. I'm not supposed to take my helmet off. Where is it? I have to go...

Almost suffocated, he lost consciousness.

22

JENNA

After quickly eating some of the provisions they'd taken from the military police, she'd left immediately. Jenna wasn't sneaking. She ran as fast as the vegetation allowed. The sun was peeking over the horizon, allowing her to move more quickly. The nature of the forest made it clear that no one had ever walked along here, and the secret owners of this place in the middle of nowhere were only interested in the bottom of the valley where they hid whatever. It took her over two hours to reach the other side and walk down the mountainside far enough to see, between the trees, the back of the rectangular building sticking up from the leveled earth just a few meters from the forest's edge.

She crawled on all fours through the undergrowth, moving to the left toward one of the large piles of wood that had been stacked up all around the edge of the area. Judging by their level of decay, Jenna guessed the clearing must have been done many years ago. Even the gigantic metal pole closest to her, holding up one corner of the huge camouflage sky, already showed significant signs of rust and certainly hadn't been erected in the last few years. The camouflage system was of such brutally crude design that it seemed to have landed here from somewhere else in time.

On the other hand, the tents sticking out of the ground like pimples looked new in comparison. Very little staining showed on the white outer walls. The whole encampment looked like the set of a science fiction movie from the 90s. The tents were larger than apartment buildings, and their entrances looked like tiny mouths. Everything about this place was eerie, like it didn't fit into reality. The camouflage sky cloaked much of the leveled area in shadows like a permanent twilight, while the surrounding forests and mountains were bright.

When Jenna reached the large pile of logs, which smelled strongly of mustiness and rot, she stood up and moved to the right until she could peek around the end. Up close, the small building she'd seen seemed more like an oversized junction box, gray and big as a truck. In front of it stood two men wearing black combat fatigues and tactical vests, and armed with assault rifles. Judging by their Slavic features, they were probably Russians. One of them smoked while the other talked and kept striking out with the butt of his weapon at some imaginary enemy. The smoker laughed throatily.

Kalashnikov AKS-74U. Russian mercenaries. Probably ex-Special Forces, she thought.

They were not to be trifled with, that much was certain. Jenna was trained as a field agent, a good shooter and a good hand-to-hand fighter, but former elite soldiers would be a problem. Of course, these men could simply be paid muscle using rifles that just happened to be used by the Russian Spetsnaz, but she didn't think that was too likely. If this was indeed a secret Golgorov Systema facility, they wouldn't be cutting corners now after having so obviously dug deep into their pockets to set it up.

The four cables lying next to the guards' legs were as thick as their forearms and ran toward the giant tents through retaining clips hammered into the ground. One cable disappeared into each tent, and about 20 mercenaries swarmed in the open spaces—quite a gathering. True, 20 seemed lost in this valley where everything was big, but still, she would have expected fewer. Such a well-hidden facility on foreign territory would never be able to defend itself if the Chinese army approached, so why all these armed soldiers? The best defense was to remain invisible.

Now would be a good time, Feyn, she thought, checking her submachine gun and pistol one last time, as well as the combat knife, flashlight, wire cutter, and screwdriver on her belt. After making sure everything was ready and seated as it should be, she watched the two guards who were still talking. They stood facing away from her and didn't seem particularly tense until a fireball appeared up on the other side of the valley, roughly where Jenna guessed the tunnel was. The thunder of the explosion followed, after a barely noticeable delay, causing the mercenaries to flinch. The one on the right threw away his cigarette and jerked up his assault rifle just as the other did.

Quick reflexes, perfect fit of the rifle, basic posture with good weight transfer, she analyzed in a flash, and ran from her cover behind the tree trunks the ten meters to the power distribution building, where she pressed her back against the wall. Only then did she peek around the corner, unable to see the men from there but able to see those between the tents, all but four of whom were now running toward the blast.

Loud shouts rang across the area like distant echoes. Jenna waited a few seconds until she was sure no vehicles were coming into play, nor were the doors of the strange tent-buildings opening. Then, with a jump to grab the edge of the roof, she skillfully pulled herself atop the distribution building, which was only two meters high, and lay flat on the corrugated composite that reminded her of a rusted shipping container.

Jenna reached the edge that faced the cleared area almost

immediately, as the short sides weren't much shorter than the long ones. The two mercenaries had lowered their rifles but only to angle them downward, and both men peered toward the other end of the valley, even though the camouflage sky obscured most of the mountain there. They whispered to each other in Russian, sounding tense.

Quietly, Jenna came up into a crouch, slowly laid the submachine gun down beside her, and pulled out her combat knife, holding it blade down in her right fist. One last glance between the tents, the first two of which were barely 50 meters away, and then she jumped off. Even as she swooped down like a shadow to their left, the two men noticed Jenna in their peripheral vision and whipped their heads around. She was still able to hit the one she'd been aiming for, driving her outstretched knee into his spine, which cracked with a loud pop.

Reaching out with her right arm, she swung the blade at the smoker's neck. He jerked back, however, so she narrowly missed her mark, slicing his larynx instead. With a forward roll, she got past the corpse and turned even as she scrambled to her feet. The stricken man was holding his neck and gasping, but she hadn't caught the artery, and he was bleeding much less profusely than she'd hoped. At least he didn't seem to be able to scream.

Jenna lunged at him and kicked the assault rifle out of his hand just as he was about to swing it up. Her swipe at his knees came to nothing as he had the presence of mind to drop back and pull his knife from his belt. She straightened and shifted her weight to her back leg as the Russian spat blood and scowled at her. Then he charged forward and thrust for her face.

She jumped to the side, realizing as she moved it had been a feint, and he used the resulting momentum of his body to kick her right thigh. She buckled in pain and reacted with lightning speed, faking a fall over her knee. The mercenary jerked his knife up to slash her stomach, but she flipped away to the right, pulled his wrist forward with her free hand and drew her blade lengthwise through his entire forearm. Blood spurted toward her, and her opponent huffed a bubbly gasp, staggered, and could only struggle powerlessly as she leapt up, twirled behind him and grabbed his chin, yanking it upward and drawing the knife across his neck in a semi-circle.

Gasping his last, he slid down her leg. Jenna stared at the backs of the four remaining guards who stood about 200 meters away between the two closest tents, staring after their hurrying comrades. They hadn't yet turned around. Good. She glanced over her shoulder and saw a small door in the container-like power distribution building. She quickly opened it and pulled one body and then the other inside, closing the door as soon as she and the second body were inside.

Still breathing heavily, she turned on her flashlight and looked around. It was a single room containing six human-sized, quietly humming cylinders connected by wires to a voltage transformer the dimensions of a coffin. The transformers were matte black and had the connections on top, where the cables stuck out like hair from a braid, and each had only one marking: stickers with the radiation warning symbol consisting of a black circle and three black trapezoids on a yellow background.

Radionuclide batteries, she thought. A quasi-inexhaustible energy source researched in the Soviet Union that had gained renewed importance in space travel in recent years. Decades to centuries of energy at a level that wasn't high, but seemingly sufficient for this facility, and no telltale connections to a power plant. That made sense.

Whatever was being researched or hidden here didn't require an excessive amount of power. That probably meant she didn't have to deal with electronic door locks, cameras, or auto-firing defensive devices. But if she did, she didn't want to take any chances. Besides, though felt it was extremely helpful that Feyn volunteered to play the distraction, she did not like being in anyone's debt. She didn't want him to have to deal with more than a dozen ex-special forces because of her.

Jenna opened the door a crack again, made sure the four mercenaries weren't looking her way—in fact, they were gone now—and reached up to pull her submachine gun from the container's roof. Then she stood between two of the radionuclide cylinders, stuffed moistened wads of cloth that she had made from gauze bandaging into her ears, and emptied the entire magazine into the voltage transformer, from which sparks flew like short-lived fireflies. Short circuits crackled behind the shot-up paneling, bathing the dark room in irregular flashes.

She wasted no time in tossing the submachine gun away, then running out and grabbing the assault rifle of one of the dead mercenaries lying on the wet soil before running as fast as she could to the left tent. With ten meters separating her from the dark entrance, gunfire rattled across the area, and the bare ground splattered right in front of her feet. She looked to her right and spotted two mercenaries heading toward her from behind the neighboring tent. Firing as they ran, they weren't too accurate, but that could change quickly if they stopped and took aim.

Jenna returned fire blindly, quickening her steps once more until she arrived, panting, in the tiny doorway of the tent and pressed her back against it. Another volley missed her by an extremely narrow margin and whizzed past her head. Then she looked down to see a small control panel where she would have expected a handle. It was dead.

No power. She pressed hard against the door, pushing it inward, which took all her strength. Jenna assumed she was struggling with the servo-assisted hydraulics. On the other side was a sort of airlock in pure white with metal grooves on the floor, below which lay a drainage basin. There were small jets stuck in the ceiling, and on the other side there was another door, above which warning lights caught her eye.

She ran over and grabbed the bowling ball-sized wheel for the manual release, pulled it, and stepped through into the gigantic dome. She locked the passageway again by turning the wheel back and then jamming the mercenary's assault rifle between the three levers. Only then did she pull out her pistol and look around.

In an area of several hundred square meters were countless cots filled with people of all ages. Their eyes—at least those she could see in the foreground—were closed, and tubes ran from the crooks of their arms to small computers and modern intravenous infusion machines. Up above, large cubes were mounted on steel racks, with wide, open pipes protruding from them, and a barely audible hiss permeated the scene.

Right in the middle, with all the cots' headboards angled toward it, was a square room as big as a gazebo, in front of which stood two figures in white chemical protection suits with closed face masks. They held tablets in their hands and were animatedly conversing with each other. They didn't seem to have noticed Jenna.

She wasted no time before running in their direction, as right between them, leading between the medical cots, was a hallway of sorts that stretched from the door to the airlock. Jenna was breathing heavily and felt like her lungs didn't quite want to fill. Also, the air smelled oddly like rotten eggs and mint. The impression wasn't powerful yet it couldn't be denied, and the back of her throat itched unpleasantly.

After she'd gone half the distance, the two figures noticed her. They wheeled around and froze, then simultaneously reached for a door handle at their backs that led to the central room. Their clumsy and panicked movements hindered each other. Still, she would not make it, so she made a decision and shot the left person in the leg. The sealed face mask muffled his scream, and as he slid to the ground, the other froze and raised his hands.

As she passed, she glanced at the countenances of the motionless figures on the cots to the right and left. They could only be the village's inhabitants, for their dress was simple and their faces possessed the Slavic-Asiatic mix of Kazakhstan. They seemed to be in some kind of comas but were still breathing on their own.

Jenna grabbed the upright one of the white-suited individuals and pushed him against the wall. She ignored the injured person, and also the thunderous pounding at the airlock.

"Get in there!" she growled.

A female voice answered in Russian.

"Get in there," she repeated in English, shooting the person lying on the dark rubber floor in the other leg.

"Shit!" her captive cursed, inserting a key into the keyhole with shaking hands before opening the door. Jenna pushed in with her and found herself facing two elevators.

"What is it? And don't pretend again that you don't understand me. I have neither time nor patience!"

"Th-th-those lead to the other l-levels," stammered her hostage. Jenna saw a small pouch hanging from the woman's belt.

"What's inside there?" Jenna asked, pointing at the pouch.

"A-a-a radio, a-a stethoscope, and a b-b-blood pressure monitor."

"What's on the other levels?"

"Th-that's hard to s-say," the woman whined.

"Why are you wearing a mask?"

"B-because the air out there is toxic after a long time."

"Are there security guards on the other levels?" asked

Jenna, pressing an ear to the door behind her. She could hear muffled sounds. Not good.

"No!"

She took the gun and held it to the woman's head.

"Really! No!" she affirmed, and began to sob hopelessly. Jenna grabbed her and heaved her next to the door as she made her way to the other side.

"Kneel down!" she ordered, waiting just moments before the door was yanked open and an assault rifle appeared. She grabbed it and jerked it into the room. A shot discharged and burned her palm, but she didn't hesitate, firing three times into the torso of the mercenary who staggered toward her and slammed into the doorframe.

Even as he tumbled, she grabbed him and spun him around to use his body as a shield, stretching her pistol past him and firing at his comrade, who'd been about to come through the door, and fired reflexively. Her bullets hit him in the chest, neck, and head, and he collapsed. The hostage was screaming in panic and had her hands pressed to her ears.

Jenna grabbed the first mercenary's radio and peered past the dead guy to the airlock, which opened again.

"Get the elevator!" she yelled at the woman, pulling the body inside and closing the door before picking up the key from the floor and locking it. "We're going down!"

"But we're not allowed to!"

"Oh, no?" Jenna raised the pistol and aimed it directly at her face before waving the muzzle toward the left elevator door.

"You don't understand. Th-there's a removal going on right now!"

"I don't care!" She shoved the white figure forward and pressed the control panel herself before ripping off the woman's mask, revealing the sweaty face of a pretty woman in her mid-40, wearing narrow glasses on her petite nose. Her lips quivered and her nostrils flared like a skittish horse. The door opened. Jenna pushed her inside and pressed the send button on the walkie-talkie. In Irish, she asked, "Feyn? Tell me what's happening out there."

For a while there was only static. Then it clicked.

"I hear you!" came the Brit's breathless reply. He sounded as if he were running, and she could hear the loud clatter of automatic weapons in the background. "What did you do? Most of those gorillas have gone back to the valley. Shit!"

"What is it?"

"I'm being followed, that's what. A lot of them have run back. Whatever you're gonna do, you don't have much time!"

"Get the hell out of there. Don't come here!" she shouted into the small radio in her fist.

"I'm trying."

"Good luck!" She knew it was goodbye, and it felt strange, even though she'd known the agent for such a short time. After clearing her throat, she added, "Take care."

"It's been an honor, ma'am."

Jenna walked into the elevator and looked at the control panel on the gray wall. There were a total of five lower levels. "Where does the removal take place?"

The frightened woman pointed to U5.

"That's where we're going." She pounded the button with the butt of her pistol and tapped her nose with her other hand. "Why the mask? What was that up there?"

"Experimental atmosphere," her counterpart replied in a rolling Russian accent. "It is t-toxic for us in the long run."

"Will I have a problem?"

"No, based on the short exposure, probably not."

"Is there security down here?"

"No, they're not normally allowed in here. Only scientific staff."

The elevator whirred and clamored its way down.

The Meteor 1

Without further ado, Jenna pressed every single button on the control panel. When the first door opened, she aimed her gun out into a large office room filled with noisy computers and wall displays. She quickly snapped a few photos with her smartphone.

One floor down, she saw laboratories with dissecting tables, microscopes, and large tanks in which bloated figures floated, some of them barely recognizable as human beings. They looked as if they had disintegrated or were at various stages in the process of doing so. On U3, all she saw was a long hallway with many doors.

"Accommodations," the scientist said as Jenna looked at her questioningly. There were about 20 hospital beds on U4, like in an intensive care unit, with oxygen supplies, IV machines, and cardiovascular equipment. They were all empty, and just like the other floors, there wasn't a soul to be seen.

"What's your name?"

"Darya Saizew," the woman answered hesitantly.

"All right, Ms. Saizew. You're going to be nice now. If I get the feeling you're up to something, I'll shoot people, and then last of all I'll shoot you, because I think our last station is where this removal is going to take place, am I right?"

Darya nodded and cringed away from the gun as Jenna grabbed hold of her and held her like a shield. The weapon extended forward over the woman's shoulder. The elevator doors opened, and the contrast with the other floors couldn't have been greater. They stepped out of the elevator into a cavern of sorts, where a dozen figures walked around in the same white suits as Darya, only without hoods or breathing masks. They wore gloves and boots sealed to their suits, and worked on long coffin-like containers of gray metal that stood on rolling racks, the containers' lids transparent. Jenna made out six on the fly. The roughly carved, dirty brown cavern walls shone damply. On the opposite side were several small tunnels with rails.

The scientists were clearly in a hurry, hooking up some of the containers to cables and tubes, while others were doing just the opposite, all of them looking down at tablets and talking together as they worked. In an almost surreal moment, all heads turned to them as the elevator doors closed behind the two newcomers. The faces displayed fear and horror, like a bunch of kids caught playing a naughty prank and knowing they were in trouble.

The white-clad figures froze momentarily, and it became so quiet that the strange machines could be heard humming softly. Then the scientists began to run amok like a flock of panicked sheep. Jenna raised her pistol and pulled the trigger. The blast was deafening and echoed like thunder through the cavern, which was large enough that three delivery trucks could have parked there. Everyone flinched, pulled their heads in, and stopped moving.

"To the left wall! Move!" yelled Jenna, nudging Darya, who immediately translated into Russian. The terrified scientists tentatively complied with the request and moved to the left wall while Jenna moved further into the room with her hostage. More quietly, so that only Darya could understand her, she asked, "What is this place?"

"The successful test subjects will be transported away from here."

Jenna had a thousand questions buzzing around in her head, but she didn't have time. The other mercenaries would be coming down to her soon enough. Even if they searched all the floors, five was not a big number. She quickly took a few photos as she had on the other floors, put the smartphone away again, and pointed her pistol at the three tunnels.

"What are those?"

"The cocoons will be carried away through them. They are

taken to a station on the Mongolian side and then distributed in different directions," Darya answered in a quavering voice.

"Are these test subjects still alive?" Jenna slid her living shield up to one of the cocoons and saw through the glass two healthy-looking middle-aged women who looked as if they were blissfully asleep.

"Yes."

"You've infecting them with Compound X, haven't you?"

"I don't know what that is."

"Is there a landline here?"

"No." Darya shook her head as the scientists on the wall followed her every move like a cornered flock of terrified sheep. "There's only one connection to the outside, and it's not here. But I don't know the code for that, either."

"What happens when your employers find out someone broke in?" asked Jenna, and the woman didn't answer. She could feel her tense in the grip of her arm, though. "I thought so. Get one of those cocoons ready for us. We're leaving."

"What?" The horror in Darya's voice was almost physically palpable. "But we can't. We—"

"No? Why not. They have their own oxygen supplies, right?"

"Yes, but—"

"Get to work!"

"I need help from—"

"Stop stalling or I'll start shooting," Jenna interrupted her roughly, aiming at the sheep. "I trust you to do your job well, because you're going to be in there with me, all right? I'm going to let go of you now."

While Darya hurriedly walked toward the container that stood directly in front of the right tunnel and had already been lifted up on the trolley to be level with the rails, Jenna pulled out her smartphone. She saved the GPS coordinates her map app had displayed before she'd gone underground and prepared a message to the Deputy Director. Once she had reception, it would automatically be sent to his work phone—not the proper way for an operation like this, but the best she could do, under the circumstances.

She added some of the photos she had taken of each floor. It wasn't much, but it was something. Next, she recorded a quick voice message, then stashed the phone in the back pocket of her jeans. Darya frantically tapped away on a display located on the side of the container, and finally the lid opened after a loud hiss. A fountain of gas escaped, and the scientist ran to a small device on a trolley, brought it over, and connected a hose.

"You need to get into it now," she said in a heavy accent.

"You first," Jenna replied, shooting near the feet of one of the white-robed men against the wall—he'd been about to reach for an object beside him on a table. "Last warning!"

Darya made a sour face and groaned as she tried to pull out one of the limp test subjects that were in the cocoon. Jenna helped her without letting go of her pistol, and they laid a young man with black hair against the rock beside her. A teenage girl with a weak but steady pulse followed. White padding lined the now-vacated container. There were leg and chest straps, and several nozzles at the foot and head ends. Jenna had to stare at Darya over the sights of her gun before the scientist settled into the container, despite the fear in her expression, and she followed. As Jenna did, she thrust the tablet back into Darya's hand, noting that the woman had subtly laid it aside.

"I'm not going to be fucked with. Let's go." A glance at the display above the elevators showed her that the one on the right had already arrived at U3 and was just changing to U4. "Take off! Now!"

"We will fall into an induced coma until we are awakened

on the other side. We were not prepared for this, and it is possible that we will have permanent—"

"I don't want to hear it! We'll deal with that when the time comes. GO!"

Darya pressed some buttons on her tablet and the lid closed agonizingly slowly. Quickly they tightened the straps, and they lay still beside each other. Jenna still had her pistol slid under her back. Darkness fell above their heads as a sled presumably pulled them onto the tracks and then they accelerated.

Jenna suddenly became unnaturally sleepy, and even as she tried to fathom whether it was reduced oxygen, or a plot by Darya, or perhaps something she had overlooked in her haste, everything went black.

23

BRANSON

The coordinates that the mysterious voice had given them during the radio call led them to the port city of Vladivostok. Here, unlike Maupiti, a very different regime ruled. They were asked over the radio why they were docking. Branson claimed it was for refueling, as that seemed to Branson the most innocuous reason. In broken English, they were assigned a surprisingly convenient berth, being on a side jetty in the sizeable industrial bay.

The sight of the town lying in the dreary gray of Siberian autumn was gruesome compared to their home port in Hawaii. The old Soviet buildings were dilapidated and marked by the damp and cold that prevailed year-round. They saw chipped plaster as they passed, crudely repaired facades, and many ruined buildings among the quickly and cheaply raised warehouses and apartment blocks that crouched under the rain-swollen clouds beside muddy meadows and diseased trees. Oil slicks, stinking silt, and indefinable muck coated the harbor water.

Branson hated this place from the moment he saw it. The

coldly, unfriendly dock worker was little more than a confirmation of his first impression. While Marv and Johnny, in their waterproof board overalls, set about mooring the *Triton One* with the longshoremen, he remained on the bridge and dialed the number Perkins had left for him.

Again it took what felt like an eternity before someone answered, and again it was the deep male voice with the Russian accent. "You're on site. Good."

Branson froze. With his brow furrowed, he peered out the bridge windows and looked across the wharf to the long flat-roofed building beyond, in front of which a number of workers and civilians stood smoking or talking. No one seemed particularly interested in his ship. The rooftops were clear, too, not the men with binoculars or sniper rifles that he had somehow expected.

Don't go crazy, man, he admonished himself. The guy probably figured we wouldn't call again until we got here. "We're just now docking," he stated calmly.

"Good. The package and payment are on their way to you. Arrival in one hour."

"Wait a minute! What package?"

"We have a shipment that you will deliver to an address on the west coast of the United States," the man on the other end of the connection replied.

"Will I?" growled Branson, as reluctance to take orders flared up inside him like an allergic reaction.

"I'm assuming so."

"What *package*?" Take it easy, man, just take it easy, he told himself. This isn't a Walmart store manager. This is someone throwing around tens of millions of dollars and snatching things off the bottom of the ocean from under the noses of several country's navies.

"That is not your concern. We're talking about four devices the size of very small cars and four people who take care of it while you're driving."

"The ones taking care of *them*, I think you meant to say?"

"We expect a smooth handover."

The connection was disconnected, and Branson angrily squeezed the satellite phone in his fist.

"Hey, what's up?"

He turned and saw Joe standing outside in warm clothing, poking his head through the doorway.

"We just got a new contract, and I didn't feel like we had a choice," Branson replied, his teeth grinding.

"Mmm. More money?" From outside came the loud hiss and roar of a tanker truck that had begun refueling. "And we go where?"

"United States, west coast. He didn't talk about more money. Just that he'd bring our agreed-upon payment."

Joe shrugged his shoulders. "We have to go home anyway, so why not take a little side trip?"

"I don't have a good feeling about this. I feel like a used tool in the hands of a bumbler."

"That's because that's what you are, I guess."

"Was there something you wanted to ask me, Joe?" Branson sighed and looked at his friend with a raised eyebrow.

"No, but I'll tell you what. The harbormaster has just informed us that we have been selected for a customs inspection. Until further notice, we are not allowed to sail."

"What? That can't be!"

"Let's hope our unknown client picks up that thing in the hold very quickly, before they come here asking questions we can't answer."

"How much time do we have?"

"Half an hour."

"Shit! Tell Xenia to hide that damn thing well, or paint it —I don't care! We'll distract them as long as we can."

"Aye, aye." Joe pulled back again and disappeared downstairs.

Half an hour later, the customs officers were there, men in dark blue uniforms and reflective vests, six in all, all armed with pistols and clipboards. Xenia had unceremoniously thrown their precious cargo into the container with the organic waste. Unless someone was walking around with a metal detector and sticking it inside the lid, they shouldn't have any problems.

It was a different story with their weapons. In keeping with the liberal gun laws in their home country, they had several shotguns and semi-automatic assault-style rifles on board, plus a handful of pistols. Johnny and Joe were absolute gun lovers, and Xenia was the only one who wanted nothing to do with them. Branson had quickly checked the lockable gun cabinets to make sure there wasn't a gun lying around somewhere, and now stood dutifully with Joe at the short gangway at the stern to welcome the Russian officials.

They returned the greeting with curt nods and then came aboard. They stuck their noses everywhere: the cabins, the toilet rooms, the stores, bridge, mess, galley, engine room. Everything was noted down like an inventory, and then finally —as expected—it was about the weapons. A lengthy discussion broke out about whether they were illegal because Russia had much stricter laws regarding private property, or whether that didn't apply to the crew because they were on a U.S. ship and not ashore.

The men wanted bribes from them and they had no real legal recourse. Branson knew this kind of 'treatment' and what helped against it. So he pretended to be constructive and assured them that he would be happy to pay appropriate fines but would need the accompanying paperwork and receipts. Corrupt officials hated only one thing more than recalcitrant victims: paperwork, because there could be no such thing. As

The Meteor 1

soon as they had to fill out official documents, others in their office could inspect them, meaning they would be exposed.

The argument that broke out on the quarterdeck lasted for what felt like an eternity and only ended when a tractor-trailer and two Mercedes SUVs stopped on the pier right next to the *Triton One*. Out of the SUVs stepped men in dark bomber jackets and white and gray camouflage pants who didn't look like they were to be trifled with. One of them came jogging up the gangway, a man with a brush cut, a serious expression, and three-days' beard growth. The others set about unloading the semi, which had four large plywood boxes lashed to it.

"Mr. McDee?" the man asked in a heavy Russian accent.

"That's me," Branson said.

"Good. We're bringing your shipment. My name is Sergey, and I will accompany you with some of my people."

"I heard about it."

"Are these guys disrupting the schedule?" Sergey pointed blatantly at the four customs officers he had studiously ignored so far, as they were eyeing the newcomers suspiciously.

"Yes, they've searched the ship, and they want bribes."

"Is that a problem?"

Branson knew what he meant and shook his head. "No."

"Good."

Sergey turned to the eldest of the inspectors and began to speak to him in a torrent of Russian. Branson thought he sounded very threatening and aggressive, but perhaps that was because of how Russian sounds to a non-speaker.

A brief argument broke out, but then the four men in the reflective vests suddenly became much more restrained and finally left the ship without so much as a final glance at Branson.

"That was... easy?" Branson commented.

"Officials have to be motivated for everything," the

Russian replied humorlessly, pointing to the crane. "Can we use that for loading?"

"Yes. However, I must say that we have no accommodations and too little food for so many passengers."

"Let *us* worry about that." Sergey glanced at his wristwatch and pointed at the crane again. "Let's get started."

Branson looked at Joe, who shrugged and looked very unhappy. He couldn't blame him. Neither of them could shake the feeling that they had just traded one evil for another.

The loading worked smoothly, as the new passengers were highly skillful and quick. Soon the four boxes were standing on the quarterdeck and were lashed down with straps anchored to the cargo eyes in the floor, which gave his ship the appearance of a delivery service.

"Sergey?" Branson asked the apparent leader of the four men who were milling about the boxes, continually reading data and making entries on tablets. He had no idea what they were doing, finding their paramilitary demeanor and their downright serious preoccupation with the boxes somehow incongruent.

"Yes?" The Russian turned to him with an expectant mien.

This is my *fucking ship!* Branson thought angrily. "I don't mean to seem impatient, but we've been promised payment." He felt uncomfortable, like he had no right to point this out, and he hated feeling that way. He felt... inferior... like a child begging from the big guys while expecting to get punched in the neck.

"Of course," Sergey replied. He made a loud hissing, "Pssst," through his teeth and when his three men looked up, he shouted in Russian to one of them, who put his tablet away and went to one of the four military crates they had brought in addition to the boxes. From inside he pulled out a backpack and tossed it to Sergey, who then pressed it to Branson's chest. "Five hundred thousand for the promised delivery and five million as a down payment for transporting the boxes to the U.S. The remaining five will be given upon arrival."

Branson unzipped the backpack and saw countless bundles of $100 bills held by rubber bands. They looked and smelled new.

"You're welcome to count it." Something in the Russian's voice sounded mocking.

"No need." He tossed the backpack to Joe, who caught it and started toward the bridge.

"We'd like to transfer the object Fred Perkins recovered now."

Branson told him about the need to hide the sphere and that they'd had to improvise, but his new passengers didn't seem to care and lifted it unapologetically out of the organic waste container. On deck, they hosed down their arms and the object, and then loaded it into another military transport crate that they carried to some of the men on the dock. After holding complicated-looking instruments over it, the recipients slid the crate into the leading SUV, the one with the tinted windows. Then they sped away, tires screeching.

"Two rules," Sergey said, grabbing Branson's arm as he was about to walk to the bridge. The Russian's grip was firm and almost painful.

This is *my* ship, you damned Klingon, he thought angrily, but kept silent and looked calmly at his 'passenger' instead. *And?*

"The boxes are off-limits."

"And the second rule?"

The Russian grinned humorlessly, and two gold teeth flashed. "Whoever breaks the first rule becomes fish food."

Branson swallowed and tried an amused snort, but Sergey quickly dropped the grin and his grip held steady. Only after a nod from Branson did the Russian let go of him. *What the hell is in those things?*

"Xenia will show you to your room," Branson said. "It's an old cold-storage room for caught fish, back when this was a trawler. There is enough room for all of you."

"We'll be staying out here with the delivery."

"Sure," snorted Branson. "You've never been across the Pacific, have you?"

Sergey said nothing and continued to look at him intently.

"Wind, spray, cold, salt. Just forget it."

"We'll see."

"Your call. I assume you brought your own provisions?"

The Russian nodded, and Branson walked calmly up to the bridge while casting glances at the boxes and wondering what they were carrying that had to be kept secret. What if they were dirty bombs or something like that? What if they were helping terrorists smuggle warheads into the U.S.? What if they found themselves in FBI mugshots in a few weeks because, unbeknownst to them, they had been aiding foreign forces?

"Did you get some bad food?" Johnny asked as he saw him come through the door. The young machinist was halfway under one of the bridge fittings, screwing away at something. He was lying on his back with the cover on the floor.

"I don't like the taste of our delivery," Branson grumbled in reply and walked over to Joe, who was standing at the card table counting the money.

"Which part of it? The weird guys who look like mafia thugs from a nineties' movie? Or the four boxes on our quarterdeck?" his first mate asked without looking up from the cash. He routinely picked up a bundle in his left hand and flipped through it note by note with his right before moving on to the next bundle.

"*Every* part of it. What does it look like?"

"It looks like we're filthy rich," Joe replied calmly.

"I hope we don't show up on a wanted list anytime soon. We better give Hawaii a wide berth and repaint when we get to the West Coast before we turn back."

"That's not a bad idea. We've got the capital for it now, that's for sure." His friend paused to look at Branson as a bright white grin split his ebony face. "We might as well just stay there and retire. It's already a million apiece, and you can say what you want: Whoever these guys are, they pay reliably and well. We've seen worse."

"True," Branson admitted reluctantly, a sinking feeling in his stomach that wouldn't go away. "Now we'll have to go through with it anyway. Johnny?"

"Yo, boss?" came the reply, and it sounded muffled and resonant, since he still had his head and half his torso inside the housing.

"When you're done there, go on deck with Marv. We're casting off. It looks like we're tanked up, and I have no idea what our new *guest* told the customs agents about turning tail and disappearing, but if they reconsider, I'd rather already be at sea."

"You got it, boss. I'll be done in a minute."

As it turned out, the officials did not return, and no one else bothered them. Whatever Sergey had said or implied, everything went smoothly. Formal clearance had come promptly, and they hadn't even been charged demurrage. His clients were either well-connected or feared, and from what he had experienced so far, he suspected both.

∽

The first few days on board were bizarre. The four Russians on the quarterdeck kept to themselves, ate their own rations, and slept outside, even though it was very chilly. They never came in, nor did they appear to talk much among themselves.

The crew felt increasingly uncomfortable, as if they had a cancer in their bodies that they couldn't cut away. No one was talking about it, but Branson could see in their faces how worried they were about their cargo. What was hidden in those strange plywood boxes? Why were these men, from whom an aura of danger emanated, watching over them so meticulously? They were all asking themselves the same questions, he was sure: *what if we are committing crimes?*

Driving a man like Perkins from A to B so he could pursue hidden treasure at the bottom of the ocean, that was one thing. They could understand that. Even though their passenger had been a little cagey and odd, the assignment hadn't seemed too crazy to them at the time. Now, they had tattooed musclemen in military fatigues and bomber jackets on board, carrying weapons and making it clear he and his crew had no business being on their own quarterdeck.

"You're not going to go and look in one of the boxes, are you?" Joe asked as they sat in the mess hall with Xenia and Johnny, slurping their instant noodles while Marv was on duty on the bridge. It was already close to midnight.

"Are you out of your mind? They're sleeping right next to them—if they're sleeping at all."

"But you've thought about it."

"I haven't always covered myself in glory when it comes to landing contracts, and I'm not proud of those oil barrels. But that wasn't about shady Russians throwing millions around to smuggle four boxes into the U.S., sight unseen."

"And who can chase armed customs officers off a ship just like that?" Xenia interjected. "I'm really scared, Branson. What are we even doing here?"

"I'm not sure."

"That's what I'm talking about. Anything could be in

those things. Why would they make such a secret of it if it's something legal?"

"What would they be smuggling? Weapons?" Branson asked a counter-question, but sounding unconvinced himself with his attempt to defend their passengers.

"Even if the boxes were full of machine pistols," Joe spoke up again, "nobody would pay ten million for them. No guns would be worth that much."

"So, something worse," Johnny said, slurping as he sucked in a mouthful of noodles. After smacking his lips, he continued, "I love you guys, man, but I think our greed has got us into a big problem. I've got a really bad feeling about this."

"I know. But what are we going to do about it? It's too late to change our minds." Branson sighed and ruffled his hair. His appetite was in the basement, and his bowl was still half full and getting cold.

No one said anything more, uneasiness filling the silence as the ship began to roll harder and harder.

After what felt like an eternity, Marv's voice boomed from the crackling old speakers above the door. "Yo, we're getting close to that bad weather front. Maybe you better get down here, boss."

"I ain't hungry anymore, anyway," Branson grumbled, pushing the bowl away from him and standing up.

"I'll come with you. I'm not tired yet," Joe announced and followed him onto the bridge while the other two set about washing up. They sent Marv off for the night, as he looked like a drop of water zigzagging down a curved window and didn't seem far from microsleep. The weather was indeed getting uncomfortable with heavy rain and gusts setting in. The Beaufort numbers were still manageable and indicated a relatively mild storm, but *Triton One* was already rolling nicely. It didn't surprise Branson much when Johnny came in at some point and reported that the Russians had retreated to the old cold storage room.

In the hours that followed, as the weather worsened and the first waves broke over the bow, flinging spray up to the bridge windows, Branson and Joe spoke little and kept their thoughts to themselves.

"You take the wheel, and I'll take a turn to make sure everything's tied down," Branson said after a while. His friend eyed him briefly before nodding and taking the wheel. Branson slipped into a waterproof thermal overall and pulled on a pair of rubber boots from the closet next to the stairwell. Then he pushed the door open to step out into the storm-lashed night and had to brace himself with all his strength against a powerful gust that threatened to yank the door from his hand.

Only when it had latched did he look around and see the gray billows that seemed to come from every direction at once with angry crowns of spray. Like a nutshell, his ship danced on the energetic sea, stubbornly making its way straight ahead.

With decades of experience and his innate sense of balance, Branson had no trouble maneuvering along the rail in the illumination of the ship's lights to check the lashing buckles of the lifebuoys.

Joe could still see him in the mirrors, though the thick veils of rain did not make it easy.

Then Branson went aft and looked down at the quarter-deck. Dark tarpaulins that had been hooked to the deck eyelets covered the boxes, keeping out the worst of the spray and rain. There was no sign of the Russians, but he had figured them for landlubbers who wouldn't be able to stand on their feet, since a couple of them had been puking and swearing for hours.

Branson went into the bow's superstructure via the lower access and enjoyed the silence for a second as the door

The Meteor 1

slammed shut behind him, shutting out the roar and foam of the storm. Then he ran to the storage room and grabbed one of the tool belts, which he strapped around his waist before putting an ear to what used to be the refrigeration room one floor up. As expected, he heard retching noises and Russian curses from the other side. Satisfied, he made his way to the quarterdeck and pulled his hood tight before exposing himself to the storm again. The noise instantly enveloped him, and the rain lashed at him as if to hurl him onto the deck.

Branson walked carefully around a box that was a little closer to its neighbor, making a slightly more sheltered area. After one last look toward the bow, he slipped under the tarpaulin, and things calmed down a bit, though the pelting of raindrops was more intense. Using the small cordless screwdriver from his tool belt, he unfastened the finger-thick screws from the corners and stowed them in his pocket. Thanks to the tarp, he was able to pull off the sheet of pressboard without losing it, as the plastic held it in place. With difficulty, he squeezed between the boxes and looked at the contents that had cost him so much sleep for the past several nights.

When he saw it—a gray coffin that reached just below his chest—he didn't know whether to be worried, relieved, or both at once. The lower part was massive and had many tubes and wires connected to it. A gentle hum emanated from it. The upper part was a bit slimmer, and as he bent his back to lean over it, he saw a pane of glass that was either slightly hazed or fogged over.

Pursing his lips, he stowed the cordless screwdriver, shifted his balance from left to right as the ship rolled more violently, and took the flashlight from his belt. He shone the beam through the glass and yelped in startlement. His head crashed against the lid, and he cried out in pain before daring to look again, holding the flashlight in trembling hands.

Two women with pale faces lay beneath the glass as if in

slumber. One looked Slavic and a little older, but very attractive. He thought she gave the impression of having just been surprised, as if someone had shock-frozen her. The other had brown shoulder-length hair and a pretty if stern face with the corners of her mouth drooping slightly and a long straight nose. She wasn't wearing a white chemical suit like the Slavic woman, but a battered jacket and jeans and a belt with tools on it.

"What the fucking hell?" he breathed into the whistling of the storm. His brittle voice echoed in that tiny cave, and the instinctive protection it offered crumbled under his angry thoughts.

People! Those are people in there! With a pounding heart he looked around. The tarp was flapping out and rattling just as hard as before. Vast quantities of foaming seawater flowed over the deck. *What am I to do?*

Branson found a control panel at the head end, but he couldn't see it very well because there was hardly any room to his right. It had only two buttons, and underneath was a large warning sign that he couldn't quite make out or read. He simply pressed both buttons and recoiled when a loud hiss sounded. The seal released slowly and the coffin's top went up with a hydraulic squeal until, after about 30 centimeters, it hit the box's lid and let out a protesting squeal. An ugly smell assailed his nose but quickly dissipated, and he glanced at the two women lying close together in the coffin.

With a heavy swallow, he put his hand through the opening and felt for their pulses. When he felt faint but steady heartbeats, he didn't know whether to be relieved or horrified. If they were transporting corpses, that possibly meant they were merely being transferred, though that seemed richly naïve to him. However, if they were still alive, he was involuntarily implicated in human trafficking, and that thought caused a

The Meteor 1

lump to form in his throat, so thick he felt like he should choke on it.

"Why are you Americans always so nosy?" A heavily accented Russian voice sounded behind him, cutting through the storm like an ax.

Branson flinched and whirled around, only to look up into the face of Sergey, who was standing behind him, completely soaked. The tarp was gone, and with one hand the Russian was holding onto the box beside the opened one. In the other hand Sergey held a pistol, tapping it against Branson's temple.

"You get millions, and you still have to stick your nose into something that's none of your business. We pay you handsomely, but you can't just look the other way, can you? It's never enough for you," the Russian continued, sounding disappointed. Out of the corner of his eye, Branson saw another figure with a gun standing at the railing to the right, securing his grip on the metal with a safety harness.

"I..." Branson started to explain, but Sergey shook his head. Honestly, he didn't know what he should say anyway.

"Forget it. I need you because you can steer this barge, but this," Sergey pointed to the coffin behind Branson, "is a violation of our rules, which I've made very clear. Didn't I?"

Branson did not reply.

"But your crew... one by one, I will slice them open and strangle them with their guts. You'll scream and curse me, but you'll obey and sail this ship anywhere we ask because you'll be traumatized. That works every time with you Yanks. You're like sheep who feel great power in the flock, but individually you're pathetic wimps."

Sergey reached out a hand and waved him over, even though they were standing only two meters apart. Branson cursed inwardly, and at the same time, was more scared than ever. He felt paralyzed as a loud bang sounded. It was hollow and hissing, occurring only so briefly that he initially thought it was a fitting or antenna destroyed by the storm, but he saw the other Russian at the railing slammed against the metal and slumped over.

Sergey leapt forward, grabbed Branson, who had no time to react, and took a half step back until he was up against the open coffin, holding his hostage in front of him like a shield. The man's arm was strong and nearly squeezed the air out of Branson as Joe rounded the corner with a shotgun at the ready. His thermal overalls shone as if greased, and the hood flapped back and forth in the wind. But his gaze was clear and determined.

"Let him go!" he shouted, but Sergey instead extended his pistol, which had just been pressed against Branson's temple, and fired without hesitation.

Joe, caught off guard, was hit in the stomach and collapsed. The shot that came from his shotgun shredded part of the open box above them, passing away in a shower of splinters. Another shot thundered through the night, also loud enough to ring in Branson's ears. The pressure on his chest suddenly eased, and as he turned with shaking knees, he saw the face of a woman leaning halfway out of the coffin. In her right hand she held a pistol with a smoking muzzle, which she pressed directly against his forehead. Sergey collapsed dead behind him.

"Where am I?" croaked Jenna weakly.

"Uh, um-on the *T-Triton One*," Branson stammered, more confused now than frightened, though the hot opening of the gun barrel on his forehead made him swallow hard.

"What's that? A ship?"

"Yes."

"What day is it?"

"Wednesday, I think."

"What date!?"

The Meteor 1

When Branson told her, her eyelids fluttered and she went slack, like a spring that had lost all its tension. He noticed then that the other woman in the coffin was stirring, but very slowly and tentatively. She, too, seemed somehow haggard and emaciated.

Branson turned and ran to Joe, who was lying in the storm, breathing heavily and with his eyes wide open.

"Hang in there, old friend," he cried out in a quavering voice, and then shouted, as loud as he could, "HELP!"

EPILOGUE
LEE

Lee sucked on his sippy cup and grimaced, already feeling better after a week in Berlin's Charité hospital. It wasn't the smoke inhalation, nor the mild concussion, nor again the laceration on his temple that had done him in, but Mean Ol' Mr. Gravity. His body was still struggling with the compressing weight of this beautiful 'gravitational sink' on whose surface he now found himself again.

Just looking out the window over the rooftops of the German capital felt more precious to him than anything ever had before. He had survived, though someone had tried everything to prevent it—the reason why he'd refused to be taken to the Medical Clinic at Ramstein Air Force Base after Greek rescue workers had recovered him from the *Crew Dragon* on the plain of Thessaly.

Despite pressure from the U.S. ambassador and various forces in Washington, the German authorities had acceded to his request for treatment in Berlin. This was both a blessing and a curse, because he did not know whom to trust. Lee felt violated, preferring to pay privately for his treatment rather than go home now in this condition and face the unpleasant questions. This problem was finally solved when he was dismissed in absentia, for defying direct orders, by an irate Ulysses Keinzman in a press conference.

The first few days had passed like a hazy dream that had been replaced by a harsh reality as soon as he had turned on the television. At first, the English-language channels he could tune in to, alongside the daily Cassandra broadcasts, reported on him and his crash landing in Greece. The speculation and political skirmishes he'd sparked were maddening at the best of times, and he felt uncomfortable constantly seeing his face on the screen.

Fortunately, it had only lasted two days, because then something seemingly more interesting had hit the news: a prime-time announcement by the Chinese president. Xi Jinping declared that a fact-finding mission to the strange asteroid was being prepared to explore the black dot in the night sky and seek answers where, up to now, humanity did not even understand the questions it had to ask.

President Xi also gave a timetable: The three-person crew would launch ten days from Sunday. While all news outlets doubted that China could even manage a human-crewed mission to the ISS in such a short time, the Americans and Russians followed suit and wanted to be even faster.

A frenetic new space race had started, and even the Europeans and Japanese were teaming up to avoid falling behind.

As Lee's smartphone vibrated and he looked at the push message on his news app, which announced another artifact shower from Cassandra 22007, the door opened and his nurse Madlen walked in.

"How's our astronaut today?" she asked in passable English, coming over to him and checking his blood pressure.

"Good. I think I might be ready for discharge," Lee replied just as he did every day, and she smiled indulgently. Like every day.

"That bad, then?" she asked.

"Not so bad that I couldn't sign the release papers."

"It'd be a shame if you left, because you have company."

"Visitors?" he asked in wonder, inwardly scolding himself for imagining Sarah and Markus walking in the door, neither of whom he'd heard from yet, leaving him not merely sad but perplexed.

"Yes. If you feel up to it."

"I'm not married, so I don't have a mother-in-law."

"Well, then." Madlen seemed satisfied with the blood pressure reading and went back out. Soon, a young man with horn-rimmed glasses and a bag under his arm came in. He had the look of an intelligent and alert mind and the demeanor of a teenager.

"Hello, Mr. Rifkin."

"Hello." Lee straightened up a little until he was sitting with his back straight against the raised headrest. "And who are you?" he asked with a frown.

"I'm Peter. I flew in from Hawthorne. My boss would like to talk to you and is inviting you on a flight to California. At company expense, of course."

"Hawthorne? Your boss's name is—"

"Elon Musk, yes." Peter smiled. "SpaceX would like to have you as a commander for a human-crewed mission."

"He wants to send a crew up to the asteroid, too?" Lee thought he was dreaming.

"Yes. In fact, as early as the end of next week. It's not that easy to put together a team that doesn't need training first. Well, there's never been any training for landing on an asteroid, but you have the experience and—"

"—the desire not to fly with NASA," Lee interrupted his visitor. "I get it. But what kind of team?"

"Well, your team from the ISS. Our mission is co-funded by the EU on the condition that one of your country's astronauts flies with us, and we thought you'd prefer to have your colleagues with you, with whom you're already attuned," Peter explained with a cheeky grin. "And Sarah MacDougall quit social media an hour ago. If you agree, we'll collect them from the ISS on our way to Cassandra 22007. I must warn you, however, that the physical preparation for the strain of a launch less than three weeks after returning to Earth will be exhausting."

Lee sighed, remembering how he had looked out of the cupola at the shining dot near the moon that had changed life on Earth, possibly forever, with its very existence.

"When do we leave?"

EPILOGUE
JENNA

Jenna awoke, as she did every morning, with a roaring headache. It wasn't as terrible as the ones from the first few days after she'd been awakened, but it was still crushing. Darya lay above her in her bunk on that ugly old trawler they'd landed on, apparently suffering as much as she was. By all accounts, their journey in the strange medical coffin, which had probably taken several days, had taken them to Vladivostok.

Whether it had been by luck or design that they hadn't killed her—even though she and the doctor clearly didn't look like the test subjects in the other devices—she probably wouldn't find out any time soon. Apparently, the oxygen supply in the container had been significantly reduced to deliberately shut down her metabolism. The effect of prolonged lack of oxygen would be with her for a while, that much was certain.

Waking up had seemed like a bad dream from which she'd been startled, only to see a Russian in the middle of a storm, pressing a gun to the temple of a somewhat disheveled-looking redneck. She'd shot more out of reflex than calculation, and she couldn't remember the rest. It wasn't until she'd awakened here in this stuffy and far too short bed that she'd felt like she was back in reality. Pain is the best way to ground yourself, she mused.

There was a knock at the door, and before she could answer, it opened with a squeak, and in walked Branson, the burly redneck with graying temples and dreadlocks tied into an impressive braid. His undershirt was stained, and the tattoos on his muscular brown arms were largely faded. He reminded her of a hapless treasure hunter from one of those second-rate cable TV shows.

"Hello," he greeted her, and Jenna left it at a neutral nod as she rested. "It's ten o'clock now."

"I'm already awake," Darya moaned, and the bunk above her head began to creak as the Russian stretched her legs out. Branson came over and helped her down. Jenna looked past him and saw a young man with blond shoulder-length curls standing there with *her pistol* held casually in front of his hip.

Every morning and evening, the Russian doctor was let out of the cabin, which was something like their prison cell, without anyone saying a word. When Jenna had asked her what was happening, she merely explained that she had a patient she had to take care of. Other than that, they didn't talk much, and judging by the looks Darya kept giving her, she expected to be smothered with a pillow in her sleep at some point.

As she was being led out, Jenna waited a while before knocking on the door from the inside.

"I have to go to the bathroom," she lied. It was a daily ritual. In the early days, the crew had been most vigilant. People were always the same—primacy effect. At the beginning of a new situation, attention is at its highest, and once everything seems to normalize, attention eases as well. She had chosen this day because her headache had faded at least enough to think reasonably clearly, and she had recovered passably physically.

When Darya went in to treat the patient, she guessed that Branson would be there as well to keep an eye on everything. That meant there were still three crew members on the ship—if she had counted correctly so far. It had always been the same faces that had brought her food. Someone had to be on the bridge, which left two. Not too bad a place to start.

It took a while before the lock clicked and the door swung open. The blond surfer dude was about to nod routinely into the hallway, as he did every morning, when she delivered a firm blow to his larynx with the heel of her hand, disarming him at the same time. Gasping, he grabbed his neck and staggered backward until she grabbed him by the collar and pulled him into her cabin. Quickly she gagged him, bound his hands behind his body and his feet together, before tying hands and feet all together so that he lay hogtied on the floor.

"Shh!" she hissed. "Shallow breaths. That helps."

Then she took his key and locked him in before looking around the small wood-paneled hallway and creeping up the stairs. She could hear Darya and Branson talking behind a door on the next floor. A third voice, deep and full-throated, muttered something unintelligible. Jenna didn't dwell on it, and crept up another floor until she had made out the door to the bridge. She ducked under the small window, listened for a while but heard nothing, then peered through.

A tall, sinewy guy in a jogging suit leaned his butt against a high-backed chair in front of a steering wheel, peering out the small windows ahead, etched by decades of salty spray. Carefully, she pushed open the door a tiny crack, worried that it might squeak like everything else on this barge, and crept on bare feet toward his back. By the time he noticed anything and was about to turn around, she had already put the muzzle of her gun to the back of his head.

"Don't," she said. "Where's your satellite phone?"

"Uh, what?" asked Johnny, who smelled of marijuana.

"Satellite phone." To emphasize her demand, she released the safety of her pistol. The click made him freeze.

"It's stuck up there by the sonar." When she didn't respond, he pointed to the fitting in front of the window on the right.

Jenna walked over sideways so she could continue to keep an eye on him, then reached her free hand out to the satellite phone with the powerful antenna.

"You don't have to do this. We saved you, after all," Johnny said.

"Quiet." She dialed the assistant director's number, waited until the line was open, then said, "Eight-four-seven-one-Washington."

"Jenna?"

"Yes. I'm still alive."

"Thank God!" He sounded genuinely concerned. "Where are you?"

Johnny eyed her with a furrowed brow.

"Somewhere in the Pacific. From what I understand, some hillbillies kind of picked me up in Vladivostok harbor. Did you get my message with the pictures?"

"Yes. That was good work, Jenna! Really! I went to Montgomery with it, and he looked at everything and increased our funding tenfold. That was really fucking good."

"What did you do?"

"I've dispatched ten more agents to the region. I want them to follow up on any other leads. As we speak, fifty analysts are going through the photos you took from the secret facility. We need to get you back in the field as soon as possible. I want you to lead our field team," the Deputy Director stated.

"No debriefing? No extraction and return to Langley?"

"No. You've been in hiding for a week and a half. That

damn asteroid changes everything. Also, there was an eruption of something in Siberia, and judging by our satellite imagery, it happened when a freight train stopped near the town of Ulan Ude. The Russian government has sealed off the entire region, and now guess what's there?"

"A branch of Golgorov Systema?"

"That's right. Do you have a way to return? We can send you a strike team and enough resources to Hokkaido. You'll have to get into Russia illegally somehow. They banned all foreigners from their country a week ago. Something's going on, Jenna, and it's not just the Defense Minister who wants to know what."

"I'll find a way," she assured him. "I have a request."

"Anything, Jenna."

"I think we should get the Five Eyes involved. This thing is a lot bigger than I thought, and I had the help of an MI6 agent who introduced himself as Feyn."

"The Five Eyes are already in. I'll see what I can do. I'll email you anything important. Take care."

Jenna hung up.

"Who are you?" asked Johnny, as if seeing her for the first time.

"I work for the CIA," she said just as the door to the bridge silently opened, "And I need this ship."

"What's in it for us?" asked Branson, coming up behind her. She didn't seem surprised, and certainly not startled.

"How does ten million dollars sound to you?" She lowered the gun and turned to face him. He, too, lowered the shotgun in his hand and put on a satisfied smile that was allowed to feign a bit of greed.

"Where to?"

"Northern Japan. Then Russia."

"Agreed," he said a little too quickly.

EPILOGUE
BRANSON

Branson was extremely relieved to find that while Joe had received a nasty flesh wound, no internal organs had been hit. The woman who had held him at gunpoint and saved him from Sergey at the same time had passed out shortly after their terse conversation, while the other woman beside her had recovered fairly quickly with some smelling salts and an IV.

The very next day—having disarmed and tied up Sergey's two remaining seriously seasick men quite effortlessly with help from Marv and Johnny—they learned that the second woman was a Russian doctor. After she had stitched up Joe and given him the best possible care with the ship's supplies, he took her out of her room on the second morning under the pretext that she was to treat him further. The American with the restless look seemed to be in a sort of stupor, tossing and turning in her bunk.

"What do you want with me?" asked Darya as Marv waited outside the door and then led her to the quarterdeck. The storm had passed, and the temperatures were picking up again. By the time they reached the stern, the four exposed coffins were already gleaming in the light of the still low sun.

"I thought you could explain what this is," he said, waving his pistol at her to approach the first container.

When she leaned forward and looked through the glass, she was startled. "Oh my God! It happened." She slapped a hand over her mouth.

"*What's* happened?" growled Branson, staring at the two figures, barely recognizable as human outlines, on the couch cushion. The nasal probes and mouthpieces that had been on their faces before now lay in a semi-transparent, sticky mass that had drawn long threads. There were stains all over the glass as if the disgusting-looking stuff formed a kind of web through which it gradually spread.

"The remedy!" Darya seemed to be talking more to herself than to him. "It has broken out, just as I predicted. The activator must have been found."

"What kind of activator? What kind of agent?" he huffed. "What the hell is this on my ship?"

"You need to take us back right now, do you understand?"

"We're supposed to be taking you to the United States."

"No! This needs to be examined. It's not ready for execution," the doctor stammered, "and we don't have much time."

"What kind of activator are you talking about?"

"Well, from that thing, of course!" She extended a finger toward the moon, still a pale disk in the dark blue morning sky. He didn't need to ask to know that she meant the large black spot that covered part of the Earth's satellite.

"The asteroid?"

"That's not an asteroid. It's a meteor."

"I read that—"

"It's still an asteroid, but it'll be a meteor soon, believe me!" she interrupted him much more gruffly than her petite stature and somewhat girlish voice would suggest.

"What the hell are you even talking about?" he huffed.

The Meteor 1

"Look,..."

"Branson."

"Branson, whatever happened here, you have to take us back, do you understand? This batch has got to go back."

"It's not going to be that easy. And what the fuck happened to these people?"

"I will assure my employer that you saved me. You'll be paid handsomely, and you won't have to worry about being followed anymore. The man who shot your friend Joe..."

"Sergey."

"Yes, Sergey. We'll just say that his people were shot by the agent," Darya said, her voice almost cracking.

"Wait a minute. Agent? What fucking agent?"

"Never mind right now. Let me make a phone call, and I'll guarantee you'll be paid more richly than you could hope for. My employers would pay anything to get their batch back."

Branson was considering. The shock at Sergey's casual manner in saying he would have to kill him still ran deep. On the other hand, the Russian had also correctly noted that his crew had kept to all agreements so far, unlike him, who had inspected the transport goods despite making other arrangements.

But smuggling people? That was completely unacceptable. At the same time, strictly speaking, they weren't *people* now, but *sick* people, or *dead* people, or whatever. In truth, he had no clue what had happened to them.

They spent the next few days making the American believe that Darya—who was also still recovering from her time in the coffin—had to look after Joe every morning and evening. In truth, however, they were negotiating with the mysterious man whose number they had and who spoke a lot to his associate in Russian.

She eventually negotiated twenty million dollars on the

condition that they were not to leave Russia for at least a month. After a thorough meeting with the crew, during which Xenia shed many tears, they decided to go for it. Branson waived his share out of guilt that his curiosity had gotten them into this situation in the first place. They were angry, no question, but the prospect of being hunted by a mysterious crime cartel scared them too much to turn down the offer, and they had a female agent on board. How else were they going to get rid of her?

At least Darya agreed not to kill the American, because both Branson and his crew would not cross that red line—except in self-defense. But there was already an idea for that, which took shape after about a week, when, as expected, she broke free. Branson was in the chart room with Joe and the doctor, one deck below the bridge, discussing the route to the coordinates they'd been given when Xenia alerted him.

Branson grabbed his shotgun and ran outside and up from there. He saw her pointing the gun at poor Marv and holding the satellite phone in her other hand before he went inside. For a few heartbeats he worried that she might have called for backup, but they were between Hawaii and Russia, and this far out, he didn't think it possible. The *Triton One* was doomed after all this anyway, but if all went well, they had enough money to go underground and make new lives for themselves somewhere.

"I work for the CIA," she said just as he silently opened the door to the bridge, "And I need this ship."

"What's in it for us?" asked Branson, coming up behind her. She didn't seem surprised, and certainly not startled.

"How does ten million dollars sound to you?" She lowered the gun and turned to face him. He, too, lowered the shotgun in his hand and put on a satisfied smile that was allowed to feign a bit of greed.

"Where to?"
"Northern Japan. Then Russia."
"Agreed," he said.
How convenient.

AFTERWORD

Dear Readers,

I hope you enjoyed the first part of my Meteor trilogy. As is usual for my works, I like to package great stories into multiple volumes to create the necessary space for what the protagonists experience. In that sense, *The Meteor* is the kickoff, the getting of Jenna, Branson, and Lee into position for the big bang. If you found the story exciting, I hope you'll forgive me for this exposition. Part two will be available for purchase in just a few weeks—I promise ;-). Of course, I'd also be delighted if you would support this book in the form of a review on Amazon. If you would like to contact me directly, you can do so here: joshua@joshuatcalvert.com

Afterword

If you subscribe to my monthly newsletter, I will keep you informed about new releases—of course, also about *The Meteor 2*. And you will receive my e-book *Rift* exclusively and for free: www.joshuatcalvert.com.

Warm regards, Joshua T. Calvert

GLOSSARY

AEGIS: Electronic warning and fire control system of the U.S. Navy

AKS-74U: Assault rifle from former Soviet Union, mainly Russian production

Altay: Town in the northwest of China, very remote and dominated by the Kazakh minority

Astron: Radio telescope of RJKK Energiya

BCD: Buoyancy Control Device, inflatable vest for divers, to which the tank is also attached, among other things

BND: Bundesnachrichtendienst; German Federal Intelligence Service

Canadarm 2: A remote manipulator robotic system on the International Space Station

Glossary

Chatanga: Village in the Krasnoyarsk region of Russia, famous for its proximity to the site of the Tunguska event

CNSA: Chinese National Space Administration

Coma: Shell-like 'cloud' around a comet in close proximity to the sun, consisting of vapor and dust

Conidia: Specific spore form of higher fungal species

Cupola: Observation platform of the International Space Station

EEZ: Exclusive Economic Zone

EMU: Extravehicular Mobility Unit, maneuverable space suit of NASA for field operations

ESA: European Space Agency

ESO: European Southern Observatory located in Chile

Five Eyes: Intelligence community of the Anglo-Saxon nations: United States, Canada, New Zealand, Australia, and United Kingdom

Fruiting body: Reproductive organ of multicellular fungal species and what is commonly considered and referred to as a 'fungus' when visible on the surface/soil

FSB (Federalnaya Sluzhba Bezopasnosti): Russian Federal Security Service

G36: Heckler and Koch assault rifle

Glossary

GRU (Glavnoye Razvedyvatel′noye Upravleniye): Russia's Main Intelligence Administration

Guangzhou: Large industrial city in China

Hemukanasixiang: Isolated poor village in the Chinese Altay region

Humvee: Military multi-purpose off-road vehicle, mainly used by the U.S. Armed Forces

Hyphae: Branched filaments of fungi, which spread in the soil under the fruiting body, among other things

IRBM: Inland Revenue Board of Malaysia

Lahaina: Small town in the west of Maui

Maui: Island belonging to Hawaii

Maupiti: Small island in the French overseas territory of French Polynesia

MI6: British Military Intelligence, Section 6

Mjöllnir: Satellite-based weapon system consisting of kinetic tungsten projectiles

MP5: Heckler and Koch 9mm submachine gun

NEOWISE: NEO Wide-field Infrared Survey Explorer, NASA's reactivated unmanned space telescope

Glossary

Okavango Delta: Confluence of rivers in South Africa and important wildlife area

Ophiocordyceps unilateralis: Parasitic fungal species from Asia that infects its hosts and controls them so that they visit places favorable to the parasite and die there in order to reproduce the fungus

Pancit: Filipino national dish made of noodles, chicken or pork, and assorted vegetables

PL-15K: Semi-automatic pistol from Russian production, shortened version of PL-15

RJKK Energiya: Russian space company

Roskosmos: Russian space agency

Spetsnaz (Voyská spetsiálnogo naznachéniya): Special operations forces of the Russian military intelligence service GRU

Spore: Developmental stage of fungi, for example. Spores distribute the genetic material of their mother lifeform via the air and ensure further distribution and thus reproduction

Stroma: Filamentous network which protectively surrounds the fruiting body of a fungus and on which the conidia are located (cf. 'conidia')

Ürümqi: Capital of Xinjiang, China

Vandenberg: Space Force Base in the U.S. north of Los Angeles with launch and landing facilities for orbital missiles

Glossary

VLA: Very Large Array, radio telescope in New Mexico in the U.S.

Vladivostok: Large port city in the far east of Russia on the Pacific Ocean

Xinjiang: Northwesternmost province of China

Yongshu Atoll: One of the Spratly Islands in the South China Sea, which are claimed by China—which claim is contested by multiple other nations, including the Philippines and Vietnam—and have been artificially built up and under military construction for several years

CAST OF CHARACTERS

Aleksander Khrogashvili: Son of a Russian oligarch, considered a rival of Yuri Golgorov

Alexi: Biochemist of the Russian scientific corps

Anatoli Timoshchuk: Russian cosmonaut who was selected, under controversial circumstances, for an ISS mission

Anton: Biologist of the Russian scientific corps

Black Widow: Shadowy underworld figure

Bobby Zurkowski: Chief Engineer at SpaceX

Boris Tatishchev: Son of a Russian oligarch, considered to be a rival of Yuri Golgorov

Boris Uljana: Director of Roskosmos

Branson McDee: Boat captain and treasure hunter

Cast of Characters

Carla: Los Angeles survivor and Branson's right-hand woman

Cassandra Miles: NASA astronomer and discoverer of comet Cassandra 22006

Chiu Wai: Chinese entrepreneur from the middle class of Guangzhou, produces school bags for children

Colin: British agent of MI6

Conny Jones: Acting Vice President of the United States

Darya Saizew: Russian doctor who works in the secret facility in the Altay

David Myers: Chairman of the Joint Chiefs of Staff (U.S. military), Army General

Delilah Jones: Assistant to Lee at SpaceX

Dima: Russian Roskosmos cosmonaut

Dwight Decker: Treasure hunter and multimillionaire with base in Lahaina harbor

Feyn: British agent of MI6

Fred Perkins: Obscure client for the *Triton One*

Jenna Haynes: Spy working for the CIA

Joe Kamaka: First mate on *Triton One* and Branson's best friend

Cast of Characters

Joe Walker: Acting President of the United States

Johnny: Machine Technician on *Triton One*

Kathryn Gerschwitz: Superconductor engineer at SpaceX

Kenneth Hauser: General and Chief of the U.S. Central Command

Kolya: Agricultural engineer of the Russian scientific corps

Lee Rifkin: NASA astronaut

Leslie Johnson: Mayor of Los Angeles

Lieutenant Eversman: Lieutenant in the California National Guard

Linnea Daubner: Physicist at ESA and head of the control station in Cebreros

Luc Breusch: Astronomy blogger

Markus Wlaschiha: German ESA astronaut

Marv: Deep-sea diver on the *Triton One*

Michael Hyten: Joint Chiefs of Staff, General of the United States Air Force

Michelle Ferguson: High-ranking NASA official and head of the control room

Montgomery Schrader: Director of the CIA

Cast of Characters

Nikolai Semyonov: FSB agent

Oleg Snietseva: Russian oligarch and founder of the space company RJKK Energiya

Paul Levendale: Homeland Security Agent

Pyotr Wolkonsky: Contract killer from Siberia wanted by Interpol

Richard Fouler: Democrat Senator

Rick Perlman: Psychiatrist at SpaceX

Roberto Camacho: ESA employee at the control center in Cebreros

Rufus: Los Angeles survivor and Branson's right-hand man

Sarah MacDougall: NASA astronaut

Sergei Morozova: Son of a Russian oligarch, considered to be a rival of Yuri Golgorov

Sergey: Leader of the Russian mercenaries aboard the *Triton One*

Tony Garcia: Jenna's instructor at the CIA

Ulysses Keinzman: NASA Director

Walt Cummings: Secretary of Defense of the United States

William Forstchen: Republican Congressman

Cast of Characters

Xenia: Assistant to Branson on *Triton One*

Xu Qiliang: General of the Chinese Armed Forces and Deputy to Zhang Youxia

Yuri Golgorov: Oligarch and pharmaceutical entrepreneur, allegedly died in the downing of Flight MH17 over Ukraine

Zeek: Los Angeles survivor, former football player, who becomes Branson's right-hand man

Zhang Youxia: General of the Chinese Armed Forces in the function of Chief of Staff in the Western sense, supreme commander of the Chinese military

Printed in Great Britain
by Amazon